SISI & SONIA

Nic Penrake

Published in 2008 by YouWriteOn.com

Copyright © Nic Penrake

First Edition

The author asserts the moral right under the Copyright, Designs and Patents Act 1988 to be identified as the author of this work.

All Rights reserved. No part of this publication may be reproduced, stored in a retrieval system, or transmitted, in any form or by any means without the prior written consent of the author, nor be otherwise circulated in any form of binding or cover other than that in which it is published and without a similar condition being imposed on the subsequent purchaser.

Published by YouWriteOn.com

CHAPTER 1

Adrift in the waters of post-trauma, my daughters' tendril-like hands sometimes touching me, their voices lapping in my ears, all I can really see in this leisure centre's recreational area is that beautiful, lissom young Thai girl clinging to the side of the pool like a flower, trembling, broken by heavy rain. The blood red of her swimming costume seems to have been branded on my brain. Even though it wasn't my fault that I knocked half her tooth out – it was a stupid accident – I feel pregnant with a sense of responsibility, pained that she's gone already. I also got hurt. Everyone's said I should go to the hospital to have some stitches put in the small gash above my left eyebrow. But I've also been asked to wait for the police just in case the accident was in part my fault. So, for the last twenty minutes, I've been sitting here on this plastic coloured chair amid excited kids and vending machines and smells of chlorine and take out food, gradually beginning to feel like a bag in Lost Property.

"Dad, you're bleeding again!" my daughters are telling me, more alarmed than I am.

The plaster I was given has finally been breached. I look between my feet to see small drops of crimson rain down in slow motion. I take a tissue from my jacket pocket and press it to the trilling wound.

Michaela, 9, and Mia, 6, five minutes ago dancing in circles around me, their arms arcing, their bodies shaking with laughter as they collided with each other in that happy, lazy and gentle way young girls do, now plonk themselves down beside me–clamouring for information about blood and cuts.

"You need to go to hospital, Dad!"

"No, I'll be fine."

The girls sit beside me. Mia hugs me round the waist–only to get a whiff of vomit from the bag between my feet and recoil suddenly – "Ugh, disgusting!"

"What… where?" Michaela asks, forensically interested.

"I think it's coming from the bag," I tell her.

"*Disgusting*," Mia repeats, waving her hands at the stink. "Is that when you were sick by the pool?"

I wish she wouldn't shout for everyone else to hear – I've attracted enough disgusted looks from strangers already this morning.

"I think so, yeah. It's mostly on the towel, which is in the bag."

Mia backs away from the bag as though the vomity towel might jump out at her. She's funny, so dramatic always. "Don't worry, I'll put it in the wash as soon as we get home."

"When *are we* going home?" Mia asks with renewed emphasis.

"Soon."

"Why were you sick?" Michaela asks in that dreamy way she has that suggests she processes all information in terms of other images, usually from movies and computer games.

"That man said you were pissed. What does 'pissed' mean, Dad?" Mia asks, ever the little perceptive one.

"Pissed means drunk. I wasn't drunk, I had a concussion, and sometimes a concussion can make you look as if you're drunk."

"What's a concussion?"

"When you bang your head and you're knocked out, or you're nearly knocked out. And sometimes that makes you feel sick…"

The truth is, I did wake with a fairly bad hangover that morning, but I'm not about to admit that to two young girls with flapping tongues–it's hard enough to get their mother to give me the benefit of the doubt when the shit hits the fan and the girls are involved.

I'm about to enlighten them further on the subject of head injuries, when my mobile starts vibrating against my thigh and I motion to the girls *hold that thought.* The caller ID tells me it's my brother and I feel immediately grateful for the timing of his call.

"Myles!" I say with the kind of unimpeachable spiritedness the British can muster so naturally in the midst of a crisis.

"Tony, are you alright?" His instant and deeply felt concern strikes me as eerily prescient, it's as if he'd had a premonition days ago that I might be in some kind of danger.

"Er, no actually, my head's killing me, I–"

"Christ, were you hurt?"

"Yeah, I–yeah I was…. how did you know?"

"It's been all over the news."

"The news?" Suddenly my heart starts galloping all over again. I look about me half expecting to see a gaggle of journalists with cameras arguing with security at the entrance of the leisure centre. But no one's there, just this steady on/off stream of scruffy looking parents and hyper kids bouncing in and out on their way to changing rooms, reception or pool gallery.

"Yeah, are you OK?"

"No, I'm not, I–I think I got a c-concussion, uh..." I just stammered, I never stammer, this is a little worrying, but I plough on. "–There's a girl with her tooth knocked out–"

"Concussion?"

"Yeah, cut my head open, smashed my knee... It's not too bad, but there's another kid also hurt–he's been wheeled off to hospital–and I think the people here think it's all my fault, I don't know, I'm waiting for the police to get here."

"Shit, why would they think it's *your* fault?"

"Myles, how did you know I'd been hurt anyway? I didn't call you, did I? I feel a bit dazed…"

"I just told you, it's on the news."

"Really?"

"Yes."

His slightly reproachful tone makes me prickle with confusion. My head's beginning to throb with a fresh surge of anxiety, exhausted adrenals are squirting what little they have left–and, now I realise, I'm shaking. I remove the tissue I've been pressing to my cut–a sopping wad of bright red that's made me a little Japanese flag. Another little red bomb explodes on the floor. I press the tissue back, even though it's probably lost its absorbency.

"But it wasn't that big a deal. I mean, I don't think anyone got seriously hurt–"

"Well, Tony, over 30 people are dead and they expect a lot more. I'd say that's a pretty big deal."

"Myles, what're you talking about? No one died."

"Tone, you've got a TV at your dental practice, don't you?"

"Yeah, but I'm not there–"

"Well, a radio or something?"

"Myles, what's up?"

"Find a TV, turn it on. There've been 3 or 4 simultaneous terrorist attacks on the tube and on a bus. Maybe you should be in hospital if you can't remember what happened to you."

"Myles, there were no bombs. I'm at a swimming pool."

Hanging up, I now have an explanation as to why the police are taking so long: they've got more important things to be doing. It's probably a fair guess they'll never materialise.

"*Daaad*, when're we going home?" Mia moans again.

I reach for her hand.

"Right now, sweetheart," and so we just walked out of there. And in spite of all the earlier uproar and panic no one seemed to take the blindest bit of notice.

Most life-changing accidents that befall us fill our mouths with spiky 'if's, like fish bones we can't spit out quick enough–*If only I hadn't gone on that day, if only I'd stayed at home, if only I hadn't looked into her eyes…* For most of you reading this, July 7 2005 brings back one memory–the London bombings. And for me, yes of course it's that, too. But even as I soaked up the repeated video playback of victims' talking of what they'd experienced, shots of the mutilated bus and street debris–all of it a thickening collage of fear and speculation that overlapped itself into slowly-gestating panic–I was still caught up in the experience of some other random collision of energies that had happened to me around the same time, in the same city.

It's an odd feeling to be involved in a public accident at the same time as a bigger public outrage, somewhere else in the same city. I was secretly excited by the coincidence, inclined to believe it might even 'mean' something, I could have believed I'd tapped into a major vibration of gathering randomness, that the events were trying to tell me something about my own destiny. Yes, I sound overblown perhaps, but those were the emotions that day. And although I was transported from my own immediate preoccupations to a broader canvas of concern, I felt undeserving of a sympathetic ear. And so I withdrew. Ironically, it would be in part the post 7/7 swell of compassion that would sweep me, months later, into my own nightmare of savage violence and loss. But I'm running ahead of myself. I should return to the pool– which gave birth to this story.

I'd been startled awake that morning by a vibration against my thigh. I was lying on my back in my dentist chair like a space traveller. I'd meant to get out of the chair and crash on the sofa in reception, but I'd been too wazzed to make it that far. I'd opened my eyes half expecting to see that I'd fallen asleep on the dodgy drill head. It was my phone, of course. The single buzz told me it was a text message. I lay there a moment longer, gazing at the crowd of happy-go-lucky cartoon characters on the poster pinned to the ceiling above my head and imagined pinning something obscene up there in its place. And just for a second or two I felt bereft of any childish mischief in my life.

A little letter icon and my wife's name, SYLVIA, soon wiped the grin off my face.

I'd argued with her the night before. Over money. I'd not only given her less of it in the last three months, I'd failed to offer up an explanation which could be accounted for in terms of the family's well-being. If I was really going through such a lean period at the practice, perhaps *she* should check my books. If I didn't want a joint account, fine, but she needed a regular monthly allowance–either that, or *I* could start doing the bulk buys at supermarkets.

"So what is this money going on?" she demanded.

I could have asked her the same thing about the money I'd given her. Surely switching to organic hadn't cost *that* much.

"I don't know what you mean? Bills, I imagine. It's not like I'm out boozing every night. Or even every weekend…"

"So what then? – because it's definitely less than you were giving me." She'd planted herself in the middle of the doorway like a reindeer blocking the road, defiant, even a little haughty, daring me to test her with evasive tactics. All the warmth had gone from her Franco Mauritian eyes. Her lips, normally full and sensuous, had shrunk to angry, cherubic knots of ruthless repudiation. With her rich, curly dark hair now like an angry mane, her long, dark eyebrows stood ready like little curled swords drawn from their sheaths. I wasn't going to be allowed to wriggle out of this one–she'd been saving it up.

I threw out some figures, but she chewed them up and spat them out–they simply didn't account for the shortfall. She didn't like being taken for granted, she said, as if for the record. Sylvia wasn't one to carp on about money, even when times had been hard; only when she felt the kids' future might be at stake would she transform herself into some kind of paragon of steely virtue–she was doing it then and I was dangling on the pin of her stare until I insisted lamely, then more heatedly, when I saw she wasn't about to soften, that I'd already given her some extra cash that month.

"When?" she scoffed.

I stammered, not remembering clearly.

"You see – you don't even remember. The money you think you gave me was months ago – for fixing the car."

"No, it was after that…" I began, honestly amused by this 'false memory' syndrome we both seemed to be suffering from more and more, recently–but of course she assumed I was being supercilious. Which was fair enough, I suppose–but, again, her reaction once again underlined the fact that we were so seldom on the same page.

An ordinary enough squabble, perhaps, familiar to any couple, except, coming through this one, like the scent of a third person in the room, was Sylvia's unspoken fear – a fear that she's always carried around with her like a wound I've never been able to heal – that I was spending my money on another woman. Ironically, although I wished I were, I wasn't in fact seeing anyone else. As the accusation in her eyes bore into me, my blood began to fizz with this heady cocktail of latent guilt and bristling indifference. It's true, both of us had been tired, dehydrated, fractious from drinks we'd had earlier that evening with our separate friends – we were as volatile as sticks of sweating dynamite – but for the first time in a long time I didn't care too much about the consequences.

I grabbed my jacket and rushed out of the house into cool, summer night air, a kind of teenage kick to my stride, as I headed off just anywhere. Not even half way to the next street, I slowed down and seriously considered rushing back to the house to pack a suitcase. Thing is, I wasn't twenty-three anymore, I wasn't even thirty-three. I was forty-three in all but a few weeks, and I was a dad. I could just picture Sylvia rousing the girls as I was heading down the stairs with a case, getting them up to come see their wonderful daddy walking out on them, a picture to remember for all eternity… OK, so I'd walk round the block, walk it down, I told myself. But then I surprised myself by hopping on a bus, the bus I take to get to work. I hopped off near the practice in North West Ealing and strolled into an off-licence a few minutes before closing. I hadn't done this for some time and I had a sort of warm alcohol feeling that a bottle of comforting Cabernet would do me some good and, by turns, perhaps even Sylvia.

With the alarm deactivated, a couple of lights on, I poured myself a glass and propped my feet up on the sofa before the widescreen TV. But after 20 minutes of flicking from channel to channel, and already queasy from the ejaculate of the reality shows, I settled on the news until I was threatened with trivial stories and golf highlights, whereupon I aimed the remote.

Silence. The faint smell of damp in the air. Sylvia had remarked on it years ago and only now was I really noticing it. Didn't help that I'd gone for a traditional toothpaste ingredient as the theme for my waiting room–the dark minty green of the leather sofa and armchair, the pale creamy mint for the wallpaper, the green tint to the landscape photograph had all lost their refreshing look in less than six months and reminded me of the girls' tropical fish tank when it got covered in algae. I didn't even much like the taste of mint, if I was honest.

I turned my head and glanced at my grey filing cabinet–I'd been uncomfortably aware of its presence as I watched the TV.

I slapped a pile of papers on the reception desk. I drew up the chair and began raking through the accounts, and all the other bumf you have to file. I wasn't sure what I was looking for–presumably, some kind of proof that we were in fact going through a lean period. But now that I was here, alone, not having to worry about losing face, I had to admit that I possibly hadn't given her as much money in the last three or four months because I was apprehensive about what I'd be left with if what was happening led to divorce–I didn't want to be living in squalor when it happened. *I'm turning into a squirrel.* Trying to convince myself that I'll put my few hoardings back on the table again if we could but somehow bridge the gap between us.

If only I'd got a pre-nup.

Sometimes it appalled me that I thought this way, but I'd once been badly fucked over by an alcoholic partner in the early years of setting up my practice–a Lebanese Jew who had so played me for my liberal sympathies, my fear of appearing to be in any way anti-Semitic–and I'd never quite regained my trust in human beings, even the women I'd loved. Still, a two-thousand-a-month allowance wasn't exactly mean for a woman who was now a full-time mature student. Would I ever see any of the money she earned from selling a painting, assuming she ever sold one? We might be divorced by then. *God, all she has to do is fuck my brains out and I'd be easy about money–well, easier.* If only it were that simple. Well it might be, on one level. But her urges aren't made that way, I know that. And I'm drunk. She probably senses I think like this sometimes and tells herself she'll be damned if she's going to stoop to being my whore. "I'm a whore," I told her only a few nights ago, in a moment of self-disgust, words I already regretted as I uttered them. "I'm a whore because I'm not even in love with my job."

"So change it."

I'd laughed. "And who's going to pay the mortgage if I do that?"

"So let's downsize – but don't give me your self-pity."

Even though I knew she'd already demolished me, I laughed louder.

"Only the week before you'd been asking me to look for a new house! So which is it?!"

But I knew the answer to that: she wanted answers not questions. Sort myself out, then she might listen and plan something together.

"What would do it for you?" I'd say, one of those nights when we'd have gotten into bed frisky enough to do something, but twenty minutes later find ourselves just lying there, side by side, gazing at the inky ceiling, strangely disembodied from our impulses.

I'd hear a gently scoffing laugh and she'd ask, Why did I only ever bring this subject up when we were in bed, when she was already tired?

"You don't seem that tired."

She'd sigh and I'd pursue the subject regardless.

"How about with other couples?"

She'd laugh derisively, denying me the irony in my question. I could have reminded her there was a time when she might at least have had fun with the idea, but this was my problem, wasn't it–*living in the past.*

"Toys?"

"I have enough of those going up my bum by accident, when we sit down to watch tele…"

She didn't like anal sex. If I liked anal sex, why didn't I go to a gay bar?

"I'm not gay."

"You might be. You've got a strong feminine side. You might be better off with them–you'd certainly get more sex than with a woman."

I could never be entirely sure whether she was being purely facetious–there was always this edge of suspicion to her tone. And yet her suspicion wasn't about my sexuality per se–her way of normalising her loss of libido was to mock my own. By making me feel desperate she was hoping to undermine my chances with other women, or–presumably–men.

"Why does it always have to be something that ends in an orgasm for you?"

"Well I always try for us both – you know that."

"No, I mean, why can't you just enjoy tenderness?"

"I can."

She thought about this. "Not really," she said finally.

Five minutes later, exasperated by our inability to find a meeting of minds, I'd said in an almost off-hand way that I supposed this sort of thing happens to most couples – only a lucky few manage to interest each other sexually beyond the seven-year itch.

"So – you just want to give up?"

"I don't know. Maybe it's best."

"Why can't you think of a different way of approaching me? Like, why does it always have to be in bed?"

"Like, when else do we have time for each other? You're always so busy with your studying, or the kids, for us to even think of doing it at any other time!"

"You could watch less TV and then we wouldn't get into bed so late, when I'm already tired."

So I'd gone on a diet of less TV. I'd got a lot of reading done, but still gained no insight into our chilled sexual relations. Ironically, the reading had inspired me to go on a course for amalgam-free dentistry, which in turn took me farther away from Sylvia. By the time I'd completed the course, she was addicted to E-Bay. Missing my treats of CSI and 24 no longer became a meaningful sacrifice. Her E-Bay habit and bingeing on comfort food became the permanent cuckoos in the nest of love. I drank to take the edge off my sexual frustration and, if she'd abstained that same night, my winy breath would be duly noted in bed as a reason, specious or otherwise, why she never really felt like it anymore. Eighteen months of this and we'd become fully dysfunctional. For the past six months we'd taken care not to touch each other in bed without prior intimation that it was sought after. I'd found the cold turkey horrendously painful. Also demeaning. My attempts at rekindling interest became increasingly self-conscious and carried the whiff of desperation. If only I could have been happy cutting my balls off, maybe that sadness I saw in her eyes from time to time would lift.

So there I was in a pool of electric light at the receptionist's desk, on my third glass, wavering between an optimistic outlook and a downright pessimistic one. I saw myself admitting to her that I'd gone down to the practice and checked over the accounts and, well yeah, perhaps I could afford to give her a bit more money after all. With the wine in my veins, I could picture her breaking into that cheeky, all-forgiving smile I saw so rarely these days. I could see her coming to give me a hug – her sweet little boy who'd finally worked up enough courage to dig out his awkward make-up-and-be-friends speech. 'Would 250 quid help?' I'd say, taking out the wad of notes I'd have drawn from the ATM on the way home. She could buy some new boots with that. Would she still be smiling as I offered her the money? Or would the gesture be taken as 'patronising'? What if I came back and her mood had hardened with time? And we had to continue with the argument to its bitter conclusion… whatever that might be.

I poured a fourth glass hoping to gain clarity as to which scene was the more realistic outcome. I took the reconciliation scene further. And, strangely, it was this scene that unsettled me more than the other one. I could picture myself recoiling from her as she hooked her hands round my neck and told me she was worried about me, I was over-working, it was time we took a holiday. I could see her jumping onto the kneel-chair at my desk and booting up the computer and logging on to lastminute.com before I could sound a tentative note of caution. I could imagine my panic; I saw myself incapable of reminding her of the conflict that had dogged our last holiday together. To have pointed out that we were now even more remote from one another than we were then might have ended it all that very night–and I wasn't ready for that just yet.

The fact is, you can't bear the thought of not waking up with the kids every day.

I knocked back the glass and took measure of my settling inertia. On balance, it was probably best just to give her some space.

Coming up for midnight, I was even admitting to the possibility she was right about everything–that I was to blame, I'd been blind to her little hints encouraging me to woo her afresh. If intelligence was defined as the ability to adapt–in this case to a very infrequent sex life, that's to say 3 times in the last six months–I was a very dumb male. I should have done what she did in her early twenties: gone travelling around the world: waking with scorpions tickling your toes, rats the size of cats scratching at your door; spontaneous sex on E on a Thai beach; living in huts with crocodiles swimming beneath you; being nearly busted for drugs planted on your friend by a dirty Asian cop; having sex with a silent Massai whose penis resembled the spears he carried; waking in the Serengeti Desert to see the silhouettes of lions through your tent covers… I'd still not heard half the stories. These days they tended to pop out in the company of friends over an evening meal. She'd be telling them her story, not quite including me in her narrative, a guilty but tenderly outreaching look in her eye as she read the left-out expression on my face. She's never said in words that I should have got all of that Wander Lust out of my system long before having kids, but I know she feels it. And she never used to make me *feel* it, until recently. *As if there was anything I could do about it now.*

Or could I?

The bottle empty, I'd gone to the pharmacy cupboard and carelessly tipped out a bunch of sedatives into my open palm. I gazed at them, wondering drunkenly whether I wasn't vaguely suicidal. Then I put all of them back but one and went to lie in the chair. Where I must have nodded off.

'Give me a call please,' read Sylvia's text message.

I'll go for a pee first, thanks.

I washed my hands and splashed some water over my face.

"Hi, it's me."

"And where did *you* go?" There was the hint of laughter and irony in her voice, as though she were fully prepared to find an account of how I'd ended up at a brothel totally hilarious. I hadn't expected that. And was instantly reminded of why I still loved her: for her tremendous capacity to forgive and move on.

"I'm at the practice, um…" I drew breath, rubbing my muzzy head. "I thought I should, um–y'know–check over the accounts… uh–"

"You spent the whole night doing that?" as if my income had nothing to do with what we'd been arguing about.

"No, I–I watched a bit of TV…um–You OK?"

"Yes," as if to a stupid question. "I hope you haven't forgotten."

"Forgotten what?"

"You're taking the girls to the pool today."

"I thought it was Thursday – aren't they meant to be in school?"

This is where men fall down so badly–it's not so much we forget about the arrangements for the rest of the week following a bust up, we can't even imagine *any* kind of future arrangements. Women, on the other hand, can always stay focused on their children's appointments, regardless of their spouse's behaviour.

"No, don't you remember? They have an audition for a TV commercial at 2 this afternoon. You said you'd take them swimming in the morning, because they have the day off and so do you. Why do I – can't you –"

"It's OK, I-I can do it. Um –"

She sighed down the phone–to blow away any germ of a lame proviso.

"What's wrong with your voice anyway?"

I coughed, trying to clear it.

"I suppose you were out drinking again last night and that's why you can't remember."

"OK, yes, I admit, I did have a few glasses of wine–doing one's VAT is very dull. I had a few to help me get through it."

"I thought your accountant did your VAT."

She was right. What a pathetic lie.

"Well, it's not very bright, is it, checking your accounts when you're drunk? Your maths isn't so good anyway, is it."

I inhaled, exhaled–a very useful practice in stopping yourself from getting further mired in a woman's pique. I expected her to continue, but she'd fallen silent, either lying in wait or on the verge of hanging up in disgust. In the past year I'd grown to read these silences of hers less as pockets of silence as I used to think of them, rather, as soundless ping pong balls that we knocked back to each other in a bid for one long, final pause.

"So are you coming?"

Yes, I was coming. I reminded her I had to be back at the practice around lunchtime to let in the engineer, who was due to come and fix the drill bit that had been playing up.

"Fine. I don't need you for the whole day," she replied pointedly, as if she might run on to point out how useless I was generally at family matters.

It occurred to me that I might still be over the limit and unsafe to drive, but I didn't dare air the possibility. Perhaps a black coffee would make all the difference.

I hung up. *Fuck. We're fresh out.*

I found Sylvia in the kitchen, wiping surfaces down, reasserting her high standards on her environment. Her shoulder-length Afro-Western-Asian hair was tied back in a simple band. The sleeves of her tight-fitting cardigan were hitched up revealing her elegant forearms and accentuating the beauty of her tapered fingers (which she'd inherited from the Hindi line in her family). Her movements were measured, absorbed in the choreography of her routine. She barely glanced at me as I appeared–I could have returned from the postbox at the end of the road–so I was immediately mindful of how I should approach her.

"Hey," I said simply.

"You OK?" she inquired with provisional warmth.

I nodded and gave a tentatively hopeful smile. As our eyes met, she paused half way through folding a tea towel and raised her chin a fraction. I detected a hint of forgiveness about the slight but telling smile on her lips and read from the glint of irony in her eyes that she assumed I knew she was sorry for her harsh attack the night before but also had enough sense to see to it that I made up for my meanness of late. I stood there, hovering by the door, suddenly overcome with a desire to kiss her, passionately, but before I could move an inch the girls and their choruses of "Hi Dad, where've you *been*?! Are you taking us, Dad?!!" were pouring into the room.

"Aren't you going to shave?" Sylvia asked over the hubbub.

"I don't think there's time, is there?"

She clucked her tongue, despairing of the lack of care I took over my appearance these days.

"Can't you change that awful old fleece top at least? It's pathetic."

As I stood before the bathroom mirror squinting at pink eyes and an impudent zit on my forehead, I heard Sylvia calling from the kitchen that she'd packed a towel for me along with my trunks. She expected me to join the girls in the water. I knew it was unwise to protest, so I called to her, Had she seen my goggles? "No! Find them yourself!" But she came into our room anyway, determined to prove how useless and childlike I was – and not hearing her, I bumped into her as I turned round. She laughed and playfully slapped me and told me I was such an idiot, never organised etc. and, as I stood aside, letting her do my job for me, I casually reappraised her behind – still in good shape after two kids, I told myself, as if merely reading the electric meter – vaguely wondering whether a beach holiday for two, (kids at Grandma and Grandpa's), mightn't give our marriage the kind of shot it was badly in need of. "There," she said, turning round, making a face as she planted my goggles in my hands.

It felt churlish not to kiss her on the cheek on the way out, but I wanted at all cost to avoid her smelling the alcohol on my breath.

"Don't forget to give Mia her armbands if she goes into the deep end!" she called after us as I herded the kids out the door.

"OK," I said, hardly listening.

Turning to see her wave, I was struck by the depth of her devotion to us as a family unit – my compartmentalising ways of the male seemed suddenly so devious and self-serving by comparison. She called a musical, faintly melancholy "Take care!" after us, which lodged in my throat like a prickly seed of sadness for at least a mile down the road.

The girls were all questions and chat about school and movies, their energy pushing us through the traffic, insisting that life goes on with minimal self-reflection.

"Oh, Dad, haven't you seen it yet!" Mia exclaimed.

"Sorry, I've been a bit busy recently. Is that the one with um–"

"You're always so busy, Dad!" they complained beautifully together.

"I know, I know, always busy," I said with a tired, sympathetic cadence that reminded me of how meaningless the word had sounded when I was their age–that's if it didn't seem even more meaningless now.

I always wish I could share in my kids' pleasure upon arriving at a leisure centre, but the fact is I find the whole experience turbulent and overwhelming, as if I'm being force fed with everything that's generic in the world of advertising. Not having eaten a thing that morning, the warm fog of chlorinated air punctuated by the cacophony of echoing voices made me feel instantly queasy as I entered the pool. I was surprised to see so many other children. Did they also have McDonald TV ad auditions to go to that afternoon? My fragile state of mind wasn't helped when the girls emerged from their changing room to fall about laughing the moment they spotted me waiting for them in my trunks.

"What's so funny?"

"You're nearly as thin as Grandpa!" Mia exclaimed as if she'd never seen me out of trousers before. She was growing up, I realised, little by little being infiltrated by social and sexual self-awareness.

Michaela and Mia trotted off like fairies to the diving area on the balls of their feet. They sat down together on a corner of the pool and dipped their legs in. I'd been close to my brother, but these two were even closer. How would they ever bear to be apart? I watched them natter happily for a minute, legs idly kicking in the water, their life stretched before them, so buoyant. I wasn't even sure I could face going in, so I parked myself on a wooden bench within a few feet of them. Michaela turned her head and smiled and waved the moment she saw me, and then Mia did the same and I waved and smiled back wishing to encourage them to explore on their own for a while.

Michaela then Mia slipped in and began swimming widths. It must have been three or four months since

I'd seen them swim and, gratifyingly, they were beginning to find their strokes at last. It hurt to recall Sylvia's recent criticism that I was 'missing out on my daughters' lives'. My friends would readily observe that as far as they could tell I did a lot more with, and for my girls, than most fathers they knew–and that was some source of comfort, but I think I knew what Sylvia meant. She meant that even when I was with them, I was mentally elsewhere for much of the time. If I wasn't preoccupied over the recent ups and downs at the practice, I was asking myself, Did I really want to spend the next twenty years of my working life as a dentist? Or I'd be with them one minute, then dreaming of adventures with other, younger women the next.

When I looked around the pool at other fathers my age or older, I didn't see myself in them. They seemed happier in their softer, sagging flesh and trunks, their baggy jeans and baggy tracksuits. Why did I never get chatting with any of the parents in the playground whenever I went to pick up the girls? The mothers who would have welcomed a chat. Where had this profound unwillingness to involve myself in like parents come from? I wasn't unfriendly, but I was invariably distant–Sylvia had told me some mothers had said I looked 'unapproachable'–which was quite unlike the person I was with my patients. I suspected it had something to do with a subconscious feeling that being a dad was an emasculating experience. Which was bizarre, really, because I don't identify with anything overtly male or macho. Valuing integrity in others, I suppose I've always felt uncomfortable being identified as Mr. Happily Married Family Man, because I was anything but and suspected I was probably incapable of ever being one.

It had been a mistake to try and line my stomach with a few Pringles from the tin Sylvia had slipped in with our things. My mouth felt icky and my head ached. I pulled out a newspaper I'd rolled in with Michaela's towel and chopped it into readable portions as though settling into a thorough good read. As usual I darted listlessly from one article to the next, often starting in the middle or even the end and reading from random points–like a film editor desperate for a fresh, 'alternative' way of telling a familiar narrative–until finally I found the rhythm of it only added to the swell of my nausea. I stuffed the newspaper away and contemplated the pool with the short, sharp shock of a swim in mind.

Mia was bouncing up and down on the second highest diving board–and off she went, the little daredevil. I cherished the warm feeling I got as I watched her, totally absorbed in her moment. Watching these two is the nearest I get these days to 'feeling in love'. When I watch them move, I'm in that same innocent space as you are when you're in love. It's not something sexual; it's something wondrous and light, buoyant with hope.

Mia's head bobbed up and she shook the water out of her face calling to her sister, "It's great Michaela, you should try it!"

I saw Michaela trot along in her funny fox-like gait to the same diving board. Her co-ordination skills as a two-year-old were so poor you couldn't believe your ears when you'd heard she'd come second behind an athletic black girl in the Summer Sports Day race last year. Now she was running straight to the end of the board and doing a little twirl in the air as she spun off, one hand holding her nose. She came up with her eyes closed tight. Mia was already showering her with fresh alacrity about how great it was. She then pushed up and out of the pool and hurried off to go again–with such great fanfare it had boys twice her age coming along to join her.

The sun came out about then, casting a multitude of dazzling scales of golden yellow on the hypnotic, shimmering grid of blue. The echoing voices sloshed around in my head like memory soup and I was content to drift off into nowhere for a minute and a day. When I next turned to see what the kids were up to, my eyes were dotted with yellow blotches from the sun. And as they slowly began to make out clear outlines again, I saw a flash of red and white costume half way up the ladder of the tallest diving board and I recognised Mia by her sheer Laura Croft energy alone. Three seconds later, I realised something was missing, it was something I'd forgotten–*You forgot to give her the fucking armbands!* I turned and dove into the bag on the bench beside me–fluorescent orange things her mum had specifically reminded me I should give Mia before she went in… My legs scuttling ahead of me toward the boards, I blew air through one of the chlorinated valves, realising I probably should be calling to her already. I got to the lower board and waved, hoping she'd see me, but her face was busy watching some boys take their running jump.

I glanced in the direction of the umpire-like chair, some 25 feet away on the other side, from which the attendants survey this end of the pool. It was empty. The guy had left his post to fix a water polo goal stationed in the far corner.

"Mia!" I called out.

Sylvia was right, my voice was lower after drink, more resonant and yet I hadn't found the wind to make it cut through the atmosphere of echoing voices and splashes. On the other hand, I was very conscious of not wanting to betray alarm. I wasn't alarmed. I'd go up there and give her the bands, simple.

I got onto the lower diving board and started up the steps. From the first board there was another flight of metal steps leading to the higher board. It was roughly 25 feet above the water, hardly a dangerous height. And yet, as I neared the top, I felt slightly faint and, for a moment, I lost the point of what I was doing there.

Level with the board I saw Mia wasn't alone. There were two boys–ages twelve or thirteen–up there with her. With their hair plastered flat to their skulls and their hairless wet bodies glistening in the light, they looked like amphibious humans. They were taunting each other, then darting innuendo around Mia who'd just stepped back from the edge and turned to beam at them with cinematic confidence. Even in my befuddled state I could tell the boys' mischievous desire to tease this little girl over the edge was being fuelled and undermined by their adolescent fascination in her beauty and courage. My arrival had introduced a new power dynamic, forcing them to back off or up the stakes.

Before I could say anything, Mia pointed at me and laughed and cried, "Daddy, what are you doing up here?!" as if I'd appeared in a clown's costume.

"Sweetheart, it's a little high, OK?"

"Wanna get high mister?" It was the skinny boy with dark hair, a similar skin colour to my lot, almond eyes, who took the first shot–leering at me with a swagger that boys show only when they know you're on their turf now.

I ignored the remark and walked over to Mia.

"It's really high," she said, gesturing expansively before her as though surveying a new kingdom she never knew existed. "Can you die if you fall?"

"Hey… let's put these on, OK?" I started to slip one of the armbands up her slender little arm.

"You're in our way mate."

I turned and realised it was the fat boy talking. His mouth was lardy and unlovable and the sloping hound-dog eyes gave him a congenitally bored look that you learn to associate with sociopaths.

"Give me a second, OK?"

Crouching, I was seized by a nasty cramp in the arch of my left foot. Mia visibly reacted to my grimace as though I'd pulled a nasty face at her. The boys were muttering obscenities behind my back–

"Guys, can you just give me a minute here, OK?" The tone of a mate, reasonable–but even then I was conscious that they might find the familiarity presumptuous–*like, no was I as cool as them brov.*

"You just 'ad a minute," the fat one said.

"Yeah, go on, this board isn't for dads and little girls, y'know," the skinny one joined in, swinging about on one of the support bars. He spoke like adolescents who push themselves to be hard, the type who's come late to the hard game. He had crooked teeth, a fidgety energy.

"I realise that. I came up to take her down."

"*Take her down, boss,*" the fat guy echoed back with a mock New York accent, vacuously conveyed. He started making rap noises that descended into farts and giggling.

"Well get on with it then!" they nagged more or less in chorus.

I turned back to Mia to put on the second armband. She'd fallen quiet, faintly troubled, the full lower lip hanging in a doubtful pout.

The boys started up their rude and impatient demands again but this time with a difference–one of them, I think the fat one, said that this wasn't the place to touch up little girls. I jerked my head round, my face creasing with disgust.

"Hey, will you just get lost. This is my *daughter*, OK?"

"No you get lost–wanker!'" the fat one bounced back at me–he looked like a pig chomping his words, as if he'd eat me next. "Get off this fucking board or we'll call a guard."

It was years since I'd encountered this kind of unprovoked aggression in anyone–I'd known how to deal with it better when I was his age.

"You're in our way, mate." It was the skinny boy, now delivering a matter-of-fact explanation as if merely to temper the full-on provocation of his friend.

My butterfingers slipped with the valve again as Mia quietly observed that the fat boy had used the 'f' word.

"Oi!" I heard needling my ear. Then snickers. It was hard to judge how serious they were.

Mia's earlier happiness had evaporated under the savage heat of the older boys' jibes and she'd become completely suggestible to heading back down. But then she spotted Michaela, who was waving up at us from the water, diagonally below. Mia waved back, calling out and I lost my grip on the valve of the armband again.

"Sweetheart, stay still a minute, can you–"

As I put my mouth over the nipple of the valve –

"Blow job, blow job!" the boys sounded off, behind me.

In retrospect, I should have realised my butt was out there like some kind of fresh insult to these two boys itching for their jump.

I heard a quick rumble of feet and the next thing I knew a pair of wet hands had landed on my back, with weight, a body flew over my back, but clipped the side of my head so I lurched sideways. As a reflex I grabbed at Mia–or was I still holding her?–and, for a second, I thought we'd steady ourselves, but then Mia toppled, and as I reached out to grab her… I don't know, perhaps we were already falling. Even as I was falling I somehow had time to feel anger first at the boy who'd pushed us–was he the fat one or the thin one?–then joy as I saw the world entirely through his eyes… but I had no fear of being hurt or of anyone else getting hurt. So that was the shock. Hitting someone. Or *something*, you think to yourself, because when you're falling into water anything you hit that isn't water is a thing to begin with. Mia went over with a squeal–but it sounded like fun, if only just. I knew I'd get a nasty smack from the surface because of my awkward trajectory and flailing shape. But then came the crack of something hard against my head, left hand and my right foot. *Don't say you've hit Mia.* In the first few moments of being under the water, I wasn't concerned with pain, I knew that was coming, I was worried I'd seriously hurt someone else. Except the worry kind of froze as I sank further into the water. My body pretended to be a starfish, waiting for the current to lift it onto a rock. Time stood still. My lungs seemed capable of holding out for minutes on end. Instincts had assumed command, the body knew to relax and let the brain rediscover coordination in its own time. Like a trapped bubble set free the thought came to me that I must somehow move to find Mia before something worse happened.

I broke the surface to see one of the attendants diving into the pool fully dressed. He swam out to the skinnier boy who was rolling in the water like a dying fish ten yards away from me. His rescuer scooped him up and safety-swam him to the side of the pool. I saw Mia had made it to the other side, a little shocked by the jump, repeatedly wiping water from her face and coughing to clear her throat of the water she'd swallowed. She hadn't seen me yet. A body was bobbing up against mine and caused me to go under. I swam back up, choking and bumped up against a young woman, her arms and legs. I sputtered an incoherent apology expecting to see a swimmer trying to get round me. But the girl, with long black hair, was treading water, a hand covering her mouth and nose. She had large eyes–South East Asian–she was frightened and she was in pain. I saw blood running through her fingers–and I may have said, "Are you OK?" but my mouth wasn't articulating properly, my teeth had come down on one side of my tongue, and my ears were full of water. The caveman-like utterance seemed to frighten her and she swam away from me as though I'd been about to hit her again.

I swam after her as instinctively as though she'd been my own child. Dazed and shook up, my breaststroke kept deteriorating into a messy doggy paddle. I flopped into a space beside the girl and clung to the side, catching my breath. I still couldn't hear properly, everything was muffled, echoing twice what it had been. The girl had her face turned away from me–whether on purpose, I couldn't tell–her long, dark hair a soaking wet curtain between us. Her dark-skinned, ultra slender body trembled in the water, but she made no sound.

A few yards further along, my daughter was clinging to the side, still coughing. But she saw me now and sent me a little wave to signal she was OK. She looked unhurt. It must have been then I grew aware of something warmer than pool water trickling over my left eye and down my face. I could taste it–it was blood. I dabbed at my forehead but couldn't feel any opening, just wetness.

Turning my head I saw the pool attendant giving mouth-to-mouth to the boy, the skinny one. He'd placed a foam float under his head. The boy was coming round, coughing and jerking about as if a return to consciousness was like being forced back to school…

I turned back to the girl and, my arm shaking, reached to put my hand gently on her shoulder. The pain was beginning to define itself now–in my head and my knee–but a way of avoiding it was first to understand this girl's pain.

She moved a fraction, darting cat-like eyes of suspicion at me.

"Please, I'm a dentist, let me take a look… Maybe I can help."

Hearing 'dentist' I thought I saw something in her eyes relax. I reached out to gently remove her trembling hand from her face, entrusting her shame to me. Blood was streaming from one nostril, but the nose didn't look broken. Angling my head to catch the light I saw her mouth must have taken a direct hit because her upper second, right, was now but a short stump.

"You've broken a tooth, OK, but I can fix that for you. I'm a dentist," I repeated. "Is there anywhere else you're feeling pain?"

She was gazing at the cut over my eye now; the stream of blood trickling into the corner of my mouth seemed to make us nearly equal and produce a calming effect on her and she made an almost imperceptible shake of her head. The new expression of trust that had entered her large almond eyes reminded me instantly of my own Mia.

"I'm sorry if I landed on you… I was pushed."

"My teeth, it's bad?"

"Could you get out of the water, please, sir!"

A female attendant–shaggy blonde, all business in her hips and square shoulders–was calling across to me from the other side of the pool, as though telling me off for sexual harassment. I ignored her, pressing on to explain to the girl that I personally could fix her tooth and it wouldn't cost her anything.

"Sir, if you would please–"

"Yes, OK! Give us a minute! We're hurt!" I was surprised at the bark in my voice as I turned to fend off the institutional drone of the bustling attendant, then surprised again by the dizziness that followed.

A stocky Thai girl, not half as pretty as my neighbour, appeared next to me, sweet-voiced, calm–

"I'm her friend," she explained. "She get hurt, yeah?"

"Yeah, we both are. Could you help me get your friend out of the pool?"

She was so light we almost tossed her out.

Mia was already standing on the edge, expressing wide eyed amazement and concern at the blood everywhere–on my face, my nose, the girl's mouth, her hand...

And then there was the male pool attendant calling across to me from the other side:

"Can you get out of the pool now, mate?" Australian accent. "I think that's enough high board antics for one day, don't you, sport?"

I turned round to see the boy still on the floor, moaning like a baby, all the puff gone from his gangsta rapper persona. I was tempted to answer back, We were pushed, but the boy's father–a broad-shouldered athletic guy of about my age and height, a few stone heavier, muscled-up–was standing on the side of the pool, short wet hair pasted to his Norman looking skull, swearing and gesticulating and darting increasingly murderous glances at me. The attendants were having a time keeping him in order.

"Dad, Dad–are you alright?" It was Michaela, standing on the side, hands clasping opposite elbows, shivering. "Dad, you're bleeding," she observed, so much more calmly than her sister.

"I know, darling, I know, it's OK," though I didn't know that and I certainly didn't feel OK. I couldn't think how I'd cut my head: maybe the girl's tooth, or that ring–a gold ring with a leaf-like design–on her left hand, middle finger, or maybe the boy, he could have had jewellery, even chunky stuff…

"Guys, can you get dressed, I need to look after this girl–she's lost half a tooth."

"Did she swallow it?" Mia asked.

"I don't think so, I think it must be in the pool."

"Oh."

My girls gasped in horror and cast pitying eyes upon the slender young woman sitting motionless beside her friend on the side of the pool with her hand to her mouth.

"Mia, Michaela, let's go… let's go!" and they duly ran off to the changing room without any fuss.

I heard the crackle of a Walkie-Talkie from the far end and saw the female swim attendant arrive with another attendant and some kind of stretcher. *Surely not.*

It was time I made a move. So I put my palms on the tile edge and thrust down. My stomach heaved with the sudden movement. I got my left knee up, but it was the one I'd just bruised, I registered a sharp pain in the area of an old injury, my adrenals surged and I fell into a zone of suspended nausea and fainting. I was no longer a swimmer getting out of the pool, I was a surfer riding a wave, and the wave was curling over me… if I could just thread through it before it swallowed me up… Half out of the pool, I hung there probably only three seconds, a proverbial lifetime, I bent forward–a serious miscalculation, because all of a sudden my stomach heaved up its contents. An ignominious splash landed on the tiles inches from the injured girl. It was so loud and sudden I couldn't believe it had issued from my own mouth. But then it came again. With a gasp and a rasp of my lungs I flopped like a wounded seal on the tiles, bruising my cheek. I could only lie there at the mercy of my spasms. I was too helpless to push the vomit away or even roll away from it. The Thai girls had jumped up with a cry of alarm and disgust and begun moving away from me. My eyes blurred and I lost all sense of where anyone was. I wanted to say I was OK, but I was retching again. How embarrassing. I could hear a round of kids' "Ughs!" bouncing around the pool… that Australian voice again, this time expressing mild disgust and disbelief as though I were some kind of paedophile drunk who'd dropped into his pool from out of space… Alcohol, hangover, Pringles flavour, concussion–Ugh… *I've had enough*, a voice said in my head, and the voice seemed to be referring not just to this but the shape my life was in at this present moment–and yet, how bloody irrelevant…

I was being hauled roughly to my feet and carried away by two very fit young men, that Australian accent no longer rasping and broad, just matey and chipper, riffing stuff about getting me cleaned up. I felt like a piece of trash I was happy for them to throw away. We torpedoed double doors and arrived in the changing area where the air was thick and muggy with body odour. I was bundled into a cubicle, but let down easy.

The Aussie was gently slapping me about the cheeks and saying, "So are you alright in there, mate? Can you hear me…? What's your name, mate?"

So this is where it begins, the blame, the shame, the legal battles that will take your life to pieces tooth by tooth…

I told him my name and clung to the belief that if I could just make him understand I was a dentist not a drunk and that I would be happy to help the girl and anyone else who'd lost a tooth today, he might give me the benefit of the doubt here.

"The kid pushed us… it was a prank… a leapfrog… He was impatient for his turn…" I blurted out. I badly needed to spit. I was slurring my words and suspected I might have cut my tongue on my own teeth... "I'm sure he didn't mean to hurt anyone," I said, because it offended my sense of decency to hold a grudge or look inside my atavistic self.

"The kid's OK, mate, just got a bit of a concussion like yourself, alright? But y'know, you really should've left it to one of our guys to get your daughter down–"

I looked at the face directly in front of me–the skin younger but having seen a stronger sun, the blond hair burnished, almost turning gold, the blue eyes, used to bigger horizons than anything you get in England–and I felt I was looking at him as a girl might before he fucked her. How weird. I saw he was wearing a badge and that he was GREG. And then I blinked blood again–

"Where're your little girlies? Are they still in the pool?"

As I told him their names, described them, told him they were getting changed, I could see people peeping in through the cubicle door behind his back as if at a lunatic. The muted and shrill pool sounds had a strangely soothing effect on me now and I began to feel as if I belonged here, the way you quickly start to feel you belong at a hospital when you arrive there on a gurney after a car accident.

I noticed a large blob of blood drip onto the dotted floor between my feet and noticed the landscape down there was dotted with blood.

"Let me get a bandage for that thing on your head there, Anthony, OK?"

At least I was Anthony now, not just 'mate'.

He'd just gone away, I was sitting there with my forearms on my thighs gazing at the blood drops on the floor, trying to count them only to find I couldn't count past 3, when there came a hefty thump against the cubicle walls. I jumped and looked up to see an angry figure leaning in menacingly, he was spitting words at me, bellowing with such force his words blew any verbal response clean out of my head. It was the boy's dad, like a pitbull off its chain leash, and all I could think was that his boy had just suffered a brain haemorrhage or something. In the first moment of this barrage it was vaguely reassuring to note that he was now wearing a spanking new navy tracksuit with cream zips and a pressed, white T-shirt underneath, a flashy diver's watch–because dressed like that he was probably less likely to beat me up. The long, squared-off features suggested a man with a passion for boxing, but his small, bulbous blue eyes and the rapidly blinking eyelids with their rather effeminate eyelashes betrayed panic and disbelief, less an intent to harm me physically. He was a barker, not a hitter, I told myself, as I sat there, taking it, weirdly fascinated by the pink lips of his anus-like mouth that kept puckering with each round of attack as though it could barely handle the volume of the words it was spouting in an increasingly piping, absurdly theatrical voice.

"I'm sorry… I'm sorry," I repeated lamely.

"So you admit it, you pushed him off the board!"

"No, he pushed *us*."

"Bollocks!" His hand slammed the cubicle wall. "That's not what *he's* saying. And my son doesn't lie – not to me he doesn't!" An odd qualification, I remembered long afterward.

"Your son pushed me!" I roared back and my body trembled as my heart and lungs pumped out the words. I was in no physical shape to withstand a physical retaliation. Perhaps my cut was saving me from a second beating.

"Well that's not what *I'm* hearing! He went to jump and you barged him sideways!"

"I'm sorry, but it didn't happen like that. He leapfrogged over me and I lost my
balance–"

"What're you doing up there anyway! He says you were being abusive, totally pissed out of your fart!"

"Alright fella! Easy now... Easy…"

My mate, Greg, had returned and was already shielding me from my assailant, backing him up like one of those cocksure Australian documentary filmmakers talking to one of his deadly matey crocs.

"Look at this moron! Half pissed, puking in the pool–"

"Hey hey hey… easy now, my friend," Greg kept saying.

"Alright alright, I'm not doing anything, I'm not touching 'im, I just want a reasonable explanation!"

"I know you're upset," Greg was saying. "Your boy's been hurt, but *he's* been hurt too, mate, so let's just take a breather for a minute, OK?"

The man continued to protest, but he was gradually being prevailed upon by another male attendant to return to the reception area.

Greg returned with a smirking half smile–

"Wo, is he a mad one!"

I got to my feet, holding on to the sides of the cubicle, fingers buttery with blood.

"No no–not a good idea, m'man. I don't think you should be moving for a minute or two. So take it easy now."

Just for a second or two I laid my mind against that soft, spongy 'e' of the Australian tongue. Then I pulled the band and locker key from off my wrist.

"Can you open it?"

"There's plenty of time for that."

"I want to give the girl my business card. I'm a dentist. I can help her."

"She's got a knocked tooth, has she?"

I nodded.

"In my wallet, there're some cards, business cards. She needs treatment. I can do that, no charge. I need to do this. Please."

He studied the card briefly.

"If you hang there a minute, I'll see what I can do."

"Thanks."

He took my key and left–with a squeak of rubber.

I sat up and rested my back against the cubicle wall. I'd give myself another 60 seconds' decompression, then I'd step out of here and go find my girls. And that other girl too.

CHAPTER

2

Pressing to my head the tissue Greg had left me with, I padded out to the lounge area in my wet trunks. My daughters, now dressed, were sitting on dual coloured chairs, talking with Greg, who was squatting before them on his muscular hind legs, his broad back like a ramp toward me. As Michaela saw me coming, she tapped Greg on the shoulder and said something. He rose to his feet,

"Ah, there you go, girls, the walking wounded. Are you gonna be OK, there, mate?"

"Did you get my card?"

"Yep, and here's your key," holding it out to me. "I gave the girl your card and she's agreed to wait for ya, if you're up to seeing her."

"Sure. Let me just get some things on. Is the boy OK?"

"I believe he's pretty much fine? But er, yeah, checking him out now, sport, as far as I know."

The girls were still and patiently awaiting a signal. I told them I'd be back in a minute, I just had to change. Greg said he'd stay with them until I reappeared.

When I next returned to the lounge area, the girls were gone. I stalled a throb of panic and headed for the reception. Greg and the girls had congregated there with the two Thai girls on a row of seats the other side of the reception desk.

"Is this your dad?" the young blonde receptionist called across to my girls in a cooing tone.

With one hand pressing a fresh tissue to my wound, the other holding our bags, I made my uncertain approach with a bravely ironic smile.

"I've just been hearing–how did happen?" the receptionist said, showering me with sympathy, as though we were old pub regulars.

I'd got as far as 'pushed' when I was rudely interrupted–by that voice again:

"Pushed?! Don't listen to him! My son's on a stretcher because of him!"

As if winged by a bullet I spun round–my brain rattling like a dry nut in its shell.

Walking alongside a couple of paramedics, who were wheeling out the boy on a gurney, was the man in the tracksuit. He paused a safe distance round the reception desk and pointed an accusing finger at me.

"It was you doing the pushing, mate! Completely pissed out of his head, this man!" he announced to everyone.

"I wasn't drunk, I had a concussion–"

"Concussion my arse!" He seemed to be enjoying the scene he was making and rounded it off suddenly with the promise I'd be hearing from his lawyer about the 'damage' I'd done. The gurney with 'damaged' goods had already passed through the doors and now dad marched on to catch up, piping still more indignation into the air as he went.

I turned back to the girl on reception. She'd turned pale just being within a few yards of the verbal onslaught. I made a conscious decision to look her in the eye so she knew the accusations to be false.

"His boy pushed me," I said simply. "And that's a fact," I added, and in that moment heard my faded American accent become suddenly more prominent, (something that tends to happen, I realise, whenever presented with making myself understood to strangers). "I hit my head," I continued. "He doesn't understand, vomiting is a common reaction to concussion," speaking with cool objectivity, and yet keeping my distance from her–I was only too aware that my breath must be awful and might even carry enough of last night's alcohol consumption to support the dad's wild accusations still ringing in everyone's ears.

The receptionist pulled a down-at-the-mouth sort of face, as if 'What can you do?' and asked politely was I sure I didn't need any First Aid or anything?

Greg said he'd take care of that right away even before I could speak.

"No, really, thanks, but could you just get a room for me and, um –"

"Steady on, sport, I don't either of you is in much condition for any of that, y'know what I mean –"

"No, I –" I was blushing, "I need to take a look at this girl's teeth."

My Australian friend was grinning and blushing to his roots – but enjoying it more than I was. "It's OK, mate, I've already got somewhere for you to do that, if you'd like to follow me..."

Five minutes later I was rolling up my sleeves in a small, windowless and overly air-conditioned office in the bowels of the leisure centre complex. I grabbed the head of the Anglepoise – the only light I had to work with – and swung it round.

"You might like to close your eyes at this point," I told my new patient, seated in an upright chair by a standard office desk.

My girls were sitting next to my patient's friend on the chairs on the wall behind me, observing like conscientious students. I switched on the light and peered in.

About half of her upper right second was missing, a clean break.

"Don't you need your dentist chair, Dad?" Mia remarked quietly.

"Yep, that would be easier, sweetie, but I think we'll manage." Then to my patient, whose name I'd forgotten to ask: "Head up just a little… that's it."

Too early to say whether the pulp was shot, might even need a pin… Diamond stud inlay on the upper right incisor–don't see that very often.

"Hm, I'm afraid you have lost quite a large part of that tooth. But not to worry, you won't lose it entirely, we can build it up. The first thing I need to do is put something on it so you can eat and drink because it must be quite sensitive now." I switched off the light and she opened her eyes, looking up into mine. I always get a quiet kick out of seeing vulnerability and trust pooling in a patient's eyes. "Hurts, yeah?"

She barely nodded.

"It will do, I'm afraid, until we can cover up the break you've got. And the quicker the better. So can you come and see me this afternoon? I'm out in Ealing. I hope that's not too far for you to travel."

She looked over at her friend and, awkwardly because of the puffy lip, said something in Thai, receiving assurances in return. She then looked at me and said, yes, she could come.

"OK? Good. How about 3.30 this afternoon?"

My patient nodded to the affirmative and asked her friend to do something for her that involved an agency and a restaurant. As they chatted quietly together, I took my first real look at her since I'd been in the pool. She was a beauty, that was clear, even if that beauty was somewhat tarnished and subdued for the moment. The line from her broad cheekbones to her chin cut in more sharply than I was used to seeing in Thai girls, and gave her an almost Western shape face. The lips were so full that the one swollen by the bang turned her naturally proud expression into one of almost absurdly gross imprudence. Her eyes were dreamy now, but I had a sense that in better circumstances they'd be alive to the charm of the unexpected. The shaggy long hair, streaked with highlights, the low cut designer T-shirt and design-ripped jeans struck me as casually thrown together and effortlessly coordinated. Even her most minimal movements suggested a potent mix of the ingénue and a woman wiser than her years. She was a sexual chameleon, I felt, a sort of female Peter Pan. I'd read intelligence in her face and suspected she had money, possibly a mundane Business major under her belt. Her voice was sweet and musical and it was already gently smoothing out the jagged bumps in my head and body. She stopped talking to her friend and turned to me and said,

"I come your place, yeah?"

"Yeah, um, my surgery… yes. It won't cost you anything," I reminded her.

"OK. Thank you." Her wince I understood as a brave attempt at a smile. She became embarrassed and covered up the front of her mouth with her hand.

"And what's your name?"

"Sisira. You can call me Sisi."

"Sisira." Even on my chewed tongue I liked the feel of her name in my mouth. "OK, well–"

"Dad–" Mia started up.

"Darling, just let me finish here, OK?"

But then I *felt* what she was looking at: a rivulet of blood had escaped the plaster on my forehead and was running down my face.

"Shit."

My blood had splashed on Sisira's dark skin.

She yelped but stayed in her chair–she was smiling as if at a curious denouement to a tribal custom. Our eyes met briefly–and their dark brilliance stopped my next breath. I had to stop myself from licking up the drop from off the nook in her clavicle.

I was finally back at reception, I'd just said goodbye to the Thai girls and I was ready to leave, when an urbane young Asian kid in a new suit and blood red tie swanned by in soft leather shoes and began gesticulating excitably–Was I the gentleman just involved in an accident in the pool?

Before I could even formulate an answer I was caught up wondering if my face had ever shone with this kid's transparent, entirely cosmetic confidence at twenty-five.

"I was involved, yes." I said, instinctively wary of people who prefer gist to meaning.

For some reason my reply caused him to smirk. Pressing his hands together in a regrettably camp gesture of entreaty he asked me if I'd mind sticking around for a while–the police had been called.

"The police?"

"Yeah, it's just routine, yeah? We just want to be sure there was like, y'know–we've got a responsibility to get everyone's details and stuff. Would that be alright?"

I felt I'd just been cast as the 'sensible man' in a comedy sketch.

"No, not really. I need stitches in my head, my kids have to be returned to their mum and I have to get back to my surgery to attend properly to the girl who was hurt. She needs immediate treatment."

"Oh, really, God, I'm sorry. Thing is, 'cause the boy–yeah? Uh, y'know he had had to go off in an ambulance, yeah? So we–like–we feel obliged to, like, y'know, call the police." His way of talking vaguely reminded me of Mia at the age of three-and-a-half. "I'm sure none of it's your fault, yeah, but the boy did have to go to hospital."

"I'm sorry if he's been hurt, but he pushed me and my daughter off your top diving board. I then seem to have fallen on him. That would suggest his injuries were self inflicted, wouldn't you say?"

He smirked again, as though my more direct form of diction suggested I had a hard-on he might have time for. "I'm sure they won't be long. You can wait in the lounge, there's TV, food and drink… Can I get you a coffee or something… yeah?"

Just for a second I thought he was offering me a decent one from a cafetiere, but no, he simply wished to point me in the direction of the vending machines. Recalling the father's public accusation that I'd been drunk, I pictured myself blowing into a little see-through bag. Perhaps a machine coffee was a good idea after all.

As the young, blood-red tie slithered off to a leafy branch somewhere, I returned to the lounge where the girls dragged me to the wall of slot machines. I threw in some coins and managed my coffee. I dropped in some more coins to a giant food machine and pulled the slot. Nothing.

"Dad, you have to bang it!" Michaela thumped the machine and the selected flavour of rubbish dropped to the collect drawer. "See!"

I could have done without the 'See?!' just then, but I figured she was entitled to express some of her own frustration with my performance that morning.

I took my instant brown water to a tucked away row of chairs and sat down. My hands around the coffee cup, I realised I must have knocked out the girl's tooth with the ring on my right hand. I sipped the coffee, which was less awful than I'd reckoned, while the kids roamed restlessly, making me vaguely dizzy again with their walking in circles as they munched contentedly on crispy carcinogenic compounds. I sat back, contemplating a trip down to the local A&E, but I dreaded the thought of running into that man again. Besides I had the engineer to get back for…

The girls had run out of games and, tired from their swim, had lain down on the chairs beside me, Mia using her sister's lap as a pillow. We'd been waiting maybe 30 minutes when my brother called. By the time I hung up, I realised the gathering buzz around the place wasn't about me, or the accident–everyone was talking about the bombs.

It was time to go home.

A light breeze was tickling the leaves of singular trees as I returned to an unseasonably cool July morning like a criminal walking out of jail in a simple disguise, completely unnoticed. It was weird, though, because I hardly recognised the car park and had to stop and squint at everything.

"Why're you going like that, making your eyes small?" Mia asked, imitating my squint.

"Can you see the car?"

"It's there, Dad! Can't you see?!" Michaela called as if to the dumbest in her class.

And then I couldn't get the key to turn in the lock. I stood back to take a second look at the car. It seemed to be ours.

"Come on, Dad!"

I tried again, turning the key harder this time and the lock made its familiar whirring noise as a light flashed on and off. I slid myself inside like a package marked 'Fragile' and started up the engine. I reversed very carefully–one accident was enough for one day.

As I pulled out of the leisure centre parking I suddenly realised I didn't know where we were–or at least, I knew the name of the place but I couldn't recall how we'd got here. I had to pull over and get out the A-Z. Lots of yellow, orange roads and white roads and patches of green to help me, but my mind was only getting lost in them. I tried again, but my mind just tailed off half way. I felt a wave of panic at the possibility I might have some kind of brain damage. *But this is still consistent with a bad concussion*, I told myself. All I had to do was get us home and take a day off work; rest. I turned in my seat.

"Michaela, can you sit up front with me, sweetheart? I need your help..."

Then I discovered that although my brain was incapable of following lines across a page, I could at least explain quite clearly to her how to navigate. When I told them that I thought my memory might be affected by my fall, both girls rallied to the cause of getting us home and took special pride in being able to direct me.

Traffic was thick because of the chaos caused by the terrorist attacks. The girls remained patient, because they saw they had an important job to do, but they were hungry again. When I groaned, knowing they'd soon be urging me to stop off at the nearest McDonald's, Mia reminded me I should let them have their way because they were helping me and if they didn't eat, they'd fall asleep and then we'd never get home because I'd lost my mind.

"My memory," I corrected Mia. I smiled to myself, amused that she could argue her case with such eloquence and moral conviction only two years on from tantrums.

"Yeah, memory," she added.

"Turn right here, Michaela," was saying.

"There aren't any shops round here Mia, you'll have to wait."

"We've got Hula Hoops in the boot," Michaela said, looking up from the A-Z.

"Yeah, in the boot, Dad!" Mia echoed.

I pulled over again and popped the trunk. As they tucked in to their snacks, I switched on the radio news. Requests that Londoners stay in their homes or in their offices went out, and then on and on. The girls grew interested in the reports and my explanations of what had happened, the background to what had happened, the dangers we all live in now.

"Was that man a terrorist?" Mia asked, referring to the man who'd shouted at me in reception.

"No no – just an angry man."

"Is he a Moslem?"

I winced at the muddle they were getting into. And yet how fitting, really, how modern. I did my best to explain. Inevitably the conflict had to be drawn for them as mainstream Hollywood would depict it–in terms of goodies and baddies–which was pretty much how Bush and Blair seemed to see it, I realised. Michaela was just old enough to remember seeing pictures on TV of people falling from the Twin Towers. I suspected she was not old enough yet, to distinguish between spectacle and reality, though–fear was only real insofar as it pertained directly to her. Which was just as well. As for me, I could see myself reacting with a typical Londoner's subdued horror before the images of aftermath TV terror. What did the terrorists hope to gain, if, even after such random carnage, people like me just got back on with things.

Worried that I wasn't going to be able to make it in time for the engineer, I called Andrea, my bright and very dependable Croatian nurse. We asked after each other and loved ones, sighed with relief, groaned at the horror. I said nothing about my own accident–it would have sounded so frivolous, almost disrespectfully self-indulgent. I did tell her, though, that I was stuck in traffic… would she mind nipping down to the surgery to let the engineer in? Yes, she could do that, no problem. Her young voice was compassionate, almost motherly, and even though I'd said nothing about my own accident, I felt soothed by her.

I got back to an empty house around midday. I put on the TV news for the girls who made little sense of the pictures of mutilated wreckage in the absence of real explosions and screaming victims.

I took a long, hot shower. Unlike some, I was still in one piece.

Through a hole in the steamed up mirror I saw the cut was in a bad way and grabbed my phone. Andrea was still at the practice, the engineer was about to leave. I asked her if she'd mind hanging on for another hour, I needed her to do a bit of suture work for me.

Washed, warm and seated comfortably in my own dentist's chair, I felt a light buzz of sexual excitement relating our pool story to Andrea as her pale white fingers worked around the gash in my head, gently pulling together torn skin with black silk. It had been a while since I'd seen her wearing clothes other than her white tunic. The morning's events seemed to have put a girlish sparkle into her warm, Slavic slate grey eyes, leant a vaguely flirtatious rhythm to her hands, and I thought I detected a mild frisson between us–which, I had to remind myself, I would not be exploring further until she handed in her notice, if at all.

When she was done, I packed the girls back into the car and–"Dad, why do you always drive so fast?' Michaela asked. "Mum says you drive too fast."

"Does she?"

"Yeah," they say in chorus.

"She says you're dangerous and you ruin the car by going too fast," Michaela said volubly, a note of hilarity creeping into her voice.

"Mum's safer, but it's not so much fun," Mia concluded, with admirable objectivity. Her sister agreed readily.

"I have to drop you off and then I have to go back to the practice, that's why I have to be quick," I explained. "I have to fix the girl's tooth, the girl in the pool, remember?"

There was a pause.

"Do you like her, Dad?"

I glanced in the rear view mirror to see Michaela wearing a slightly embarrassed smirk that made me feel, ever so briefly, like a junior school boy with a hopeless crush.

"Don't tell Mum about what happened, OK. Let me tell her… later."

"OK, Dad."

As I arrived home, I saw Sylvia had also just got in.

"Hello!" she called, not bothering to turn round, lots of shopping to unpack.

"Hey. Did you hear what happened?" I said.

"Hear what?"

"Dad knocked a girl's tooth out and smashed his head and then he was sick in the pool," Mia blurted out.

"Mia," I shot at her. "What did I say?"

She slapped her hand to her mouth and ran off. Michaela following her.

"What's she talking about?"

"If you haven't seen it, turn on the TV. We've had five bombs – in London. This morning. Many dead –"

"What happened to your head?"

"Oh, nothing, it's um, I'll explain later, OK. I've gotta go to the practice, I'll see you later – " and I rushed back out before she could ask any more questions.

Half way down the road, Sylvia called me, worried that we'd narrowly missed being blown to pieces at the swimming pool. I could hear Mia in the background shouting, "No, Mum, you don't get it! A bomb in the bus, not in the pool!"

I arrived at the practice around 3.15. Andrea had gone by then. I switched on the TV in reception and sat in the receptionist's chair to be closest to the phone. I began to worry that the turmoil caused by this bigger event would create irrational fear and confusion in the Thai girl's head and she'd decide against coming to see me. In any case, she was late. I berated myself for not having taken down her number. Perhaps I'd alarmed her with my first diagnosis. Perhaps I couldn't be trusted because I was Caucasian and she was now phoning around for a Chinese dentist. I worried she might lose the tooth if she waited too long. And it put another crack in my skull thinking I might never see her again.

After switching off the TV, I began pacing up and down the rickety flooring until the sound of the creaks became too irritating and I had to sit down. I decided to make some calls to friends and family– checking everyone was alright, that no one had a friend or relative who'd been caught up in the bombings. Of course, for every other number I dialled I got the engaged tone because everyone else was doing the same. At every other turn in the conversation I came close to relating my own disaster story for the day. I knew I'd make light of it, though, and to all but my closest friend I could picture myself admitting to having unduly provoked the boy, even though I didn't believe I had. I think even then I suspected that what had happened was only the beginnings of a story, not the whole of one. What if the boy's concussion had resulted in brain damage, for instance? What if the father really was about to contact a lawyer? I wondered in a tired sort of way whether the day's carnage mightn't bring Sylvia and me closer together. More likely, though, she'd see this as further evidence of a deterioration of my parenting skills. Rather unsettling was the realisation I had no one to talk this through with. Or at least no one whose reaction would clarify and renew my own wobbly trust in my own take on the experience. Maybe it was time for a shrink… Dammit. The Thai girl wasn't going to show, was she. I could have had another couple of hours with my daughters...

Shortly before six, as I was picking up my keys ready to close up shop, the phone on reception began to ring.

"Anthony Price?"

I didn't recognise the voice, but for a moment an instinct prompted me to withhold my identity to the late caller.

"Is this Anthony Price's dental practice?"

"Yes. I'm Anthony. How can I help?"

"I think we need to talk, mate, don't you?"

Now I was certain, it was a man whose voice I'd only heard till now in its angered state.

"Um, what about?"

"Well –what happened, obviously. My name's Neil, I'm the father of the boy you landed on in the pool."

"I think I already explained to you what happened at the pool."

"That's right, you did, you did. Um, I'm sorry. I did rather lose it with you. I, um, I was just freaking out. He's my son and… I'm sorry.' There was a pause.

"Apology accepted."

There was another pause. "Do you think we could talk? It doesn't have to be now, I can fit in with you, but I feel – it would just be better if we did. Is that OK?"

It seemed like a reasonable request, but I withheld an immediate answer and then asked after his son.

"Yeah, I think he'll be alright. He didn't have to stay over night or anything. They let him home." The tone had turned strangely familiar, as though he were now informing a member of his family. "So would you be alright if I dropped by your place of business tomorrow around six?"

He said he already had the surgery address from the internet. And then he hung up in the middle of my first line of directions. Which again was odd, given he'd concluded the conversation in an otherwise polite tone of voice. My instincts told me I shouldn't have agreed to see him on my premises. But I was in a strangely fatalistic mood by then.

CHAPTER 3

About a couple hours before my own appointment to see the father of the boy who'd pushed me into the pool, Andrea came into the consultation room with a certain cheeky glint in her eye to tell me that that woman was back again, wondering if she could speak to me.

"Christ, you didn't tell her I was here, did you?"

I knew whom she meant–she meant Georgina P–P for psycho–my stalker. Ever since I'd allowed myself to become her de facto shrink while in the chair, this garrulous fiftysomething divorcee assumed my polite interest in her calamitous life bore the hallmarks of an incipient romantic interest. She'd sent flowers, left gifts, and clogged up our answering machine on several occasions with her barely contained breathy excitement for things she imagined we could do together. And the joke was wearing thin.

"Andrea–"

But Andrea couldn't hold it in anymore and she burst out laughing like teenager.

"I'm sorry, it's not her. I shouldn't do that to you, should I?"

"Thank God for that. What made you pull that one? Is there someone there I need to be worried about?"

"Well," she began, still in a teasing mood, "there is a young girl in reception asking for you. Very pretty. Dark skin..."

"Black, Indian?"

"Maybe Thai."

My back went quite rigid for a moment–fear of my own desire–and I left the room as Andrea was still speaking lest she catch me blushing.

Usually when I step into the reception to greet one of my patients, I find him or her in some state of apprehension. I found Sisira, the girl from the pool, reclining as though the sofa were made of something unusually buoyant, which, from overnight experience, I can tell you it was not. She was dressed in jeans, sandals and a faded, red cotton shirt, her luxuriously long hair hung loose, over her chest.

"Hello… how are you?" My voice was strangely intimate to my own ears, as though I'd come across her hiding under some stairs, not in my own waiting room.

She sat up suddenly, looking lively, immediately apologising for not having shown up the day before.

"I thought I'd lost you!" I cut across–and the words echoed around in my head with amplified meaning.

"Yes, me too!" She'd meant to come, she said, but the traffic had been so bad because of the bombs and then she'd lost my card and she only just found it–

"That's fine, don't worry, don't worry," I cut across, perching beside her. As she sighed I felt an urge to lean forward to inhale her breath, the expression of relief was so charming. She smiled forgetting the unsightly tooth. "Oh," she went and clapped her hand over her mouth.

"So how are you coping?" I had to stop myself from reaching out and touching her arm; not simply because I was attracted to her but because I saw her as a fellow victim of an accident which still resonated for me with the bombings of the day before.

"Yes, I'm OK. How is your head?"

I'd felt slightly embarrassed to be asked about our little secret in a public place.

"Why don't you come through–we can fit you in now," I said, casting a coded glance at Rebecca, my wily old owl of a receptionist, who enjoyed nothing better than some sexual speculation to get her through the day.

Getting to her feet Sisi was all lightness in her limbs, like a marionette. Following her down the corridor, even in the low light, the craftsmanship to the line of her back, the exquisitely carved groove of her waist, easily visible through her diaphanous red blouse, was so shockingly beautiful I had to pause to catch my breath. Standing a yard or so short of the door, like an actor suddenly fearful of stepping onto the stage, I told myself to get a grip, now, before my nurse started to take notes that she'd later be comparing with the receptionist's. The moment I heard Andrea's voice welcoming Sisira into the chair as if she were just another patient, I regained my composure and strode into the room.

"So…" I began breezily, a propos of nothing really, just resetting my brain to 'light and professional'. "…Upper second on the right, if I remember," I said to Andrea.

Now that I was on my comfy stool, skating on rollers from trays and worktops to my patient in the chair, Classic FM playing, by chance, a rousing Waltz by Strauss, I was Anthony Price BDS LDS RCS M.Sc. once again.

I started off by asking if she could describe the pain, if any other teeth were hurting–short, simple questions that tend to reassure my patients. I pulled on my surgical gloves and mask and wheeled in to her bruised but gorgeous mouth and a cloud of erotic perfume, which momentarily robbed me of my next thought. I was glad to see that my patient's lip, though swollen, was healing nicely of its own accord and was not going to scar. I tried to express sympathy and calm with my eyes only to find myself wondering at the absence of reproach in hers–after all, I'd caused this damage, albeit inadvertently. Andrea placed the safety specs over Sisira's eyes–following normal procedure, although her glance at me made me feel she thought that I was already becoming unduly distracted by their beauty. I adjusted the overhead light and fixed my own specs or, more accurately, loupes (which are essentially magnifying glasses supported by fibre optic light) for a bigger picture on the detail of her broken tooth.

As I feared: telltale pink dots on the remaining stump that suggested irreversible trauma to the pulp. We were therefore probably looking at a root canal. As she opened her mouth a little wider, I slipped my mirror round the back to check for other, less obvious fractures to adjacent teeth. Her oral hygiene looked good. She had only three, small white composites, no extractions. "All four wisdom teeth have come through, no obvious sign of impacting, the two lower ones partially erupted," I dictated to Andrea. I gave the broken tooth a little spray. The second she twitched I felt a rippling in my own skin as though I were the earth for her little shock. I gently removed her specs.

"A little painful, yeah?"

Her face told me she was a little afraid of what was to come, but her eyes that told me that she was probably no wimp when it came to pain.

I got the seat upright and we took X-Rays. Then we had to do a few tests to check for the tooth's vitality. The cold test first of all, which involves soaking a cotton wool pellet in ethyl chloride and placing it on the front teeth, first on the unaffected teeth to get a control reading, then on the broken one. As I suspected, she wasn't feeling much of the cold on her broken tooth; the tooth's vitality was poor. Using an electric pulp tester, I also tested the tooth's vitality as against electrical stimuli, ranging from 1-10 in strength. But again, her poor vitality meant she wasn't experiencing much sensation until mark 8, only two notches below the maximum, whereas a vital tooth would have been tingling away at 3 or 4. "Still, at least the tooth isn't loose," I announced cheerfully.

I could have opted for a temporary sedative dressing and crown in case the trauma eased up over the next 48 hours, but I wasn't optimistic about her chances, so I told Andrea we'd start on the root canal straight away. I took a look at the X-Rays. No sign of fractures to the root, which was good. I gave her a local and asked her to return to the waiting room for a few minutes. I could deal with my next patient while we were waiting for her to turn numb.

"First we're going to do a bit of cleaning and filing, OK?" I explained fifteen minutes later. "And then we put on a temporary crown. Do you understand temporary?"

My patient nodded. I nodded to Andrea and we got to work.

I popped the saliva ejector in her mouth, gently picked up her hand and placed it on the tube, saying that she could be our assistant in the procedure. I made an access hole into the pulp chamber and cleaned it out with a series of graded files. Her root canals were a little narrow, but I took my time and finished roundly pleased with my craftsmanship. I disinfected and measured the canals and put in a temporary filling. Next, the stump. Sharp edges that needed filing. A gentle squeeze on the acrylic gun, a gooey paste that hardens in five minutes to make a temporary crown. File that down… polish… Do the impressions… Make a few notes that would be pertinent for my guy at the lab… And, finally, floss.

Pulling off my gloves I explained to Sisira what would happen next. I could skip the talk about the different kinds of crowns I could offer her because I was going to give her an Empress crown, the top brand, free of charge. She'd need to pay a visit to my ceramicist. No, she didn't have pay, *I* was paying. He was a nice bloke and very expert in his field. He worked out in Beaconsfield, about 30 minutes out of Marylebone. If she had email I could send her a PDF that would show her how to find it from the station. Yes, she had email. Good. She seemed a little nervous about travelling, but I impressed on her she needed to go along or we might have an imperfect colour match to the rest of her teeth. And she didn't want that, did she? By way of further reassurances, I tried to sell her the trip as educational as well as practical: it would be interesting for her to see how many varieties of shades of porcelain she could choose from. She'd find my guy very accommodating... I found myself pausing and smiling, rather as I do with children, except that my pattern of speech struck me as oddly fragmented, as though my 'script' was coming back to me in stops and starts. I was reminded of Anthony Price as he first started out in dentistry, a little hyper with his overall delivery. When we were done, I offered her my hand before I could stop myself.

Stepping into reception with her I had Rebecca book her in for a fitting in two weeks' time. When my receptionist angled her solicitous smile at Sisira and quoted a price, I was still hovering, ready to fan away the slightly odious smell.

"Becky, um, no, it's alright, there's nothing to pay." For a second I thought to explain why, but it was far too lengthy to go into now.

"Oh… OK." Rebecca turned back to Sisira, now with a little candy in her smile. "So, how's Thursday?" Sisira nodded. "What time would you like?"

"Five thirty, could you?" I leaned over the table to point at the computer and the gap I'd seen in Thursday's diary.

"Right, OK, five thirty, Thursday 21st."

Rebecca was doing her best not to appear overwhelmed by my guardianship of the new patient, who I noticed had mentally drifted off as if bored with waiting for the adults as they wound up their circumlocutory arrangements. She re-emerged languidly from her reverie as I asked her if she could give me her email so I could send her directions to the lab.

Opening the door for her, I was aware of my blood fizzing in my veins as if I'd accidentally jabbed myself with adrenaline. I handed her a fresh card and urged her to call me if she was worried about anything. What did I mean–*anything*? She smiled grotesquely (as you do when half numb) and thanked me.

As she appeared the other side of the window, walking away, I remembered I was due to get a visit later from the father of the boy who'd knocked half her tooth out.

Tom, my gentle-mannered Malaysian hygienist, Andrea and Rebecca left that day at around 5.30 pm. I stayed behind, flipping through an out-of-date Vogue in our waiting room, wondering what kinds of fashion magazines Sisira might look at, pausing only to reflect on the remote possibility I might myself need a dentist later this evening if my visitor exploded again. Around six I heard a car draw up in front. Through the half-drawn blinds, I saw a figure approach the front door. I opened to a solid man, wearing an anxious expression and a crumpled Boss suit, playing nervously with the car keys in his hand.

"Is it OK to leave my car here?" No hello, just straight in, a bit nervous as he turned to point to his old, blue BMW as though she were a dearly loved but troublesome dog.

His eyes didn't quite meet mine, they kind of scanned my face as if measuring it for warning signs that I might be about to find truck with his request.

"Yeah, sure, come in." I hadn't reckoned to respond with such breeziness.

"Cheers." He fired off the fob at the car alarm. I held out my hand and he shook it with a solemn, "Cheers," he said again.

I caught the smell of minted chewing gum just over my shoulder as I returned inside.

"I'm not pulling you away from your patients or anything like that, am I?"

"No no – we're done for today."

I held the door open for him as he entered the reception with a kind of 'am I trespassing?' furtiveness. I could hardly believe this was the same man who'd thrown a fit at the pool. I invited him to take a seat and offered him coffee or tea. He declined with a rush of whispered "No's" and "Cheers" and "Thanks anyway", chewing hard on his gum. "How about a water?" I asked going to the water cooler. OK, he'd have water.

"There you go." I sat on the same settee, not too close and took a sip of mine.

"So… how's your boy?" I asked. My gut feeling told me I didn't think we'd get on to whether my own daughter had been adversely affected by the fall.

Elbows on his thighs, he looked sheepishly into his cup of water, then up. The summer fruit of his yellow tie and sky blue shirt clashed badly with the shrapnel grey of his suit. He let out a pained sigh and, for a horrible moment, I feared I was going to get that man in the tracksuit again.

"Danny's fine, he's OK, but um… " He drew breath, wrinkled his nose, frowning intensely, looked into his cup again, then at me–I think for the first time noticing the plaster on my head. "I've been a bit disappointed. I, um…" He paused, glanced at me. "It took me a while to get to the bottom of what happened. I didn't know about the leapfrogging – not when I was there. I just thought you'd, uh – y'know – you'd jumped off on top of him. Um…" he looked me straight in the eye, a cold focus. "…you really deserve an apology," he said, in a tone that could just as easily have delivered: *You really deserve a fucking kicking*. "I'm really sorry about my behaviour at the pool–I was totally out of order–I–D'you have a bin for this?" He'd gotten to his feet, taking out his gum. "Sorry."

"Sure."

I fetched him the wastebasket. He picked out a piece of discarded paper, wrapped his gum in it and chucked it as if it were poison and returned to his seat.

"You really didn't have to come along, it's OK, I – y'know, kids his age, they uh –"

"No no no – I did have to come along, it's not right; I couldn't just leave it. Not if my son is the one at fault. No."

His eyes boggled at me, demanding acknowledgment of his moral standpoint.

"He wasn't skiving, in case you thought that. The school was closed for teacher training."

"Mine neither."

He nodded without comment. "The thing is, I'd been *misinformed*, y'know? Totally misinformed. The first person I spoke to, one of the attendants, she said–she said a man had pushed a boy and a little girl off the diving board." He gestured to me as if to say, Why would she lie? "I get to my son and, when he's able to talk, he says the same. He said he'd been pushed. And then when I saw you throwing up on the side of the pool, I just *assumed*–which was wrong of me, right?–but I *assumed* you were some kind of piss-head fruitcake."

He stared into my face as though I might be about to turn into one. Then double-blinked. His tongue flicked out to wet his lips before he went on.

"Fucked up, man, fucked up." I was getting a Nottingham or Coventry accent softened by maybe 15 years of living in London. "Later in the day, yeah? I went back to the pool to ask if they'd got your contact details. They wouldn't give them out – which is, y'know, fair enough. So, anyway, I got talking to one of the attendants, Greg, and *he* says, *he saw* my boy push you and your little girl off the board! So I go back home–have it out with my son…" he was shaking a sorry head now– "…finally he admits it was all his fault, he said his mate had put him up to it. So, yeah… apologies on my son's behalf." He gestured expansively with his arms. "I would have brought him along but he's, um–" he paused, tucking in his chin to deal with some indigestion–"he's with his mum tonight and she and I… If you did want to see him–"

"No no–honestly–it's fine. I appreciate your coming along. Uh–" I was finding the man's protracted apology somewhat oppressive and laughed nervously–"to be honest, I wasn't sure what you wanted and uh–"

"No I know, I know, I know–you must've thought, 'Oh, who is this guy, he wants a fight,' but no, I just wanted to clear this up I felt really bad."

"OK, great… Uh, I'm sure your son didn't mean to harm anyone, it was..."

"It was bollocks, mate, it shouldn't have happened. I wasn't raised like that, I don't expect it of my son." He wasn't shouting but his vehemence resonated with my memory of being cornered by him in the cubicle. "He's been behaving kid of strange, though, recently. We don't–It's kind of a… it might even be a medical condition. 'Cause I've um–I've taken him to psychologists, psychiatrists... His school keeps writing us letters… I think they'll kick him out before long." He smacked his lips together and sat back a fraction, briefly fussing with his sleeves. "He's abusive to me, to his mum, kids at school feel threatened by him... I think that's why I was so on edge that morning, y'know."

He dry-sniffed, shuffled his shoes again.

"Thing is, I'm not at home, that's the trouble. Me and his mum, we split, 'bout a year ago, y'know, so…" he inhaled, exhaled, tensing his back. "…Things got ugly, y'know? Very ugly… And, anyway, this–this bloke she's with–they both let him do whatever, y'know? No discipline, none whatsoever, man. But guess what? It's my fault. Not hers, not the new bloke she's with, it's my fault. It's my fault she had an affair." He knocked back his water like a man about to leave. "Sorry, I'm going on, aren't I. You're a dentist not a social worker– "

"It's OK, I–it all sounds pretty… trying."

"Yeah, it is."

There was a pause. I sipped my water.

"How did you track me down, as a matter of interest?"

"Oh, that Thai girl you were looking after, she showed me your card. But then I forgot your number and had to look you up on the internet.

"Right."

I made my understanding smile. Neil rustled his classic, black Clarks shoes on the floor. They needed a polish.

"You knew she was Thai?"

"Looked that way, to me. Is she not?" he gave me a strangely startled look, exaggerated.

"Yeah, no, she is."

He rubbed his nose and sniffed, drank his water, no longer interested in this person.

"You married?"

I said I was and braced myself, hoping he wouldn't ask me how it was going – he didn't:

"Is your little girl alright?"

"Yeah, she's fine… Bit of a mad day, all told."

"God, yeah, wasn't it? Fucking terrorists. People from *this* country. I'm not BNP or anything, but fuck. It's gone too far." He jutted his chin forward, as if his next words were stuck in his throat, before adding, "They just don't fucking integrate, do they?" He threw that goggle-eyed stare at me again, and I felt anything less than a clenched fist salute and cry of vengeance would be an inadequate response. I nodded soberly and managed a flickering half smile of accord. His gaze softened finally, and we fell into a trough of bleak, male silence. I thought to speak, but as the silence grew, I felt us both drifting into a stream that was bigger than our own worries about the accident–it seemed swollen by the collective anxiety and anger that had arrived in the wake of the bombings.

"I was going to ask you," he started up afresh, "I've got this dodgy tooth… here." He put a finger in his mouth, pointing toward the back. "I keep meaning to sign up to a new dentist, but I just haven't got round to it since I moved out and now I'm getting this–I dunno–like, sensitivity on my back teeth? Up here," pointing again. "You wouldn't have a minute to look at them, would you?" I sensed he was hoping for a freebie, off the books.

By the time Neil left the surgery around 6.30, I was in a state of complete bemusement at the outcome of our meeting. I was also enveloped in a warm glow of unlikely optimism of a kind that I hadn't felt since I was at school when enemies had occasionally and miraculously become friends overnight. Even after the check-up, seated upright in the chair, he'd chatted away, asking me all sorts of questions about my business from the mundane to the downright prurient. For a man who talked a lot, he also injected his observations with sharp and timely remarks. In spite of his earlier sour note about fractious family life, he struck me as an optimist, a searcher, who was also willing to share the things he came across. I'd expressed spontaneous surprise–then apologised for doing so–when he told me he worked for the government in Immigration; I'd taken him for an entrepreneur. He was pleased by that impression–he wanted to be one, he said. "But, yeah," he groaned, "for now, I'm one of the government's minions," he said with chiselled irony. He told me he hated his job. In fact he was looking for "the right kind of business opportunity" so he could get out of it–he wasn't going to be a 'lifer' like most of the people he worked alongside. He already had a few things "moving in the right direction", he said, nothing he'd want to reveal at this early stage, though. He told me "the job" was mad half the time–no consistency in the cases, wide abuse, hundreds of foreign criminals being put out onto the street, some of them mental cases. It was all going to come out sooner or later and he didn't want to be around when it did. He said the experience was turning him into a racist. He was adamant that he was the last person on earth to be like that–his ex, for instance, she was Chinese, he said, as if that settled it–he'd gone into the Department wanting to help genuine asylum seekers but everything had turned to shit, we were being flooded, the people above him were spinning stories just to hold on to their jobs or climb up the slippery ladder of politics.

I was just beginning to think to myself we might have to break into the practice's last bottle of Argentinean Viognier, when he segued back to the pool.

"What happened to the girl then, the one who got a knock in the mouth?"

Perhaps he was just shy asking about a pretty girl, but his casual prurience elicited in me a professional response. I described what had happened to Sisira when I fell into the water and what I was doing for her and that it was free of charge.

"That's bloody good of you. I mean it wasn't your fault you fell on top of her. Y'know who you should send the bill to? My ex. That's where the trouble's coming from. Maybe I could chip in something – maybe not the whole thing, but –"

"No no, really, please, don't worry, it's fine." I couldn't help feeling this was a man in the habit of making 'offers' like this to people he knew were unlikely to call them in; had I accepted his offer, I would have wasted days chasing the bill.

"Pretty girl, that one," he remarked, as though referring to a model of car that was good value for money–I felt he must have been eyeing her in the pool. "I'm sure you'll do a good job, mate." The hair on my back bristled at the tone, but he probably means well, I told myself. "And thanks for the check up, much appreciated." He hoisted up his trousers by the belt. "You're sure it's OK to settle up next week when I come for the filling?"

"Check-up's free," I said, "but yeah, you'll need your credit card for the filling."

"Oh God, is it that deep?"

His look of mock horror made me laugh.

His handshake was more gripping than when he'd stepped inside. He thanked me for being so understanding.

As he headed for the doorway, something in the slight hunch of his right shoulder, a hesitancy in his feet, told me he'd got some other burden he'd want to disclose to me at a later date.

Thursday 21st July I had a text from my brother stating simply: 'Are you OK? We are.' It took me less than five seconds this time to realise he must be referring to another bomb, or series of bombs. The sheer brevity of his message conjured a faintly absurd picture of a future peppered with these kinds of missives between friends and families–a sort of lotto which, when you won, meant you hadn't been blown up today.

I walked in to the reception to find Rebecca and two rather worried looking middle aged ladies already talking about three or four packages that had been found on public transport that had failed to go off. Glancing over Rebecca's shoulder I saw Sisira was due to come in for her fitting at 5.30 and thought *how uncanny* that we should meet again on a day with news of bombs in London.

Later that afternoon I was in the reception when I saw Sisira run across the road heading for the practice. I'd already let Rebecca go, but Andrea was still around; (as much as I wanted to be alone with Sisira, you can't be too careful avoiding possible sexual harassment cases from patients).

Her scent–this time I was catching a stronger note of vanilla and a tree sap deliciously roasted around the edges–induced a brief spell of confusion to my syntax as she floated passed me and into the reception like a butterfly that might fly out the nearest window if I didn't catch her. She spun around as if the absence of a receptionist had disoriented and slightly amused her at the same time.

"After you," I said–and again my stomach was doing somersaults as I filed behind her down the corridor.

The way she got comfy in the chair, you'd have thought I was about to send her up and around on a fairground spaceship. Andrea bibbed her up as I pulled on my gloves.

"We've got your new tooth. Looks very good!" I said, perching on my stool.

I unwrapped the porcelain I'd received a couple days before and skated over to her.

"That's what you chose. Was it an interesting visit?'

She gave me a polite smile–the type of girl who probably didn't care too much for museums as a kid. "Let's take a look…" and, holding up a mirror for her,

I compared the porcelain with her front teeth. It was a good match, very good.

"So how've you been?" I asked.

Considering how nervous I'd been earlier, trying to imagine how the hell I was to find a moment to ask her out without Andrea catching on, my outward manner was very relaxed. It wasn't until I began to sense that my banter and questions were affecting her like a breeze alternately refreshing and irritating that my confidence started to congeal. Still, she seemed happy with the porcelain, so I resigned myself for now to focusing on the job in hand. I sedated the area at the front of her mouth and asked her to wait in the front room till she was nicely numb. After she'd vacated the seat I realised this was probably the best time to ask her out–before she was too numb to talk properly–but then Andrea volunteered to go on reception – Rebecca had left already – in case we got any late callers, so I was left to potter about in the surgery, agonising over half-finished versions of how the dialogue might go.

Both women were being ever so quiet. The silly voices on the radio commercials were beginning to grate. So I punched OFF. Then dropped something. It went off with a terrific clatter. Was I waiting till she was so numb that she'd find it easier just to give me an affirmative 'Mm' to my proposal? Would she feel I was taking advantage of her by asking her before the work was completed?

"How's that then?" I asked five minutes later, arriving at the threshold of the reception to find both women gazing out the window like cats. "That numb now?" I asked tugging at my own lip to describe 'numb' for her.

Even with that lopsided, numbed-up mouth her smile was charming–because the eyes that lit it were so alive, so willing to engage.

When she was settled in the chair, I wheeled my stool up to her. The temporary crown came off a treat and everything looked fine. I cleaned with alcohol and flicked off bits off cement. I asked her what kind of music she liked.

"Buddha Bar?"

I hadn't thought she'd pick something I actually had in my small, if half decent dance collection and was delighted to be able to oblige – and asked Andrea to put on the CD.

Now for the drill. Whittling away at the stump till it was a peg. We were ready to fit. First with a temporary paste. You can shade the crown further with the pastes you use to stick it in with, but as Sisira's teeth were a healthy white, and the match was already good, I didn't need to vary the colours–we could go with neutral. I showed Sisira the final temporary fitting in the mirror and she was happy. I checked her bite while Andrea prepared the luting resin with which I'd cement the crown permanently. As I worked, I began to grow aware that my chest was pressing up against her right hand. With the repeated contact–rolling back and forth on my stool, from worktops to the chair–I was reminded of those first weeks of contact between me and my children, when they were very small, nestling close beside me. I kept expecting her to take her hand away but she didn't, presumably because the warmth of my chest, the rhythm of my contact, had a soothing effect on her mind.

Pushing the crown on, ever so slightly lifting her head up as I did so, gently forcing her neck to arch, exposing her throat, I swooped briefly into the strangest vampire fantasy. Still pushing I reached for the mirror. She was happy and yet the music of her voice seemed to denote a fond farewell, and suddenly I was panicking that I'd let her leave my chair and walk out of here with no promise of seeing me again. Marriage had left me so out of practice at this sort of thing.

"Andrea, do you mind, um–could you tidy those things away and I'll, um– "I gestured feebly in the direction of the reception. Andrea sweetly agreed to my request without her customary, if lovable, smirk.

"Sisira," I called catching up with her in the reception. As she turned I saw she hadn't a clue what I was about to propose. I seized on the openness in her expression, but only managed to say, I thought she'd be fine. "–And if you have any problems, please call."

"OK, thank you. Bye!"

And then she was out the door. *Fuck*. She was leaving. I felt as though I were falling down a lift shaft. I counted to three and dashed for the door. I caught her as she was reaching for the latch on the front door to the street.

"Sisira!"

She turned, unperturbed by the fracture in my voice.

"Sorry, uh–I was just wondering, could we–could we meet for a coffee or something?'

She looked utterly perplexed by my words, as though I'd suddenly switched to Swahili. A younger me would have gabbed on, but I knew I was better served by a beaming smile, however forced.

"A coffee?"

"Yeah, not now, but, um–next week? Say, Wednesday?"

When she said yes it was as if I'd merely asked her to change the time of a six-monthly check up.

"I give you my number?" she asked, as if she had only the vaguest notion as to what use I'd have for it.

We went back into the reception to exchange numbers, discuss a time, my heart like a bass line beating away in the next room as I wished very hard that Andrea would not wander in. Sisira had school in the mornings, she said–and she must go, she said, she'd been very lazy recently. How was 4 in the afternoon? Perfect, I said. Wednesday was my half day. I already had images of us both in a local Starbucks, me with a decaff, because a real coffee would make me tremble with excitement, painfully working my way to asking her out on a proper date. We agreed I'd call the day before to confirm. And then she went.

As I headed home, that old friend Cynic spoke up, reading her yes as no more than an expression of gratitude for the work I'd done gratis on her tooth. I saw us parting on the sidewalk somewhere in her neighbourhood, me mumbling stuff about staying in touch and reminding her to book a check-up in six months' even as I saw myself falling further from her playfully evasive eyes before letting go and heading toward the nearest tube station, smarting with the embarrassment of having let myself run so hard and so far with such an impossible fantasy.

But I didn't care. I just wanted one more 'hit' of being alone with this girl. Because when I was with her, everything that was stale in my life flipped over, exposing itself to healing fresh air. I simply had to find out what it meant.

CHAPTER 4

Chemistry, that elusive thing–some of us spend our lives looking for it… Few of us expect to find it on the end of a blow to the head–and yet how much more rousing is the prospect when it happens.

So anyway, there I am, surfacing at Paddington tube station, sweaty and fractious after delays on the tube, courtesy of the bombs a few weeks ago. I'm running a bit late, and I don't like to be late–*for a very important date.* She'd sounded sleepy on the phone when I called and first off I figured she'd forgotten or had changed her mind, but no, the date was still on, if I didn't mind meeting her at her place.

Entering the leafy square of Queen's Gardens, W2, I walked along a row of white-stone, Victorian four-storey terraces noting the numbers till I came to number 63. I climbed stone steps to a large black door and checked the intercoms. Flat C's buzzer was half punched in. I pushed it and waited. No answer. I checked my watch. Only ten minutes late. Had I gotten the number wrong? I buzzed again. This time I got a response. The voice sounded like a woman of forty something, irritable, as if wary of stalkers.

"Hi, it's Anthony, the dentist. Is that Sisira?"

My only reply was the sound of the buzzer. A bit off, I told myself, but allowing for cultural differences and all that...

I stepped into a spacious hall, lofty, quiet. Bundles of mail lay in untidy piles on a ledge, a soiled beige carpet rolled up a wide stairway slightly to the left of me. I heard a latch bounce up further down the corridor and headed in that direction. Half way along I came to a door marked 'C'. It was an inch ajar. I knocked. When there was no answer, I nudged it open.

"Sisira?!" Her name seemed to hang in the air a moment like a weave of spider's silk.

I closed the door and stepped into a newly furnished kitchen/lounge in the style of an Ikea showroom. The kitchen was in front of me and to my left. I caught a lingering and delicious smell of Thai cooking, but everything was washed up and tidied away. To my right, summer sunshine from the square filtered through the slits in new but economy Venetian blinds.

"Hello!"

I turned, to my left–a voice I thought I recognised–now a slender, long-haired figure emerging from the end of the long, dark corridor. This at-home Sisira didn't float as she had in my practice, she shuffled–in a pair of pink leather moccasins–across the wood panelled floor, with a lazy swish of her hips. She was wearing a white cotton mini and a red, short-sleeved top slightly revealing of her breasts. As we kissed lightly on the cheeks, she shuffled off to the fridge.

"Sorry, I fell asleep after you called. Very tired today."

She opened the door to her fridge and leaned back on one leg as she looked inside for something.

"How's the tooth?" I asked.

Still holding onto the fridge door, she swung round and cast me a for-the-camera smile. I grew conscious of the nimbleness to her movements as if gravity was slightly less weighty for her than for me.

"It's good. Sometime a bit funny, you know–like boom boom, like–"

"Throbbing? Like throbbing?"

"Throbbing?" she queried.

"Yeah, the beating sensation in your tooth."

"Yeah–yeah beating."

"Yeah, that's normal, don't worry, that should calm down soon. That's totally normal."

"Please, take a seat. You want a beer, wine…?"

I took the corner seat of the sofa, in sunset orange. "Uh–" 4.20 pm was a little on the early side for a man keen to cut back on his weekly units of alcohol.

"Oh, wait a minute, please."

She ran in the direction of the window, turned right up a few wooden steps and disappeared. I racked my mind for ideas where we might go for a café that wasn't a chain, but realised I barely knew the area.

She returned shuffling quickly to join me on the sofa. "Sorry, I left tap running," and smiled to let me know she had my complete attention from now on. *God, don't say you have to wait for her to have a bath first...*

Her thigh came up against mine–not calculated, it just seemed to land there naturally. Before I could speak she took my hand in hers.

"Oh, hands cold."

"Yeah, I get that sometimes, even in the summer."

"Cold hands, warm heart," she said, rolling it off pat.

I smiled.

"You very kind to me."

"Well, I'm just glad I was able to do something for you. It was just such bad luck I hit you, wasn't it?" I was thinking the very opposite, of course.

"Yes but– you know – some people, when accident happens…" she tossed her hair back, "they just walk away. You didn't walk away."

Looking into her beautiful almond eyes I wondered how she could even imagine a man would walk away from her.

"I think it might have been this ring that broke your tooth," I said and pointed to the suspect on my right hand.

"You married?" touching the silver ring.

"It's not a wedding ring, it's –"

"Ah, yes, I know–other hand," which she duly noticed carried no ring. "What does it mean, this picture?" She leaned closer to study the carvings in the silver ring that had smacked her in the mouth.

"I don't know. Looks like coral or leaves. These look like claw marks. It's Indonesian, hand-made. I've had it a long time."

"You went to Indonesia?"

"Yeah. Just before the bomb in Bali actually. Bombs seem to be a theme in my life at the moment," I added with faint, ironic laughter. She didn't seem to recall too clearly the bomb in Bali. She'd have been a teenager back then.

"You want bath?" she said, segueing off like a young person easily bored by talk of bombs and killings.

My heart jumped –

"A bath?"

She turned slightly in her seat. "You know I'm working girl, yeah?"

I felt a pressure behind my eyes forcing me to blurt: *Yes, of course*, as though it were the most natural presumption to have made the first time I set eyes on her, but I couldn't speak. I'd so readily assumed she was a full-time student, supported by rich parents.

Not once had she eyed me with a lingering look that suggested she could use the extra trade.

"Yeah, I'm working girl, so…" her words trailed off and I worried my inability to speak had offended her.

"Hey, that's–that's–that's fine. Is this so you can pay for your studies here?" As if I needed a reason– *money's money, man.*

"I told you I'm student, didn't I?" She pulled the face of a naughty girl. "But I don't go to school every day. It's impossible–I finish work very late, maybe 2AM every night."

"Right."

"I come here to make money, you know? You don't make money like waitress, yeah?"

"Sure. Um…" I looked away, feeling vaguely stupid, as if no one had made it clear I should turn up in fancy dress. "…I thought we were going for a drink, uh… I just didn't – I don't even have any cash on me, so –maybe twenty pounds, but –"

She was waving her hand before my chest, my mouth–

"You don't pay – no no. This time no pay, OK?"

Her hand caressed my inner thigh to reassure, it seemed, not seduce.

"To be honest, I'd really prefer to get to know you a little?" I said, lapsing into the Americanised note of inquiry that's supposed to bring the other person into line with your naïve assumptions about the way the world works.

"You get to know me now." I was about to protest when she cut me off saying, "You don't want sex with me?"

My chest tightened around conflicting emotions. It's true, I couldn't pretend that it hadn't occurred to me that a beautiful Thai girl living in Paddington might be prostituting herself, but somehow the violence and the timing of our encounter, the bombs going off, the care I'd shown her afterward had all conspired to create this hopelessly naïve and romantic vision that I might be let into a beautiful woman's heart because I'd made her better. Too many movies, obviously.

"You don't find me attractive?"

Her look of disappointment pained me because I couldn't tell whether it was generic or genuine.

"I find you very attractive, but I also…" I looked over at the kitchen sink, then back at her.

"Quiet day today. It's good. We have time. You can get to know me a little."

Before I could say another word, she had hold of my hand and was on her feet–

"Come."

I was led down the corridor to the end door. I entered a neat bedroom draped in masked sunlight. A robust bed was positioned in the right hand corner, left of the dropped Venetian blinds. A small electric fan, on top of a wardrobe, was blowing quietly, as if for its own amusement, and next to it stood a framed photo of Sisira, posing in swimwear. She'd placed lit candles on the chest of drawers, several on the wooden floor and two beside her bed. For me.

She was already unbuttoning her blouse. She discarded it, light as chaff, on the back of a chair. Seeing me watching her, she came over to me, and slipped her hands under my linen jacket and off my shoulders with lubricious ease. Wrapping the jacket around a hanger, she politely remarked on its cut, brightening as she noticed the Armani name.

"Yeah, it's a bit tatty now, but–yeah, I like it." I fell quiet, remembering how Sylvia had nagged me to give it away to a charity shop.

Now I felt her fine, long fingers against my skin as she lifted my T-shirt up my body and over my head. I'd almost forgotten what it was like to be undressed by a woman–and it felt good, immeasurably soothing. She gave the end of my belt an authoritative tug, as though I were her suitcase, popped the studs as if shelling peas, then withdrew – the rest I could do – to resume her own undressing.

"Are you having a bath with me?" I asked.

"Yes… It's OK?"

She slipped out of her mini and thong as if before her little brother of four, not a trace of self-consciousness. She re-pinned her hair, which fell in arcs of grass-like thickness about her ears. She handed me a fresh white towel and picked up one for herself.

"You come?"

I wrapped the towel around my middle and followed her down the corridor with a sense of being about to join her in a ritual in a Buddhist temple. Her shoulders back, yet relaxed, she seemed to glide across the floor in her bare feet.

A foamy bath was waiting for me. The blinds were down, candles by the washbasin. We lowered ourselves in and yelped and then laughed at the same time as our bottoms kissed the hot surface. She turned around to fiddle with the taps, her lovely bottom now wearing a funny soapy beard, only inches from my face.

"OK? Not too hot?"

"No, just right."

She turned off the taps and we sat together, our soapy legs slithering against one another. The only sound now was of water rippling to the movement of two bodies like a secret whispering in counterpoint. My hands caressed idly over her thighs and came to rest about her pelvis. I felt like a collector who had found his Ming vase years earlier than he'd ever imagined, and was in a state of awe at the unexpected suddenness of his acquisition. She soaped a sponge and started to bathe me, no words for a moment. I was reminded that it was this kind of intimacy that was the first to go for Sylvia and me after Michaela was born. I'd had my daughter's hands washing my body and my hands would wash their bodies and that was a beautiful experience and yet often a painful reminder that there was no longer a woman who touched me that way. And then, before long, Dad got too big to share a bath with his girls, so there was no one to touch him when he was in the water. I'd been washed before by a call girl, years ago, but never with this slow, caring hand. I felt no need of conversation – Sisira's beauty and grace were as absorbing as watching a Japanese poet paint kanji. Perhaps I could be different from other customers because I'd saved her tooth; even if I was the one who broke it, she appeared to accept without a trace of suspicion that I wasn't to blame for falling on top of her.

"You very tin."

"You mean thin?"

"Yeah. Why? You don't eat much?"

"No, I do. I have a quick metabolism."

"Maybe too quick," she added with an almost maternal smile. The diamond stud in her eye-tooth seemed to sparkle in the candlelight.

We made the kind of small-talk I'd imagined sharing over a coffee–but without any of the fidgetiness that accompanies the sexual anxiety of a first date, our voices velvety in the shrouded daylight. There was a perpetual impish happy smile on my face–I could have believed I was in the midst of an epiphany.

Placing my hands on her hips, I drew myself closer to her–the sliding of our soapy legs sweeping an arousing current to my groin. I searched for her big eyes that seemed so wise one moment, so naïve the next. Then, finding her elusive, I felt a twinge of disappointment as if I'd almost kidded myself that I could have the whole deal–love–right now. I ought to get clear in my head that the deal was in fact her body, this one time and maybe never again. I let the smile go before it curdled. I ran my hands up her sides, I cupped her breasts, which struck me now as more mature than she was herself, prepossessing in their firmness and bold contours. With my wet fingers, I began 'painting' her flesh with water and soap bubbles as a childlike diversion from my turbulent arousal. When I brought my face to the side of her neck, her quietly industrious hands fell still. I held her very lightly, my every sense finely tuned to reading her reaction to this moment of close contact. I inhaled her scent, notes of sapping wood, vanilla and lemon grass, half believing its effect might inspire me how best to win her affections. But then I heard her ask, with just the slightest hint of dismay perhaps, "Are you OK?"

I withdrew, smiling guiltily like the only one at the party on E. "Yeah. This is so nice, though..."

Her eyes averted, she dipped the sponge in the water and squeezed out the water over my shoulders as if to bring me back from paradise. *How beautiful wet skin looks in candlelight.*

She met my eyes finally and I asked if I might kiss her.

She gave an almost imperceptible nod, which told me I must start with the gentlest kiss imaginable. As if she were a virgin.

The tips of our lips touched, like two tongues of blood gently merging into one another. She closed her eyes. A thin line of deep turquoise ran across her lids. I kissed her lower lip, then even more delicately the upper one, the one I'd cut open. Something in my chest trembled. I slipped the tip of my tongue between her lips and ran it between them, as if teasing open a partially sealed envelope. I kissed once more. Five long seconds. As she parted from me, she eased me back, gently, hands on my chest, pushing me down, til the water was lapping about my earlobes. She took my swollen, bendy cock in her hands and pulled back the foreskin to wash me–thorough but tender with her actions. Watching her clean it, knead it, caress it, my cock seemed like a mere appendage of a vaguely ceremonial significance. It was also a reminder of the promise she had made – to take it inside of her.

"Can I wash you?" I asked.

"It's OK. I showered already."

"Oh."

"We rinse?"

She turned on the shower, testing the jet with her hand. She swung the spray over my legs. I jumped–it was cold.

"Better?"

It was still cold, her eyes shone, she was playing a game with me now. I laughed along with her and we started splashing and spraying each other.

"Now it's OK! Turn round, please!" she said in a mock matronly voice that took me back to bedroom pillow fights with the au pairs when I was a kid… those strange moments when as a pre-pubescent boy I'd rubbed up against a pretty young woman for the first time and experienced a strange sensation throughout my body and a head-rush of confusion…

She rinsed my back, turned me round and rinsed my front. I'd gone semi hard with the excitement of the spray of cold water and my thing bobbed blindly against her groin, though she didn't even seem to notice.

She handed me my towel and held my hand so I wouldn't slip getting out of the bath. I felt I ought to be doing this for her, but she was already washing between her legs to finish off and, from the angle of her back, I sensed she preferred to be left alone.

Returning to her room, she gathered our towels and hung them up. She laid a fresh white towel on the bed and told me to lie down. Getting on the bed with me, she invited me to tell her about my life as though I might dazzle her with a box of tricks. I smiled. I couldn't imagine someone like her would be remotely interested in amalgam-free dentistry. But I gave it a go–peppering the dryness of a common procedure with ironic asides and vignettes of peculiar cases in a bid to make my world at least vaguely exotic to my listener, if in fact she was really listening.

"It's good job, yeah?"

I smiled bashfully.

"Well–how about you?"

She'd been here nine months. She said her English wasn't good. I said, it wasn't at all bad and perhaps I could help her with that. She gave a half-shrug of indifference as if bored of hearing men saying this.

She asked me my age. I smiled and told her my sign instead. She didn't know what her sign was in English. She was born in November. "23," she said.

"You'll be 23 in November?"

"No, 24."

"Sorry, I'm confused."

"November 23."

"Oh, 24 on the 23rd?"

"Yes. I'm on the edge,"

"You mean, on the cusp," I said, smiling at her choice of phrase.

She seemed proud that she was a little bit Scorpio, a little bit Sagittarius. "Scorpio rising," I said, pointing to my chest. She didn't know her rising sign. She knew she was Virgo moon, though. "Me too," I said. She laughed as if I were tricking her into loving me. I hadn't had one of these New Age chats for a long time, hadn't missed them either, but with so many thousands of miles between us, it felt like a common ancient language upon which to build trust.

She laughed girlishly as she talked, so I was constantly losing her words, but I didn't care, not for now, I felt privileged to be lying beside her, feet lazily caressing hers. I felt no immediate urge to begin in earnest, though the urge to kiss her was already a beating wing in my chest.

She grew up in Chiang Mai. Her family was not poor, not rich, she said. Middle. She had a younger brother who was very smart; he was expected to become a monk. It was tradition, she said for young son to be monk for parents because this bring them luck. Her father was Singapore Chinese; he had relatives from Laos and Thailand. He left home when she only nine. She remembered crying every night for month and month, going to bed, clutching to her chest his photo in a frame. She'd always been his special one and she couldn't understand why he'd left. He had an affair, she said. She didn't like the other woman, she was cold and didn't like his family. She wanted her father to cut off from them. She blamed her mother for his drinking, she said. She always nag about money. Kind of mean to him. But she'd grown closer to her mother in recent years and now they very close. She had to start a business from bottom, she said. She do OK now, but *very* hard in beginning. But still she choose her men badly. Like her step-father. He drink worse than her dad. He always bothering her. Sometime he hit her. He treat her like a–She paused, possibly about to say 'like a whore', but instead she said, "–like slave". He always interfering, even come in to her bed, try to have sex with her, that's why she had to leave home. She was worried for her mother and her brother's education–her brother was nine year younger than her. Big reason why she was here was so she can earn money quick and get mother free.

She'd gone to university in Bangkok to study tourism – her uncle paid for her to go – but she got bored and was spotted by a scout to do some modelling. She did catalogue stuff for a while, but it didn't pay well. Then a friend introduced her to an agency in Bangkok that recruited girls to work in London as escorts. She said it had been difficult at first. When she paused, I felt a void open inside of me at the notion she had now grown used to it and was even enjoying it.

"How long d'you think of doing this job?" I asked.

"We don't talk about that now, yeah?" she said, looping an arm over my shoulder, drawing me in. Frankly, I was relieved, because I'd begun hating myself for my increasingly tabloid prurience.

"What you like? You like massage?"

"No I… I like this," I told her as I brought my body over hers–her skin warmer than mine, silky delicious–and kissed her neck. She'd added some scent since leaving the bathroom and it intensified the rush that I was getting from touching her with my lips. She giggled, as if tickled, as I ran the tip of my tongue round the tender whorls of her auricle. Was I being too personal? She reached for my sex, turning putty into erection in seconds. But I wanted to taste her first…

'Her between legs', as Sylvia had taught the girls to call it, (in opposition to their dad's apparently scary grown-up term, 'pussy'), was neatly trimmed and shaved at the sides as if to guide the man's nose and tongue along a runway to her clitoris. I lifted her thighs, opened them wider. And then I was feeding on her. Licking each of her labia individually, then back up to her clitoris, teasing it up into the shape of a proud bud. I wormed my finger into her slowly moistening vagina, still working on her erect clitoris, sometimes sucking on it hard as if slurping oysters from their shells. She began to move against my licking tongue, groaning, losing herself in her thickening bubble of pleasure. Out of the corner of my eyes I saw her fingers clawing the bedclothes. Then she was pulling at my arms, urging me–in a fake delirium, though you dare to hope it's real–to get up from there and fuck her. She reached for a condom under her pillow, ripped it open. I laughed, confessing that I'd gone soft, I'd lost myself through giving her pleasure.

"It's OK," she said, and masturbated me with an expert hand. We kissed and the taste of her made my heart race. She popped the condom over me and used her mouth to peel down, her fingers to secure the ring...

And now I'm there, working her, a man's job, the beginning always so mechanical somehow… I'm already close, but I keep slowing it down, because I'm so happy simply being inside her–looking down at her beautiful face, the flecks of blazing green in the deep woody brown of her iris, marvelling at the tightness of her unlined skin across those proud cheekbones. I never want this to end. I draw the back of my cock against the back of her vagina, as if to rake over nerve endings other men don't think to reach–and with each stroke I seem to bring her to the brink. I scoop her small, round ass in my hand–she's maybe 48 kilos, very light for 5'7"–and rock her over my sex as if to spark a flint. I'm doing OK, I think, just a little puffed, *need to get back to the gym, maybe even go swimming...* when I have to pause.

She rolls me over and gets on top, facing me.

So now it's her turn, showing me how it's done–on the balls of her feet, strong thighs, so lean you can see the ligaments at cable strength, as she rides me like a jockey. I lick my thumb and rub it gently against her clitoris–more rubbery than my wife's, which is silky and tender–till it seems to melt even as it grows engorged. I press my tongue against my palate, holding back, her speed blinding now, frenzied, I could be in a car hurtling toward a wall at 100 mph, no brakes...

I had to sit up, holding on to her. She slowed down, making me stir her slowly, a sorceress, as I whispered into her ear, urging her to come...

I would never have expected a prostitute to come with such force–a loud groan, for sure, but not this: arching her back she dug her nails into my forearms, her knees locked about my pelvis and I couldn't move. So focused on maximising her pleasure, I forgot to reconnect with my own saved orgasm, and so she finished before I could join her in her magnificent slo mo crash.

"You didn't come?"

I shook my head and smiled–happy for her, happy I'd still got mine to come.

I suggested we continued, doggy-style. She assumed the position readily. Her engorged sex all mine. I slipped the back of my hand between her thighs and gently eased them apart, like a cop with a suspect in an alleyway. It was surprisingly tight getting in from this way. Resting on my knees now, sometimes watching my cock shaft in and out, I fucked her at a pace that made me think of time. The long time I hadn't done this. The time I was spending on tasks that gave me no joy anymore. The time I had left to me to fall in love with a young woman who wouldn't be repelled because I was turning grey. The time I had let go by without dealing with the stuff that made me unhappy. The time it took to fall from the diving board and land beside this girl I was now inside of… But I was taking my time, wasn't I? I sensed she was getting bored. Perhaps she had a booking with a customer after all. Or maybe she was the type who liked to change positions every few minutes... So I got onto my feet like a jockey, as she'd done with me – and I rode her. At first it was like any other good fuck from behind, my tight, wet balls banging up against her wet pussy, the delicious bounce of my groin against her firm buttocks. But then something happens, something I can't remember experiencing for years. I'm inhabited by some other me and I want to fuck her hard, as if to punish her for some unconscious hurt that I've been carrying around with me for all my life. Is it something about the breathtaking beauty of her back, the vulnerability of the groove of her sunken spine, that long elegant curve from her slender shoulders to the pelvis where my hands grip her like the pommel of a saddle? Is it that extravagantly ornate dragon tattooed on her right shoulder that spurs me on? The quaking of her slender but muscular arms that moves me and angers me so, as I thrust harder and faster inside of her? …This is a girl I first met through a punch to her teeth, her ring tearing into the skin above my eye, a girl I have cared for in my chair, whose diamond stud winked at me and put me under a spell, a girl who offers herself to me today without payment–it's all happened so much faster than I'm used to. My wife would have shrieked that I was being brutal–and yes, I hardly recognise myself–but this girl isn't complaining; you could believe she has an infinite capacity to absorb a man's anger, which of itself makes me even angrier. Why? *Though right now, I need all my concentration in order to finish.*

As the finishing line comes into sight, I dig my spurs into my own 42-year-old horse as if it were a race to the death. And when I come light bulbs shatter in my chest, my brain; the violence of my finish is shocking and magnificent. Winded and straining I look down to see her lock her elbows hard, my knuckles blanche as my fingers dig into her pelvis as if they wanted to break into a ripe tropical fruit from which I could quench my thirst. My body bows, my forehead comes to rest on the dragon like a felled tree.

Do women ever fall in love this way?

"Are you OK?"

I was still catching my breath, but laughed a hot laugh of pleasure. She didn't move for a moment, except to place her hand on the base of my cock feeling for the ring of the condom, wary that I might pull too quickly from inside of her.

"It's OK, I can do it," and I took myself out from her, carefully.

She dropped to her belly and reached for nappy wipes. She flipped over, took the condom from me and wrapped it in a little packet, which she threw hastily in her wastebasket.

"Are you OK? I'm not normally so… crazy," I was saying, still panting. I laughed, feeling vaguely foolish to be expressing bemusement–there was no hint in her expression that I'd gone too far. She probably had guys a lot heavier than I was, all sizes of penis, guys who flattened her, probably pummelled her into the mattress till they were only aware of fucking something warm, wet and soft cushioning their bulk.

She asked me to lie on my front. "I give you massage."

She wasn't very good, though–it was more like a prodding with fingers, which I soon grew tired of. I sat up and offered to give her one, but this seemed inappropriate. So we lay side by side, a few inches apart, radiating heat to one another. There was a rested quality to her eyes that suggested she really had come earlier. I imagined I could look into them for another hour and still be happy, like a child in a warm rock pool. I slipped my feet over hers, our only cold point. Perhaps I was wrong about the customer, because she seemed in no hurry to have me leave.

She told me she was thinking of moving soon. She was being watched by Arabs or Pakistanis, she said. Sometimes they were there, sometimes they weren't. She was afraid to answer the interphone sometimes. A friend of hers, living five minutes away, had been assaulted recently–by a dark skinned guy, not black–who had been loitering outside her apartment for days. She'd screamed and someone had heard and the man had run off, but she'd been seriously freaked out. I swelled with protective instincts and wondered what kind of courage I might be capable of if challenged to defend her in a similar situation.

I asked her about boyfriends. She admitted grudgingly that she was going out with a sort of ex-boyfriend sometimes, an English guy she'd met here.

"A customer?"

She nodded. "Used to be," she said. "I think I stop seeing him, but then sometimes he's nice," she added vaguely. "Agency don't like us to have boyfriend, you know. I only see this guy because he friend with a Thai boy who friend of someone at agency. Not time for boyfriend when I do this job."

"No time, no time off?"

She shook her head.

"But surely, when you have your period, you're not working then, are you?"

She smiled, as if acknowledging I'd caught her out, but fell solemn just as quickly, averting her eyes. I didn't know where I was going with this. I didn't want to spoil the moment, but maybe it had already gone.

We showered together, our hands no longer searching and tentative, but rather, caring and gentle, like children when they're nice with each other after a fight. As I was getting dressed I asked her if she was busy now.

"Nothing else, no customer," she said, as if school had closed today for an adult function. She had to deliver something to a friend, she said, but afterwards she could join me for a drink. "Yeah, why not?" she said, and laughed as if in defiance of the notion a working girl can't socialise with her john. "You friend," she added with fresh emphasis. "You my dentist!" Laughing with her at her little bit of theatre let in the even funnier notion that her dentist might also be allowed to become her boyfriend one day.

She stepped into some black-laced pink underwear, threw on some jeans and a loose top, her Birkenstock sandals and was ready in five. Sylvia would still have been curling her lashes.

The sun was winking at me as we stepped out onto the street beneath tall chestnut trees. The balmy air further ripened the post-coital bliss coursing through my veins. Sisira took my hand as if for the hundredth time in our friendship and set off at a jaunty pace. We cut through side roads and squares until five minutes later she stopped at the door of another Victorian terrace and pressed the buzzer. An elf-like Japanese girl came to the door in her nightgown. Wouldn't step out onto the street, stood behind the door, bowing like a Japanese girl, but speaking seemingly fluent Thai, darting curious glances at me as she gratefully accepted the bag of food Sisi had brought her.

"Is she also at your agency?" I asked as we walked on.

"Yes. She's good girl. Very funny. And speak good Thai."

Arriving in Queensway, I asked her if she had a place in mind. She shook her head as if it hardly mattered and suggested the first rowdy pub we came to. In the company of anyone else I'd have pulled a face, but I felt almost as unencumbered by experience as I'd been when pub crawls were the order of the day and I'd once been entertained by all the noise and the smoke and the wash of hormonal laughter, the tinkling, whirring slot machines and the slop on the bar. I expected her to order a cocktail or wine, but she wanted a pint of lager; I was the one with the white wine.

We grabbed a table as it became free and sat opposite one another. The lighting was garish and, with anyone else, might have evaporated the already fond memories of seeing her face in candlelight–but she was still beautiful. She looked about the room as though time and place were infinitely elastic to her. She's like a butterfly, I decided, that seems to want to rest and enjoy the flower it's landed on, but must fly off again almost immediately. I wanted to play. But how would I ever keep up at 42?

Fishing out a cigarette, she told me she wouldn't normally go out with a guy she's 'seen' – but *she'd looked in my eyes and I seemed OK*, she said. A woman capable of split second decisions, going with her gut–I liked that.

I smiled and lay my hand on hers–it was cool, more like mine usually are. She reciprocated, just as though we were lovers. Her palms were a little dry–from all the baths and showers she must be taking, I figured.

The post-coital feeling sweetened by the alcohol cast us as the best of friends, even though the reality was that we were more like two business partners celebrating a mutually beneficial transaction which might be repeated at a later date – albeit not without a renegotiation regards the fee.

She remarked that I didn't seem typical of most English, either in looks or manner. I don't know why that pleased me. Perhaps it was because she was so exotic and having her tell me I was atypical brought me a little closer to her. When I told her I was born in Boston, she laughed, pleased she'd guessed right that I wasn't from England. "Ah, but let me finish: I came over here when I was, like, ten, so I've very little accent, if any... At eleven I was already saying, 'Bloody hell.' I had an Irish dad, a British mum. They'd been working over there and then they came back to the UK when my dad got a job at a hospital in London… So, no American blood; English, Celtic, some German blood, but way back." She had some Chinese blood, on her dad's side, she reminded me. Which prompted me to tell her about my father's parents who left England after the First World War to go teach in

Hong Kong in the 1920s. "…And here's a curious thing," I said. "My Grandma–in photos of that time?–she actually looked Oriental, especially about the cheekbones and eyes… I've often wondered if there wasn't something in my blood that drew me to Oriental women… My 'ex', for instance,"–why was I referring to Sylvia as my 'ex', just tidier perhaps than 'the woman I feel I'm virtually separated from but am still sleeping with' – "she was originally from Mauritius, her father was half Indian, half French and her mother was half Malaysian and half Chinese."

"So you like mixed blood?" she said, as though determining my preference in sauces.

"Yeah, I guess so."

"You're in good city for this. Lots of pretty foreign girls working here."

When I realised that she'd just assumed I was in the market for a certain kind of prostitute, my heart sank. I wanted to say, I wasn't like that, I wanted love, but I said nothing, because that's the kind of thing I would have said at thirty-five; at 43, it just seemed so much wiser to answer with silence, the kind of silence that just might make a beautiful woman think twice about you–and if it didn't, at least you'd saved your breath.

After a pause, completely out of the blue, Sisira looked me in the eye and said she was going to tell me something she would never tell a customer – not that I was a customer exactly, I was her friend, her dentist! She blushed a little, confused by her own system of distinguishing friends from customers.

"OK," I said, excited by this early development.

"I just heard my sister got breast cancer."

"Shit, I'm sorry."

"Yeah. And, you know, this happen only one month after my dad die," she added. "Same year my older brother killed in car crash."

Christ–and I'd expected she was about to tell me something intriguing in an uplifting sort of way.

Her father had died of liver disease, drinking too much, two days before the pool incident. She wasn't sure if she wanted to go home for the funeral. It was expensive to fly back–she went home only recently and she was still angry with her dad for letting her and her family down since his divorce.

"I wanted to go home, maybe start business, but now my step-father, he take lots of money from my mother–yeah?– all the money I sent home for her. So now I have to stay here to make more money. Maybe I have to stay one more year–"

"Doing this job?"

She nodded, puffing on her cigarette. "It's OK. I don't do too much, yeah? –"

"Good."

"But I feel bad, yeah? I don't know…"

I touched her hand again, like a father, a true one perhaps, and she let me hold it as she made a brave stab of looking nonchalantly around the room with tears in her eyes.

I asked her if she could stay for one more and, to my delight she agreed to another pint of lager. Standing at the bar, I turned to observe her. There was something about the lithe curve to her slender back–in the tight-fitting, almost kiddie-like pink cardigan–that moved me so ineffably. As if I'd finally found the 'material' that most perfectly embodied a vulnerability and strength out of which I could make a staff that would help guide me on my way. Men were watching her more keenly now that her male companion had gone to the watering hole. *What would you do if one of them recognised her, having tasted her, and felt he had an equal right to sit at your table?*

Half way through my second wine, I asked her, with a sudden tremulous note to my voice, if we might see each other as friends. "I mean, I realise–you have this job, it can't be easy, but… there must be gaps," I said, laughing to hide my fear of rejection. "We could cook together, watch a movie at your place…"

"OK, but when I'm free, yeah?"

"Sure." There was a pause. "Not for sex," I added. "I mean, as a friend… see how *that* goes."

"Yeah, OK, I understand." As if I hadn't needed to spell it out to her. She said I was to call her and that was that – I'd been sent to the end of a queue.

A few minutes later she opened her silver, light-flashing phone to take a call. I braced myself thinking it would be the agency calling, but it was a friend. Hanging up, she said her friend had locked herself out so she was going to have to go home and put her up for the night. *So sorry.*

Leaving the pub I had the impression she'd enjoyed our drink together but was glad of an excuse to cut it short. I told her I'd walk with her to her flat, then head home–*home*, that completely different world.

We were just entering her square and a pool of dense, yellow light from a solitary lamppost, when she got another call. Immediately I had the sense she was being told off for something–by a man. She gave a little wave to me that I couldn't quite read–it could have been an apology or a request that I go on alone–then she moved away, turning her back to me. She began protesting, but reined in, going, "Ka… Ka…" every few seconds. When she hung up, her face was drawn with worry lines. I asked her what was up. She just shook her head, still preoccupied by the call, now glancing up and down the street.

"Someone's watching me," she said finally.

"These Arabs?" I said. And I winced inside. Since 7/7 and 21/7, I'd hardly dared to use words like 'Moslem' or 'Arab' for fear of being overheard and judged as racist–ashamed and suspicious of our own anger, how hopelessly liberal was that!–and now I was with a girl who had good reason to be a little more paranoid than most of us.

She shook her head, but it didn't read like a denial, it was more like, 'I can't tell you'.

"Are you in trouble?"

"Scuse me," cutting the life from my question. "I have to make a call. You go if you want."

"It's OK, I can wait–"

She was already on the phone, talking in urgent Thai, head in her shoulders, complaining about the person who'd just called or someone connected to him. One hand abstractedly fiddling with her left earlobe, she finished up with a softer round of "Ka… ka." Then turned to me: "It's OK, we can go now."

"You're OK?"

"Yes, I'm OK."

And she set off at a swift pace. We said not a word for the rest of the way. She gave me a hasty kiss by the railings and ran up the steps to her front door. As she was fumbling with her keys, she turned but not to look at me, rather, it was to look over my shoulder into the shadows of the square. She slipped inside and slammed the door.

I looked about me. There was no one, just rows of parked cars. A small handful of windows showed lights. It was only nine thirty, but it felt much later. The square was still and silent save for the flutter of leaves high above my head. I had the distinct impression, though, that I was being watched. Fear was highly contagious in London's Zone 1.

I moved off slowly, keeping my wits about me until I reached the main streets. A glorious evening had ended prematurely in paranoia. I told myself it was probably nothing serious and on the tube train home I became absorbed in writing a text message thanking Sisira for the evening and looking forward to the next time. Getting off the train, I checked my phone for a reply. Nothing. Still, she'd probably be busy putting up her friend for the night. Wouldn't she.

Just as the ten-minute walk back to the house, in the refreshingly cool summer evening, re-enlivened my memory of the evening's best moments, it also filled me with a bold indifference to whatever might follow. Perhaps I'd never even see her again, I told myself, like a novice who'd won a few hundred quid on a one-off, impulse bet. And yet I couldn't deny that it hurt to remember she'd offered to put me in touch with other pretty girls, as we'd been about to leave the pub. As if everything I'd said was just 'customer' talk and any liking I had of her could just as easily be transferred to another 'working girl'. Perhaps being so beautiful she had more than enough customers and could afford to palm me off to her friends and this gesture would hold her in some esteem among her peers. Or perhaps she'd been testing me to see whether I was interested in her only as a sex object. Her cynicism was so gentle and without sarcasm, yet so profound, it intrigued me already.

As I was getting undressed in the sliver of light from the corridor, I felt my phone vibrating in my pocket and stepped onto the landing to check caller ID.

"Hey."

"Hello." She made the 'lo' rise warmly, round, like a bubble escaping to the surface. It was as if I'd phoned her and she was happy to hear from me.

"You OK?"

"Yes, OK now. Sorry about that."

"Oh, don't worry about it. You're OK, yeah?" I could hear a childlike excitement in my conspiratorial whispering.

"Yeah, I'm OK. My friend here now."

"Good."

A pause.

"You very good to me."

"Really?"

"Yeah." The conversation was becoming vaguely incantatory already. "Men don't usually say such nice thing in my ear when we fucking, yeah?"

"Really?"

We laughed and my spine tingled up and down.

"No… makes me excited! That's why I come with you!"

"Well – great." My ears burned with pride and incredulity.

"Yeah… so take care, yeah? You call me again."

Hanging up I had a bendy hard-on. I had to beat off in the toilet, like a teenager.

I switched off the small light Sylvia had left on for me and got into bed beside her. Enjoying the warm glow about my groin, I lay on my back in the dark, thrumming with a cocktail of emotions. The call was unexpected, it had excited me–why deny it. But I wasn't convinced she'd called just to say she liked my sexy whispering in her ear as I fucked her, and it was something more than a customer-care call timed to reel in a nice guy as a regular; I felt sure her call had something to do with that other call that had shaken her in the street. I'd already proven to her I was a sympathetic professional UK citizen who had fixed her tooth–maybe, I could be called upon to fix something else.

"Who was that calling so late?" It was Sylvia, in a sleepy, somewhat peeved voice, interrupting my thoughts.

"Um–" I couldn't say 'wrong number', I'd been too long, maybe she'd heard. I couldn't say 'my nurse', she'd think we were having an affair–"…my brother. He uh–women problems. You know what he's like."

She sighed and said, why did he have to call so late, and, sighing noisily, rolled over onto her side.

CHAPTER 5

I wake up the next morning, reliving the anger and violence that so unexpectedly defined the last minutes of my fuck with Sisi. I've used anger in sex before, the way an athlete would to optimise his performance, I've used it to whip resentment into love, I'm sure we all have… but I can't recall having used anger as an end in itself. In fact, to talk of anger doesn't even properly describe the emotion that swept over me. It was as if I'd gone riding into a valley of joyful death.

I've grown used to finding this half of the bed empty when I surface properly. It's like a gap in the teeth, instantly evocative of pain and loss. By now Sylvia will have had her shower and done her chanting or daimoku and be preparing the kids' lunch. When your libido dwindles to nothing, it's amazing what you can do for other people. Your social conscience swells with the sweat of your own self-sacrifice. While your 9-5 dentist husband carries on more or less as he has done for the past twenty years, you create new demarcation zones of self, marshalling children, conquering house chores and adapting to new challenges such as a BA in Fine Art at thirty-five. In spite of her feminist credentials, she's programmed to act in such a way that makes a man think he must always try harder, do more, be more. To show appreciation is just a tactic for hooking a man; to show it when you have him is tantamount to giving him a free pass to exotic pussy…

It's hard to believe now that Sylvia had been drifting when our paths first crossed. She'd recently got back from her 18-month world trip, not knowing what to do with her life, career-wise. Brought up in Mauritius and West Hampstead, London, she'd studied History at Sussex University and finished with a 2'2 and not a clue what to do next. She'd gone on the dole for three months, moonlighting as a waitress, before signing up to do a TEFL course at International House in Piccadilly. Just days after she passed her exams, she packed her bags and set off for a teaching post in Malaysia. After about four months there, she set off again–Singapore, Philippines, Thailand, Vietnam, Laos, Hong Kong, Sri Lanka… teaching on the go for about six or seven months. She hopped from Bali to Australia, where she learnt to dive, left after six weeks and spent a month catching up with distant and elderly relatives in Mauritius, before moving on to Brazil to teach in Rio for 3 months, where she took up capoeira and fell in love with a black guy from Bahia. After she split up with the capoeira dancer with a body like a god (and a small harem to prove it), she came home to take a part-time job doing the same in a small language school in W1. Now under the close, grey skies of London, she found the teaching experience such a pale copy of what she'd been used to, she chucked it in and began temping and, having done some acting at college, took a shot at getting back into that, putting herself up for auditions and castings. Blessed with good looks and some natural talent, she picked up a few minor parts in TV, short films and one commercial (which kept her in pretty clothes for a year). She was also doing voice-overs – mainly in

French, as she was bi-lingual – and, for a time, she seemed poised to make a career of this newly reignited passion. But back then there were so few decent parts for girls of a mixed race and she began to despair of ever being put forward for anything meatier than a nurse or traffic warden. And then came along an Irish lad with a shock of dark hair and a fondness for breaking young girls' hearts. Totally humiliated and exhausted by bad boy Jamie, she lost her rhythm and her spirit for drama. Doors closed on her, her phone cooled off and she was forced to take a job – as my receptionist. She'd heard about the post through my hygienist, Tom, whom she'd met in Kuala Lumpur. My immediate impression when I saw her walk through the door was that she was far too pretty and exotic to be my receptionist, she'd be off in no time. But her natural charm on the day, blessed with an enticing spice of indifference and candour, were so disarming, I couldn't possibly say no to her. She was restless back then, a young deer learning to walk, often breathtakingly spontaneous. She was open–if not bold–in her request for the occasional day off for auditions and castings, but she was never self-important about her prospects and I respected her for that. Every now and then she did throw us all into chaos, begging for time off the day before, or even that same morning, but on the whole she was good at her job and true to her word in making up for lost time. I'd read a mutual sympathy in her eyes from the outset, but I was always so conscious of her heart and mind being elsewhere, romancing about some other life only just out of reach – I couldn't imagine why she'd want to get involved with a relatively non-creative person like me, someone who at best could only confess to having a rather private, barely explored ambition to write. About two months after she started with us, she joined me, Andrea and Tom for a drink in Soho. I'd been looking forward to it, I was even a little nervous because I saw it as the step before asking her out. But to my surprise, I found her strangely lacklustre. After that I sort of crossed her off the list and wouldn't have asked her out but for the fact she stayed late one night offering to make up for lost time for an audition I'd let her go off to the day before. I happened to be around too, not even by design and we just casually asked each other what we had on that night. I was surprised at the contrast between our first drink and this impromptu date and even more surprised when we ordered a second bottle of wine, throwing caution to the winds–we were colleagues–by talking into the early hours about our previous love affairs. Seeing we'd missed the tube, I offered her a taxi back to mine. The passion was revelatory–I'd never underestimate the possibility of chemistry in a woman again, not one I liked anyway. But I wasn't about to drop my style of life and seeing other girls, just because of one night, or even three or four. Which seemed to suit her anyway, as she claimed she'd been pretty "done in" by her experience with the wily James and wasn't about to take a fall again any time soon. I think it was probably the fact I was so relaxed about her and my sex life at that time which held added appeal for her. Until of course, this sort of casual minding-one's-own-business attitude to sex lost its charm and feelings started to kick in. That's to say, her feelings. As for me, I'd not had half the sexual experience of some of my contemporaries in my student years and now that I was finally able to exercise some financial muscle, I was in the mood for making up for lost time. Sylvia understood this, but said, in that case, she needed some 'time off from us'. And so we agreed to 'give each other space…and see how it goes.' But within a few weeks of separating, we threw ourselves into unsuitable affairs. Hers hadn't ended as swiftly as mine, and she seemed to relish the fact. It was the first time in my life I was seized by a need to possess a woman, a belief that I might belong with her, that I'd be happy waking up beside her day after day–and I was suddenly appalled with myself that I'd so casually given her up. But this realisation came too late, I think. Even though I surpassed myself in winning her back, I think she came back to me with a broken wing. The wing healed, but from then on, even through our happier periods, I was aware of a sadness in her that leaked up from the wound caused by the frivolousness of my behaviour at the time she'd fallen in love with me, and from my having failed to live up to her ideal.

We weren't even yet living together when she got pregnant. Before we'd even begun to exhaust the sexual chemistry. Her acting might have been about to take off–now, at 25, if she went to full term, it would wither and possibly die. My own creative side, which had come to life again inspired by Sylvia's acting ambitions, stood to be buried under diapers and wipes and toys. Surely we should abort. But we dithered and in the end, I think we went for it because we believed that our combined DNA would create a person more special than if we'd waited to have babies with someone else. Which is to say, we admired one another more than we loved one other.

To her credit, Sylvia took to motherhood with great élan, no morbid looking back and moping over the acting life she might have had. As the children began to walk and talk, she started going to life drawing classes. And from there, she progressed to part-time courses and a Higher National Certificate in Fine Art. She had talent, that much was clear to everyone. I was proud of her ability to transform herself, even as I was a little worried she might never crack the even harder world of contemporary art. With the start of her part-time BA, I sensed she felt justified in putting our physical relationship on hold–she now had heaps of essays to write as well as the kids to look after. It would seem that my unwavering support of her efforts to get back into higher education had made me complicit in the demise of my own sex life.

The mistake so many men make is to imagine the event of having kids as some kind of temporary hiatus to one's sex life, or to any of the playfulness of the life before the first child came along–but of course it's more like a revolution. Some men kick and rail against the bars of the new confined parameters of their sexual playpen, others seem to sleep through the post-baby years just occasionally remembering to shake their rattle. I was one of the difficult ones, banging at his cage day and night, even though, according to friends, Sylvia's lack of libido was no worse than average. For a time, after Mia was born I felt I was beginning to adjust to a less active sex life. But then came my fortieth and, with no change in Sylvia's interest, I grew restless all over again. The life ahead wasn't an open road any more–things, experiences, pleasures had to be seized NOW, or you'd wake up at fifty something to find you could only perform on Viagra washed down with shark fin soup.

As time has gone on this one thing has become clear to me: it didn't matter that she chose to go to full-term even as I'd poured doubts on the viability of our relationship at the time; the fact is, my sperm had contributed to the demise of her acting career. With child bearing behind her, she didn't want anything I said or did to deflect her from her new objective: to be a good mum and a painter. It wasn't inconceivable that she looked forward to a day when she could paint me out of her life altogether.

Under the hot shower I close my eyes and picture Sisi beside me, naked, a smile forming on my lips as I remember that soapy beard on her cute behind.

Entering the kitchen, I find Sylvia spooning out pasta into Tupperware, but not so busy she hasn't time to pause and cast me a welcoming smile. It's not just a smile that belies the long absence of sexual contact between us, it's a smile that sweetens the strangely inappropriate cheerfulness a man wakes up with after he's had sex with another woman. Do you hide that cheerfulness for fear she'll know where it came from, or do you use it to reawaken her interest in you?

If only she saw it as the chance it was.

When the phone goes Sylvia takes the phone into another room. Returning to the kitchen she looks troubled. What's up? I ask. Her sister has had another bust-up with her bloke. We both know this probably means there's been violence or a threat of violence. She'd stayed with a friend overnight but was now back in her flat clearing up the mess. Why doesn't she leave? I ask incredulously. She draws a breath and holds it, her eyes inclined over the table. Does she think I'm thinking the same about us? I want to reach across the table and hold her hand, but I'm afraid she would find any gesture I make glib or even insincere.

As I step off the bus on the way to the practice Sisi appears beside me with a skip and a jump and I actually stop mid-stride and consider calling her on the phone–but then I remember she wouldn't even be up yet. She's there again, in my dentist's chair, as I sit on my stool waiting for an elderly patient to return from the toilet. Later that afternoon I slip furtively into the back yard with my phone. I leave her a message, feeling happy with myself that I could sound casual when I'm so peculiarly het up.

A day goes by and no reply. That's normal, right? But I feel my sense of what's normal already beginning to warp under the pressure of emotions I am so not used to. I call again, but hang up before the message service clicks in. I begin to fear she's changed her number. She had two phones that night I saw her. Maybe she's junked the one I'm calling or given it to one of her forgetful friends. I call again from the back yard of my practice, pacing up and down the cracked concrete patio. I'm about to close the clamshell over a long ring when she picks up. She sounds sleepy, groggy. My name should have come up on her phone, but she asks, "Who is this?" I remind her I'm Anthony, her dentist. Yes, she'd like to go for a coffee but not now, honey. *Honey*, I think to myself, not Anthony. She's sick, she says. It's her stomach. My mind reels at the graphic picture of her stomach awash with her daily cocktail of DNA and bacteria deposited by countless customers, and I wonder how many men she lets kiss her. I perch on one of the shabby garden chairs, elbows on my thighs, the tip of my toe molesting a despondent weed. She's been throwing up, she says. I ask questions she doesn't understand, doesn't have much patience for. But patience is what I am good at, it's part of my job; I hope she appreciates this because I really have got it down to a fine art. But she only asks if we could speak later and barely waits for me to round up the conversation before hanging up. When she goes I feel as if I'd just lost something precious down a drain, *how the hell to get it back?* I'm suddenly consumed with concern for her, though it's probably nothing more than a stomach bug she has. Andrea is calling me back inside. I have patients to think of, some of whom are in pain, but I wave and call, "One minute!" I open my phone and start jabbing at the keys: 'I have the day off tomorrow, so if you need any shopping, food or medicine, just let me know – I can help. Anthony.' I press SEND and wonder if she'll even see it until the early hours.

To my surprise she calls me the next day, that same day around five. Hey, I purr, immediately ready with my warmest bedside manner. She thanks me for offering to help her, but she'll be OK, which is perhaps just as well because I don't have a day off, on the contrary my day is packed with appointments, one dental emergency and kids homework and babysitting, though I might have cancelled it all had she needed me. She asks after me: "What have I been doing?" But she isn't quite there behind her own line of inquiry, her voice a languid soup of generic concern for one of her potential regulars. In no time she's telling me she has to hang up, she's got a booking, could I call her tomorrow? A booking. A fucking. Sure, no problem.

I call later. Twice. I leave messages. The earlier nonchalance in my voice is showing strain. I wake at dawn in a feverish sweat like a junkie missing his fix. And then in the tubes, the buses, I'll suddenly be missing her so bad that I find myself in the grips of a mild panic attack and have to step outside, onto the platform, to calm down. My nerves tingle, my skin crawls just thinking of her–and I realise I'm terrified of the chemical excess she induces in me. In almost every dream I try to cajole some clue from her as to what it is about her that fills me with such a maddening mix of tenderness and anger. It's as though her origins lie deep inside my own DNA, which I must somehow unravel if I'm ever to understand my past and my future. Is it her uncanny resemblance to my youngest daughter that haunts me? Wait, that's kinda freaky–don't even to go there.

"Sisi–" finally I get through and she sounds awake, lively; in fact she's laughing, I have to hope it's not at something a customer just said, "it's me, Anthony."

"Hello! I'm sorry, I have no time to see you today."

She must have seen my number come up nearly a dozen times in–what? 5 days?–but she betrays no impatience as she says this, which, sadly, suggests I must be one of several men who regularly call her up for a 'coffee'.

"I want to book you," I blurt out.

"For sex?" her voice sweetening as it rises to the 'x'.

"Yeah." I feel like a detainee who's finally confessed to a crime he didn't do, unable to hold out any longer. I'm deeply disappointed in myself, but so relieved to have a solution to this agony of withdrawal. I laugh tremulously – "It seems it's the only way I can see you!"

"I'm sorry, I have to work, you know–"

"No, it's OK," cutting across her, digging into hidden depths of stoicism. "So, um, what do I do?"

She gives me the number for her agency and tells me to ask for Sonia.

"Sonia," I repeat, scribbling the name on a Post It. "Is that your booker?"

"No, it's my name on website."

You don't need drugs, you don't need drink, you don't need to excel in your career – all you need is one more hour with Sisi, that's to say, Sonia. But this time you see her for what she really is, OK? A whore. True, a lovely girl, but a whore. Think of it as therapeutic to have great sex with someone who would make no claims on you after the event.

I call the agency and talk to a Thai man, who speaks to me in a low-key, velvet voice synonymous with shady discretion and the sensuously grotesque worlds of David Lynch. I book Sonia for 3.30 Sunday. He politely requests that I call the next day any time after 9 a.m. to confirm. For two eternal weeks I've been longing to see her, afraid that I might be in love with her, afraid that I might discover she would from now on prove a disappointment – and at last I'm booked to see her! I could still cancel, but I won't; it's not like she'd get a kill fee, the way I do. So what magic can I conjure in that hour so that I get Sisi rather than Sonia? How do you hide the desperation when the very fact of going to see a call girl is desperate? Maybe you need two hours. That's 300 quid. Why would I need two hours, though? I'm not twenty-five any more. More to the point, I'm not even feeling so good. Ever since the accident–no, even before then–I've been experiencing unexplained surges of adrenalin spurting about my system at the slightest excuse, sometimes unprovoked. Seems like I get to forty and suddenly I can't process the stress properly. *That's why you need to get laid*, says a voice in my head, *siphon off some of the excess cortisol.* Sonia performs a service that keeps men from losing it. The NHS could set up sex clinics and shave off some of its burgeoning debt and reduce crime into the bargain. Why, all of a sudden, have I become a sponge for my family's stress? For instance, I hear from Dad that my mother's so far unexplained bout of chronic diarrhoea has meant diapers and I'm so *moved* by her predicament I have three days of IBS. I never used to be so wired in to people's upsets. My mother's voice, when she comes on to the phone, sounds breathy and weak. I admire her cheerfulness and humour, but her inability to follow my advice in opposition to my dad's is growing ever more exasperating. She tells me, with such moving gratitude in her voice, that Dad's ever so good; he's never once shown any irritation with her when she shits her pants half way to the toilet. But he's also a stubborn old pharma-head, who refuses to accept my prognosis that she's almost certainly suffering side effects from the anti inflammatory drug she's been on! And why? Because a) I'm his son and b) the dumbass consultant she's been seeing hasn't raised the issue of side effects; instead, to my amazement, he's told her she needs *more* fibre. *Hello?!* Even your average bod in the street knows fibre makes you go to the loo more. The whole thing's depressed me. I should be visiting her, not Sisi. Well, never mind, I'm doing neither. I'm down at my own doctor's. Dr. Patel. He frowns when he sees me, as if merely my presence in the room is an anomaly. This makes me want to be cheerful, but what would I be doing here if I were cheerful. I talk to him as if he were a colleague, but then wonder if he finds this a little condescending. He draws a deep, wheezy breath. Fifty going on six-five, the poor guy's bulging with ghee – and I wish I hadn't noticed bits of wax hanging like tiny dead insects in the web-like hair of his ears. Seated in the plastic bucket seat next to his desk, I feel like a witness of my own condition, he the judge of my dubious testimony. I am here to discuss the results of a set of bloods and the CT scan I had done ten days after my collision with Sisi. They're probably fine, or wouldn't they have called me already? I wait a small lifetime as his podgy hands sift through my notes as if they were old indecipherable archives from a Hindu temple. I chip in a reminder as to when the tests were done, hoping to speed things up a tad. He nods, frowning more intently as though he'd finally come to a turd. "Well," he says finally, "everything appears to be normal." He gives me a checking glance as though I were about to rebut these not entirely conclusive findings with alternative medicine heresy. I find myself expressing relief more out of politeness than anything else. "You're a dentist," he notes, prepared to ponder the case a little further–in my opinion, from the wrong end of the stick. I suspect he's inferred from this nugget of information that that I'm probably depressed; it's a well-known fact now that dentists have a high suicide rate. But how could I possibly confide in a man who doesn't even look at me as he asks me if I'm depressed? I return home, thinking about my older brother, who still suffers bouts of high anxiety even years after giving up gluten, of which he has an enteropathy. Now I seem to be getting the same kinds of symptoms. Perhaps I should have asked Patel for an IG test for gluten. But perhaps I'm feeling this lousy on account of the alcohol I've been imbibing so freely–caffeine and alcohol are pretty pernicious on the nervous system. Maybe I go for a colonic… So, anyway, will I be fit enough on the day? As if Sisi could care less. OK, never mind *her* for a minute. You're *paying* this time, so you want your money's worth and that means lasting at least 30 minutes inside her, because anything less won't give you the high you crave or bring her off. But why're you going over this? You were fine last time. Eat a banana on the way over there–the potassium in banana's good for easing cramps, boosting energy. Second thoughts, don't, you might get indigestion eating on the train.

I wake to see Sylvia sit up in bed and look past her at the pencils of early morning light growing between the slats of the Venetian blind. As she moves, haltingly, I reach out to touch her, my hand on her pyjamas about her hip. She seems barely to register my touch. I slip my hand under her pyjama shirt, I mean nothing by it really except to feel her skin, for her belly to feel my hand without clothes between us, but she stands immediately, losing my hand, an unwanted encumbrance. She glances behind her and smiles in case I might be offended, a fond smile as if to say 'it might have been nice, but you know we have no time', and yet I read it as I should surely only see it in retrospect – as a sad farewell. She picks up her clothes and takes them from the room to escape my possibly critical eye, noting again the stretch marks, the loss of a full cup-size since her last failed attempt at breast-feeding. But there's also my hungry eye she'd be wary of. It used to make her smile and giggle, now it only serves to make her feel guilty about her post-natal libido and then resentful of me for having inspired the guilt she feels. I shouldn't assume that she could just switch herself on, should I. I should approach her differently somehow. I can't help feeling she means she wishes I looked different as well – a different man altogether beside her in bed might just awaken her desire. Ironically, it's been she who has neglected to explore new ways of making the sex feel fresh. It hurts that she goes away. How can I be creative with her if she acts as if she's ashamed of us. I remember, even before the sex ebbed away, she'd begun changing into her clothes in the kids' room, or the bathroom. When I'd joked of buying her a beautiful Chinese screen for her birthday, she'd smiled sourly as if to say, 'the laugh is on you if you think your humour is the solution'. And she's ceased to watch me whenever I slip from a bathrobe into my pyjamas–because that would have meant having to decide whether she still wanted me.

As I turn back to face the wall, I escape again to the memory of being naked with Sisi. The silkiness of her skin over mine. I lie there for a few more minutes cradling that imagined experience as though it were a baby, a baby that might not live to see another day.

As I sit up my eyes come to rest on the tray of ash of burnt joss-sticks placed mid-centre at the front of Sylvia's gohonzon near our bed. It occurs to me Sylvia hasn't spoken much about the bombs, or the paranoia that's settled like a fine toxic dust in the bronchial passages of the city, making our chests a little tighter whenever we contemplate the future. Men and war, she'll sometimes say, as if that explains it all. She and I used to talk politics, comparing notes of favourite journalists, such as Simon Jenkins in The Times, but in the last couple of years, as she's grown more interested in Buddhism, she's become more ambitious for her day, as opposed to her life. Her focus has been on things she might do for her local Buddhist group members, whom she meets on average once a week. By degrees, she's withdrawn from having any opinion about the Bush-Blair-Bin Laden madness, just as she's withdrawn from sexual relations with me. While my social life has slowly eroded away, hers has grown… more diffuse. Her network of virtual and real friends has gradually superseded anything I can give her. Even in conversation my opinions count less and less–and not so much because she disagrees with them, it's more that they seem only to clutter her mind, her seeking of something outside of anything I long for.

It's kind of sad, she's observed of me, that when the sex was vibrant I used to be full of plans, but that once that faded I became a person who simply collided with other people's plans. It's true: she sees the bigger canvas of life, whereas I squint at the detail immediately in front of me; (I've gone 'snowblind' from looking at too much enamel). Ironically, in the early days of going out with Sylvia I used to say to my mates that I thought Sylvia was too laid back with her acting ambitions, even naïve; I'd imagined I was attracted to the alpha type, but now I was living with one, we were less happy. As I became more frustrated she became more evasive. When our respective frustrations collided we were explosive and, as Sex was no longer in the First Aid box, our wounds festered. The centrifugal force of family and professional life have kept us whirling round and round and, in our moments of quiet, I think we've harboured the hope that we would one day come across a clearing that was ours again, where our doubts and fears and longings could be reconstituted into something new and vibrant. But now, with Sisi on my mind, I feel further than ever from such a place. I am not even sure I would have any use for it if I got there.

"Why don't you try chanting, just see if it works for you?" she'd put to me whenever she caught a whiff of my mid-life crisis talking. "You've tried yoga, you've tried alternative medicine… you've opened your mind to the risks of amalgam fillings, why is this any different? We're not a cult. You don't have to come to meetings–"

"I just don't have that spiritual dimension that you obviously have."

"It doesn't have to be spiritual, the way other religions are–"

"But you still have to believe in this… other entity. You sit, or kneel before your shrine, you put your hands together holding some beads and recite a–a what-do-you-call it."

"Nam-yo-ho-reng-yo-kyo."

"Yeah, that. And it's just not me."

"How do you know if you won't try? I didn't think it was me, but I tried and now I see how it's working for me."

I couldn't deny the fact that her deepening interest in Buddhism had coincided with a galvanising of her confidence and creative potential, but, as my brother had found with his Buddhist wife, in terms of *us*, her chanting and meetings had to a large extent supplanted the physical with the spiritual. So was I trying to say Buddhism had killed her sex drive? How stupid. Two pregnancies had killed it. Or at least squashed it. Some of the women in her group wanted sex 'all the time', she'd remind me.

"But those women have Buddhist practising husbands and boyfriends, don't they?"

"Yes," she'd say defensively, only to smirk with embarrassment as we simultaneously understood the implication of where this was going: that all I had to do was become a member and my member would be better served.

Desire–or animality, as she sometimes preferred to call it–was limiting because it kept us tethered to materialist cravings. Sorry, I'd say, but I wasn't ready to be a monk yet, even though I seemed to have become one by default over the past two years. Well, she'd counter, if only I could clean up my karma, I might even find a solution to my sexual frustration; whether that was through her or another woman, interestingly, she left open to question.

"So you think we're all victim types, with low self-esteem."

"Not exactly. But you have to admit, most of your members do tend to be people who started practising when they were in a crisis. I think you had low self-esteem for a long time–"

"Yeah, OK, and now I've changed. It's helped me. How else do you think I would have found the courage to study for a BA in Fine Art–at 35? You tell me you feel your life lacks sparkle, you feel down–so why don't you at least explore something that might inspire you?"

Sylvia, who was already more than half way there to becoming a Buddhist by virtue of her heritage–Indian, Malaysian and Chinese blood–thought I wouldn't try because I was embarrassed, but it went much deeper than that; I was incapable of entrusting my 'fate' to anyone's hands but my own. It had taken years to persuade her that I might not think less of her because she was a Buddhist. And therein lies my problem with all religions: if you're not a member, you're a sort of enemy–albeit in her eyes, a benign, possibly rather pathetic one.

Later that day, in such turmoil with my emotions, I send Sisi a text cancelling our appointment, pretending to be ill. I receive no acknowledgment from her, no wish that I'll be feeling better soon. But what was I expecting? She's not my girlfriend. Arguably not even my friend. So what will she do with that hour? Will she fill it up with someone else? The funny thing is, having cancelled, having expected to feel calmer about things, I now feel even worse. I'm like a junkie who's just cancelled his dealer in a spasm of self-possession only to realise he can't handle his withdrawal symptoms after all. Ironically, I'd decided to spend my planned time with her reading a recent paper on toxicity from amalgam, but I'm reading the same paragraph over and over, caught in a loop of reliving the intoxicating pleasures of locking myself inside Sisi. I go over to the window to look out into the street, my hand grips the edge of the table, and I remember the pressure I brought down on the small of her narrow back, the soft clap and bounce of my groin as it slapped against her buttocks, and that same anger she invoked in me rises again, only this time I think I identify a healing quality about it and curse myself for having cancelled. I see her long, permed hair swish across the middle of her beautiful back, I see the dragon on her shoulder lift its head and breathe fire at me... I close my eyes and relive the fullness of her lips, the evasive playfulness of her tongue. How can I think about detox, possessed by such an intoxicating woman?

I wake the next day and hear another year of my life crash to the side of the bed like a corpse. It's my birthday. I check my face in the mirror and, for a moment, I can't understand why the face I'm looking at isn't fifteen or sixteen anymore. Always a late developer, I've grown leaner, more muscular, even in the last five years. It's as if my soul were whittling down the physical me in order that I might finally look in the mirror and know better what it is that I want out of the rest of my life. But the years are coming too fast. I never used to be able to see the next birthday, it was always around the corner somewhere, but now on my forty-second birthday, I see 43 already hurtling toward me as unstoppable as a meteor.

My wife spends the morning taking shots of Mia hiding in a bin liner for her next art project.

"What is this about?" I ask her.

She doesn't like to be asked. It's an emotion, she says. It's about feeling trapped as a child. But how do we know a child is in there? She shows me the little window through which a grinning Mia is calling Peep-o! to me. I'm happy she's chosen my birthday to work on her art and not worry how we should celebrate the day.

I bring her a glass of wine as she continues to explore her subject. I park myself on the bench where I'm joined by Neo, our Burmese Blue, who curls up on my lap, purring loudly. As Sylvia prepares the meal, I even get up onto the trampoline and jump with Mia and Michaela, holding hands. Then Mum joins in and we spin round and round holding hands until she and I become children again and all the bad things fall away and I feel intoxicatingly at one with everything.

That night I'm hopeful and reach out to touch Sylvia. She smiles and I raise myself a few inches to kiss her. She kisses me back and smiles, eyes still closed.

"Sorry," she whispers. "Tired."

I kiss her once more and thank her for a lovely day.

The practice is busy. Which is just as well because whenever I pause for five minutes, Sisi is in my head, my blood. I return home in the evenings determined to make an extra effort with my kids and whatever homework they might need help with. One sunny Sunday morning Sylvia pops her head round the living room door and, finding me reading a multi-ethnic version of *Alice in Wonderland* with Mia remarks on my frowning. Was I? I say. She frowns back at me like a kid, then smiles as if to a potential convert, hopeful that I'm enjoying this extra time I've been putting in with the girls. I smile back, but her encouragement mostly rankles, as it reminds me that part of my dedication here is a strategy to overcome my 'addiction' to Sisi.

I go for a game of badminton with my hygienist after work. *I'll sweat her out of me.* But the truth is I'm thinking of picking his brain for some insight on Oriental women.

My mind's not on the game. So of course I'm losing. I can't keep up with his younger legs even if I do have the clever shots. I leave the court in a philosophical frame of mind, arguing to myself that my below par performance is not just about my general level of fitness, it's about reality – I'm 43 to his 33. Having found something inelegant and mechanical style about his style, I'm no longer inclined to ask him for any tips. Besides, I'd probably embarrass him hinting that I might be seeing another woman; worse, he might worry that it was a patient and that I was about to involve him in a conspiracy.

My voice re-oxygenated, I step out of the changing rooms dialling SONIA before I can stop myself. I connect to a Scottish guy, who says in a lyrical Glaswegian accent, that he thinks Sonia will be free the time and date I've asked for, but would I phone the next day to confirm? Of course. I know the drill. I give him my name. He sounds friendly, professionally warm, as if he understood intimately my state of mind, like a psychiatrist. Minutes later I remember it's my turn to pick up the kids from school that day. *Damn, you have to cancel again.*

The following day, while killing time for a friend who is held up on the tube, I walk into Piccadilly's Waterstone's where my wandering eye locks onto 'Languages' out of all the subjects on five floors. On the second Floor I walk along to 'T' and pick up a book entitled *Colloquial Thai.* Checking that no one is close by, I read aloud a couple of the sentences at the front of the book. I used to speak a bit of Cantonese ten years ago, which I picked up while going out with a striking and wiry, if painfully exacting, Chinese girl, so I have some experience of a tonal language. I see the price is marked 'reduced' and think, 'Might be interesting…' It's only as I leave the shop that I realise I'll be hiding the book and CD from Sylvia as I used to hide porno mags from my mum.

Another couple days go by before I call again. This time Sonia isn't free. Unless she's ill, I figure she's probably got her period. So if she's got her period and she can't work, Sisi must have time to meet me for a coffee. But she doesn't return my calls.

The next day I speak again with the Thai man with the velvety voice. When he calls me back to confirm Sonia's availability, I feel as relieved as a cardio patient with news that there's a new heart waiting for him in an icebox. I simply have to make the appointment no matter what comes up at home; my bottled up hormones are scaring the kids.

CHAPTER

6

I get to Paddington tube station in good time. I file through the turnstiles with the rush hour crowds wondering if I'm the only one among us who's arrived for paid sex in the afternoon. I walk up and down Praed Street looking for a flower shop, but all I can find are shabby newsagents hoping to get lucky with overpriced, wilting Chrysanthemums, roses and other funereal clichés. So I double-back and walk down the hill to the main station. I find a flower stall back from the milling crowds and choose some white lilies–five for £7.50. Modest enough, I tell myself. But as I walk back up the hill to Praed Street a black guy heading downhill smiles at me and cries, "She's gonna be pleased with them!" I smile back, charmed by the man's spontaneity, and I wonder if he'd seen a man in love coming toward him.

I enter the square of chalky white stone and white pillars on porches and black, spear-head railings just before five. I feel like a young student again coming to visit a girl in digs. I wonder how many more flats down this street accommodate escort girls like Sisi. An almost invisible commerce if these quiet squares are anything to go by.

Number 63. I climb the steps, slightly weak at the knees. There's no answer when I press the buzzer. I call Sisi's mobile, but her phone is off. Vexed, I call the agency. That warm Scottish voice comes on the line again. He apologises, addressing me by name, and tells me he'll call Sonia and find out what the problem is. He returns with a gracious apology–she'd be coming down in just a moment; there's a problem with the buzzer. Waiting, I feel exposed to invisible eyes from neighbouring windows, but remind myself I'm not likely to become a celebrity. The heavy door eases open like a sleepy jaw. Sisi stands by the door, hair tousled, eyes brimming with playfulness. She's wearing just a light dressing gown, catholic purple, which she keeps pinned to her chest as if she were cold, or rather, perhaps just vulnerable standing out here in the hallway. She waves at me to come inside. I watch her funny waddle, very Oriental, as she makes for the open door at the end of the corridor, then follow.

Once inside her flat, she pirouettes about and glides toward me. Her lips enveloped mine, even fuller than I'd remembered. I hold out the flowers and her eyes brighten as if she'd only just noticed them.

"Oh, thank you!" and she kisses me again, briefly. She rushes off to the fridge, carefully depositing the flowers beside the kitchen sink, and asks me if I'd like anything to drink.

"Water, thanks."

"Wait, please," she says, raising a finger and she doubled-back and scurries off down the corridor.

I take a seat on the sofa. I hear another girl's voice. Thai language. Presently, two people enter the room: a dapper man in his late forties with short hair, greying at the sides, wearing a suede jacket and clean, pressed jeans, a leather briefcase in his hand, and, just behind him, a Thai girl who is topless. Seeing me, the man says a polite, almost chirpy "Hello", like an actor embarrassed by the lateness of his exit from dressing room to stage. The girl, now with one hand covering her breasts, beams at me and calls "Sorry!" as she scuttles over to the door to see her customer off, giggling as though it were all a carry on–which I guess it is. He calls a goodbye to Sisi and says to the other girl:

"See you next Tuesday!"

They smack lips and he spirits himself through the door, refreshed, like an old suit put through the dry clean.

I feel momentarily pleased for the bloke. On the other hand, Sisi had come to the door late with barely anything on, had she been taking part? I make a mental note not to book on a Tuesday afternoon in future.

"Don't worry!"

I turn my head. It's the girl, now with a top on. "He with me, not with Sonia! You OK!"

I smile graciously and wave to signal my appreciation of the heads-up. She disappears and I hear a door close. My wait already feels like I'm waiting for a girl to come back with the size shoe I want to try on. Except I don't think I could do sex as shopping. I'm too sensitive, not macho enough… I was actually considering leaving, when Sisi reappeared, hurrying past me on her way to the bathroom. I hear her turning on taps, scrubbing on enamel. She returns a minute later to fix me my glass of water. And finally she comes to sit beside me, straightening a gold medallion on a chain around her neck – a recent gift from a Columbian drug dealer? – which has slipped out from her dressing gown. She's put on some blusher, perhaps to hide a few spots – and I wish she hadn't. There are dark rings under eyes I haven't noticed before. She puts her hand on mine, slips it across to my leg, then almost immediately bounces out of her seat – (and my wife complains that *I'm* restless) – "Oh, your flowers!" she exclaims.

"The girl who sold me the flowers, she told me they'd open more fully later today," I tell her, just needing something to say.

As she holds the flowers out before her, her restlessness falls away from her like the wrapping; her face suddenly blossoms with such pure happiness, I could believe this were the best present she's had in years. I was touched, the way perhaps a film director is touched upon discovering a beauty in the movie he has made that represents something more resonant than his own emotions.

She fills a vase–which I can see is going to be too small–and tries to put the flowers in.

"Is that OK?" she asks of her hasty arrangement.

I get up asking her for a knife. I pick up her chopping board and crunch the heavy blade over the stalks, about eight inches up, and hand the flowers back to her. They sit in the vase a little too low now. Never mind, we say, laughing.

Back on the sofa, as she asks me what I've been up to, I realise all guys get this: a little how-are-you attention in here and then business in the bedroom. I surprise her, though, by telling her I've been teaching myself Thai. I show her the book I was reading on the train.

"What can you say?"

"Koon soo-yay mahk," I say [You're very pretty]

"Korp koon ka," she thanks me, smiling like a beauty queen.

"You see, I know the most useful phrase," I quip and she laughs politely.

She seems to have forgotten I booked her through the agency and for a few minutes I hope that we might agree to do something else together.

"You can come through now."

I was wrong.

"Could you take your shoes off please?"

"Sure."

In the bedroom, I continue telling her about my life, trying to animate the daily stuff, as though I've come to pick up a sick person confined to her room and a mind-numbing routine. But what do I know, really? Maybe she has great sex half the time – and, of course, plenty of it.

"And how are you?" I ask. I tell her she looks tired and she admits she's been "working harder than before." I can see she's uncomfortable with my inquiry, so I quit talking and begin caressing her gently.

"You pay me now please?"

Of course, how rude of me. I pluck the twenties and ten from my wallet, dropping them in a heap on her cover as she kneels behind me, massaging the top of my shoulders and nape. She disappears with the money–doesn't she trust me?–and returns shortly.

Her breasts in my face as she straddles me, her gold medallion swinging before my eyes, a montage of gangster scenes come to mind – except, I don't feel sleazy, I feel joyous as I run my hands up her thighs. I cup her two round cheeks, smooth and cool like breathing pebbles. My middle finger chances upon the single cord of her thong, which I trace till it disappears into her crack. Pleasure travels up my fingers and arms like sweet electricity. When she brings her lips to mine my blood surges.

"I got something for you," I say reaching for my bag. I hand her a couple of Chill Out CDs and immediately feel old not for not passing her the mpeg versions. Expressing surprise, and a warm thank you, she deposits the CDs on her side table as though they were forgettable items I could redeem at the end of my stay. "You can keep them," I add, in case she's not understood. She smiles and kisses me. Now I see how deluded was my gesture. I hadn't bought her the CDs to impress her, I'd bought them because I wanted to leave a little bit of me behind. If only she could read, I'd bring her books too.

She lights three little candles placed on the corners of the bath. She places a cushion behind my head and tells me to lie back. Then rides her soapy body over mine with an urgency that suggests she knows I'm here because I am in medical need of this silky therapy. When she stops, she slides her legs all the way under mine, lifting me out of the water, and goes to work washing my sex as though she were polishing a special ornament. Finally done, she rinses me. She checks the peg in her hair then bends her back–but the angle's too sharp and she has to manoeuvre under me before she can bend far enough down to take me in her mouth. We still haven't said much, I realise, since getting into the hot water.

"Mm, you very t'in, but you have big son," she remarks, stroking me rhythmically.

I laugh at the concept of 'son' and she assumes a mock serious face, then smiles playfully as though to remind me she's a pro at playing to a man's vanity.

As if to prove her interest in my 'son' she pushes her bottom back in the bath and, lengthening her back, begins to blow me, still with her legs lifting me a few inches above the water line. I watch her, trying to imagine what she's thinking, if anything at all. She's going a little too fast, so I sit up, obliging her to stop; (I'm not young enough any more to come twice in under an hour, not with a condom on anyway). She looks a little peeved as if she'd hoped to bring me off in the bath and be done with that side of things.

"That was nice," I say, in the hope she might have enjoyed it too in some way.

But she's avoiding my eyes, simply opens her legs to let my body slip between them, and resumes her washing of my body–the armpits, the arms, the fingers–in a preoccupied mood. After she's rinsed me down, we sit facing one another. She becomes perfectly still. I kiss her… draw back, briefly sated with the taste of her. Out eyes meet with a shy, fleeting elation that surprises us both and makes us laugh. Now I feel ready. I feel confident.

"KOOn wahn mahk," I say, now on the bed, my lips wet with her juices.

She can't get my pronunciation.

"Wahn," I repeat. "Sweet. Your pussy…"

"Wahn," she corrects, crushing the sound with her palate, making it fatter and broader. She laughs. Good–at least I'm entertaining her with my efforts to learn her language. How many other punters can say the same?

She puts the condom on me too early, so I'm all hands and fingers getting myself inside her. It takes five laborious minutes just to get fully hard, during which time I begin registering her sounds of enjoyment as bordering on fake. I shift off my knees to lie over her, my pubic bone grinding against hers. She begins tightening her thigh muscles every so often, forcing me to brake, draining me of energy. We've been fucking in a kind of competitive lock for maybe 15 minutes when she makes a sudden abrupt thrust at me and I pop out of her. My blood recedes fast. My confidence turns to limp salad.

I reach for the glass of water I brought in with me.

"I got so hot on the train," I explain, getting my excuses out fast. "Dehydrated." I find I can gulp down the water as if I were on E, the liquid barely touching the sides.

I take a break, laying my body over hers.

"Your heart is beating very hard," she says, almost alarmed.

I want to tell her this is my passion for her. I want to tell her that I've thought of her every day since I last saw her, but I know it's only going to sound corny.

"Y'know what… " now combing my fingers through her thick hair, moist with perspiration, "I had to come back. There's something special about you, some connection…" But already I'm nearly choking on my own words. It's so futile even to attempt to describe what I feel.

The look in her eyes, as they search mine, suggests she might feel a little pity for me–pity is one thing whores know how to do, though; it's the mothering part of the service.

She tells me to relax now, lie on my back. She works on my sex with her hand. The sensation is delicious but my sex has lost interest in penetrative pleasures. Even when she rolls her breasts against my cock, I get only half way hard. She puts the condom on even so and begins sucking me. Every time she rolls her tongue over the tip and round the back of me, I get a little harder. When I'm nearly ready, I want to fuck her with that same anger I experienced before, as though she's been mocking me with her oral play.

Picking up on this rising primal anger in me, wanting to gratify it, she suggests we try from behind. Her sex is tight, though, I'm already tired and I can't get a rhythm going. I slip out of her like a jockey losing his stirrup.

"Can we lie down a minute?" I request.

So she lies flat on her belly, waiting. I remain seated, though, intrigued by the band of darker skin, like the reverse of a suntan line, around the edge of her firm round buttocks, the flat V of skin around her coccyx like a dark arrowhead directing my gaze to the crevice of her sweet anus, as yet unexplored. I so want to penetrate her again, and yet I'm soft as putty. I peel off the condom and lie across her slowly rubbing myself on her thigh. I grow a little harder, but it's taking time and I know I don't have much time remaining to me and I have no more cash in my wallet. When I pause, she gets up off the bed. She goes to look at her clock on the wardrobe on the other side of the room.

"Oh, it's time. We run over 15 minutes already."

"You have someone else?"

"Yes, sorry. I have twenty minutes and I'm not ready yet."

Twenty minutes?!

"OK."

For a second or two I figure she's going to pack me off like that.

"Could you use your hand?"

Yeah, she can do that.

She comes to sit beside me on the bed. She squeezes some KY onto her palm and begins working on me as though shaping clay on a potter's wheel. Her eyes on the job, professional. Finally in good shape, I have the same angry urge to fuck her as a younger me would have done, but I know she'd want to clean off the KY, and then of course we'd have to find a condom, pull that on, maybe she herself would now need some KY, we'd fuck fast and furious, it wouldn't be enough time to bring me off, though, and after five minutes she'd tell me that was it. So I surrender to the mastery of her hand and fly off the wheel.

I open my eyes to see the ejaculate has shot further than I'm used to, the first nearly clear blob landing just above my right nipple. She looks surprised, and I think, *Not bad for 43*. Even as a wave of gratitude rides through me, I feel an afterburn of shame for having failed to bring her off too.

"Finally," she says, and reaches for the nappy wipes to mop up the creamy islands of sperm. She could have been my nurse, her voice modulating between praise and mild admonishment.

"I know, I'm sorry. I shouldn't have come to see you when I was so tired."

"You working too hard? Hard work pulling teeth, yeah?" she jokes, acting out a sort of Marks Brothers version of my job.

I smile quietly and explain I don't in fact pull so many teeth, the fatigue comes from trying to preserve them. *But why am I being so pedantic?* What I want to explain – not that I would, it'd be grossly inappropriate – is that my performance was under par because I'd masturbated that same morning: I'd wanted to slake off some of my desire before meeting her so that I might better understand whether it was the sexual experience alone, or something more besides, that made me think about her throughout every gap in my day. But what has that achieved? I'm little the wiser for knowing what she feels about me and I just feel old, past it for having had to ask for her hand at the end. So used to sex without condoms, I'd kidded myself I was still the same I was the last time I had sex with condoms, maybe seven or eight years ago. I lie there, quietly panicking about my decline even as my body enjoys its post coital bath.

"Don't worry, you come with me next time, yeah? You want take shower?"

"No, it's OK." I smile, aiming to reassure her as if we were lovers, which I accept now can never be the case. "I know you have to get ready." *Another cock going into that pussy–wahn pussy, wahn–where I'd put my mouth, my tongue, my heart, less than an hour from now.*

She slips me a token smile of gratitude and slopes off to scrub and refill the bath.

In the kitchen/lounge, as I stand ready to leave, against my better judgment, I return to that old song of having a simple coffee together; but for the irony that laces my proposal, I'm being as importunate as an undergraduate.

"Anthony, you very nice, but I can't really be your girlfriend, OK? Cos I'm working now."

"That didn't seem to stop you with this other guy."

Her whole face tenses and darkens and I see I shouldn't even have gone there.

"He wasn't really my boyfriend. We friends, yeah? Maybe when I stop working something can happen. We see, OK?"

I look away, trying desperately to blanket my frustrations with indifference.

"OK, I–I know you're not really free to see me, but–how about if we met every now and then to exchange Thai for English? You said you don't get much time to go to school, so… let me help you with that."

"Maybe after, OK. When I'm not working."

"Don't you think it's a waste of an opportunity to come to London and not improve your language?"

"Maybe you should try dating agency if you want Thai woman, yeah? Lots of pretty girls want to be with educated Englishmen–"

"Sisi, come on–" I laugh down my nose, insulted by her suggestion, the detached air with which she delivered it. But why do I even address her as Sisi, this is Sonia. And maybe I'm not even Anthony; maybe I'm, say, Angus. How will I ever get to show her the real me? She has her hand on the latch already–it's time to shut up and go.

"Could we do that?" I persist. "I mean, you told me you want to open a business in Thailand–so look, you'll do better with better English. Right?" I smile like a salesman.

"OK, maybe," she answers with a sigh that carries her 'maybe' out the door ahead of me like a bag blowing in the wind. "If I have time," she stresses.

I smile again, gracious in defeat–my grace, my only consolation.

"We talk on the phone, OK?"

"Sure."

She dives on my mouth for a kiss–which throws me, because it 's deep and lingering and seems to engorge the earlier lite 'maybe', but of course it's the equivalent of a vampire's bite claiming you for another visit, another £150 or more. She smiles and says, "Chok dee ka."

"Say again."

"Chok dee. Good luck. Good phrase to know."

"OK."

As I step into the shadowy corridor, the door closes swiftly behind me. I feel as though I've been fired, someone else will soon be taking my place. I don't want to move. But this isn't the place to ponder my emotions–another five minutes and I'll run into Sonia's next customer.

CHAPTER 7

The following morning, I step into our reception in a mood to improve the place. Or do I really just want something here that reminds me of Sisi? I give our receptionist £20 and ask her to nip out to the nearest flower stall–it's actually an act of faith that we have a vase somewhere. Depositing the false flowers out back, I wonder if Sisi looks at the flowers I bought her, the CDs by her bed and ever thinks of me with fondness. A patient is waiting, but this is more important… Yes, here we go. Looks like one of those vases Sylvia bought from Conran when she used to shop there. I wonder why it's here–and then I spot a chip in the glass; *it'd be good enough for Anthony's reception.*

"Blue eyes are sometimes very beautiful. Like glass," Sisi had said, on her knees, looking down at me, just moments after she'd brought me off. She'd made a movement with her hand that suggested a play of light through glass. I wanted to believe she'd never said that kind of thing to any blue-eyed customer before looking into my eyes.

What the hell. I get on with my day, my week. I wish I could be busier. Even when I am, my mind switches a little too frequently to automatic pilot. I narrowly make some serious mistakes: one afternoon my nurse stops me from filling an upper fifth instead of lower fifth; the next day I'm hooted from a dream that nearly swept me into the back a van… I continually forget things like my keys, pens, mobiles.

On Friday afternoon, after everyone's gone, I lock the office from the inside and drop the blinds in the back room. I log on to Sonia's webpage with my wireless laptop and sit in the chair. I hook myself up to the Nitrous Oxide and unzip my trousers. I close my eyes and remember the sensation of Sisi's head in my hands as we kissed. (The shape of it had shocked me because it was so like Mia's, a shape so precious to me.)

"Oh baby, oh baby," I cry, as she'd cried when I'd made Sisi come that first time.

I wipe up, muttering in appalled disbelief that it's time I found myself a shrink.

Within twenty minutes, the pleasant drained sensation has turned to irritability with things I can't find in the reception. A final knot of irritation drives me to the store cupboard. I dose myself up with sedatives. This is my Friday night out. Or rather, *out of it.*

I burst into the house like a man rushing for the bathroom–only I'm rushing for a suitcase. I can't find one. Sylvia's stashed them in the shed. My quick getaway is going to get messy. She enters the room, worried by the violence of my homecoming.

"What's the matter? Where're you going?"

I look at her boldly in the eyes, trying to express a million emotions at once. Manic, like a hailstorm.

"I'm sorry, I… I'm just not coping."

"So don't work so much."

I consider surrendering this impulsive mood I'm in and simply agreeing with her–everything can be made better with a glass of white wine and some adrenaline-fuelled show like '24'.

"I'm sorry–I have to leave, I–I have to be near her. I know this is totally fucked up, but I can't–it's just not fair on you and it's not fair on the kids, I'm going absolutely fucking insane!"

I'm trembling now, my mouth is dry and rubbery, but she… Her face has begun to crack down the middle, not metaphorically speaking, literally. I suppose this is why she can't speak. I blabber on until her mouth snaps with a question that is less a question than a lancing, "She's a prostitute, isn't she?'

I can't answer because I'm struck dumb by the spectacle of a humourless, vengeful other Sylvia pushing out of the crack in Sylvia's skull like a snake shedding its skin. I'm about to attempt a reply when I hear a bang.

I think it's the door.

And I wake from the nightmare.

I'm in the chair. Disoriented because the blinds are down and my head is woozy. I wonder if the bang was Andrea arriving early for work, unable to get in because I've bolted the door. I open the blinds. It's eight in the evening not the morning. The sun is slipping between clouds enjoying a colourful bath of orange and purple on the horizon. I pull myself together and call home. Sylvia's voice sounds pleasantly tired. I tell her I've been working late and finish with a tired sigh because I don't want to sound as though I might be fucking the nurse (which, oddly enough, I've never done, though it's been a constant source of teasing from mates over the years ever since I dated Sylvia, a former receptionist.)

As I'm re-setting the alarm, my mobile starts ringing and vibrating. I have 45 seconds to get out of the place. I step outside and flip to: Unidentified Caller.

"Hello?"

"Anthony, how are ya mate?" The voice is pitched deep, intimate.

"Uh, fine" still racking my brain for an ID.

"I need to see you."

Does he think I'm some guy he picked up in a gay bar last night?

"One of my back teeth–I think I've cracked a filling or something. It's very sensitive, I can hardly chew on it and it dances like Tigger on speed when I have anything hot or cold. Are you able to see me tomorrow? I can come down whenever's good for you."

"Neil?"

"Yeah, sorry sorry sorry–didn't I say? Apologies – just rushing ahead like that. How're you doing?"

Talking to me as if we'd known each other for years–which I find unsettling and comforting in equal measure.

"I just stepped out of the office, Neil, but if memory serves, we're pretty chocker until five thirty. Is that any good for you?"

"That's fine, yeah, perfect. Maybe a drink after, if you're not too pushed?"

Grasping at some kind of antidote to the emotional mess I'm in, I say, "Yeah, let's do that," and he says, "Great, look forward to it."

I rush from the practice with just seconds to spare before the police would have received sign of a potential break in. All I had to do was override the damn thing, but I chose to chase my adrenaline around the block. Call it practice, I told myself, never for a minute suspecting that adrenaline overload would soon become an everyday occurrence for something far scarier than unrequited love.

I have a few colleagues, I have patients, of course, and I have old friends–but it's rare, almost impossible to conceive of making a new friend at 42; even the idea of one strikes me as anachronistic, a throwback to childhood. And if the potential friend is male, there's always a creeping suspicion he might be gay. But Neil wasn't just some stranger knocking on the door of friendship – he'd been one of the vectors that had brought me into contact – or collision – with Sisi. And I hadn't been able to talk to anyone about Sisi. Male friends were either getting engaged, about to have a baby or on the verge of a 'messy' divorce (as if there were such thing as a 'tidy' divorce), and all of them were generally too preoccupied with career and money – or their own therapist – to have the patience to listen to an old friend confess to making the kind of mistake for which only a much younger man could be excused. As for my female friends, essentially ex-girlfriends, three had gone back to Brazil, Japan and Singapore, respectively, and were only in touch by email, and the last remaining close ex was being treated for breast cancer. Five, or even two, years ago I might have had a stab at entertaining some of my closer friends with my visits to Sisi, my conflicting emotions, but in the last couple of years, I'd felt less in need of sharing my dramas with anyone; I'd re-rooted them to a sort of off-line blog in my head. I'd noticed too that most of my friends around the same age had also given up seeking opinion on their private lives. Feelings, it seemed, had rather had their day.

Which struck me as strangely at odds with the culture we live in -- everyone being in such a hurry to score 'celebrity' points for showing the anonymous public every little stain on his or her underpants.

I slipped off my mask and addressed my patient, my potential new friend.

"Over-brushing?" Neil said, horrified. He laughed. "God, I thought that brown stuff was staining. I was about to apply some Harpic!"

"No, that's your exposed dentine, I'm afraid. You need to go at them a little less rigorously… The filling's fine."

I put something on four of his teeth showing gum recession that would soften the jabs from hot and cold and advised him that he apply Sensodyne twice a day like an ointment.

I expected to have just a glass of wine, possibly two, after we were done and then to gravitate home to wife and family, but Neil went at our topics of conversation like a dog with a bone. And when it came to Sisi – I'd only meant to tell him that I'd seen her for a coffee – he worked us both into a lather of fascination for Oriental women in general –

"So you fucked her?"

I hesitated, only to realise my hesitation was already a confession. "Yeah," I said.

"How much?"

I tucked in my chin, pulling a face at the boldness of his presumption. He could at least have followed with, "Any good?"

"You knew?"

"It's obvious, isn't it!" He put down his pint. Then, counting on his fingers for me, he went: "She's beautiful, she's Thai and she lives in W2 – has to be on the game, *has to be*."

He picked up his pint to wash down this morsel of insight as if it had some nutritional value. He then glanced at me as if fearful of having to deal with any embarrassment he'd caused.

"The first one was free," I told him.

"Cos of the treatment you did?"

"…Yeah."

"And the second one you had to pay for."

He wasn't asking, he already knew. I nodded glumly.

"So you're like her regular, are you?" He wasn't being judgmental, just gathering the facts.

"I don't know if I'd call myself a regular–"

"Don't get sucked in mate. I'm sure she's gorgeous, but all they think about is money. Once they get into that game, overnight, man, they're like–kching!–like those Japanese slot machines. Pachinkos. You put your cock in, they take your change, they go *ping ping!* and flash lights and smiles at you and you walk out of there *majorly* lighter in the pocket. And in London, it's bloody expensive. You'd be better off saving your money and going to Thailand and having a different girl every night if that's what you're into."

"The thing is, I'm not into that. I'm into *her*."

Neil raised a sceptical eyebrow as if to suggest, '*You think you are*'.

"So are you, like, seeing her for *coffee*?" I read the thinly underlined sarcasm and short laugh as being directed not at me as such, but rather the sad notion of there being anything real about spending time with a prostitute outside of bed.

"Don't get me wrong mate, there's definitely a time in your life when whores can really sort you out, but you can't afford to have any illusions about them. Of course she's nice to you. You're a professional, you're probably better looking than most of the guys she gets – I bet she gets mostly Asians, doesn't she, Arabs living round Paddington? – and I know Thais don't like Arabs – they find them dirty and macho; the ones she sees – unless she's 300 an hour – probably are. But you're cultured, Anthony, you're obviously kind." He paused. "You're soft."

"Soft? Why, because I'm not working class and come from south of Watford?"

"No!" He'd recoiled as I alluded to a common northern presumption that Southerners were basically poofs. "I mean you're – you're just too nice. They don't know nice. They only know rough, tough, big mouths, bullies."

"Battered wives syndrome–"

"There you go–you're getting it." He paused. "Most of them like it. Treating them nice just confuses them. Because it's not business," he added emphatically.

I stared at Neil a moment, as though horrified by his cold-blooded analysis, though I already knew it made perfect sense.

"That's quite a club I've joined."

"I tell you what you should do. If you think you really have got something special with her, test out that feeling, go and see someone else from the same website. She'll probably do it for you as well. And if she's any good, give me her number."

I pulled a face.

"Seriously–I only go these days when I get a recommendation."

"I don't want to start seeing other girls and giving you recommendations–"

"Why not? I'd give *you* a recommendation."

"I don't want a recommendation, or anyone else."

He looked offended.

"Honestly, get some perspective, man. Fuck another whore and wake up. I'm serious." He said this as if it were just sound business advice he was willing to impart for free.

I felt justly admonished and clammed up. His crassness was beginning to grate, though–that and the probable truth of what he was saying.

"Tell you what, let *me* find you someone."

"Neil I'm forty-two, I really think I can tell by now what sexual fantasy is and what's…" I held back, the word 'love' forming a ridiculous bubble on the tip of my tongue. For a moment Neil was listening without appearing to be about to pounce on me with sarcasm. "–y'know–deeper."

"I don't mean to talk down to you, Anthony, don't get me wrong. I've been where you are now – I have, I have, but…" He paused to level his bulbous blue eyes on mine – his expression suggested that my obduracy was giving him indigestion– "… it's a phase, it's confusing, it's… it's a whole different world, to be honest with you. It's got its own rules–"

"I know that–"

"–You have to respect them or they fuck you up. Like I said, your best bet is to indulge on holiday – where it's cheaper. Brazil's a good place. In Rio you'll get girls coming up to you in bars offering to have sex with you after, like, half an hour of small talk. It's totally normal out there. All you have to do is give them a good time, pay for their drinks, give them a sort of tip the next morning. They'd be offended if you called them whores, but that's what they are," he said.

"And now?" I asked.

"I'm more into fitness at the moment. I dunno why, but I really don't miss it. I'm more into watching."

"Watching?"

"Yeah, clubs. Fetish nights, that kind of thing. Dressing up. I don't think it'd be your scene really."

"I dunno–" I said, rising to the challenge. (His epithet 'soft' was bad enough, I didn't want him to think I was square as well.)

"It's not romantic, Anthony, and the girls aren't usually all that good looking, but I get off on the spectacle."

He said he used to film himself and his wife having sex. She wasn't comfortable with it, so he'd bought a secret camera. He'd taught himself Final Cut and made little porn movie "collages", as he called them. It wasn't long before he found he had to recall these films to stay hard as he was fucking his wife. Toward the end of the sex life of their marriage, he said he couldn't come during sex because he needed the films to be happening before his eyes and she wouldn't allow that. And because he couldn't come, she began to suspect he was having an affair. So *she* went and had an affair and that was that. He'd moved out of the little terrace he'd spent all his savings on and taken an impoverished flat a few miles away in order to be near his son.

He told the whole peculiar story with a furrowed brow, jutting his jaw forward in a sort of rowing action (his tick) during pauses, his eyes staring straight ahead with a fixedness that made me think he might possibly be bipolar. Every so often he'd release himself from the intensity of his own narrative with short bursts of laughter, a tight, knotted sound, as if he were coughing up fur balls of unresolved anger and regret. He finished off descending to a trough of silence, his back rigid, eyes gazing blankly at a mid point a few inches above our table. His lips moved, rippling like dying flames, soundless, before he said,

"Fucking pervert… moved in after me." The chin tick again. "That really didn't help, I can tell you." He picked up his drink, knocked it back.

"Pervert?" I queried.

"The bloke she was screwing, yeah?"

"How do you mean, 'pervert'?"

He blinked in quick succession like someone surfacing from hypnosis, then glanced at me, the lips pickled by embittered spittle.

"He's a PE teacher – gets on very well with the boys, if you know what I mean. I don't have any proof as yet, but…" nodding to himself, fixed eyes again, "my son's behaviour's – it's completely changed since I left. Completely changed."

"That's probably got more to do with your not being there, y'know? Some kids, especially boys his age, they find it hard to adjust to the father's moving out, especially if there's been some acrimony over an affair. Maybe–"

"We're still fighting over stuff even now. He picked up his drink, shaking his head solemnly. "She's…" He wrinkled his nose. "Chinese, yeah?" He drew breath. "They're very hard, y'know. I mean, once they're against you, there's no reasoning with them. They become 'the enemy', whether you like it or not. You look at them – I look at my ex," he corrected himself, "and I can't even see the woman I used to know. I'm–I'm just this thorn in her side, y'know, and she's going to cut it–me, this thorn–out with anything she can get her hands on–even our son, if necessary… play on his adolescent confusion, turn him against me, turn me into a fucking loser, not worth knowing." He paused–on a knife-edge, then shot a querying look at me, which was unsettling, as it seemed to look less for empathy than contradiction or confrontation.

"Hey… I'm sorry."

"I've actually contemplated joining Fathers4justice. I should get my Batman kit on and fight for a cause, y'know. Actually that's one kit I don't have," he laughed in an aside to himself. "But anyway there's fuck all else I can do fighting with her, so why not – if it makes a difference…"

I finished my wine, placed the wine glass carefully on the table.

"Well, on that cheerful note, fancy another drink?"

Neil didn't seem to hear me.

"You have another one?"

"Yeah yeah–why not? You need some money?"

"No, that's fine. What you want?"

"Oh, same as you, whatever. Cheers."

As I returned to our table with two glasses of wine, Neil dove into fresh topic of conversation – my practice. I was quite thrown by the change in his mood. And again he was poking around in there like a dental student after a night on the booze–in fact to the point I was getting slightly uncomfortable, not just for my sake but my staff as well. He ran on to ask if I'd ever thought of investing in some other line of business – property, say? I told him I was saving my cash for a rainy day – divorce. He laughed and shook his head in sympathy. Yeah, wise decision, he said. But maybe I could double my nest egg if I had another business on the go. Forget pensions, they were a bloody con. Internet. It's the second revolution. Money was flooding in to digital, he said. He was particularly interested in using the net to interest foreigners looking for property here. He'd been approached by a Russian millionaire to find him a place in Knightsbridge. He'd be looking at a 1%

commission on 2 to 3 million pound houses if he got a sale to go through.

"Well, great," I said. "How did you come across this guy? Is he mafia?"

"*Ironically*," his rounding tone seemed to embrace the concept in all its various manifestations, "it's someone I got to know through my wife, before it all turned to shit. She lived out there in the diplomatic service for a few years."

"Foreign office?"

"Yeah – one of the minions. Yeah. Like me." He gave a short deprecatory laugh. "The thing is, it's all very slow; I can't rely on it; it might not even happen, they're stalling. I'm getting paranoid. Maybe Ling's found out and she's trying to sabotage the whole thing, I don't know." He paused, as if he suddenly feared we were being bugged. "The idea's good, though…" He went on to describe, in something of a hush-hush, this website he'd got someone to start building that allowed rich foreigners to view online little video films showing the interiors and exteriors of luxury homes.

"But why wouldn't they go to an estate agent?"

"More personal service. But I've got to get this first sale to go through – I need that to create some word-of-mouth."

He asked me if I'd bought to let. I hadn't. Had I thought about it? He'd listen to my ideas if they were properly thought out. Maybe we could go into partnership on a purchase. He'd come round and film me with this girl I was fucking, he said. It would be great! He knew how to operate a camera, he wasn't bad on Final Cut… I was laughing, but he kept talking, as if pitching me the climax scene to a movie he'd written.

"Neil, Neil," I said, amusement struck across my face, "I'm a dentist, not a porn star."

"We could hide your face–"

He reined in–he was only pulling my leg, he knew I was a professional, had a reputation to think of. His words echoed, betraying a hint of invidiousness. The point was, he said, he was seriously interested in working with me on something.

"Neil, I couldn't possibly invest in anything just now."

"That's because you're spending all your money on this girl." I cut him a sharp glance. "Sorry. Sure, no worries, mate. I need to develop the website first anyway. I've got a young designer on it already. He's a bit slow, always wanting more cash, but, y'know, it's getting there." He pushed back in his seat, put his arm up and turned his head, almost regal. "When I'm ready, I'll show you what I'm doing. I think you'll be impressed."

I wanted to admire him for his passion to transform his life, even mine in some way, but I couldn't shirk the suspicion he might be a bit of a charlatan. Or was my reaction to his entrepreneurial drive more indicative of my own play-it-safe outlook than proof of any shortcomings in him? Wait and see, I told myself.

Stepping outside, Neil changed his tone completely about my seeing Sisi. He said maybe he'd been a bit harsh and cynical earlier, maybe she really did find me special, maybe I should see how it goes. I'd have to marry her, he warned, if I was ever to really have her. I was charmed briefly by his sudden willingness to enter into my fantasy even as I told him I couldn't imagine it ever coming to a proposal of marriage and wasn't even sure I would see her again. Most of my friends would at that point have dropped the subject, but Neil, I was beginning to realise, had this compulsion to run with things. Now that he was optimistic on my behalf he was committed to a vision of Sisi and me living happily ever after. Finally I had to cut him off with a "Well, crazier things have happened, but right now I've got the wife to deal with." He laughed heartily at my turn of phrase and grabbed my hand with a passion I'm not used to in people who've lived in London for ten or more years.

I headed off down the road with a smile on my face. And yet I had this unsettling, ambiguous feeling running through me that I was going to be answerable to Neil from now on as regards my relationship with Sisi. I could so easily imagine him saying at a later date, 'You do realise, don't you, you owe me one, because if it hadn't been for my boy you'd never have found her.' Then again, he might say that with only the best of intentions.

I gave some serious thought to Neil's advice about seeing another prostitute. I even visited escort agency sites, prowling for girls as alluring as Sisi. There were a few. I felt tempted. But I couldn't get past the sense, however ridiculous I knew it to be, that making a booking would be a disloyalty to Sisi and that any alternative experience would cheapen my feelings for her.

I think it was possibly while talking to my mother on the phone, the weekend after I saw Neil, that I came to a decision about Sisi. It was the words 'stability' and 'routine' that did it. We'd been talking about my brother, a copywriter. He'd just been made redundant for the third time in two years and was on the dole, occasionally picking up a few days of freelance but still desperately short of money. We both oozed fatigued sympathy for him. As far as she could see, everyone was expendable, she said – loyalty was now just a marketing concept. (I smiled inwardly as I realised she'd picked up the phrase from my brother himself.) She knew the cultural differences between my brother and his Japanese wife accounted for much of his recent talk of getting a divorce, but she was sure the biggest source of conflict and unhappiness had to be the lack of stability in his career. If only he had a regular job, like me, for instance, with a steady income–not as steady as my mother seemed to think, but anyway–then he might one day be happy. *Happy*, I thought to myself afterward. It tends to sound so advertising glib when most people use it, but when your mother uses it, it seems to regain most of its true meaning; you have to stop and ask yourself…. Well, yes, I was happy when I was with Sisi – even if it wasn't the kind of happy my mother could possibly relate to – but I wasn't happy with the situation. So maybe a short-term solution was to commit to seeing her on a regular basis and learn to accept it for what it was. I'd never win her love if I didn't learn to relax about her availability to be with me. So make it a routine thing. Wednesday afternoon looked good – the day we usually closed early. Treat yourself like a dog that recognises the sound of a bell for dinner time. And be happy.

How mature this plan seemed at the time.

The next Wednesday, a muggy August afternoon, I travelled into Soho to revisit a favourite ceramics shop in Marshall Street. I bought a beautiful big vase bearing a simple floral design over a light sandy colour. I smiled as I noted the price, £150. I could have spent that on having a threesome with Sisi's flatmate. What a giggle that would have been. Except that I would never again have been able to claim that Sisi was special to me.

I left the shop in glorious sunshine and, to avoid any knocks to my purchase on the tube, took a cab. I got out at Paddington main station where I went straight to the flower stall. The woman recognised me and we had a chat as she put me together a beautiful bouquet of sunflowers and lilies, a more generous bouquet than last time.

Sisi was overwhelmed by my gifts. Turning the vase around and around in her hands, marvelling at its beauty as she marvelled at my generosity, she could have been playing with my inner core, unawares of how hollow I felt without her. I was happy to hear her say this vase was one thing she would definitely take back to Thailand when she went, but, then, immediately sad as I realised that one day she would probably vanish from my life without a trace.

"Now I have a vase big enough to take your beautiful flowers!" she exclaimed.

Her eyes shone like I hadn't seen in a woman's eyes in a long long while – my kids' eyes, yes, but not those of a woman – they could almost have fooled me into believing I still had my whole life before me.

She comes into her room with a cigarette and lies on the bed with me, her bathrobe falling open, only skimpy panties on underneath.

"We talk, yeah? It's been a long time since I saw you."

I tell her I haven't been too well recently, which is true, but I regret saying this, I don't want her pity–she might encourage me to overcook it anyway. When I begin scratching an itch in my nose, she sits up, waving the smoke away insisting that I tell her if the smoke is bothering me.

"No, don't worry about it, I'm fine."

She stubs out the cigarette anyway.

"I really missed you," I tell her and smile as she lights another candle on her chest of drawers.

"I missed you too. You are the only one who is so romantic, no one else!"

"Really?"

"Yes. You are so romantic!" she says smiling and gesturing something like a rising star.

"I think you are too."

"No, not like you."

"Well, you probably have to be more business-like at the moment."

She purses her lips as if to say, 'That's true'.

I take off my shoes and socks and lie beside her on the bed.

"It's quiet at the moment," she says. "People on holiday." I picture the dads she knows, their knees in the sand as they rub Factor 25 into their wives' cellulite while dreaming of leaner bodies available to them when they get home.

I look into Sisi's eyes and observe: "You look a little tired again. Eyes, skin…" I reach to touch her, as if painting over blemishes about her face with my finger.

"Yeah, I feel tired all the time. It's not fucking lots of guys, I get tired waiting, you know? When they come? Will they come? Do I have to wait more? Sometimes you go a bit crazy thinking all this."

We kiss tenderly and she responds similarly, as if she really has missed me. I strip off – the bath can wait – I explore her, urgent, feeding on the lips and juices between her legs with an appetite I can't comprehend… But I'm tense somehow, unable to come and I wilt inside her after only fifteen minutes.

"It's hot, huh?" she says.

Like an animal I watch her bottom and her exposed, shaved sex, not shy about letting me look, as she clambers across the bed to open the sliding window. "You want to take a break?"

As we get in the bath, the water overflows onto the floor and we laugh as if we're always having these kinds of funny mishaps in the bathroom together.

"Don't worry!" she says, throwing a towel onto the puddle on the floor. She insists I stay in the water as she stands and lets the water out.

Before she gets in with me, she hands me her hair clip as she re-pins her hair and just that simple gesture of trust lends an aspect of teamwork to our bath time.

Now she bathes me. Lavishly. And when she's done and lays her silky body across mine, I let slip my feelings for her, as if I've been squeezing a slippery bar of soap all these minutes. Before I've barely begun, I rein in with a gasp that makes her think I've sat on something sharp–well, I have, haven't I, it's called reality. I smile and say it's nothing.

"But what do *you* want?" I ask.

"I want everything!" she says, smiling and throwing her arms up. "Some people say I have magic, but I don't know… I want to… I don't know." She smiles, discouraging further inquiry.

"You could act. Not here – Thailand."

But she shrugs away my romantic suggestion as though it were some old garment pulled from the bottom of a drawer.

She rinses me down and I look at my body in the candlelight and feel pleased by the new improved muscular definition of my arms and chest, the result of extra hours and heavier weights at the gym, and I wonder if it pleases her too.

Back in her room, "It's getting cold now," she says closing the window.

"Yeah," with my hand gently on her waist, guiding her back to me.

"Shall we go again?" she asks with genuine élan.

We start, sitting face to face, as if to equilibrate our energies. As she looks into my eyes I believe I read genuine fondness there. My vase and flowers have opened some new buds of feeling in her, perhaps. We embrace as she rides me, as I rock her over my sex. Our skins begin to cook, till I'm breathless and I have to pause. My arms slip round her back, something about the willowy shape of it moves me to utter softly, "Oh, sweetheart… where did you come from?" As I kiss her, and she rolls her tongue thickly over my teeth, I am intoxicated by her saliva, the faint Thai food smell of her breath. I break off, gasping, and she asks me if I'm all right and I laugh, too high even to begin to explain. Being medically trained, of course there's this diagnostic voice going off in my head referring me back to the concussion I suffered at the pool, even though it's my heart not my head that seems on the point of exploding.

She says, "Lie back," and gets up on her knees and takes a sip of beer, then bounces off the bed and goes to her chest of drawers, where she picks up her hair-clasp, making her body into a ballet dancer as she pins up her mane of hair on her way back to the bed. I watch as she takes my soft thing in her hand and pushes it around and about like some spare end of pastry on a board, kneading it into shape, teasing it with her breasts and erect nipples. My heart aches studying her beauty in the absence of any normal arousal. I tell her to leave it for now and I lay her down hastily and dive on her pussy, as insatiable as before. She's horny too and puts her fingers in, my tongue and her fingers competing to bring her off. She gasps and asks me to take it easy. But I don't want her to keep anything back for the next person, so I work at her even faster–the same kind of fucking I'd done that first time when I'd wanted to break something in both of us, only this time with my tongue and my lips sucking at her as if she were a ripe peach.

When she comes, she says my name for the first time. She says 'No!' and 'Oh!' and grabs my hair in one hand. I feel my roots tingle as her inner thigh muscles contract. A cry escapes her mouth like a little devil falling into a well with its tail on fire.

Sucking on her pussy, bringing her off, my whole body aches to fuck her now, the way teeth can ache after you've been grinding the whole night. I turn her around, pull her up with my palm flat across her groin and roughly push myself inside her. I lock into that same anger I discovered the first time. But just as the anger is bringing me close to release, a wave of tender emotion washes over me, the anger buckles, I totter, so dizzy with love that I cling to her as though she were sucking everything out of me and I were powerless to stop her… And as I lose pace – can you fucking believe it – she reaches for her clock.

"It's time now, you know?"

I freeze.

"…We can do more but I gave you more than an hour already, so I'm sorry, but…"

I flip back on my haunches, a hint of cramp in my shins, as I run into extra time. I feel a sulk coming on – the defeated sportsman; the condom, like some sodden rubber sock hanging off my drooping end.

"Can't you come?"

"Yeah, sure, I *can*, but…. the thing is, I hold back for you, I need *you* to come or I lose it."

"But I come twice already, and you not come with me, I can't come again, I think."

"I know... I know."

Serious now, I ask her to lie down. One last try. I kneel before her, pull off the condom and begin chugging on my string–slippery, floppy, out of commission… That I'm in front of this beautiful woman, eyes feasting on her shaved pussy moist from my mouth and her own juices, and I still can't give it to her totally shocks and horrifies me. And that look on her face, the same look every woman gives you when this happens–embarrassed for the man, vaguely guilty, too, because maybe she's doing something wrong.

The clock is ticking. And I know that to be the problem–but I'd chosen the time I was to spend with her, hadn't I.

She gets me to lie back, urgent now, squeezes some oil into her hands and starts to work on me with her oily hands… The pleasure spreads through me, but my sex shows no sign of getting hard. *Try the defibrillators*–but she wouldn't get the joke, so I can't even laugh about this. I'm as tense as if my balls were wired up to a volt metre. I detect impatience in her–can you blame her? Perhaps she's becoming concerned for me as much as worried about the time.

"Could you give me a blow job?"

She doesn't look too pleased to be asked.

"I'm sorry, but you know I have to tell you about the time."

"I know, I know. Do you want me to wash?"

She answers by way of plucking nappy wipes from their packet as if they might have been pubic hairs on my balls. She wipes, meticulously, as if swabbing me down for surgery.

She takes me in her mouth, this time without a condom. Growing hard so instantly I feel foolish, like a little boy who always needs a favourite sweetie to get him out of his sulks. I'm close to coming in her mouth, when she stops to ask me if I want to put the condom on. We scramble for it like a torch it the dark. She gets on her fours… I line myself up, but I can't get in, then I can, but slip out. We try the other way. I can't believe she's gotten so tight. I squeeze in finally, but go soft inside of two minutes and slip out. I tug bad-temperedly at the condom, but it sticks to my cock, before snapping off with a pesky *tsk* against my thumb. As she turns round, I jump off the bed. I can't bear to face her. I circle the middle of her floor like a wounded animal and then some madness overtakes me and I lash out at the door of her closet.

"Fuck!"

I could hit the door again, but I've come to my senses–if only just.

I retreat swiftly and shamefully to the chest of drawers, my boyish bare back to her, my heart pounding, my hand stinging – but it's nothing compared to my pride. *So this is forty-two. You finally fall in love–it's with a prostitute and you can't even finish because your heart beats with so much passion.*

"I'm sorry," I begin, mumbling as if to my flaccid cock, my forehead pinned to the hands I've pinned on the corner of her chest of drawers. "I'm sorry."

I want her to come up to me and stick a knife in my side, yes, let me bleed out and be done with it. There's a miserable pause of suspense, then a draught passes my back and backside. I don't have to look up to know she's left the room – I suppose in disgust – giving me time to cool off; dangerous male.

By the time she comes back in I'm already half dressed. I look at her with apology etched into my face, half expecting to be told she'll never see me again. But she overlooks the apology, barely meets my eyes, now tidying something away in her chest of drawers as she asks, from behind a rehearsed facade of indifference and humility, tinctured with a pungent anger that I fear and crave to see more of:

"You don't like it with me?"

I can't help snorting with derision at the question–it pains me that she could even imagine that my desire for her has already burnt out.

"I'm sorry, really. That won't happen again." I pull on my sock. "I just got so tense and I – I have too much feeling here," touching my heart like an Indian brave, "so all the blood is going here and not... down there."

"But I'm not your girlfriend, Anthony. If you need more time, you have to book longer– *for your feeling*."

Touché. "Yeah, I guess so."

There's a static pause.

"Will you sit here, please?"

I can feel her contemplating a punitive measure, but then she heads over to me, showing turquoise lids, her eyes to the floor.

"That was bad of me–"

"I feel bad–"

"No, really–don't, it's OK. Next time I'll put my watch by your pillow–I just forget the time, it's my fault."

"I feel bad I didn't say before. Maybe–you know–you had a nice time, talking, being with me, even if you didn't come."

"Sure."

"One guy, I said, 'I'm sorry you didn't come,' and he said, 'It's OK, I enjoy talking.'"

Her remark is meant to ease my pain, but it only serves to rob me of any uniqueness I might cling to that is *us* and to remind me that there are other guys with my problem.

She puts on her bathrobe and leaves the room–*so we don't get into a conversation, just before she has to look smiley for the next customer.*

When she returns, I'm dressed, nearly calm. She comes and sits beside me.

"It was good to see you anyway."

"You too," she says.

We hug.

"I so missed you." My chest burns as I say these words, as if to brand my ribs against hers.

"I missed you too–I want you to know, even if I don't think of you every day. I missed you, and I thank you for saying you missed me. It means a lot to me."

She gives me another hug. I'm surprised when it lasts so long and, for a fleeting moment I wonder whether she's not shedding tears over something. But no, she's not.

As I make to leave, she picks up the bouquet again (still in its wrap) and tells me how perfect the flowers look, and that she loves the other flowers I gave her and that she's amazed they lasted so long. For a few minutes she's just so charmed by my gift that she seems oblivious of the time, oblivious I'm watching her the way I do.

"Well, you're certainly worth it," I say, grasping at the fashionably crass as a means of distancing myself from the welter of my emotions. (She seems to miss anyway the lame reference to the L'Oreal tag line.)

She gives me a lover's kiss at the door and says a warm "Take care."

"You too," I say.

I hang by the door patting my pockets, and realise it's not my phone or my wallet I am missing, it's my hope of her ever agreeing to a social get-together.

"You have everything?"

I smile, pained, thinking, *Yes, everything but you, it would seem.*

As I return to the street, I feel as though I'm walking away from a duty to protect her even as I reason to myself she chose this way to make a living and, for all I know, she'll enjoy her next customer as much or more than she enjoyed me.

I don't know how to resolve this problem of time. Logically, of course, I should book her for longer–as she said, *for my feelings*–but I doubt this would make things any easier, it might even make things harder. Sisi-time is on another plane from what I'm used to. The nearest I can compare it to is the kind of time–or absence of time–that I'll experience while watching a completely absorbing movie. The moment I step into her flat and into her arms, I am on the big screen, I am acting and she is acting, we are both committed to creating magic from the scene we act out again and again with one another. Magic with pain, it's true, but magic all the same. This tight framework in which we act together is our prison and our escape. We've grown to love or admire each other's characters, but perhaps not each other. Not truly, not yet.

On the Piccadilly train I open my Teach Yourself Thai book–a secret window I could get back to her by, as if her language were the medicine that would keep me calm (and hard) when I saw her next. I repeat a few phrases in my head, but I'm too mad at myself to concentrate. The experience I've just had reminds of *Maria's Lovers*, an early Natassja Kinski movie about an American POW who returns home to rejoin his true love but can't perform because he's used his memory of her ethereal beauty as a mental trick for staying sane in a Japanese camp of war, and now that he's back home and has her in his arms, he experiences the act of penetration like a desecration of that precious entity he's made of her in his head, a profanation of his survival. His case I understand well, my own I'm simply baffled by–I've never been a POW, after all. He'd been cured through the anger that came from seeing her leave him to go out with another man. His anger had brought him back to being a man. But Maria had wanted him. I still can't be sure Sisi wants me, not in the truest sense. Because I always get her for £150 an hour.

CHAPTER

8

If I'm honest, I've never been passionate about what I do. Yes, I can get fired up about the post-war conspiracy of silence over the toxicity of amalgam. I feel personally soiled by the mismanagement of resources in the NHS and having to put children with aching teeth on the waiting list because their parents are too poor to pay for private treatment. And yes, I can *talk* passionately about new practices and advances in dentistry. I can get quite worked up over a patient's problems, oral and otherwise, and feel a pang of disappointment when the work I do doesn't achieve all that I hoped it would. But, privately, I'm dogged by this feeling I left my passions on the side of the road somewhere, some twenty years ago, and it's only fairly recently I've begun to wonder why I did that. It's true *I* chose dentistry, no one pushed me into it, even if I was only seventeen when I made that choice and the choice had in some ways already been made for me–that's to say, Mum was a physiotherapist and Dad was an anaesthetist. Our mealtimes, our walks in the country, were often gentle meanderings through the vessels and organs of the human body. Both my parents had creative interests, but that's all they were–'interests'. From twelve to sixteen I wanted to be a journalist, but my parents' constant reminders of what a journalist's salary and security now amounted to prevailed (this was at a time when Thatcher was crushing the newspaper unions with an 'iron fist'), and gradually I returned to the family current of medical pursuits, albeit setting course for a territory not already colonised by my parents. I must have been fifteen when I had my first root filling–without anaesthetic. For one long, interminable moment as the dentist drilled deeper into my upper second right–by coincidence, the same tooth as I'd broken in Sisi's mouth–I felt as if a large part of my face might rip off with the drill. It should have been an experience to put me off dentistry for life, but perhaps some of that early humanitarian idealism that had drawn me toward journalism at eleven and twelve had combined with my inherited interest in medicine to fire up a desire to contribute something to raising the standard of dentistry in this country. Now that I was talking about science A'levels my parents wanted me to go for Medicine. Why would I want to look in mouths all day? Bad breath, discoloured tongues? As if carcinogenic lungs and aneurysms were somehow more illustrious. As if teeth were a mere cosmetic matter, or at best the medical equivalent to plumbing. How would I keep intellectually stimulated? they would invariably put to me. But I wasn't convinced the intellect was all that demanded in what they did. They seemed swamped in admin and petty politics. I didn't want to be like Dad, so overworked he could be anaesthetised by a weekend movie he'd been looking forward to even before his family had counted back from 10. Not for me. I'd have my own little team and we'd fight our own little battles against caries and dental trauma, 9.30 to 5.30 thank you very much. And I'd be driving a Merc before I was thirty. But then I arrive at dentistry school, and it's clear from the outset, that I'm not like most of my fellow students.

I've grown my hair long. I'm left in my politics, while most of them are not, or only pretending to be until they start earning and having to pay tax. I play bass in a band. I even write poetry and paint oils. Is this just a phase, or am I headed for the wrong 'vocation'? In my final year, I briefly flirt with the notion of chucking it in and joining the VSO and going out to Africa, (in part inspired by what was going on with Bob Geldof's first Live Band Aid for Africa). As Sisi had said, I was a romantic. But then I saw what my older brother was going through, doggedly pursuing his artistic dreams to be a writer and songwriter and I came around to thinking that for now at any rate I should just knuckle down and make sure I didn't join him as a statistic of the long-term unemployed. Middle of my third year I got my head down and qualified. In for a penny, in for a pound, and I went straight on to do a Ms.c. Around the age of twenty-seven, as my older brother was retraining and flunking his law exams, I was starting to make money. Money meant I had a girlfriend and he didn't. I had a holiday twice a year and he was at the doctor's a lot. I began to see the Arts, media, TV, all that, as a trap I'd nearly fallen into. My brother and his mates had the occasional break, but the breaks were always followed by long periods of deadly silence–they were all starving for the Big-one-that-never-came. Never imagining I'd marry and have kids, I began to see myself retiring at fifty and travelling in South East Asia, Africa. With money saved I could more than make up for not having taken a gap year. I might even try my hand at travel writing. When I got married and the girls came along, I realised my plans for retiring at forty something would have to be put back ten years, but essentially I was on course to get out of dentistry young enough to try something else–without being broke. For most of my thirties, life was productive. There were a few financial crises, like when I had to set up on my own being owed a serious amount of money by my former partner, a closet alcoholic, an, sure, Sylvia and I had our ups and downs, but I was essentially OK in myself, my skin, until I hit my fortieth. We had a huge gathering at the house on that day, a beautiful August day. Sylvia's spread of delicious African and French food on tables outside in the garden. Friends declaring with genuine envy how well I looked for forty, how beautiful Sylvia was, how together we seemed (we were always so convincing in public), how adorable the children were. It was the kind of heart-warming occasion that dispels many of those fears we all have that we're not loved enough, we're not appreciated enough. But in just a few months', I began to notice that the job's moments of satisfaction were growing fewer and less pronounced. Whereas, before, I'd seen my work as improving people's lives, somehow now it seemed to be all about patching up, making do–which I knew not to be the case, not entirely anyway, but it was how I felt. And then, my brother finally started to get the breaks he'd been striving for for years in filmmaking and he was travelling the world, returning with colourful anecdotes of celebrity madness and a healthy tan and a revived light in his eyes. I was thrilled for him, but because we were so close his success also fuelled my inner doubts about my own choices. The possible 'me's I had buried rose from the past like zombies. Just as my body was slowing down, and my life rooting itself deeper into the fabric of kids, mortgage and patient list, life seemed to be accelerating out of control. To hear that other male friends were feeling the same way was a comfort as short-lived as if you'd spotted someone else falling out of a window at the same time as you. There had to be more to life than removing amalgam from people's mouths–but what, I didn't know. None of the usual diversions for fortysomething men appealed – golf, house extensions, gardening – because they aroused in me no sense of the passion for adventure I had long ago exchanged for security. Essentially the story had run out of twists–all but those that would take us to our graves with cancer and heart disease. Even London, a city I loved, the way a boxer loves his punchbag, the dancer his beam, had become less that boundless, unmapped wonder of my twenties than a matter of journeying time. The electricity of the streets had lost its buzz n' sizzle; the place seemed more and more like a fairground for other people's twentysomething children. Cut off from my own twenties, somehow I'd become a tourist. I needed the Sylvia I'd met ten years ago to make it come alive again, but she'd moved on, viewing the city in terms of its gallery spaces. Whereas my sadness over us was made of missing the motherless Sylvia, her sadness lay in the fact that I still missed the person she'd left behind. I'd remember how she used to come so alive at night. Once the babies came, the night was for staying in and curling up on the sofa at nine and nodding off in front of a TV show, or reading in bed and turning out the light long before most parties were kicking off. Those rare occasions when we'd returned to the city at night, she no longer wished to communicate her desirability to anyone. I imagine for many husbands this would have given them a warm sense of ownership, but for me, it was the equivalent of drinking flat Champagne. I had a sense that going out with me reminded her too keenly of her former acting ambitions and left a bitter sweet taste in her mouth. Having made our appearance on the stage we'd left behind years ago, we'd arrive home in a state of desultory conversation, verging on the argumentative, but in plenty of time to pay the babysitter. We'd drink a glass of water, brush and floss our teeth and get into bed, as if we'd just been on a perfunctory exercise to remind ourselves that we'd actually grown out of having fun. I'd vaguely entertained the hope that by the time Michaela was, say, five, some of those earlier nocturnal energies would return to her, but they never did and never have. In the absence of desire, the sinewy ivy of a new moral tautness grew up alongside the flower of her earlier joie de vivre. For some years my own thirst for nightlife seemed to have been slaked off too by the habit of 'babysitting' and helping the girls with their homework. Over the past year or two I'd felt I was in risk of becoming passive and pliable, a mere dogsbody for wife and kids, in short, henpecked, in a subtle, insidious kind of way. I was beginning to think I'd lost the person I thought I was, or was capable of being, to a permanent sense of quietly desperate resignation verging on hollow indifference. And this is where I was – flailing about in the mush of self-help literature – before I met Sisi. The moment of shake-up. More than just a sexual fantasy, a bit of fun – she was a doorway back to something I had lost in myself.

Now dusk and night beckon like never before. I imagine the smell of her every time I step out at night; the breeze conjures up her caresses, the coolness of her beautiful bottom in my hands. Considering how hooked I am, it's a wonder I can keep to two visits a week. It's never enough. I get headaches after three days of not seeing her. Masturbation barely eases the craving. Every evening, even through drizzling rain, I'm out there on the patio with my skipping rope, my bench and bar and dumbbells to work off the excess desire. I do heavy weights and low reps to raise my

sexual stamina and bulk up, so I don't have to look 'tin' anymore. I've cut back on the alcohol and cut out all caffeine and bread and pasta. I get my hair cut more regularly. I buy face scrubs, even moisturisers. When Sylvia remarks on these changes in my behaviour with a sly, knowing – almost sisterly – smile I pretend that I'm finally listening to her advice. She knows I'm lying, but it's her way to tease me rather than corner me into a confession –
by embarrassing me with my lies I sense she's confident of dampening my deluded attempts at impressing someone else. Then, as the moment passes, though prickling with guilt, I'm struck by the bitter irony that it's been her burgeoning array of creams and moisturisers that have ushered in the years of libidinal decline. *At least I still want to,* I thought sulkily to myself.

Pepped up by a recent visit to Sisi, I'll find myself seeking out the prettier, more interesting women at 'networking' events I occasionally go to with media clients, as if I were newly qualified to attract their attention. Whereas I'm normally reticent about my job, if not vaguely apologetic, given our nation's reputation for ghastly teeth among my American colleagues, I now happily talk up the benefits of our 'unique teeth whitening system' like a sunshine state plastic surgeon selling lipo and implants. It's been years since I was able to make my own subject sound this sexy.

But within one hour of arriving anywhere, I'll find myself standing alone with my tumbler of aqua-coloured drink and ice, my three little straws and glistening cherry, looking around the room, the club space, the hotel foyer, my own hubris congealing upon my face–because I'm missing Sisi and because I don't know whether she genuinely misses me. It's almost as if she were another breed of woman altogether–I feel a fool for imagining that I might find her double or even her shadow in among the crowd I have been invited to spend an evening with. A girl comes up to me, drunk but on a mission – apparently 'rather concerned' to note that I look 'lonely' or 'distant'. Not wanting to seem churlish, I re-animate myself out of respect for her interest in me, and for a few minutes I light up with conversation–but I burn out quick like magnesium, I recede to my dark island again, mute witness to all the sexual tics and tricks of a life I suppose I used to belong to. Around midnight I slip away without saying goodbye, without making excuses, 't'in' as a ghost.

Sonia, the escort agency website tells you, is an ex-Penthouse model – (presumably, fucking guys in London pays better than modelling in Bangkok). At 5' 7", 34B, Waist 24, Hips 34 she has long legs and a gorgeous slim figure. Under the thinly veiled pretence of visiting her for her scintillating conversation, you're invited to come and fuck her brains out at her nicely furnished flat in Paddington at £150 an hour. Or, for £50 extra, she will come and see you for a true GFE (Girl Friend Experience–you gotta learn the acronyms, guys). Not sure? Click on the reviews to see how she did, scores from 1–10. Or how about write your own review. What could Anthony Price add to enlighten readers? Reviewer Don describes how he got 'hard in seconds'. How 'responsive her juices were' to his tongue. Reviewer Mr G says she put some 'real enthusiasm into her OWO'? (Oral Without Orgasm) 'Her skin tone is a bit darker than honey almond,' another reviewer observes, 'but she certainly is sweeter.' Boom boom. Can Anthony honestly claim, anonymously perhaps, that he's larger than average and that this made for an 'oh so tight experience' with Sonia? That's how Al remembers it. 'It seemed she sincerely climaxed with me, as her heart was really pounding,' says B. Would you say, Anthony, that perhaps she was one of your 'best 'punts' ever'? This is how Andy rated her. And did you note that her 'IQ is very smart' and 'her English is pretty good for a Thai girl' and that she is 'not a machine like most of the encounters that you get when you pay for them'? 'TRY WHILE YOU HAVE THE CHANCE!' says V. 'Eventually, someone very lucky will win her love and get her into a relationship or marry her for sure!!' says 'Your Dream Lover'. Would Anthony Price like to write a review? Would that be a 10 or a 10.1? Anthony, you look so pale. As if you'd just discovered that the fast food boys have been wanking on your cheeseburger all this time and you didn't know it till now. Do you understand yet why it's not too healthy to develop any sensitive feeling for a girl like this? Well do ya?

'One month of being a 'regular' and the visits have begun to resemble prison visits with conjugal privileges,' I write in my diary in September. 'We're not to step outside together. There's a clock, and her phone, the agency, is the guard knocking on the door announcing time up whenever we run over. We have a few minutes for a chat, fifteen minutes for a bath, half an hour to have sex and make it work.' Every so often we make confessions to one another that conjure for me the image of two lifers revealing their darkest secrets to one another, figures so removed from the normal world that they're convinced their words will never pass beyond these walls.'

I set out to see her equipped with all kinds of mental strategies for controlling my emotions. I tell myself, It's the fantasy you're in love with, not her. I tell myself to treat the hour, or 90 minutes, as I would, say, a yoga class. I tell myself that I'm on a course for focusing on the self and the other person through the senses. I tell myself that because she's more or less forbidden talk of any kind of a future together, I'm getting a more pure form of sex, one I've never experienced before, not even as a younger man. But after fifteen minutes of being in the bath water with her, all those mental strategies melt away like bath salts. I spend the rest of my time with her in a maze of ecstasy and torment. And before taking my leave of her, I underline again the already noted fear that with each successive visit, as my passion for Sisi grows, my performance is becoming increasingly erratic–at least, as judged by my own standards.

As for the money, I've already grown so used to shelling out tens and twenties on her easy-wash bedcover I could believe I was buying a house on Park Lane–a little plastic one, that is. For someone generally very careful with his money, generous perhaps, but seldom reckless, it's a strange experience. When I'm in her presence, I'm as blind to the money as a gambler. The notes represent merely another go at winning–another a go at winning her heart. To anyone else I'm even acquainted with, it's just squandering. Even out of her company, whenever my conscience starts to bite reminding me I could be putting this money toward, say, the children's education, a voice'll argue back with something like this: *But you've cut back on all sorts of day-to-day pleasures for yourself – and maybe that represents a saving of at least £50 a week.* My conscience: *Maybe if you bought Sylvia flowers once in a while, your marriage might bloom again.*

Sonia's regular: *But then again, you have friends who spend the same on shrinks and recreational drugs. If Daddy had no pleasure, he might rustle up a cocktail from his pharmacy cupboard one evening and numb himself up, permanently.*

I've never really got porn as a regular source of satisfaction. Sat there in front of your PC widescreen with your box of tissues to hawk up and mop up the congestion of desire. Nor the striptease, standing before a bare stage, drink in hand trying to look only casually interested while your balls turn to cream. It's got to be tactile to be real. It doesn't have to real in the sense of a 'real' relationship – because I know what you're thinking, that my 'relationship' with Sisi isn't real – but being with Sisi is to take part in a form of theatre. I bring my props – my 50 Cent and Julee Cruise CDs to create alternative moods, from angry street to ethereal dreaminess, my D&G perfume to conjure glamour, my Kiton for its instant arousal of the libido – while she has her perfumes, costumes, sex toys etc. and we play out mostly my fantasies. Escapist? Maybe. But you wouldn't dismiss cinema and theatre as merely that, would you. All during my thirties I longed for permanence in a relationship. Why at forty something it's less important, I don't know. Perhaps because I've had my children and am longer propelled by the biological need to procreate. I no longer seek happy endings, but, rather, beautiful little moments. Didn't one great poet say, it's only through knowing that we must die that the flower is so beautiful?

Every so often Sisi shows a part of herself I know that she would never show just any customer–and this is always exciting, because you're in a territory where trust is so hard to come by. But just as I stumble upon this clearing in her where money and customers appear to have no access, the phone rings, or she pushes me back on the bed, getting us down to business.

I like to think I must be unique among her customers, if only because our first time didn't involve money and I hadn't asked to see her knowing she was a prostitute. On the other hand, Sisi might have viewed that first time as a quid pro quo payment for the free dental treatment I'd given her. And she must have known, too, that I might enjoy her and return as a 'regular'. Neil was right: she was an opportunist. Some days I wonder what I'd do if my career disappeared overnight. Say, I ran into one of these people Sisi says is watching her and he decided to teach me a lesson by cutting off my right index finger. Would she make any concessions for me if I ran out of money?

How careful was I being?

'She hasn't been out with me since that first drink,' I note in my diary, roughly two months after our collision in the pool. 'She seems happy enough for me to drop in every now and then for a 'coffee' as long as I can cope with the fact she might have to see a customer at any moment and have to turf me out onto the street. It concerns me to see her so often with a beer in her hand–the Tiger beer joins us on the edge of the bath, beside the bed, at five in the afternoon. She smokes too much. I never see her now without rings under her eyes. She needs to get out more, exercise, quit smoking. How about *we* go swimming together, I say when she tells me she hasn't been to a pool since our accident. She says her friend has gone back to Thailand and she has no one else to go with really. So go with me! I exclaim with laughter.

She looks longingly in my eye, then rests her hand so gently on my shoulder I just can't press her further when she lamely offers up another of her 'maybes'. I know I should quit caring, but I'm looking at a big bruise just under her ribs and it upsets me, upsets me that she's OK with it somehow. Today she flinched when I fucked her. In a fond note of entreaty she says, "Darling, be gentle, I'm sore today." So I stop and, instead, I lick her sore pussy, oh so gently, til the soreness melts away and she claws at the sheets, arching her back toward a sweeter pain.'

She tells me she thinks the agency watch her flat sometimes. Which presumably means they know my face. She once said that they might even get it into their heads that I was trying to recruit her.

"Are you serious?" I say.

She shrugs and smiles, languidly amused by the possibility and my alarm. "Don't worry," she says, as though it were a meaningless afterthought, "I don't think so."

That week I skip a visit, but I'm back the week following, having chewed the paranoia into digestible pieces.

"Why you want to learn Thai? What's it good for?!" she exclaims one afternoon, all of a sudden exasperated with me for no apparent reason. "When I go back, what you do? Not so many Thai in London."

"I'll go to Thailand."

"When?" she snaps, as though I've postponed my date of departure several times already.

I can't quite explain her pique unless she thinks I'm using her so I can go to Thailand better equipped to chat up other Thai girls. Or do I flatter myself? Maybe she's contemptuous of the very idea of a middle-aged man with two daughters planning on going over to her country to explore her culture, the women, his own stupid fantasies.

‘I would never leave my girls for long,’ I want her to know.

Her smile seems to tell me she’s glad and also that this is why she could never ask me to go back to Thailand with her. I make sure my smile outlasts hers, quietly urging her to keep an open mind.

“Best time you go in April. It’s hot, but nice. June is rainy season, not so good. Go in April.”

She likes to tell me about Thai women. Their strength, their pride, the unique attention they give to their men.

“You know why Thai prostitute so famous?” she says, one afternoon, as we lie on her bed, inches from each other’s face. “Not so many, really, many more from Singapore, China, Japan, but men know Japanese girl selfish, materialist, Chinese too. Thai women give good –“ she pauses–

“–service.”

“Yes. Give good service. Because our culture to be like this.”

She impresses on me that one day she will completely devote herself to a man. She will look after him totally, so he will never look at another woman. “Good sex, massage, good food, always support him in what he want. This how Thai woman is.”

I see a stark dichotomy here, even as I admire her longing for this utopia she envisages marriage to be. On the one hand, there is this strong will to be free and express herself, and on the other, there’s this cultural submission to a man’s will. Even as she says she appreciates my point that her hopes very much rest on the man not being a prick, she is convinced she will be lucky. Despite the men in her life having let her down, or perhaps because she cannot relinquish her quest for some kind of validation of her love for the father who abandoned her, she still holds on to this ideal of a happy marriage. It would be easy to dismiss her optimism as third world naiveté, but why wouldn't that be preferable to my all-knowing western cynicism?

"I think you're right," she says. "For me, Thai men, big probrem. They want young virgin as wife. They want to control her. I don't want to marry for five or six years. I want to be independent business woman. Then maybe I get married."

"Well good for you."

"But maybe not, because I'll be thirty at that time and by then I'm old, no one wants me." And she laughs heartily at the conundrum she's faced with.

"Old?!" I exclaim.

"Yes, 30 is old for woman to get married with someone in my country."

"That's crazy."

She assumes a suitably doomed expression as she nods in reply.

"So maybe I marry with farang. You know this word?"

"Foreigner."

She smiled. Our eyes met. As far as I could see, she was talking hypothetically, and that was all.

"Sisi? It's me, Anthony."

Silence, then coughing. Her throat, clogged with phlegm, croaking as she cries, "I'm not good, I'm dying..."

"What?"

I hear her blowing her nose. She coughs again.

"I just got up."

I glance at my watch, it's 4.30 in the afternoon.

"Sorry, I call you later, OK? I've got customer now."

"Sweetheart, that's me."

"What?"

"The customer you're seeing–that's me. I'm coming round and I'm bringing some medicine, OK?"

She's been seeing guys the whole week when she should have been resting up, and now she's got flu, real flu. I'm ten minutes waiting in the rain outside her door, poking her crappy buzzer before she opens. Some drug addicts look better. She's got a raging fever, no food in the kitchen, barely any clothes on–and the only thing she's worried about is whether the agency will be mad that I've cancelled and then come round to visit her to look after her.

"Who cares?" I say, popping two Ibuprofen from a blister pack.

"Can you pay me?"

"Take this." I hand her a glass of water and the two pills. "I cancelled the booking already, OK?"

"Cancelled?"

"Yes. Now I'm going to make you a soup, OK? Miso soup. It's very good for fever. You gonna let me do that?"

She swallows the pills and nods.

"And then if you want me to go, I'll go, OK? I didn't come for sex, I came to look after you."

I hurry to the kitchen area looking for a suitable pan.

"Why you kind to me?" she asks, now seated cross-legged on one of the armchairs.

"Fuck knows, I must be crazy–maybe I love you."

"You love me?" I glance round to see her smiling as if I'd just said something quaint and quirky about myself.

"You break my heart," I say, sassy with the sarcasm, and twist on my heel back to the stove.

"You brought flowers for me?"

"Sure. Always."

She's just noticed them, not my finest bouquet to date, left lying on the kitchen table.

I up-end the packet of Miso soup. Already she seems to have cheered up a little, talking about some shoes she bought and wants to show me. But five minutes later she's concerned that 'agency security' saw me coming to the house–

"You mean they have guys sitting out here all day long for every girl on the website, watching their place, to see if some guy turns up with some food for them?"

She shrugs, unsure, but fearful.

"Fuck, do they own you or something? Do they have your passport or what?"

"No."

"So forget about them for a minute, can you? You're sick. If you keep on working you could end up with a bladder infection, if you haven't got one already. What good are you to them if you're sick! If you don't rest you could end up in hospital," – *as if her agency would give a damn.*

I whack off the heat and grab her grater.

"Why don't you go independent? You could charge twice as much and do fewer hours."

"I have contract."

"Well when does it end?"

She's coughing. It's hardly time for a business consult–and what am I proposing exactly, that I 'manage' her? There's another word for that and it begins with 'p'…

As I bring her her bowl she tells me she's supposed to be meeting all the girls from the website later for a girls' night out–and she goes *yap yap* with her hand so I get the idea–but she only wants to go to bed, she says.

"Yeah, that's what you should do. You need rest."

"You're not having soup?"

"OK, I'll join you."

I grate some more root ginger and sprinkle it over my soup.

"It's good," she says. "Dee," she adds, meaning good.

"Arawi," I add.

"Delicious, yes. You still learning Thai," she says, impressed that I haven't given up already.

"The ginger's good for your gut, your fever, please use it."

"Yes, I know. I'm eating very bad since I come to England. Thank you."

When we've finished she tells me I'd better go now, her flatmate is expecting a customer soon and if she sees me here she might talk to agency.

I dig in my bag for the other stuff I bought for her: Night Nurse, Ibuprofen and vitamins. She thanks me. Holding the vitamin C bottle, she asks me how many she should take. She can read, but she wants me to tell her. As if I were Dad.

At the door we embrace as if war were tearing us apart. I fly out the door like some 21st century caped crusader and rescuer of prostitutes in distress. Well, just the one, anyway.

So is this cheating? I'd ask myself.

"Nah," Neil tells me one late September evening as we lounge in soft armchairs, side by side, knees touching, in Soho Hotel, our midnight conversation suitably enhanced by sightings of lone, fragrant females nursing flat cocktails at the bar. I can read from the way he shakes his head that whores don't count as cheating any more than masturbation does.

"The thing is," I continue, "I can't really find any meaning in that word when I think that Sylvia and I have been cheating each other of physical affection for the past twelve months. Any guilt I might feel over my visits to Sisi is swiftly overridden by the anger of having been denied sex with Sylvia for so long."

"Go for it, man."

"Not so much anger toward *her*–obviously we've both failed to find ways of interesting each other that way–anger at life."

"Absolutely."

"But what's the point of any more anger, when you can leave all that behind in the pores and orifices of a girl like Sisi."

OK, I'm drunk–I thought I'd hit on an amusing, if not poignant, turn of phrase, at least from our point of view–but when I glance at Neil I see him staring darkly into his glass of melted ice and wonder if my words haven't nauseated him all of a sudden.

"You OK?" I ask.

"Yeah yeah yeah – yeah I'm fine." He shakes the ice around in his glass, still staring at it. I grow concerned as he begins stabbing the ice with his straw. "Where you're going wrong… you're mixing your drinks, mate. You're mixing you're drinks."

"How do you mean?"

"Whoring and love–it's a head-fuck."

"You've said already–and I know that."

"Well… *your* life mate, but you're heading for a fall if you ask me."

I remember looking at his face and thinking, how haggard he looks. I could almost believe that if I took his shirt off I'd find lumpy scars over his heart, scars made by the surgical savagery of his acrimonious divorce. My heart went out to him, even as I was smarting from the reminder of my folly. I sensed he saw himself in me, as his marriage had been about to end. He had used prostitutes and, though he denied it, had possibly fallen for one or two–and he didn't want to see me go down the same path. Or perhaps he did; perhaps he wanted to be the one who'd be there to pick me up. And in my fallen state, we'd go out whoring together, talking wildly of setting up a second business, something sexy in media or real estate–celebrating our last blast of post-youth defiance before our prostates got tricky.

"Have you ever thought of men?" he asked, an hour or so later.

He'd crooked an eyebrow at me as if to suggest I was well qualified for such a 'thought'. His small sensuous mouth knotted in cherubic delight at the possibility he might have found the hole in my 43 years' heterosexual identity.

Belatedly I laughed.

"No, seriously," he put to me, "I'm not saying you're gay, you just might be both." A beat. "I've had sex with men."

"Yeah?"

"Oh yeah. Gay pubs in Soho – oh yeah. Not for years, but I did do it. Cruising, brother," and he laughed at the self-parody. "You're never too old to change," he added with a giggle of irony.

I smiled to myself and sat up in my seat.

"So is this why you've been so friendly?" I was grinning, so he knew that I was pulling his leg.

He laughed amplifying, my own amusement, then added. "It could be. When can you fit me in for a blow job with the laughing gas?"

Had my life been any different, I would probably have been quietly repelled by Neil's prurient ambivalence, but because everything that had happened since smashing into Sonia had shattered so many of my assumptions about who I was or where I was going, I was quietly thrilled by it. I didn't want to be gay or bi, but I was clearly ready to come out as something other than a dad and a dentist.

CHAPTER 9

"Hey! How are you, mate!" I winced at the 'mate' (never sounds right coming from an Oriental) but I could hardly believe my ears. It was Sisi. She was finally over her flu, she sounded truly vibrant and *she* was calling me for once!

It was early October, beginning of the week and I'd had a tedious morning with a young woman's bite, but already my voice was barking back–"I'm fine."

She asked me what I was up to and did I like Thai food.

"Yeah, you know I do!"

"So do you want to come and meet my friends and have dinner?"

The moment I hung up my elation snagged on the possibility that Sylvia would want to go out at the same time and expect me to look after the kids.

"I got some steak fillet," Sylvia told me over the phone. I could tell she was hoping that this might be enough for me to change my arrangement to some other night.

"Well, can't we do that tomorrow night?"

"I'm out then."

"I'm sorry, sweetheart, it's just–I haven't seen these guys in a while and the American guy's going back to New York tomorrow, so–"

"It's OK, don't worry, do what you want." And she hung up.

I arrived at Sisi's with a bottle of Viognier around six. A small, dark-skinned girl opened the door to me and turned her head announcing my arrival in Thai. Sisi jumped up from the sofa with laughter and skipped over the floor to welcome me, giving me a kiss, wrapping one arm and a can of Stella around my neck. She introduced me to her friends: her flatmate, whose real name I now learnt was Tasanee, and who laughed and blushed on recollection of our first encounter; the dark-skinned girl who'd opened the door to me and an older girl, too plain and stocky to be a 'working girl', who seemed to welcome the effect the arrival of a male had on the group. I was invited to sit on the sofa where Sisi joined me, curling her bare feet under her slender legs and bottom. I was given a glass from which to drink the wine I'd brought along and generally made a fuss of. They all ran around like choreographed nymphs helping each other with various aspects of the dinner, then pausing for a moment to show each other a recent purchase or photo or have a stab at practising their English with me. Every now and then one of them would translate for me, but really it didn't matter too much: I was enchanted by the simplicity of their child-like spontaneity and warmth. The last dinner I'd been invited to, I'd gone with Sylvia to a large, eighties-built house in the suburbs, with an interior design that reflected a generous blend of the best in American and Greek taste, contemporary and old. We'd all been couples. Seated in a rectangle, upon black olive armchairs and sofas. We'd drunk excellent Greek and Spanish wine and chatted eagerly about our children, the fears we had of the fast approaching teenage years. We were witty and delicate with our turns of phrase. It was very pleasant–but so familiar I had to pinch myself to be sure I hadn't turned into my dad. Here I was in the heart of London, in a little bit of native Thailand, a male guest Sisi had perhaps had second thoughts about in spite of her job, and I was someone I wasn't used to being, yet still myself.

We sat in a circle on the floor around a dozen dishes of food and a huge pot of fragrant rice. I was given a bowl, chopsticks, a plate and a flannel for my hands. Two of the girls were impressed that I could eat more than a mouthful from their hottest vegetarian dish, a kind of spicy Chinese broccoli. And all of Sisi's friends applauded my attempts at Thai.

"You must stay with Sisi. She very good teacher!"

Glancing at Sisi, she was busy with her food and appeared to ignore their remarks. Determined not to be discouraged, I stretched myself, throwing out every phrase I could possibly recall, asking the others to correct me when I made mistakes. Every other thing I said, whether in English or Thai, sent a ripple of amusement through the group. Was this because I was here as Sisi's possible future boyfriend, or was I genuinely amusing them? The two younger girls openly vied with Sisi for a sign that I was at least some way attracted to them to the point I fleetingly conjured for myself a fantasy of a threesome after dinner.

As plates were being cleared away there was talk of what we might all do next–a karaoke bar, a night club, local or West End–when Sisi received a call that blew a hole in all our plans as if they were made of rice paper. She had a booking. Not in an hour, not two hours, 25 minutes. She put a consoling hand on my leg apologising for the sudden interruption. Why had I dared to think tonight was a night off? I felt a rotten pit hollow out in my stomach even as I betrayed not the slightest disquiet or disappointment. In fact I was as accommodating as if she'd just told me she needed an hour's privacy with her brother.

"Well," I said, "if it's only an hour, I can wait."

"You can wait?" She looked surprised, even impressed.

"Yeah, I can sit in a bar outside, read the paper."

"You sure?"

"Yeah. And when you're done we can go out... Yeah?"

"Yeah. OK."

She told her friends what I was prepared to do and they voiced amazement and wonder, too. *I must be some Romeo.* Her flatmate was on the phone now, and it sounded like business. The other two girls prepared to leave. It was time to evacuate.

I found a Bistro Spanish bar restaurant in a side street five minutes away. I sat at a small table not far from the entrance and ordered a glass of red wine. I perused the newspaper pretending I was a man waiting for his train. I glanced at my watch. Ten twenty. Her customer would be fucking her by now. Or she'd be sucking his cock. I ruffled the newspaper and turned a page. More inches warning us that the police feared further suicide attacks, not just in London, possibly centres of commerce. They could happen at any moment. Somehow I doubted Sisi paid any attention to the news. She barely stepped out of her apartment for more than a few hours every week; the world outside W2 was almost a fiction.

I folded the newspaper and looked about the restaurant, observing the people. It occurred to me that since meeting Sisi I'd stepped out of a 'normal' existence; to people here I'd probably stepped into the 'gutter'. For me it was more like I'd stumbled into some kind of virtual world where expectations, gestures and words had a uniquely ephemeral quality. Inhabiting this space I had the strange impression I was becoming invisible on the street, even less visible at work. The day I'd gone out to buy vitamins for Sisi, I'd been standing in a queue in Borders in Oxford Street and looked down the shop to the entrance, through the open doors to the street and through the gaps in the passing cars straight through to the back of the shop opposite and I'd registered all the visual information as though it were as unreal as a film set– presumably because I'd reached a kind of fever pitch over my mission to help Sisi. But how did I manage to kid myself that waiting an hour for this girl while she fucked a stranger for money was not going to fuck with my head? It wasn't so much the sexual jealousy that hurt, it was more the realisation that our time together could be shattered at any moment by a phone call.

At 10.50 she called.

"I finish now."

"Great. That was quick."

"Yeah, he don't stay long."

"OK, so shall I come over?"

"I'm sorry. I have 'nother call come in. I have to do job."

"But Sisi," and I hear the legs of my chair scrape as I move sharply forward on my seat, "I've been waiting an hour for you."

"I know, I'm sorry!"

I felt the skin about my head tighten like a drum.

"You want me to cancel him?"

"Well yeah, sure. Please."

"And I see you instead?"

How beautiful that sounded at first. But as the tone and the words unveiled their ugly meaning something in me buckled. She didn't even have to say it, I knew what she was asking: go up there and replace the next customer's 150 with mine. *Hey, fucker, why should that be a problem? You been doing this for weeks at a time.* But I couldn't get passed the hope of earlier that evening when I'd dared to believe that her invite meant we'd finally entered a new stage in our 'relationship' – but now, apparently not, we were still on the fucking meter.

"I'm sorry…" she began regretfully, in a tone that told me she knew she was hurting a generic man, but possibly not even me.

"I can't do this anymore," I said, choking, cutting her off and I snapped the clamshell shut.

That's it, I told myself. You gotta wake up. For the sake of the kids, if no one else, you can't go on punishing yourself like this.

But did I get up and go? No, I sat there another ten minutes, glancing at my phone every so often, hoping that she'd call back and make the concession I so desperately needed.

"Is there anything I can get you sir?"

A Spanish girl, pretty enough to be a whore–but she'd chosen £4 an hour instead of a £150 because at least that way she'd have some love to give a man.

Yeah, a shot of cyanide, no ice. But I couldn't speak and had to make do with a polite smile and a shake of the head. Half a minute later, I waved and gestured for her to bring me the tab.

Heading up the street to the tube, I felt like a soldier in retreat, rows upon rows of customers like a vast, impenetrable army at my back. Perhaps that last call had given me the concussion I needed in order that I finally come to my senses.

CHAPTER 10

"… I never knew…" Sylvia said one October evening.

"What?" I asked, looking up from the newspaper.

"My tutor–he was on the train, the Kings Cross train, the day of the bombs."

We were in the kitchen, I'd just got back from the practice and she was pouring herself a glass of Chardonnay and seemed excited by her news as though the man's experience might inspire her in her next art project.

"He just casually referred to it when he was talking about the Munch Exhibition–all this thick smoke swirling around them as they walked along the tracks to the next station. He said he thought he was going to die. He has asthma. Must have been horrible."

"Yeah," I sympathised quietly.

My mind flashed back to my own crash into water, so much softer than shrapnel.

"Want one?"

"Yeah, thanks."

She brought me a glass and continued with her mealtime preparations and I remembered how we used to love this about each other, our respective restlessness and searching moving around each other during daytime, a sort of dance; but now there was a wariness and evasiveness about our body language, a picky quality to what we would and wouldn't share in sympathy with one another. Except for the big things, like bombs.

"He said he didn't know whether he'd got – y'know – post traumatic syndrome but– " she paused, a peeled onion in one wet hand, "–every time he smelled smoke, he'd think of that tunnel, and the dead people he had to climb over to get out of there." She placed the onion on her board and cut through with a clunk to the board. "He said he felt guilty that he hadn't gone back to help, like some of the others, even though he knew he couldn't because of the risk of having an attack."

"Human nature."

"Yeah." She sniffed and wiped a tear from the corner of her eye.

"So you like him, you get on?"

"He's a bit odd, but yeah – Shit, can you pass me a sheet of that?"

I got up to tear off a sheet of Kitchen Towel and handed it to her.

"... Thanks." She dabbed her eyes. "That onion's strong." She picked up her knife. "Yeah, he's very approachable. He's always very good at finding the good in your painting – he's sensitive how another artist might feel, he's got tact... unlike the previous one I had... I told him that the other day and he said he hadn't always been like that–it was the bombs that made him that way."

"Well, I guess we're all less sure of ourselves right now."

We said nothing for a minute or so, until I added, philosophically:

"I wonder how long he can keep it up before he reverts to who he was. I think we all do in the end."

She clucked her tongue. "Why do you always say that kind of thing?"

She was right, why did I say it, it was enough to think it.

"I just mean–like after the bombs? People so polite to each other, concerned–as the news reporters said, 'unusual for London' – then again, we are famous for our 'Blitz spirit'. A month later, though, people are walking over your feet on the way out of a tube train without so much as a glance back, never mind an apology. So–"

"Can you shut up a minute? We were talking about the bombs in class today, right? Not just the bombs, the war in Iraq, how all this killing and torture, these executions on the internet, all that–how it might be affecting how we paint and what we paint–'

"For sure. It probably affects the way I file down the peg for a crown."

She pulled a face, unsure whether I was being sympathetically ironic or mocking of her train of thought.

"Can I finish? The thing is, I don't know if I want to go there with my mind; I don't know if I want to explore these subjects in my art, because sooner or later they're going to get into my life and affect–" she paused and said, "the girls…" She paused, reflecting, but didn't go on to say: 'us'.

Later that evening I realised she hadn't painted my portrait for three or four years. Only the girls interested her now. She wouldn't want to study me as a subject, because that would involve her in studying what her feelings were for me.

As the room was beginning to fill with the rich aroma of her African curry (mild for the kids), she asked what I was doing on Thursday.

"Not sure. Might be out."

"Do you mind if I get a babysitter then? I've got something on too."

Neither of us saying what or where or with whom. Did parenthood necessarily entail so much shorthand, so many omissions, in order for us to keep our focus on our children's lives?

CHAPTER

11

Seven points down and my game's gone to shit. Something's eating me even as I run around the badminton court chasing Neil's better placed and harder hit shots. Ever since I decided to try and come off seeing Sisi, it's like I've got worms in my moral fibre and now they've spread to my limbs. I glance at my opponent's face. The bulbous blue eyes, glacial in the midst of so much ruddy skin, show me a mind focused only on one thing: beating the shit out of me. I want to tell him, I'm just not worthy of his effort, but some indelible residue of defiance keeps me hanging in there.

"Oh, good shot! Good shot, mate!" as I defeat him with a lob.

So I've clawed one back. I soak up the praise as if it were drops of morning dew on an empty can left in the desert, and admonish myself to get back in the game. I serve weakly but he whacks wildly and the shuttlecock embeds itself in the net. I get to serve again. The rally lacks flow and rhythm, my contact lenses are sticking to my eyes and blurring in a way they never used to… Should I get laser treatment? I lose the point. I should have opted for squash, but when Neil gave me the choice, I'd felt him lean toward squash and, of the two, I had at least once been a good amateur player at badminton. But that was twenty years ago, in the garden with friends and family. I've lost the wrist action you need to whip the shuttlecock around the court; I'm all arms like a tennis player and easily over-hit. I can tell Neil senses I'm not happy with myself–he wants the best of me. But even as my mind sharpens up a notch, my body seems locked into a kind of teenage sulk all of its own. And then my knee goes off, a sharp twinge, bugger, I crash into the wall and that's it, we have to stop.

Neil's hands on my back, helping me up. His concerned, matey tone of voice pulls up pictures of me in the pool cubicle, Greg's kindly remonstrations, Neil's other face, twitching with rage–

"Yeah, I'll be fine," I say, gently bending it.

His hands seem to stick to me as I move in the direction of the door unable to admit even to myself that the pain demands I slow right down.

"It's an old injury." And nearly blurt out that it's gotten worse since it collided with Neil's son's head.

"You need to warm it up before a game, y'know? A few laps round the court. I should have done that as well, I can feel a hamstring tightening up…"

I laugh suddenly and stand upright.

"Look at us whinge on, eh!" he says cutting across his own chat.

It's been a while since I had any male camaraderie that's made me smile.

In the changing room, like most men, Neil is comfortable slopping about naked. He's a fraction bigger and longer than I am, and though I remind myself there might not be much in it at full length, I waste no time in wrapping a towel round my narrow waist. As we chat under the shower he turns his whole body toward me as if to flag up his flaccid superiority. Given his hair is dark, turning grey like mine, I'm surprised to see his pubic hair is a fluffy blond, almost pretty, and I can't help glancing at it like a child fascinated by a funny little wig. When our eyes meet I register a mixture of fear and warmth in his eyes, a familiar enough electric contact when having any kind of sustained chat with a man in a shower–each of us checking, is he gay or bi? Except, with Neil, there's something else going on, it's as if he's contemplating my shadow, my feelings about something or someone else.

"You shave?" Neil asks.

I rub my chin, a bit stubbly. "No, I forgot this morning."

"I mean yer pubes, man, yer scrotum!"

My jaw drops. I'd forgotten I'm hairless nowadays.

"Yeah–"

"Bit porno, isn't it? You always done that?"

I can't admit that I started shaving there since seeing Sisi. I hadn't done it just for her anyway, though she'd said early in our meeting, among her dislikes in men, were giving blow jobs to men with sweaty, hairy crotches. I'd never liked a woman's bush. Sylvia had used to trim hers when we were first going out, but gave up once the kids were born. When I'd said she might see more action down there if she trimmed once in a while, she countered that she didn't like oral sex anymore, anyway; worse, she'd never really liked it. At a later date, as if apropos a completely separate issue from oral, she said she was still getting the discharges she was getting shortly after she'd had the kids. Even after a shower? I'd thought to ask. But what was the point, oral was simply out for her.

"You think I should do mine?" Neil is asking me. *Very definitely*, but I don't want to get into it, so I turn away pretending I've water in my ears. "Maybe I should get a wax," he carries on to himself and sucks in the air between his teeth as though he's just felt the burn.

"How's your knee now?" he asks, turning off the tap.

"Yeah, not s'bad. Hurt it years ago in kung fu. Over-kicking."

"You, kung fu?"

"Yeah, me."

"Interesting. I used to do tae kwon do for a bit. Dropped it to do boxing. Didn't go in for all that nonsense with the kicks." He jabs the air a couple of times as if to make his point. "Anyway, tell you what, you should get in the sauna for a few minutes, give it a rub. The knee, that is."

"Yeah?"

"Yeah, definitely. Come on, dry off and I'll show you where it is."

We towel down, then up and I follow Neil through some doors, round a pool edge, past one swimmer and a couple of older flabby guys talking very chilled on the other side, to a small hut. Neil instructs me to shut the door. We've got the place to ourselves. He stretches out on one of the wooden benches, puts his knee up, then drops it when he realises I'd get an eyeful of his scrotum the moment I turned to look at him.

We indulge in talk of injuries, past and present, tales that lend us a sort of shambolic heroism that would make us blush in the cool light of day.

"You wouldn't believe it but I used to be slim not so long ago," he tells me in a philosophical sort of tone. "Divorce took its toll–nothing but junk for six months. I think that's why I needed to see you about my teeth as well."

"You were thin?"

"Yeah, not as slim as you, but I didn't have this," pulling at the soft flesh about his middle, then under his chin. "It's a shame you don't do a bit of lipo on the side, then you could crown me and suck m'fat up the same day!"

I laugh along to his piping laugh.

"My problem's the other way."

"Mate, if that's a problem, pass it here. You're built like an Oriental–no fat, just lean muscle."

"Wrong climate to be lean in."

"I dunno, global warming, milder winters… I sweat like a pig in summer."

"Sweating like a pig now."

"The only time I enjoy it," he says and we laugh again. And if I were even ten years younger I'd find this 'male bonding experience' entirely gratifying, but for some reason I'm fidgety–I don't need words, advice, irony, I need–

"So how about that girl, the Thai girl from the pool? You still seeing her?"

I honestly don't know how to answer that question–so I laugh, slipping my hands under my thighs, rocking slightly, as if he'd knocked me on the funny bone. I start to describe my last visit. Neil wholly enters into the spirit of my narrative, relishing every little observation I make as if the story meant more to him than actually experiencing it for himself. His gasps of surprise and envy are amusingly theatrical and, like any story-teller given an appreciative audience, I grow zestful with the telling. I so wish the end could have proven Neil to be wrong about her. I'm a little surprised that he doesn't shower me with mocking laughter–his gently admonishing groans are almost paternal.

"What can I say mate?" wiping sweat from his face with his hand as though it were a windscreen wiper. "You're better off leaving that one where it is, I'd say. You had a good run for your money, now walk away, walk away… not worth it, it's just not worth it if it's not moving on."

"You sound like you've been there yourself?"

"No no no no…no. Just wouldn't let it happen. No offence to you but–no." The drawn look to his cheeks and craggy expression seem to refute the truth of his words, then again it is hot in here. "Suicide," he adds finally.

"Maybe I'm suicidal," I say breezily. Except, perhaps, I'm not joking, I really am very down.

"I tell you what," Neil says, a few hundred newly gasping pores later, now sitting up, re-pinning his towel. "Why don't you come out with me?"

"Where?"

"A place I know. Very comfortable. And I *know* they have Oriental girls there. You up for it? They're very good."

"You mean tonight?"

"Why not?"

I ponder the suggestion. The oozing sweat has lubricated my mind, unstuck me from my fixed and exclusive need for Sisi. "Dunno, I'm a bit tired, t'be honest… " I start off lamely.

"You're not you're not–honestly, you're not as tired as you think you are, it's just the heat. You'll be fine when we get back out there on the street. Come on," tapping me on the knee and getting to his feet. He undoes his towel again, flaps it and goes "Ooh, feel that breeze," in a camp voice and belts out a laugh, before tightening the wrap, the stance very macho, although his eyes regard me now with a young man's coyness. "Come on. This is the antidote. And it's just up the road."

"Sorted." Neil flipped shut his phone and knocked back the last mouthful of his bottle of beer.

In the Gents of a corporate wine bar, standing at opposite ends of the urinals, I said I wasn't sure I'd be able to any more.

"Nah, you'll be alright, you've only had a couple glasses of wine, you'll be fine," Neil said zipping up on his way to the basins.

As I washed my hands Neil was tearing into a blister pack.

"Here."

"Is that what I think it is?"

The pill stuck to his skin and he had to flick it into my palm.

"The future is… not orange but blue. Extra horse power."

I studied the Viagra pill in my palm as though it might start to effervesce and, out of its foam, produce a genie.

"I use 'em even when I'm sober. It's a sure thing!" He laughed to pep up his slogan with irony.

He popped his own into his mouth and washed it down with a gulp from a bottle of Evian he'd picked up at the gym. He passed me the bottle. A new ritual for fortysomethings out on the town? I was still looking at the pill when he picked it up and popped it into my mouth and put the bottle to my lips. I drank. "Seriously," he said, screwing the lid back on. "You won't be disappointed."

"You do this often?" I asked strapping in to the front seat of his old BMW.

He laughed–"Not often enough!" and turned the ignition. "How's the knee?"

"OK," I said quietly.

"How's that knee?!" he shouted giving it a squeeze then roaring with laughter as he put into first. I couldn't help laughing along. He wanted to have fun–more to the point, he wanted me to have fun and why should I argue with that.

"Actually, it's the left one."

He leant across me and squeezed the left knee, repeating the question and laughing with that absurd piping sound I was beginning to think of as his signature. I rested back and prepared myself for a night of chemical and sensual excess.

Neil drove like a chauffeur, his leisurely turns of the steering wheel lending a soothing rhythm to our conversation. He talked about a Dutch friend of his who was making loads of money with girls on webcams taking their clothes off and talking dirty for invisible voyeurs and plenty of dosh. He wanted get into it, too, he just needed some extra cash, maybe a partner, to start it up with him. His glance lingered on my profile until someone behind us began hooting.

"Tosser."

"I'm sure it's lucrative," I said, a little tired of my non-committal voice–and yet, unlike the first time I'd gone out with Neil, I was aware of a growing appetite for some extra curricular excitement.

"Oh man, when you've got it set up, it almost takes care of itself! Just give it a little rub–" he caressed the gear stick and laughed–"and there's your result."

I smiled as I pictured myself as an entrepreneur in the European sex industry. I'd just assumed my forties, fifties and sixties would consist of one long queue of mouths, not nubile girls on webcams and extra windfalls of cash that would freak out my village-living accountant.

"Think it over," Neil was saying, "and I'll show you some of my ideas some time."

"Sure," I said, and realised I'd got a hard-on.

As we parked in one of the squares at the back of Earl's Court Road, I grew a little nervous. Neil popped the trunk and we got out. From the back he took a black canvas bag with stiffened sides and slung it over his shoulder.

"What's with the bag?"

"M'gear."

"Gear?" I laughed.

"Yeah, I told you, didn't I, I'm more into the theatre than I am the sex." He shut the trunk. "Don't worry, you don't have to do it… unless you want to…?"

I laughed and again experienced that feeling of conflict within that took me back to my childhood, having to make decisions in front of the big boys who would dare you, just to see you squirm.

"These girls'll do most things. I don't mind paying, really–I feel I owe you one for that last filling you did, that posh new composite or whatever it was called.'

"Yeah, should last you, very hard-wearing…"

Neil was pointing to an ATM and we crossed the street.

"Is this going to be… expensive?"

"250. But you won't *believe* the service."

Standing before the ATM I felt as though I were at a urinal in the middle of the street, up to something dirty–except that no one looking at us could see what we were up to. I pulled the wad of notes from the tray and we pressed on, Neil drumming his bag as we went.

"If we're lucky, I might be able to persuade them to give you a sandwich."

"A sandwich?" I laughed.

"Oh, yeah, it's delicious!" and he laughed, this time with a note of mischief.

Well, he obviously didn't mean the Prêt à Manger type and I was too embarrassed to ask for 'the ingredients', so I just carried on walking, hoping that I didn't look too stupid with the nonplussed smile I was stuck with.

Another fifteen yards and we came to a tall block of modern flats made of grey-brown brick and double-glazed windows, close to where Earl's Court Road meets the A40. Neil pressed a buzzer and said he was Nick, come to see Charlie.

"Nick?" I queried.

"Oh, yeah, never give 'em your real name."

We got out of the lift on the fifth floor, passed along a narrow carpeted corridor, until we stopped outside one of the block's uniform wooden doors, 117. Neil knocked. The latch clicked soon enough and the door opened with a yawn of warm air. A short, dark skinned girl, with full breasts, few clothes on, beamed a practiced convivial smile at us both, stepping back on high heels to welcome us inside. I figured her for Indonesian or Malaysian, looking around twenty-five, but probably closer to thirty-four years' old.

"Ah, Nick, hello! Long time no see!"

She reached up to give Neil a kiss on the mouth.

"And your friend?"

"Jack," Neil informed her. "He's a dentist, a very good one."

She offered me her small, warm hand. She struck me as very low-key for a maid or madam–preferable to the cloying, snake-like familiarity of the two hostesses I'd encountered through telephone box ads in my youth. She asked us immediately if we'd like something to drink. She returned promptly clutching two bottles of Corona in her hand sporting three fat gold rings and asked us what type of girl we'd like to see. She had three girls, she said. The place was so padded quiet, I wondered if she meant life-like dummies, not the flesh and blood variety.

"Fantastic," Nick kept saying as she attempted to whet our appetite with a brief, flowery description of each one. He seemed a little nervous suddenly, going to sip his beer, then pausing, sipping then apologising and talking all sorts about what we'd been doing that evening, where we'd come from, why he had such a thirst.

"Ah yes, sauna, very good for health, yeah," the woman was agreeing.

"So, what d'you fancy Jack?" he asked me finally. "Chinese, Thai or Indonesian?"

Our hostess, who went by the name of Charlie, proposed that we each go to one of the rooms and she would bring the girls in to us, one by one. There was no pressure to make a choice, but she was sure I'd like someone. Neil said I could have first choice. "I might even have you Charlie," he said, "you're looking gorgeous tonight."

Charlie's cheeks coloured slightly and she gave him a playful slap for his insolence.

"I not working tonight, have to look after everybody!"

"I know I know, just pulling your leg–come on," Neil joshed.

Charlie fluttered her long-lashed eyelids at him and smiled as she turned on her heel. She took my arm and quietly led me off down a corridor of pale blue carpeting. I experienced the tremulous pleasure of submission in my loins as I went, my ears excited by the swish of chiffon against flesh… I followed her into a small, spotless bedroom–an Ikea space unblemished by any sign of real living. A solid double bed took up most of the space. Covering it was an easy-wash polythene drape similar to the one Sisi had on her bed. Sunset orange curtains hung from the double-glazed window. A bulbous bedside lamp, with a simple shade similar in design to a Vietnamese hat, was already on, lending a showroom's homely atmosphere to the room. A portable TV and CD player were stationed on the nearest bedside table. I noted a few things not normally found in a catalogue: nappy wipes, KY jelly, an 'erotic' photograph in a frame on the wall. Charlie said she would send the first girl to me "in one moment" and left the room.

I sat down on the bed. The quietness of the apartment suggested my experience was likely to be a muted one, not quite the way Neil had painted it. I could have been in a private hospital. I heard the faintest squeak of hinges, then silence. I sipped my beer. When I next looked at the door, a dark-skinned Indonesian girl appeared in just her underwear. Long hair, a tired, bored smile, which she tried to make appealing. When I said "Hi", she schlepped over to the unadorned pine dresser on high heels, with an obvious roll of her hips, and asked me if I'd like her to stay.

Having sent off the second girl with a polite no, I worried that Neil's good humour would evaporate if I turned away the third girl. But I was in luck, the third girl was more my type, bolder than the first two and lithe as new rope. She said her name was Sophie and she was from Singapore.

"So you want me?" she asked, getting straight to the point.

"Yeah."

"OK darling. You pay me now. I go tell Charlie, OK?"

"OK."

I waited again, sipping my beer. I felt an unnatural surge of blood to my groin, a kind of pinching heartburn sensation around my heart which I suspected was the Viagra kicking in.

In the shower, I asked Sophie if she was Chinese or a mix. She counted on her fingers the various nations running through her blood: Thai, Indonesian, Laotian and Chinese.

"Wow!"

"Yeah!" she said and returned to being absorbed in washing me, very business-like, as though I were a car. As she rinsed me down, she dropped to her haunches and dove on my semi hard, bobbing penis. I asked her to slow down. She withdrew, licking the tip and tickling my balls with her fingers like a conjurer. She wasn't just good, she was expert.

In the bedroom she folded our towels neatly and hung them on a rail. When we kissed she sucked hard on my tongue as if she wanted to pull it from my throat. She bit my nipples to just the right degree of pain, scratched my backside just deep enough to make me tingle without crying out. Her eyes met mine purely as a ploy to re-establish my interest in fucking her, disappearing behind fan-like eyelids before I could seek any meaningful contact. Her stamina was unlike that of any girlfriend I'd ever had, including the one-night stands. We fucked like intertwining snakes, legs and arms competing for a dominant, even fatal hold on one another. Her thighs clenched as if forcing me from her, then released as she tightened her flat belly, pulling on my back, arching her own as if her orgasm were like a demon inside of her battling to get out.

Whereas with Sisi my hard-on had waned after thirty minutes, tonight I had that wake-up-want-a-pee kind of hard-on even though my body felt sapped of water.

"You can't come?"

"Uh, no I can, I…" I was panting, she was not.

I came to a rest and smiled. She wasn't smiling. She was considering something, something *alternative*.

"You want more with 'nother girl?"

I said I didn't have any more money.

"Your friend pay, I think. He want you to be guest."

She rose up, easing me off her.

"I'm not sure, uh…"

But she didn't wait to discuss this with me, simply seized my hand and pulled me from off the bed.

"Hang on…" I grabbed a towel and had just enough time to wrap it around me before she dragged me from the room. To my relief, no one was in the corridor. We turned left, and further along the corridor to an end room. As she opened the door we arrived in a larger room, aglow with candles and a low wattage orange light. A black girl I hadn't been introduced to before was resting on the bed and sat up and smiled at me as we came in. She was wearing white panties and black suspenders, no top, her hair in cornrows. She had piercing, intelligent eyes. In the corner of the room stirred a figure in black. He wore a mask, a sort of black corset and black leather pants with a hole at the front, his cock poking out. He had on a cock ring. It was Neil.

"Hello, I'm Aisha," the black girl said. I thought I detected a French accent.

"Jack," I said, feeling momentarily liberated using the false name Neil had given me.

"You have been summoned," Neil droned aiming for obviously bad theatre–but with the mask on it was kind of spooky.

Sophie led me to the bed and lay down beside Aisha as if her job were over.

"So this is it, John– " Neil declared with mock ceremony, "your chance… to experience… an exotic sandwich! The exorcism of Sisira!" Aisha smiled and gestured to me with her hand as if to say we should all indulge Neil's fantasy for a few minutes longer. "But first…" Neil produced a small mirror and two chopped lines. "Come on mate," he said under his breath, suddenly dropping the act, "I've got your marching orders here."

Before I could say anything he pushed the mirror and a rolled tenner at me as if throwing down the gauntlet.

I took the tenner.

"Good man," Neil said. "You OK?"

In for a penny, in for a pound–whereupon I hovered up both lines. Sherbet on the back of the throat, a rush to the groin. So that made alcohol, Viagra and now coke in the blood–I just had to hope my heart could take it *and* rustle up an orgasm.

I had no time to fidget with my tingling nose, Sophie was astride me, kissing me with that unreal appetite of hers. I felt a slap on my thigh. Aisha was telling me, "Come on, turn around, we show you." Sophie seemed to have other ideas, pulling me on top of her. But as I lay across her, Aisha took hold of one of my arms, then my wrist, and before I properly realised what she was doing she'd handcuffed me to the iron bedhead.

"It's OK," Aisha smiled. "You want this. I know. Chill."

With only one arm tied, I could still kick or punch, I could thrash–but I found I was just submissive in her hands, precisely because she seemed so confident I would be her willing captive. When she'd secured the other wrist, Sophie slipped out from under me. Aisha tied a blindfold over my eyes. No longer able to see, it suddenly occurred to me that Neil had waited this long to exact some horrible revenge for my having hurt his son. I twisted about, trying to locate him by sound alone.

"Neil, what's going on?" I called out, hearing fear and amusement in my voice.

"Have no fear, Johnny boy. The blindfold is only to maximise your senses!" he boomed, reverting to the silly theatrical voice.

Instinctively I pulled at the handcuffs, but of course they only tightened, nipping my wrists. The skin on my back was rippling with fear. My sex was tingling with arousal but I wasn't hard. I felt an evacuation of limbs from the bed. A seductive, yet eerie silence appeared and sat down beside me. I'd been abandoned. Unless Neil was sitting in that chair behind me, watching without making a sound. I called his name. No reply. I concentrated on calming myself. Perhaps a couple minutes later, I heard a squeak of hinges… I felt fingers and nails gently scratching from the middle of my back across my backside… I felt someone get onto the bed, skin rubbing against my hips. I recognised Sophie's perfume. She was snaking her way underneath me. She kissed me hungrily and my erection grew rapidly. I kissed her in a sort of trance, instincts telling me that my only way out of this situation was to follow her cue. I felt another body arrive on the bed. My arse and balls were wet with fear and excitement. I felt a hand touch my legs and remembered the smoothness of Neil's hands in the sauna… I called out to the second person, but I received no answer. This other hand of this second person stroked my cock, a tongue was licking my balls from behind. I gnashed my teeth and called out Neil's name, but I still got no answer. A condom was being peeled over my cock and guided into Sophie's lubricated pussy. Sophie moved into me, grinding rhythmically. I needed something to hold onto, but my hands were too far from the iron bedhead and I was too low down the bed to use the mattress as leverage on Sophie, so I had to let her do the work. Suddenly, the sting of a slap on my arse. I grunted, though the immediate afterburn was pleasurable. It came again.

"Hey!" I called out. I wanted to laugh but I was too anxious. "That better not be you Neil!" The panicky attempt to express threat evaporated even as I said the words.

My only answer was something hard and wet nudging at the hole between my cheeks. I froze as my sphincter resisted, burning under the sudden pressure of penetration. The pushing eased off and I relaxed.

"Come on, don't fight it, you love it!" It was Neil's voice, inches from my right ear!

"Fuck!" I cried out. "Stop!"

But the pushing came back and was followed by a sudden thrust. My sphincter let it in, whatever it was. There was a pause, then the penis, real or toy, withdrew half way… and thrust back in. I was glad of the coke taking the edge off the pain. I strained my senses to identify whether the penis was of blood or plastic, whether the gender of the legs brushing against the back of my thighs was male or female. Now it was fucking me. Would a girl know how to fuck like this? Aisha was about the same height as Sophie, around 5'6", but much more solid in build;

her legs were muscular, her hips had looked powerful. But I still hadn't heard her speak. If this was Neil, I swore I'd kill him. But I could hardly think for the banging I was getting from both ends.

"Come on, fuck 'em, man, fuck 'em!"

It was Neil's voice again–but now it was definitely coming from the other corner of the room. I was filled with such relief I began giggling.

"Yes, come on. You want it, so take it!" It was the voice of the French girl this time, like silk stitched with strips of sandpaper. From the ennui in her intonation it sounded as though she were in the habit of fucking guys with a strap-on.

Absurdly I obeyed the voice and moved with Sophie and the girl behind me, whose cornrows were now dancing over my back like so many beaded little demons. All manner of thoughts ricocheted through my head, but they barely penetrated the wider-than-normal sensual pleasure I was experiencing. I wondered vaguely whether this was some kind of prelude to Neil trying to seduce me at a later date. *You wanted it up the arse, I saw how you loved it…* When I came, the French girl pressed up against me and rocked as if to skewer a knife into my insides for the final kill. I registered a spasm deep inside my arse, similar to but separate from my own orgasm, and a sensation that transported me back in time to the peculiar pleasure I'd experienced as a child at that moment of tugging free a large milk tooth from its socket; I'd perhaps just got as close as a man could get to experiencing a vaginal orgasm. *So this was a sandwich.* I felt as a coke-head might when he upgrades to crack.

The girls withdrew like a tide of delicious and armoured flesh. The condom was carefully removed, I was wiped down, the handcuffs were removed. I lay still in the belief it was for one of them to remove the blindfold, but they left me as I was. I waited a further ten seconds or so, ears pricked, half expecting to be surprised again by a giggling cue from Neil. But all that filled my ears was that padded silence of earlier. I was alone. I slipped off the blindfold.

Had I been exorcised of Sisi?

A strange tension inhabited my body–as though parts of me were cooling at different speeds creating a buckling effect on the original version I thought of as myself. Had I been raped actually? The French girl had behaved as though she knew I was the type who would secretly enjoy a strap-on, but she'd been acting under Neil's instruction–I hadn't asked for this service, hadn't even hinted at it. I vaguely remembered having revealed to Neil that I'd played with toys, but the word strap-on had never been mentioned. Sylvia and I had bought a couple of toys–for a laugh, or so we thought. We'd given them a go but she'd always found them fiddly, and wrote them off as the equivalent of sitcom with canned laughter. I could see her now, giggling as something popped out of her. She'd gotten fed up with the mess on the sheets and on our hands. *I was making her dirty, dirty in a way she didn't like.* She glowered accusingly at the toys as though they were depersonalising our love, might even take it over, the way machines would one day take over the world. At my suggestion we made them 'bath toys' and that was more fun, (less messy) but when the first baby bath came along Sylvia stashed them away in a bottom drawer in our closet and they'd lain there, as sad as discarded prosthetics, for the past nine years... So, anyway, you're not supposed to enjoy being raped. Or maybe the pleasure aspect is beside the point–it's the loss of control that disturbs you most. No, I hadn't been raped; I refused to see it that way. It was OK being fucked by a girl. Being fucked by a girl didn't mean you were gay… right? On the contrary, what seemed clearer than ever to me now, as I lay there in the seconds before I sat up, was this: that in spite of my willingness to explore a 'kinkier' side to my sexuality, I'd always been drawn to very feminine women. This 'kinkier' side of me was only ever drawn out by more masculine types, for whom control was an issue. When making love to Sisi, in spite of money passing hands, our sex was romantic; it was all about finding harmony through intercourse. The same I could have said about Sylvia. The more adventurous girlfriends I'd had, the ones into anal occasionally, or even frequently, tended to have had drink or drug problems, then or in their past, or control issues with previous boyfriends and, it often turned out, with me as well. I could see the attraction of wanting to control, and of being submissive, but as a long-term proposition it just wasn't me.

"Hello," said a voice softly.

Still rubbing my wrists I looked toward the door to see Aisha enter the room. Walking over to me wearing a smile that seemed both to mock and celebrate the allure of a catwalk model, she asked if she could get me something to drink.

"Wine?"

She turned and went to a fridge in the far corner, opposite where Neil had been sitting, which I hadn't noticed till now. It was stacked with a range of juices, Red Bull, a Guaranna drink, white wine and Coke. I studied her behind, parted by a thin strand of white panty line, two round, muscular cheeks.

She poured two glasses and came over to me.

"You're a kinky one, aren't you?"

I laughed.

"Yes. Such a pervert."

"Really?"

"*Yes*," she stressed frowning with a smirk that told me she was just playing with me. "And why not. It's good to try something different, explore your sexuality. Santé."

"Santé," and we clinked glasses.

She drew her cornrow hair back with her hand and sat on the bed. I noticed she had minor acne, but it did little to impair the effect of her striking features, the sensual mouth, her challenging, sensuous gaze.

"Did you enjoy it?" She smiled at my hesitation. "*I* did. I can really have fun with my strap on. It makes me come."

"You came?"

She smiled as if to say, 'almost'.

"Would you like to smoke weed?"

"Uh..."

"Yes, come on," and she was already out of her chair, taking a pouch from the top drawer of the bedside table. "I think you need to come down gently from your high." Her voice undulated with irony, the therapeutic lilt of a woman who still believes she's amused seeing again and again men's most intimate secrets on open display. Pulling a face she said she didn't like to do coke, it was too aggressive. Strange choice of words, I thought, given the way she'd used her strap-on.

She kept checking me with her smile and inquisitive gaze, suspicious of me yet hoping to be intrigued. The elongated Picasso-esque curve of the strong cheekbones, the equally proud and rounded chin and strong nose suggested a mix of Arabic and African blood–an intriguing collision of cultures.

"Yes, you're right. That's very perceptive of you. My mother is from Sierra Leone and the other one you'll have to guess."

I watched her handsome hands prepare the joint.

"I guess that would be Lebanon or Syria."

She smiled, her handsome fingers busy with the papers and weed. She lit the joint. I sipped my wine, vaguely wondering where Neil had got to.

"You're very slim, aren't you," she remarked with an appraising look.

"Yeah, I am."

"Very unusual for a man," she said, as though I'd had a choice in the matter, like maybe I could have chosen something off the rack that was a little more conventional, but no, I'd opted for the Christian-Bale-in-*Machine* body... *intriguing*... "Your body is almost as slim as the girl you were fucking." She passed the joint to me. "You'd look good in women's clothes. I would be interested to see that." I laughed. "Would you like to try that?" I laughed again. The night was becoming increasingly surreal. "Yes, but why not? You don't know until you try." I dreaded to think what she might pull from the closet if I even jested that I was game. "You know, English men are the most perverted men I've ever come across."

"Well they're bound to be with you as their personal stylist."

She laughed–"No, come on–but *really*!"

"Are they?"

"Oh, God, yes!" taking the joint back. "They are such sexual hypocrites."

"Are they?"

"Yes. And I should know, right?"

"I guess."

The weed was very smooth like a gentle infusion of syrup into the veins. I hoped it wasn't one of those with a delayed kick to it.

Aisha moved away from me and leant against the cushions as if we'd been too close physically for her to get a proper measure of my sexual hypocrisy or other sexual foibles.

"Well, they say we're repressed, don't they?"

"I guess." She smiled, the light twinkling in her dark, passionate eyes as if to reignite the pilot to her unique blend of wilfulness and cynicism. "Are you repressed?"

"No."

"That's good. I mean, what's the point, you know? If these things give you pleasure, why not explore them. Do you explore your fantasies with your wife?"

"How did you know I was married?"

She shrugged. "Your girlfriend then."

"My wife–though we're not really together anymore–"

"Oh, that's a shame!" she cried, in tones both mocking and sympathetic–again, rather surreal. "How long were you together?"

I thought of lying but then told her the truth. I told her we had two girls, their ages, their names, the shade of their skin. She assumed they must be uneasy with their parents living together in the same house but not sleeping together. I said they were coping very well with my and my wife's estrangement–which I genuinely believed to be the case, and yet now that I lay here naked airing these thoughts to a topless stranger, I suddenly had serious doubts.

"If the sex isn't working any more that's probably because you didn't explore your other side with her."

"I think it's a little more complicated than that."

"Yes, of course," she said, withdrawing gracefully. I suspected she'd be back in a moment's time with her sting raised.

"So, do you work here?" I asked, wanting to get off the subject of my marriage.

She didn't. She'd come by tonight to see Sophie. She wasn't supposed to be working, but then Neil and I had shown up. When he'd asked one of the girls to put on a strap-on, she'd volunteered–as a one off, she said. She didn't like working for agencies, she said, she was independent. She had her own website, put up her own ads, worked to her own schedule. She didn't worry about security, because if you had security, there were people controlling you. "These escort girls have no time for anything else. But in a way they are like the rest of the world," she said with elevated pessimism. "We're all lost. Running around after the latest new mobile phone, the cheapest holiday… more hours at work–and for what? Nothing lasts, everything breaks up, everyone becomes a let-down sooner or later, it's inevitable." Her hard won cynicism would ordinarily have repelled me, but it was tempered by a sweet look in her eye, a genuine curiosity in human nature–or rather, men, I felt, more than women. She may have thought she was being charming with this smile, but the eyes were too obviously trying to bewitch, seeking out weak points in my character, for me to be seduced by it.

She paused, then, smiling at me, said, "What, why you smiling?"

"You've been let down, many times over, haven't you?"

She laughed and cried, "Oh the stories I could tell you! And maybe one day, if we meet again, I will."

"And you're from Paris?"

She nodded and picked up her drink as if to wash down the distaste that her most vivid memories of the place would inevitably bring with them.

"What brought you to London?"

"Why all these questions?"

"Sorry, it wasn't meant to be interrogatory–"

"No, it's OK, I like you, but I don't open myself up so quickly, you know. It takes time for me to trust."

Somehow I didn't think we'd ever get around to spending that time together. And yet, she was growing on me and she seemed in no hurry for me to leave.

When, some twenty minutes later, she noticed I was growing cold, she left the room to fetch my clothes. I put on just the vest. She asked me if I'd like a shower, then immediately said, "Wait, we do that when you go." I thought it politic to reveal I had no more money. She said, that was fine, there were no other bookings so far, I could chill; she was enjoying our conversation.

Around eleven PM she showed me the bathroom and helped me step into it, as if I were an invalid–or a king. Then she shut the door.

My anus felt silky and soft like a vagina. I put my middle finger up there and it felt good, reminiscent of licking the bloody socket of a missing milk tooth. I felt vaguely thankful I hadn't been fucked by Neil. I figured he must have cut me nearly 2g gram of coke because I still had no sign of the come-down. As I soaped my body I saw my cock was still semi hard. It tingled maddeningly with sensation, as did my contracting perineum. I began to masturbate with an almost manic desperation to be rid of the over-arousal. But in seconds my heart was going at a gallop, my legs began trembling with over-excitement and I told myself to stop–I couldn't possibly hope to orgasm again so soon. And yet, even as I let go of the thing, it stiffened angrily, snarling at me to continue. I slammed off the shower and drew back the curtain with a dramatic sweep of my hand as if I were about to take my bow before performing another trick. Drying down I was actually considering going down to the street and pulling more money from the ATM and coming back here for seconds. Aisha had said I could go back with her if I wanted. I could fuck her up the arse this time. She was sure I wanted to do that; I preferred to give, she reckoned. "Which is how it should be–you're not gay, are you?" she said, alluding to our little secret and I wondered how many other straight men she had tempted into discovering their 'anal' side. And then she'd smiled her temptress smile. And, clenching my teeth, I was sorely tempted. But I knew already that I was more intrigued by her dark and turbulent personal history–which I could just catch a glimpse of behind the veils of gently spoken but prurient questions and coaxing–than I was by her body, so I proposed we do dinner one evening, not as escort and customer but as 'friends'–or, at least, conversationalists.

I returned to the room. Aisha had gone. Her card and number were on the bed. Had she meant it, had I meant it? I put the card in my pocket and got dressed. With my clothes on, I felt calmer, less interested in sex, but still buzzing for something–something I could get my hands on or my gnawing teeth into.

Heading back to the hallway, Charlie appeared before me like the Cheshire cat. The glazed expression with which she asked me if she could help at all suggested she'd never seen me before and was ready to take my first request of the evening.

"I'm looking for my friend."

"Ah, Nick, yes… he go already."

"He went?"

"Yes. He left you this for taxi," and she handed me a twenty-pound note. I hesitated as I spotted a few grains of coke, then took it, thanking her.

She accompanied me to the front door. The flat was still embedded in hush. She told me to take care. The door clicked behind me like the click on a medicine cabinet.

I started off down the street with an uncommon swagger in my shoulders like a modern day Mr. Hyde, sniffing at the city air like a rogue hyena setting out on a hunt, his muzzle still tasting of blood. *But how was I to top that?* I didn't know, but I was pulling another 200 from the wall anyway. It was 11.30 PM and a Thursday night. Not a bad night for revelries in Soho. And if I remembered rightly the appointment book was half empty for Friday.

My phone chimed and vibrated once in my pocket. It was a message from Neil:

'Hope you enjoyed. Call u soon.' That simple. As if he were only referring to the badminton game.

From the log I saw there was a missed call, too, and it was from Sisi, time 10.03 PM. Neil was right about one thing, I told myself, Sisi was just a high I could find by other means and without any emotional entanglements. Totally confident that I could enjoy talking to Sisi on the phone without experiencing the slightest frustration afterwards that she wasn't able to see me, I stepped into a side street and dialled her number.

"Hello." That sweet voice, reeling me in–except this time I felt far far away on some other planet.

"Hey, how's it going?! You called."

And just like that she bursts into tears. It's so sudden and unexpected the sound rips through my post-coital coke-buzzing lining and everything I thought I'd got neatly packed away spills onto the sidewalk. I was sure someone close to her had died. And I might too if she didn't stop soon.

"Sisi, calm down, can you–calm down. What's up? Are you hurt?"

"I can't–I can't do this anymore–"

"Sweetheart, you gotta cut down on the number of guys you're seeing–"

"I know I know, but something happened–"

"What happened sweetheart? What?"

"I can't tell you on phone. Oh, baby, I need your help, can you come, *please*!"

Call me callous, but a part of me was thinking, only a whore knows how to cry this convincingly in order to pull a stupid favour, so I was stalling, hoping to work this out over the phone. Until she said, between sobs:

"Do you love me, Anthony?"

And I just hung there in the cool October breeze, like a puppet swept up by a force more powerful than rational thought, my feet dangling in the air. *She knows I love her*, I told myself, *and yet she's never spoken of love before–why now?* And what had love got to do with those terrified sobs of two minutes ago? So, look, it's not as though I wasn't asking myself the right questions–even in the state I was in, a part of me was thinking lucidly, I just felt I had no choice but to go where that first heart-rending cry of pain had come from. I could have left her, but I couldn't abandon her.

CHAPTER 12

Still buzzing on C17H21NO4, I arrived outside Sisi's house around midnight to find her molar-like buzzer had fallen out since I was last round. Her cries still echoing in my head, I called her on my mobile. I hadn't expected her to sound so calm now, an emotionless calm that was ominous after what I'd just heard, though I pushed open the door telling myself that perhaps she was just lonely.

There was just enough streetlight filtering through an upstairs window to allow me to make out the grainy outline of the timer light switch in the hallway. I pushed it and walked down the corridor. The door was already open an inch. I knocked and entered. Sisi was suddenly there–in her panties and a shirt–and we startled one another. The room was barely lit–a couple of corner lamps were on–but it was enough to see her face was creased with worry, to the point I actually saw her as almost ugly.

"Hey, sweetheart, so what's up?"

She hugged me and breathed close to my ear, "Thank you for coming," she said and broke away, her eyes nervously searching mine for signs of trust. My gaze, so brazen from the coke, wanted to burn my love into hers. For a few seconds I was prepared to believe that she'd summoned me here to take part in a mysterious ritual of sacrifice.

"You having a bad night? You gave me quite a fright."

She turned as if to describe a worried circle, then stopped half way.

"Very bad."

"OK…"

She ran a hand through her tousled hair. "I didn't know what to do–a man tried to kill me–"

"*Kill* you?"

"Yeah. He tried to rape me."

"A customer–a *customer tried to rape you*?"

"Sit, please, sit," taking my hand and leading me to a perch beside her on the sofa. "I don't have much time to explain, OK?"

"I don't understand. How could a customer–"

"He tried to fuck me without condom–in ass. I tell him, 'I don't do anal. Why do I want to do anal! My friend does it and she have to wear Pampers after two year. She's twenty-five and she's like old woman. She go–*pth*, like that, when she go to toilet every time. Horrible!" I reflected fleetingly on my experience of only a few hours before and told myself, *Don't make a habit of it.* "So I tell him–yeah?–'No no, stop, you got wrong girl for this'–yeah?–"

"OK–"

"–But he gets angry, he calls me a stupid bitch and we fight, yeah?"

"Is this someone you've seen before?"

She was shaking her head before I'd finished the question. She'd put her hands together and was squeezing them between her thighs, trembling a little and I'm like, *Did she take something too?* The injection of fresh excitement had got me trembling too, at the base of my neck–

"He's dead the guy–he's dead."

"He's dead," I echoed and, for a second or two, this seemed like a simple, satisfactory conclusion to her nightmare.

She nodded. There was a pause. Then she asked me if I would like something to drink. I could have murdered a drink, but–

"This happened here, this evening?" I asked, and felt I was reading lines from a play.

She gave me another worried nod, waiting on my thoughts.

I looked around the room. My ears pricked as I heard sounds of movement at the other end of the flat. I asked her if her flat mate was in.

"No, she moved out last week. It's my friend."

The sound was getting louder, a sound like something soft and heavy being dragged over smooth wood… I looked down the dark corridor to see a stocky figure, Oriental, male, heading toward us, dragging something behind him, something long in a roll of carpeting, whose tail had just run over one of the little candles that Sisi must have placed by her former flatmate's doorway. He stopped at the threshold of the living room and gestured a greeting of sorts to me. I put him at around twenty-eight years' of age. But for the weak chin and a small, down-turned mouth, which robbed him of any natural charm, he might have been handsome–in low light, at any rate. My gut told me he was like a guard dog trained not to attack men who were friends of Sisi. By his feet, I saw strands of thick, dark hair poking out from the nearest end of the carpet roll and recalled with a jump Sis's fears of having been pestered by some Pakistani customers back in July.

"What happened?" I asked, inviting versions from them both.

The man said something to Sisi in Thai. Sisi made a short reply and turned to me:

"I tell him already, you good friend, it's OK."

I couldn't have cared too much either way, but I offered a polite nod to the man, which he returned with a more accented one.

"Have you called the police?" I asked Sisi.

The Thai man spoke again, more briefly this time.

"We can't go to police," Sisi seemed to be translating.

"Why not?"

Sisi glanced at her friend, then at me. "Customer is dirty police from Thailand, my friend say. He's tourist," she added. I noticed her fingers kept interlacing and re-interlacing.

"So we go to the police and explain that you were assaulted, surely–"

"No no no no, I can't do that!" suddenly waving her hands in my face.

"Yeah, no no," the friend is saying at the same time–in English. "No possible."

"It was self-defence, right? I mean what happened?"

"She use knife," the man said as if these three words captured the full story.

"Where did it happen?"

"In my room," Sisi answered. "I used knife for cutting apple and then…" She let her words trail off, gazing briefly into my eyes till I'd more or less got the picture, whereupon she glanced across me to her friend again. I was beginning to feel like a stand-in umpire, unfamiliar with the rules of the game.

"I working girl–yeah?–no visa," Sisi resumed, "they send me back to Thailand if they find out. Kill a policeman, it's very serious. I probably get torture in jail and raped, you know? And they–" she drew her index finger across her throat and made a noise. "It's very bad in Thai jail, you know?"

I'd seen movies, and the best you could hope for was you still had some of your natural teeth when you got out.

"But the crime happened here–"

"No no no, Thai cop, they find a way–yeah?–they bring me back to Thailand."

"No, I don't think so–"

The Thai man was interrupting me with a flow of Thai. Sisi answered with a question. I listened, recognising some of the words I'd learnt from Sisi and my *Colloquial Thai* book, but it was hardly enough to make sense of their exchange. I sensed a taut energy, like an invisible line, between them as they arrived at a final pause.

"He says, even if I don't get in trouble with British police–yeah?–then I have to go back to Thailand because Home Office send me back. And then I get picked up at the airport–and that's it."

Fucked, I thought privately. *It's late, I'm buzzing, I've just done some pretty weird shit and had something pretty weird shit pulled on me by a guy who claimed he could offer me a 'cure' for the very girl I'm now sitting beside admitting to murder.*

"So what're you going to do?"

"Get rid of body. My friend help me. He's quite strong."

"So… what d'you want *me* to do?" I put to her, finally able to express my irritation at having found another man here and at not having been formally introduced to him. "I don't understand–why you've involved me in this? I mean–if you have your friend here–"

Sisi placed her hands on my thighs wishing to calm me, but I stood up, moving toward the door. I should have gone, my god I should have gone, but I couldn't. Maybe the coke was making me fearless to all I'd seen and heard, but most of all I had to hear Sisi explain to me why she'd asked me here.

"My friend couldn't come, but then he came."

"So why call me?"

I could sense the friend tensing every muscle in his body.

"I call you before he get here. I didn't think you gonna come."

This struck me as true–I'd seen surprise on her face as I'd stepped into the flat–but I still insisted that she should have waited.

"I'm sorry, I was upset! I didn't know what to do!"

Now we were all on our feet. The Thai friend said something quietly to her and I sensed he was proposing that she ask me politely to leave and forget everything I'd seen.

Sisi schlepped distractedly about the floor space then zeroed in on the fridge. She pulled a bottle of beer from the bright yellow interior – hardly the time for alcohol – and asked me again if I wanted something.

"Water?" she asked.

"Yeah. Thanks."

The Thai friend pointed to a beer. Sisi passed him one. His hands were strong like a Thai boxer's, a latent violence revealing itself through that simple reach for the bottle of beer. The light was too low to get an angle on his eyes, which anyway he gave mostly to Sisi to read. His behaviour was that of a boyfriend itching to be left alone with his girl, and yet I could detect no sexual frisson between the two.

I took a sip of cool water. The taste of life, the coolness of death.

"So what're you gonna do?"

My company sipped their beers. The Thai man spoke first:

"She need to move ow' [out] now, to-night. I can deal with this." He jabbed lightly the motionless bundle on the floor with his foot. "She need take everything and go."

I looked at Sisi, those long naked legs crossed at the ankles as she leant her perfect little backside that some nutter had arrogantly assumed was all his for 60 minutes against the kitchen sink.

"OK. I can help with that," I said.

The Thai man nodded. "I just need help to get this into bathroom," he added.

I froze up.

"It's OK, we pay you for helping," the man said.

"I don't want money. But if you're getting me involved, at least tell me what you're gonna do with this–this–this guy you've killed," addressing them both.

The friend took out a packet of cigarettes and tossed a cigarette up so he could easily extract it from its packet with his lips–kind of cool 20 years ago and, actually, in the circumstances, still cool. He offered me one and I accepted, anxious to delay the coke come-down.

"Sisi got sharp knives," the man was saying, in a billow of smoke. "I make body into pieces and bury in concrete and then–" he gestured a throwing action– "into sea. I got friend with boat. It's OK; I can borrow. Not so difficult."

Was it his accent or something else that made me think he was an amateur? Then again if he'd come across as a pro, I might have been even more terrified.

"You gotta car?"

He gave a solemn nod and said, "Van. It's OK."

I dragged hard on the cigarette and my lungs felt fortified by the injection of smoke and tar and nicotine. Everything else inside me was hurting with angst.

For maybe a whole minute no one said anything, just smoking the Thai man's cigarettes. When I saw him stub his out in an ashtray on the table, I got up and stubbed out mine. I passed the ashtray to Sisi and she stubbed out hers. I took the ashtray to the bathroom and wrapped the butts in toilet paper and dropped them in the toilet bowl and flushed. I waited till the water reset itself. It was clear. *If only I could be.* At least my memory hadn't failed me. But now I was thinking like a CSI, I realised the whole flat needed a wipe-down. I rinsed the ashtray, gave it a quick dry with toilet paper and returned to the living room. Neither of my Thai companions had moved, though they were mumbling to each other in pharsar Thai. I placed the ashtray back on the table as if opening a chess game.

"You can't leave any trace of your being here tonight," I said pointing to the man.

He didn't seem to understand, so I said it again, whereupon he grunted. After a pause he walked off, back down the corridor. He turned round when he got to the foot of the rolled corpse. He lifted the feet and waited. For me to join him. I walked over to the other end. The carpet was wrapped tightly in thick cord. I picked up my end. I felt something sticky on my hands, but there was no time to look–the friend was pushing the elongated package toward me, forcing me to walk backward, quickly, in the direction of the bathroom. The dead guy was heavy, a brute; I pictured a cliché fat guy bad guy from movies featuring corrupt Asian cops. I got up the steps. We carried the package to the bathtub and set it down. I saw now there was blood on my fingers. I went to the basin and washed it off straight away. I dried my hands with toilet paper and flushed. The man was at my back urging me to go help Sisi get 'ready for go'– he was going to do job now.

I tripped down the steps to find Sisi gone from the kitchen. I headed down the corridor calling her name softly. I entered her room to find myself in the actual crime scene, my first. Her framed photo was on the floor, smashed. The sheets and cover had been pulled from the bed and there were patches of blood on the sheets. A professional chef's knife with a 4" blade lay on the floor covered in blood. I struggled to connect the use of such a weapon with the Sisi I knew. But if I thought of the anger I'd experienced in her fucking sometimes, the anger I'd felt rippling within her when my questions about the possibility of a future together had become suffocating, I began to picture her in action.

"Fuck," I said, in awe of the scene.

Sisi was busy, now rolling the bloodied sheets into a tidier bundle.

"Excuse me, just a minute," and she left the room carrying the sheets as if they were everyday laundry.

I heard words in the kitchen, then Sisi's moccasin-schlep back to the room. I turned to see her sail straight toward me for a hug. I wrapped my arms around her.

"Thank you for coming," she said.

"Sure."

With her warm, slender body pressed against my own, I felt some of my coke-fuelled excitement pass out of me into the bloodstained floor. I was moved by her predicament, of course, but I was also alert to the possibility I might be about to let my romanticism get the better of my judgement. *Heroics can fuck you up sooner than you think.*

As she broke from me, moving into a refulgent tongue of light cast from her overturned bedside lamp, I noticed marks on her neck, a bruise around her eye, which in the low light of the living room kitchen I'd figured were the sad signs of overworking that I'd almost gotten used to.

"And here, look," she said, lifting her shirt and showing me scratches on her fire-breathing dragon.

When I reacted to the sound of the front door opening and closing, she explained that her friend was going to pick up some extra strong plastic bags from his van. I didn't have to ask what for. At last we were alone.

She set two medium sized cases on the bed and started packing as I began running through options as to where we might go.

"You decide," she said, finally growing exasperated with my dithering and my thinking aloud. "Wait, I get you Yellow Pages."

The snappy speed with which she executed her packing and tidying made me think that we might be ready to leave in an hour. In 10 months she'd accumulated no more than someone staying in a hotel for 10 days. This trip had never been about living in London, learning the culture, the language–this had been all about money. Money for her, money to send home.

I scribbled down some names on a chit of paper and made some calls. I explained that my friend had been subject to an inordinate delay at the airport, information which was probably more helpful to my state of mind, I realised, than any of the hotel staff I was speaking to. I finally settled on a 2-star between Park Royal and Edgware.

Once she was packed, she wiped the floor with a rag, still in her underwear and shirt, me standing there sometimes gawking at that pretty arse in the air thinking what a fool I was. We decided to wash the knife, replace the blade, bag it and I would dispose of it later. It was I who insisted we wipe down surfaces–not to erase her fingerprints, I said, rather, the prints of the guy she'd killed.

I heard the opening and closing of the front door again. She signalled to me and disappeared to the kitchen/living room.

An hour later, I was standing at the front door amid bags and cases waiting for a mini cab. Sisi was talking to her friend from the top of the bathroom steps–he'd forbidden her to enter, the sight was too disgusting, she reported back to me. I expected to smell human offal drifting round the corner, but perhaps he hadn't got that far yet.

My mobile was ringing. Our taxi was here. Sisi called to her friend. I heard a nasal grunt in reply. We opened the door and stumbled forth with her things. I led the way to a smoking exhaust. A door opened, a man got out, suitably funereal with his greeting. I handed him our things and told Sisi to get in the car. The street was as quiet as an empty stage. I got in the car, having to take a couple of bags on my lap. I gave the man directions and we set off.

I felt strangely calm, as if we were heading off for a spa weekend together. I'd done what any other man would have done. I couldn't let her be dragged back to Thailand, raped and executed for killing a bent and violent cop. My thigh, warm against hers in the back of the car, the road moving with hopeful speed beneath our feet, my eyes returned again and again to those dark, bushy eyes reflected in the slit of glass our driver was checking every few seconds. Was he committing us to memory? W2 went rolling by like waves on a harbour charged for a storm. I took Sisi's hand in mine. Our palms kissed, cold and dry. She didn't look at me when I turned to look at her. I squeezed her hand, but she didn't squeeze back. She was looking obsessively out the window, chewing the end of a finger. She could have been bored or anxious. She looked like a girl who is used to this kind of shit. Lonely. She was harder than I'd figured her to be. I had no confidence that I would hear from her again after tomorrow. And perhaps that was for the best.

CHAPTER

13

We stepped out of a coffin-size lift onto a third floor, passed along a strip of algae coloured carpet through some double doors–with a comical cacophony of luggage. No other sounds but the atmosphere of the building, our breath, as we stopped outside the room with our key and its chunky ring and number tag. I unlocked the door and gestured for Sisi to walk in ahead of me. I followed with two heavy bags, returned to the corridor and picked up the two lighter ones I'd been carrying, and closed the door behind me. The room was furnished in dark woods, crimsons and salmon pinks. Very English. The air reeked of old polish and toilet lemon. Also very English. I threw open the window as Sisi sat on the bed. I could see the mattress lacked the firmness she was accustomed to. Our journey had taken us just over ten minutes but I felt as though we'd taken half a lifetime to arrive at a room that wasn't her FUCKING room, a space where we might stand a chance of behaving like a couple together. There was just one slight problem: someone had been murdered.

The night was chilly, so I soon shut the window.

I was thinking about Sylvia when Sisi said, "Perhaps you have to go?"

It was already 2.15 AM. If I got a taxi outside the door I wouldn't be home until nearly 3AM. If I stayed and returned at first light, Sylvia would no longer have mere grounds for suspicion, she would know. Sisi didn't wait for an answer–she was on her feet, moving about the room, opening closet doors and drawers.

I went over to stand by one of the open drawers.

"Sisi."

But she acted as if she hadn't heard, kept pulling garments from her case, until she stood up again and I put my hands out and said her name again, gently contriving a way of getting her to stop a moment without seizing her by the wrists. She paused, darting me a glance that hurt because it told me she was thinking I now reckoned I had some right to fuck her and spend the whole night with her for the first time.

"Yes?"

Suddenly I didn't know what to say.

"You're tired, yeah?" she said.

This, I realised, had been the question forming on my own lips. Grinding my teeth involuntarily, I said, Yes, I was–not that my mind was even close to rest, but to have said I wasn't would have signalled immediately that I wanted more details from her about what had happened.

I sat on the crunchy end of the bed. Her shoulders dropped and she sat with me–out of courtesy, it seemed, not because she wanted to talk things through. I could almost believe I'd have to shell out notes on the bedspread before she entertained me with an account of the events leading up to this murder.

"I told you," she began flopping her wrist on the bed, a little stroppy, clearly tired, "this man bother me, always want anal sex, I say, 'Go to other girls if you want that, I don't like it, OK?' He didn't come round for long time, so I thought he's gone away–yeah?–but then he come tonight, using different name… He had knife."

"I thought you said you used your own knife?"

She looked blank for a moment, then, "Yeah, I use my knife, but he t'reaten me with *his* knife first."

"OK. I didn't see it, I didn't see another knife."

She just stared at me like my own Burmese cat tensing as he sensed a possible hostile reaction.

"Arun deal with it."

"Arun – your friend, back at the flat?"

"Yeah."

My heart was beating faster as I pictured the scene, which disturbingly I found strangely arousing.

"He tried rape me–without condom, without condom, yeah?" I might have expected tears to flow, but her eyes were dry, she seemed only fractious–what had happened had been an everyday hazard, except that tonight the guy had violated agency protocol, namely, that a girl had to consent to a sexual practice outside of the norm. "I was scared, I tried to stop him–"

"Sweetheart, it's OK–"

"I hit him on the head," gesturing the motion, "with beer bottle. It was on the side of bed, near window, you know?"

"– it's OK, I'm not challenging you, OK? I just– Did he ejaculate inside you?"

"No. He nearly get inside but not come."

"Well that's something, I guess. At least you won't have caught Aids if he had it."

"I hit him again," she continued, apparently uninterested in the Aids angle, "and again, but he still not down." I watched her chest rising and falling, waiting for her to finish, but she'd drifted off into a sort of reverie.

"And then?" I prompted gently.

She was looking at the fingers of her right hand on the bed between us as she said, "I got the knife... I killed him."

"How?"

"Many time in the back, when he was on the floor in doggy position."

"Doggy position?" I struggled to hide my nervous smirk and was relieved when she smirked too and briefly we laughed.

"Yes, you know, right?–"

'Yeah, I know, sure, I–Christ. So then you stabbed him–before he could get up?'

"Yes. He was going to kill me. For sure."

I took her hand in mine to console her. She took it away after only a few seconds saying it was over now, nothing we could do. She reminded me I probably should go now. Sending me away, back to my middle-class home and wife and kids, a world she'd been working so hard to reach through the sale of her body.

She moved up the bed, toward the pillow, kicking off her shoes. Bringing her knees up to her chest and, linking her fingers round her shins, lay her forehead on her knees, her long mane of hair cascading over her thighs.

Looking at her in the grainy yellow light in this strange hotel room, I was reminded of Sylvia's recent college work. She'd taken a series of digital photos of Mia and superimposed them on digital shots of her own oil paintings of bare and isolated spaces to create a new synthesis of loneliness, longing and latent hysteria evocative of horror movies like *Ring*. Thinking of those images of my own daughter caught in a contemplative state, I pictured myself trying to engage Sylvia's sympathy in Sisi's plight, but of course the image scrambled in a second. How naïve. Why did I even want to involve her? It wasn't that I wanted Sylvia's pity–sadly, I think this would have been her immediate reaction to my telling her the truth of what had happened tonight–I wanted greater understanding between us; in that moment of sitting on the bed facing Sisi I imagined that if Sylvia were a witness to what I was seeing right now, she might be moved enough later to find some new way of expressing her own sense of loneliness and vulnerability to me other than through paintings and gestures, those aloof silences of hers. Except, of course, that could never happen. A mere concept in my head. No one could know. The reality was bleak and I feared the worst. A Thai girl far away from home and now afraid of returning there. That Thai corpse I'd carried to her bathtub had raped her. A customer. I was a customer. She had never truly given herself to me, I had always paid for her. Even the first time, which she said was 'free', had been repayment of a kind for the dental treatment I'd given her. As I chewed my cheeks, my mind spinning on the spot, then racing off like a bat into the night, it occurred to me she might even lash out at me if I so much as touched her with any overt tenderness. I was floundering for a means of eliciting some sign of trust. Poor girl. She'd had enough for one night. And, frankly, so had I.

I got to my feet.

"OK. I'll let you get some sleep."

Slowly she raised her head and looked at me. I read stubborn impassiveness. I tried to smile, but felt I was almost twitching. Finally a look of relief and gratitude arrived in her eyes and her full lips smiled for me the first time that night.

"We'll speak tomorrow, OK?"

She nodded.

I moved to the door, paused on a creaking floorboard.

"I think you should tell the agency you can't work. This guy might have told someone he was going to see you."

"I don't think so. I'm not regular for him. I don't see him for two or t'ree month, no connection!" She was moving about on the bed, unsettled by my lingering instruction.

"Sisi, you just killed someone," I said, suddenly sharpening my approach and dropping my voice to a harsh whisper. "This friend of yours is cutting him up as we speak, and you just disappeared from your flat without warning–you have to lie low."

"Yes, I know. I do this." She dropped her palms on her naked thighs, expressing exasperation.

"OK." *So why's she shouting at me, that's all I wanted to hear.*

"I have saving," she added, returning to a more reasonable manner. "Maybe I go to other city."

"So you mean like Birmingham, Manchester?–put your face on an agency up there and now there's an address for you in Birmingham, Manchester? What's that tell people? One minute you're in London, the next minute you're in Birmingham. And for all you know there's a friend of this guy you killed checking all the oriental escort agencies looking for a girl who–who–who's just made a sudden house move. Sisi, I know you want to make money, but don't get careless, or what you fear will happen."

My little outburst had drained me precipitously. I was afraid she'd notice I was trembling and ask me if I were on drugs, so, grinding my back teeth, I reached for the ledge of the nearby radiator cover and gripped hard.

"I'll be OK," she said simply, like a recalcitrant teenager.

"You involved me in this," I didn't mind adding. "It's called obstruction of justice and it carries jail time. Now, I want to help you, but I have to believe you won't do anything stupid."

"I want to stop anyway. I'm very bored."

So maybe the guy hadn't 'raped' her, maybe she'd just got bored of number one hundred-and-whatever… "OK, good. You'd better give me that packet. I'll get rid of it."

She got to her feet to root out a bag–we'd wrapped the knife she'd used in the murder in plenty of newspaper and then in a cellophane bag. I took it from her. I hadn't a clue what I'd do with it yet.

"Are you OK?" she asked me.

I looked at the door, knowing I couldn't leave yet, before saying this: "Sisi, I want to be with you, you know that, right?"

She stared back at me impassively and I nearly added: 'always', but perhaps my pause made that clear. As I drew breath, containing an impulse to go to her and gather in my arms, she jumped off the bed and came to me for a hug. The softness and flatness of her belly against my groin, the fullness of her lips, the rich sap of her scent flipped my doubts about us and I was hers again, so utterly hers.

"Take care," she said as I opened the door. "And thank you."

Stepping into the corridor I felt that nitty gritty seed of hope again scratching in the cracks of my cynical heart, trying to find root.

I arrived home just after 4AM–clutching the bag with the knife like a lunatic, paranoid that the police would pick me up and charge me for possession of a deadly weapon or worse. I'd been in such a state of preoccupation I'd completely forgotten to think of stashing it somewhere. So I walked back up the street. I came to an overflowing skip and buried it there, under some rubble and returned home, hoping for the best.

I took the toothbrush and toothpaste into the other bathroom. The Sonicare's tingling sensation on my coked-up gums was so pleasing I thought to go again. But didn't. I slipped into bed, cold and shivery. Sylvia stirred, but her breathing remained deep. I stared at the facing wall and imagined a prison cell. The events spun around and around in my head like a crazy merry-go-round that would never stop.

I was finally nodding off when the alarm went at 6.30 for Sylvia. She'd expect me to get up at 7.15 to help rouse and dress the kids. Less a marriage than a team operation. How would she manage all by herself when we split? People do. Perhaps she could quit making lunches–perhaps school dinners aren't as awful as they used to be now that celebrity chef Jamie Oliver has kicked up a fuss about our deplorable British standards on TV.

Pulling my trousers on, I was surprised to find I wasn't noticeably tired. That would come later, I supposed–hopefully not in the middle of anything fiddly at the practice.

"So what time did you get back?" Sylvia asked with a beguiling smile as I entered the kitchen scratching at stubble, ruffling my hair like a younger chap.

"Dunno, 'bout 3.30?"

She pulled a face, busy making toast for everyone but me, so she wasn't likely to exact a full inquiry now. But knowing that she was bound to ask later, when I least expected it, I volunteered some information: shortly after my badminton game with Neil I'd received a call from a mate who'd just had his teeth kicked in by some happy slappers and was in desperate need of help. She scoffed and said, I'd been getting rather a lot of these emergency calls recently, but my little faux detail about happy slapping, seemed to deflect some of her suspicion, probably because she herself had been talking about this recent, disturbing phenomenon only a few days ago, a apropos a newspaper article.

"Is that what he said–happy slapping?"

"Yes."

The oddity of the phrase plucked the girls from their semi slumber and they began giggling, Mia repeating the phrase louder and louder as if it was the funniest thing she'd ever heard.

"It's not funny," Sylvia said, "it's serious; it's bullying."

But the girls carried on slapping each other in play, laughing, until Sylvia snapped and banged the table with the flat of her hand and told them to stop it. "How would you like to be bullied by a gang of teenagers, kicked to death maybe, in the street, just as a sick joke?" she levelled at them.

They looked bewildered by the intensity of their mother's seriousness; they simply hadn't the years in order to comprehend it.

"Your dad just had to fix someone's teeth because of this–these types of people."

The kids looking duly admonished, Sylvia resumed with me:

"So did you go down to the practice and treat him there?"

"Yes."

"Wouldn't he have been better off at the A&E?"

"Sylvia, all I know is this guy calls me up, he thinks he's going to need a couple of crowns, he doesn't trust the NHS lot–" I paused to take a mouthful of cereal.

"Why couldn't you call, though? Or text?"

"I know, I'm sorry–I was distracted, I guess."

She might have been about to remind me that my recently distracted mind was in fact a selfish mind, but the girls, sensitive to early signs of parental storms, were talking over us in faintly pleading voices about costumes for a school play and the subject was swept aside for the time being.

"Is he going to be OK?"

"With a couple of crowns, yeah."

Her shoulders sagged with despair. I nodded concurrently as I pictured Sisi's hand scissoring down on the back of a bent cop–in the doggy position.

As my family filed out the door, Sylvia turned and waved a fond goodbye, her eyes seeking mine as if checking on where we were together, whether I was the person she still had a future with. I felt she wasn't interested in nailing the truth about what I'd really been up to–perhaps I'd done some emergency work, but then where had I got to?–only as to whether I was intent on keeping up the lies I was telling her. Something had shifted and she wasn't saying what. I did a complete 180° in my thinking and considered the possibility she was seeing someone. But if I thought of her pattern of coming and going, unless she was skipping college, which I thought unlikely given how committed she was, it couldn't be 'serious'. Then again, it seems nearly all relationships start as 'not serious'; it's the 'not serious' ones that surreptitiously grow roots.

I stood by the window as the car engine started up. I thought to wave. How I ached to wave. Sylvia hadn't noticed me, and nor had the girls. Was I becoming invisible to them? Like a figure who doesn't know he's a ghost.

CHAPTER 14

For weeks my sleep has been troubled. I've been having this recurring dream which I'm sure is in fact a lost memory that seems to have been dislodged by the fall into the pool and the July bombings. I'm with my older brother at the end of the garden at our home in Surrey. We're messing about by the canal bank and a bonfire we've got going. Myles is rolling oak leaf cigarettes and we're puffing away like old Red Indian Chiefs on the Westerns we used to love. There's a whole heap of leaves and trash to burn through and we keep topping up the fire as it burns its way down the bonfire frame. I must be about ten or eleven years' old and my brother two years my senior. It's our first summer in England and we still speak with strong US *aksents,* which fact just about everyone at school has to make a joke about even 6 months' on. In among the rubbish we find some aerosol cans. We throw one in, not really knowing they'd do anything but slowly melt into the soil. It's just as well we're standing back lighting up another oak leaf cigar as the first one goes off–just like a bomb. *Wow, that's cool. Let's go again.* We'd never made bombs before. So we throw another aerosol on the fire and duck down behind the belly overhang of the compost heap. After a time we get bored and a little scared of these things splitting apart about our heads and we start ruminating over the kinds of things we'll do when we're big enough to drive cars. By and by we hear a crack of twigs and peep over the edge of the compost to take a look. It's that pretty tomboy girl who comes to play with the boring idiot we got for a next-door neighbour. She's about my age, and she's so pretty–not that I admit that to anyone–it hurts like when you want to pee and you can't. We duck down. *Shh.* She's sniffing around the bonfire. We could pop up and say, Boo! It occurs to me to stand up and warn her to keep away, but the fire looks pretty dead, so I just keep watching her, fascinated by the sweet vulnerability of the nape of her bare neck in the summer blouse (she had short hair, unusual back then). I've just ducked down again, worried she saw me, when all of a sudden there's this big bang and my brother and I, we have to clap our hands over our mouths to stop from shrieking with laughter. But then, as we stick our heads up over the compost heap, there's this godawful scream. And you just know it's never gonna stop, tearing through the air with even more violence than the bombs, singeing the roots of our hair and ripping into your chest like a hot poker. *Oh, man, why's she holding her face like that, why's she doing that? It wasn't our fault, we didn't know, we didn't know, we thought that last one we threw on there was a dudd…!*

And that's usually when I wake up–with a cough, as though I could taste the smoke from the bonfire.

I try to remember the girl's name, what happened to her. Didn't she lose an eye? No one went to jail. It was all just a terrible accident. Maybe the fall-out of that bomb helped Myles and me knuckle down to some studying from that time on. Somehow mucking around with dangerous shit wasn't such a cool idea any more. We could have gone to visit her, but we didn't, we avoided her, we nursed ourselves through our guilt until we were whole again. So we thought.

Now I wake wondering where that girl is, what became of her. And I realise there's something going on here between Sisi and me that has some bearing on what happened at that bonfire. Can I honestly say I haven't imagined myself as Sisi's guardian angel and that some of what draws me to her is a long residing sense of guilt for what I did thirty years ago?

Sometimes I'm woken not by dreams but by a headache or numbness in my fingers. I shake my hands like castanets and the feeling returns in seconds, but then some nights the numbness comes back every hour or so. All this since the accident. My tossing and turning has begun to piss Sylvia off–because I ought to have insisted on being referred to a specialist. The point being, I'm affecting *her* with my headaches. When I offered to sleep in the spare room, she sighed as if I were trying to make a point of feeling sorry for myself. "I suppose if we had sex every night you'd sleep like a baby," she said caustically on one occasion. Almost out of childish spite, instead of digging out a number for BUPA, I'd called Sonia. And for a few weeks after that my sleep did improve–significantly. So maybe Sylvia was right–I just needed regular sex again and I'd be fine, I told myself. But the relief must have been due to a kind of placebo effect, because the sleeplessness and headaches and numbness returned with a vengeance, even though my fitness–from all the gym work–had improved. But I didn't wake in the middle of the night asking myself, Do I go back to the uninterested GP and insist on seeing a specialist? I woke with the fear of the hunted, asking hundreds of questions about a murder I was in on.

Newspapers. Local newspapers that covered the area she lived in. My fingertip black from the ink and feverish licking. Local TV, local news on bbc.co.uk.

Three days go by and nothing. No word from Sisi, either. I feared calling her in case she'd already been arrested by the police and the police had her phone and would trace the call through phone records.

"Have a nice weekend, Tony!" my staff called out as they left Friday afternoon.

"You too!" I called back breaking out in another cold sweat. I took a lungful of nitrous oxide to decompress before returning home. I pictured myself at the police station in a bare interview room, doubled over in giggles before photos of a dismembered Thai cop.

I badly needed to be alone with my worries.

"But you don't live alone," Sylvia reminded me Saturday morning–when I thought I caught a glimpse of her being about to add: Not yet anyway. "They're probably picking up on your mood," Sylvia remarked when I vented to her about the girls' own listless and intransigent mood. "What's the matter with you?" she needled. I simply absented myself from the room. At around six in the evening Sylvia announced she was going out. She busied herself with the buttons on her coat, avoiding my eyes and omitting to say where–I felt I had no right even to ask.

Sunday started in a similar vein until an entertaining episode of *Six Feet Under* Sylvia had taped some days ago provided a medium through which she and I could resume civil dialogue. Quite unexpectedly gasping over the mess of the characters' lives led us to a clearing that was free of the thick bracken of emotion of the past few weeks and laughed, freely expressing old longings and there was warmth between us. But neither of us had the courage to linger. So we got up and, within minutes, were busy tidying the kitchen and doing our respective toiletries, winding down to that routinely awkward moment in the bedroom when we'd turn away from each other as we undressed and got into our old pyjamas in low light.

Monday's return to the work and school routine offered the fresh possibility that everything bad that had happened in the previous week was already drifting swiftly away from me – rush the kids' teeth, remind Michaela to floss, yelps from Mia as Mum tugs at the knots in her hair because she's pissed off at me that I forgot to read and comment upon her college essay… I pulled on my gloves, my mask, my loupes… and burrowed my confusion into a few hundred teeth…

But the pungent sour sweet of resin kept reminding me there was a corpse in my cupboard.

How I longed to smell that delicate breath of sweet basil and garlic with a hint of lingering tobacco. But she hadn't called.

And why hadn't Neil called? Just walking off like that. But then I saw he had – twice, (missed calls) and remembered I'd put off calling him back until I could better control the chronic trembling that had attached itself to my voice, a parasite of fear.

By Friday afternoon, more than a week since I'd last seen Sisi and the seventh day of leaving messages on her mobile, worry had given way to anger and indignation. It was time to DO something. So I finished early that day and took the tube to Edgware. I needn't have bothered. Doing his best to refrain from a disdainful smirk, the acne-scarred man at the desk said, Yep, the Thai lady had checked out on Monday morning. Nope, she hadn't left a message. His guttural exhalation that followed seemed to intimate he had more pressing concerns to be dealing with than the comings and goings of the tarts of Siam.

So that was it, was it, I'd lost her. Disappeared. I couldn't blame her; I might have done the same in her shoes. I was still mad though. Like a father who's fallen out with his own daughter. But no, I mustn't confuse things, she wasn't blood. Just *blood on my hands.*

On the weekend I took the girls to see my parents. My mother had recently been to a second consultant who, after the second visit, suggested her diarrhoea might have been caused by the anti inflammatory drug she was on. My father had come down from the mount and said unto his wife, Thou shalt give it a go. And miracle of miracles, her diarrhoea had eased off dramatically. He was so pleased and relieved I hadn't the heart to say, I told you so.

On arrival, my parents gave a display of being sorry Sylvia hadn't been able to come, too, which I read as their discreet way of intimating that they hoped we weren't about to divorce. I smiled and made little of the fact it was the second time in a row she hadn't been able to come. With a second glass of wine in my hand, I found myself talking of her various activities as devoted mum and mature student in quietly edifying terms–less her husband than her personal manager and PR person–even as I wondered vaguely whether she mightn't be using the afternoon for rather more fucking than folio work. And yet, for the first time in days I managed to push Sisi from my thoughts and immerse myself in my mother's recovery–she looked surprisingly well considering the way she'd lost all that weight, almost getting her old figure back–and the girls' sometimes delirious counterpoint and theatre as they engaged so charmingly with their grandparents.

In fact it wasn't until the middle of the new week that I thought of Sisi. And I might not have thought of her at all but for Neil's phone call. He caught me at a good time–with time to kill, as I'd arrived early to pick up the kids from school one afternoon–and I was happy to hear from him. His tone and approach were cagey to begin with, clearly he still felt he might have overstepped the mark that night in the Earl's Court apartment, though he made no allusion to it and nor did I, except to thank him for the twenty pound note.

"Was it enough?"

"Yeah, sure!"– and I insisted on repaying him when we next met.

"Oh, no worries, next drink's on you."

He asked me about Sisi–Had she begun to show any sign she might be interested in jacking in her job? Was I still seeing her? There was nothing in his voice that intimated he would scoff if I were–which struck me as slightly ironic, given that he'd taken me to Apartment 117 as a 'cure' for Sisi. Instead of saying, 'Well that's probably for the best,' when I told him I'd lost touch, he began raking around for clues as to her whereabouts like a novice sleuth.

"What about that Japanese girl you visited with her? She might know."

"I don't remember her address."

"Call the agency. Maybe they know something."

"They possibly do," I said, not wanting to believe my own words, "but they wouldn't say anything to a customer, would they?"

"They might. You were one of her regulars."

I winced inwardly at *'one of'*.

When I finally cut him short to tell him that actually I thought I was getting over her and that I believed it was for the best to let her go, he said that was a shame, and I really felt that in spite of the scorn he'd poured over the very possibility of my ever having a future with Sisi, the story had so spiced up his life, the better part of him had bought into my dream–he appeared genuinely sorry to see it disappear.

"You never know," he concluded, "she still might call you. Women often call you when you least expect it."

The call exhausted me, even if, strangely, it had lifted my hopes a fraction. It was windy and cold and I fancied stopping off at a local café, but I had a call to make and didn't want to be overheard. So I found a bench in the park near the church on Turnham Green, fifty yards across from a Homeless Guy and his carrier bags and dialled SONIA on my phone. I got through to Andrew, the gently-spoken Scot.

"Sonia? Yeah, the Thai girl you like… I'm sorry Anthony but we had to let her go."

"How come?"

"We were having so much trouble with her, it just wasn't worth it."

"Can you tell me what kind of trouble?"

"Well, I can't really go into it, I'm sure you understand, but she was messing us about–when she was available, how much she was making... Customers were complaining that she was very moody. She'd probably had enough. Y'know some people can't do this for too long–it's not what you'd call a long-term career unless you're very thick-skinned."

I could hear a young child's whine in the background growing louder. The stay-at-home dad who sells girls' bodies for nappy money.

"Excuse me a minute, Anthony "

I waited a half-minute while the child's noise drained away.

"Anthony? Sorry about that. Yeah, well, I'm sorry if you've missed her and she's not contacted you but as far as I can tell she's left the country."

"The country?"

"I've heard rumours from her friends that she's in Australia."

"Australia?!"

"Yeah. I've seen her face on sites out there, so she must be doing the same kind of work out there."

"OK. Uh, did she–did she leave an e-mail, any kind of contact details?"

"I don't think so. We didn't leave on favourable terms, but I'll check and get back to you on this number if you like."

I thanked him and hung up. Absurdly I saw myself at Heathrow Airport with passport and e-mail ticket, checking in with a single bag. I saw myself saying to Sylvia that she'd suggested I take a break, so that's what I was doing, as if Australia was the equivalent of Brighton for an afternoon. It wouldn't be that difficult to track her down if she was working out there. I saw myself in Sydney on my mobile phone, making a booking under the name of Jack. A man who travels half way across the world to find her–surely that was all the proof she needed. It was more than Julia Roberts ever got in *Pretty Woman.* And of course I'd bring flowers, flowers more exotic than I'd ever find in London flower stalls.

I smiled wanly to myself. Pure fantasy. I had a family to look after, even if it was on the verge of breaking up and perhaps precisely because it was breaking up I was needed even more. No, that was it. Sisi, aka Sonia, was out of my life.

Except, she wasn't, was she.

"You want to come and see me?" It was her, only two days after my last call with Andrew, and she was purring into my earpiece so close I could practically feel her body rub against mine, catch a whiff of her scent.

"Australia?" Clearly she wasn't amused by the rumour. "No. Who told you that?"

"Andy, the Scottish guy at the agency."

Silence. Her call had found me watching the TV news. Sylvia had just stepped into a shower. I needed some answers quickly.

"You didn't call, Sisi, I asked you to call."

"I've been very busy." *Fucking.*

I sat up sharp and lowered the TV volume just enough so that if Sylvia got out of her shower earlier than usual the volume would mask my words. "Where are you?"

"I moved to new apartment. It's OK. I'm with my friend. She's nice." I detected a slur in her voice, and thought, *beer again.*

"She's a working girl?"

"Yes."

"You can trust her?"

"Yeah, sure. I knew her in Thailand. She's Chinese but she speak very good Thai."

"So what're your plans, what're you–Did everything go alright with–y'know–the guy, Arun and his, uh, his package?"

"Package? What's this?"

"Y'know, the, uh, his job, in the bathroom?"

There was a pause. It didn't sound good–

"Yeah… the customer, you mean?"

"Yeah, the dirty cop."

"Yeah, it's OK."

"You're sure of that?"

There was a further pause, or rather, a sort of vacuum of intelligence, until she said: "Wait a minute, will you?" But was she addressing me? I wondered.

Her mouth had been away from her phone as she'd said this. She had to be speaking to someone in the room or just coming into the room. And it wouldn't have been her flatmate, because she spoke 'good Thai.'

"Sisira?"

Silence. Then a rustling of paper out of which her voice reappeared as if lunging back at her phone and mine–"Hello?"

"Yeah, I'm here. Is everything OK?"

"Yeah, everything OK." Jesus, she could really work on her reassurance technique. "Are you angry with me?"

I said, no, I wasn't angry, I was worried about her.

"You want to come see me? I get lonely."

I bit my lip. "Not tonight. I can't."

"You call me?"

"How about tomorrow night?"

"Anytime." Anytime sounded good, if only because it suggested she'd had the sense to quit working for a while; I'd been afraid she'd go and join a new agency straight away. I asked her to text me her new address, more probing questions could wait 24 hours.

Just before Sisi said goodbye I heard the clink of metal on glass. It sounded as though it were coming from the other side of the room. Just how lonely was she?

CHAPTER 15

I arrived at Sisi's new address, a three-storey terrace, some ten minutes from Royal Oak, around 8.30 the next evening. I walked down the steps to 1A, a basement flat. A dodgy bell again, but at least she heard it. A slender figure emerged from shadows; Sisi opened the glass door, squinting at the light. Though I was happy to see her, my heart sank decoding the dressing gown and underwear. I didn't want that, I'd come to talk, hopefully have a bite to eat together. OK, I'd brought a wad of cash with me, but I'd told myself this was to help her through the week if she looked as though she needed it.

As we embraced–"Hi, baby–my back stiffened. There was something choreographed about her move on me. And yet, why shouldn't she be glad to see me, hadn't I helped her out of a tight spot, hadn't she invited me round for dinner?–(just the two of us, she'd promised). Determined to overcome my initial awkwardness, I smiled graciously and handed over an economical if fresh bouquet of white roses, which she greeted with refreshed laughter, as if in acknowledgment of a now enduring ritual, and an expensive bottle of French Viognier, which she took from me as though it were a piece of rubbish she'd carelessly left in the corridor.

As I stepped into the lobby of her new, shared apartment, she slinked off to my right, to the kitchen, carrying flowers and wine, saying I could walk through to her room at the end. Heading down the low-ceilinged, dark corridor, I passed a closed door showing a pencil of light, to her bedroom. A robust double bed took up its job-important position in the middle of the wall on my left, a pine chest of drawers stood straight in front of me and to the right of the window, and to my immediate right stood a beech-veneer closet. She'd lit some candles, but they didn't quite dispel the forlorn atmosphere, not entirely created by the drabness of the interior or the paucity of natural light. Already I missed that front living room kitchen where we'd had the little gathering, the table with the vase that had waited for me to adorn it with flowers, the clean wood floors…

I sat on the bed and waited. Like a customer, but telling myself I wasn't going to be one today. At the top of a couple of steps a doorway at the far corner of the room led to her bathroom in which she must have lit a few candles that flickered out of sight like quietly gossiping tongues. On the floor beside the bed I noticed an overflowing ashtray, something I'd never seen in her old room. Was this good or bad? On the one hand it suggested she wasn't seeing customers; (why clean up if you have no visitors?) On the other, it suggested she was letting herself go. In the beginning she'd claimed she had a way of dealing with the job– "It's OK… it's just sex… sometimes the guys are nice"–but more recently, she'd complained of the long nights, the hours of waiting up for customers who didn't turn up or arrived drunk, smelly, leery-eyed and argumentative. But until that call and that terrified cry on the phone that had squeezed my adrenals dry, it had been a means of making pretty good money. Who knows how much. Maybe 2,000 a week–tax-free, presumably. People can have the stupidest, most mind-numbing jobs and then miss them when they're unemployed. She was now more vulnerable than she'd probably care to admit: smoking, drinking… what next? Without agency work, she was prey to the sharp eye of a local pimp with a sideline in smack. He spots her at a local deli in her unwashed perm, her high heels and sexy silver jewellery. He gets her on his white horse and the rest is what you've seen at the movies, ad nauseam.

So it was with sadness in my eyes that I looked up to see her coming in to join me. But, hey, she had a glass of wine in each hand–it was the first time she'd joined me with wine–and she was cheerful; it was a brittle cheerfulness, I suspected, but it deserved every bit of encouragement I could muster for this reunion.

"Kampai!" we said, clinking glasses.

I took a sip. The Viognier's peachiness carried a band of tangerine, a pleasingly delayed hint of oak… and I dared to look forward to summer and better times for us both.

"How have you been?" her hand already on my thigh, caressing me.

I suppressed an absurd laugh.

"Why you laugh?"

"No, I'm fine, just–y'know–a little concerned as to your whereabouts. The dead body… boring stuff like that."

With Sisi, I realised, I frequently surpassed myself in the art of understatement.

"I've been here," she answered, as if she felt I was unjustly accusing her of hiding from me.

"Well yeah, I can see you've been here, but…" I glanced away at the walls as if I might use them as a surface against which to whack the balls of vexation popping up in my brain. Was this some kind of cultural divide, or was she just being so fucking obtuse in order that I crawl back into my role as 'nice customer' and shut the fuck up? I put my hand on her hand, the one resting on my thigh–to stop it and to hold it and to earth my own temper.

"So you're OK?"

She nodded. She withdrew her hand and slipped from the bed. She took a packet of cigarettes from off the chest of drawers and turned round.

"It's OK if I smoke?"

"Sure."

She lit up and returned to the bed, blowing the smoke away from me like a sixties film star.

"Just tell me if it bother you."

"It's OK."

"Last time you were coughing, so…"

"Yeah," nearly laughing, because this time I was practically choking with the need to quiz her on her friend's body disposal skills, "but that was weeks ago; I had a cold."

"You're OK now?"

She was talking on automatic pilot again, the kinds of questions I'd weeks ago asked her to quit asking me, I didn't want my ego stroked, I wanted *her,* not Sonia; or, at the very least, Sisi's attention. And she was so much brighter than this. OK, maybe a Thai degree wasn't an English degree, but simple she wasn't. She had a raw and nimble intelligence, a natural canniness I'd always found so exciting for being a little scary. Those sudden animal-like flashes in her eyes had kept me on my toes whenever I'd challenged her wit or her will in conversation. So why this fake, low-key bullshit?

"What happened with the guy, your friend? Did he manage to get rid of the–y'know–the bags?"

She pursed her lips, exhaling and nodding at the same time. It wasn't entirely convincing, but then again, what would have convinced me?

"So what are your plans?"

"Are we going to talk about the future all night?" extinguishing her cigarette over any such presumption she was game. "I don't know what my future is." It hurt she hadn't used my name in that reply, or even 'baby', something warm. She gave a shake of her mane of hair, her cheeks flushed, her chin tilted, full lips pouting. The fan-like eyelids flashed warnings at me in the silence suspended between us. But I felt my blood rise, too, I didn't care any more if we didn't enjoy a bath together or fuck, we had to thrash this out–

"Sisi, look–" I got to my feet, I put down the wine glass on her bedside table, beside a purple lampshade, "I'm involved in a murder–"

"No no, you not, *I'm* involved, my *friend* involved–" she interrupted adamantly.

"How can you say that?" She leaned back, contriving to look down her nose at me. "I mean, I can think of at least *one* person who saw me with you that night. No, two. The taxi driver *and* the hotel receptionist. That's excluding your friend–about whom I know fuck all really. How do I know I can trust him? How do *you* know?"

"He's good friend in Thailand."

"Well great, but y'know what? Even best friends have a habit of turning bad when murder's involved. I need to know you're going to be sensible and I need to know you're going to be–OK… and whether I can help. There's no–given the circumstances, you're so casual about communicating with me."

I saw her chest tremble as she inhaled the next breath, either finally moved by the feeling in my voice, or about to explode in a temper.

"I'm scared," she said–but she looked more fed up than scared.

"I thought we agreed you were going to lie low for a while. Surely that makes sense after what's happened. But instead, I come here–and–and you're sharing with another girl, who no doubt works for the same agency that sent you that thug, the man you killed," suddenly lowering my voice.

"How do you know I share with working girl?"

"Because that's pretty much the only company you keep." I paused. "So why not introduce us. I bet all the money in my wallet she's slim and very pretty. And I bet this flat is owned or leased by the agency. Right?"

She refused to look at me.

"And I'll also wager too that you're working again."

"London's very expensive city."

"I know, I know it is! But surely you have some savings that would allow you to lie low for a while. You seem to be acting as though nothing happened!"

I thought I caught the earliest beginnings of a childish smirk before she threw her hair back over her shoulder to re-establish an air of self-propriety.

"Maybe I go to America. I'd like to see New York."

Her face suddenly lit up as if right there on Broadway looking up at the neon signs.

"America?" I queried, newly deflated.

"I can't say yet. Maybe."

I sat back down on the bed with a sigh. I interlinked my fingers and despaired of ever being able to bring Sisi and me together like nicely interlinking fingers.

She came to sit beside me.

"You want bath? It's cold, isn't it?"

"You ran a bath?"

She nodded. Her hand came to touch mine.

I let my head drop back and sighed and, still looking upward, said, "I've so missed you." I sighed again and felt some peace enter me finally, even as I wondered if what I missed was the idea of her, the idea of us, not the reality. I felt her arm slip round my middle and, as I turned to look at her, she pressed her body against mine.

"You're trembling," I heard her say as I rested my chin on her shoulder. She parted from me. "Heating not very good here. The boiler keeps going out."

"Are we eating?"

"If you want."

"I thought you said we'd eat."

"You want to stay long time?"

Gazing into her eyes I asked her if she was expecting any customers.

"No, I'm free whole night. But you pay me one hour? You he'p me, so I can pay rent?"

"I got–I dunno…" I pulled out my wallet–told myself I wasn't gonna do this–started counting out the notes. "190. I might need 40 for a taxi home."

"Thank you."

She scooped up the notes and took them to her chest of drawers and deposited them in the top drawer. It was the first time she'd let me see where she put her money. She closed the drawer, then went to check on the water.

I thought I'd lost her to Australia, now I could expect to lose her to America and the dejection I felt coloured my mood in the bath. When she asked me if there was something wrong, I said, no, I was fine, caressing her sides, her breasts, like a lunatic finding calm again now that he had his precious crystal to touch, over and over. I was simply so happy to be with her again my voice seemed less to convey words than echoes of longing.

When she'd finished washing my sex, she pulled out the plug. As I began to stand, she touched my knee and told me to stay. When the water was level at about six inches, she replaced the plug and urged me to lie back. She took my cock in her hand again and, squatting over me as if to pee, started rubbing herself with it, eyes closed. She'd done this before on the bed, but with a condom on. I lay still in the shallow water, gazing up at her, mesmerized by the play of candlelight on her honey coloured skin, her taut muscle tone, as she played into me as if I were just a tool for her pleasure. Finally she opened her eyes, very wide, and said,

"You go inside a little bit, but you don't come, OK? Just little bit."

She slid over me, a wet, silk purse. So long since I'd been inside a woman other than Sylvia free of rubber protection. The sensation was too much, as was the love surging back, the fear of what was happening to us–and I grabbed her waist with a slap of my palm, sucking in the next breath.

"Sisi–"

But she kept riding.

"Sisi, I can't hold back–"

"It's OK, I take pill."

She reached for my hands and squeezed. I thought to say, But what about Aids? But presumably she hadn't done this with anyone else… unless she'd turned suicidal.

When I came, she was still riding me, she planted her hands on my shoulders and rode harder, forcing my head down the bath into the water on the now soaked towel she'd put there as a cushion, squeezing every last drop out of me until I thought my stomach muscles would rip.

When she came she cried as if she'd spiked her foot on a spiny fish. Her nails dug into my skin as she tensed, as she bucked a few last times to eke out more from the spasms of pleasure. I'd never imagined we could be this naked together and I laughed, the way you laugh at the beguiling prospect of drowning on a tiny boat in calm waters. I squelched at my waterlogged ears. Why had she done that? In recognition of a new trust between us, or a farewell gift to remember her by? As if hearing my thoughts, she said: "You couldn't come last two times, so..." she gestured, "now you come. I wanted you to come." Still inside her, still semi-hard even, the cock more alive, eel-like without its customary skin of rubber, I hauled myself upright, my hands clasped firmly around the small of her back. We pressed close together. I was trembling again, a little cold in this dingy, draughty bathroom where there was no radiator–and my feelings naked again. She reached for the hot tap, then returned to my arms. We held that way until long after I'd slipped out of her and the water level had climbed up to our armpits.

"Please don't go," I whispered in her ear.

"Go where?"

"America... Anywhere."

She placed her head back on my shoulder and held me again. I had never felt so primal.

In the cramped little kitchen, arranging the flowers I'd brought with me as Sisi did her magic with garlic, ginger, chilli and Thai basil, I began airing all sorts of possibilities she might have were she to stay here as–

Christ, did I say that aloud?–as my wife! The word had just popped out and I hadn't even proposed, and then I just ran off with the concept as if it were a pot of magical fairy dust that would transform our fortunes if I simply cast it about. With indefinite leave to remain, she could act, she could dance, she could model, she could go to college… I had to rein myself in from saying we could have kids. Instead, *she* said it, as if it were the punch line and we laughed, almost dizzy from all this romantic folly in the air, the wine in our veins. Divorce could be done in just a few months through the Internet, I told her. And while we were waiting for that to go through, I'd pay for her rent and anything else she needed. She frowned and laughed and said I was crazy–Would I really do all that for her?! We hugged again in the kitchen, kissed deeply and I grew hard against her belly, believing I wanted nothing more in life than to have a baby with this girl. My muse. A dentist with a muse, fancy that–but why the hell not?

Right in the middle of all this madness, I grew aware of someone else in the room–a girl in a white dressing gown, black hair loose, no make-up.

"Hi," I said.

She looked surprised, as if she'd thought of herself as a ghost and now turned to Sisi apologising in Thai for having interrupted–and yet she must have heard I was here.

"I'm Anthony," I said and would normally have stepped forward to shake her hand but she looked so under the weather, I felt the gesture might strike her as unduly invasive.

"Hello." But she didn't give her own name. She had a deep voice for a slim girl of only 5'5"; I found it sexy, evocative of forties film stars like Lauren Bacall.

Sisi told me her friend wasn't so well. "Headache. Migraine."

The girl nodded, wincing as though another spasm were just coming on.

"Name?" I asked Sisi.

"Oh, Li Mei. We know each other in Thailand."

"Yeah, you said."

"Li Mei like me, she wants to stop working. She just do few jobs every week."

"Same agency?" I asked Li Mei.

Li Mei nodded solemnly. "I take break soon, go on holiday."

"Good for you. I wish *she'd* take a holiday," I said, glancing at Sisi. "Where're you going?"

"Bangkok. See my friend." She reached for a bowl from a cupboard.

Sisi had her back to me now, turning down the heat on the stove.

On a second look, even though not at her best, I could see Li Mei was quite beautiful. And infinitely watchable. Whereas Sisi's allure came so much from her lightness and changeableness, this girl's appeal lay in her smoky sensuality, her languid timing, her natural cinema.

"Li Mei wants to set up bar in Bangkok," Sisi was saying.

"OK. Why not Hong Kong?" I asked.

"You know I from Hong Kong?"

"Sisi told me you're from there."

"Mm, yeah, too much mafia in Hong Kong. My parents have restaurant there and it's always difficult. Bangkok better." She paused to break open a blister pack of Ibuprofen. "You the man bring her flowers, yeah?" she asked suddenly venturing out from the frowns with a delicate, approving smile.

"Yeah, he always bring!" Sisi exclaimed.

Beaming at them both, I warmed instantly to the air of longing that had been revealed as Li Mei opened up a fraction.

"You speak Thai?" she asked of me, beginning to relax now that she realised who I was.

And so we amused her with what I could say and with Sisi joining in, praising me in English, as though I were a rare exotic berry that tasted better than I looked, the atmosphere came alive with a sense of possibility, all the more poignant given our quietly desperate situations. As a pause fell, Li Mei picked up her bottle of pills and excused herself.

As we returned to our cooking, Sisi reminisced about her last night out with Li Mei at a karaoke bar. I wasn't as amused as she was by her own story, but I was happy to think of her out somewhere with a group of friends, just being silly. As there was no table to eat off, we took our plates into her room and rested them on our laps. The food was delicious and I ate hungrily until I noticed Sisi was only picking at her food. She'd eaten late, she said. She was still living the timetable of a call girl–going to bed late, getting up late, eating at odd hours.

"That's gonna change," I said, briefly taking hold of her hand.

Later, we lay under the bed covers, chatting like children the night before Christmas. Now that we were sober she wanted to know, was I really serious about marrying her? Wouldn't it be a problem for me? I had kids already, what would they feel? I said they'd be only too happy to meet her, they were still young enough to adapt easily, they were open and friendly, she had nothing to worry about.

"But your wife?"

"I told you, we're separated." I said this with such icy passion I almost believed it were true.

But a minute later, I was beginning to suspect I'd let myself run on ahead without her. I was willing to reassure her, but only so long as she truly wanted me. I couldn't leave Sylvia and the girls only to discover I'd been up my own arse the whole time.

"You know I got a friend, yeah?" she said, changing the subject.

"The guy who helped you?"

"No, different. He kind of boyfriend, yeah? But I don't go out with him any more."

"Boyfriend?" I went rigid.

"He's kind of ex. But I still like him… sometimes."

I regarded her coldly for a moment.

"Where're we going with this? You wanna be with this guy?'

"I don't think so."

"You don't think so…" *All coming out in the wash now…*

"He kind of mad with me when he see you come to my flat in Paddington. I tell him you very good friend, I trust you, but he's bit funny about it."

"Like how 'funny'?" I sat up on an elbow, narked.

"He say, you just customer, how can I trust you, you just want young girl for sex, you not understand Thai woman, really, but– "

"That's not true–"

"–I know. I tell him you're not like that."

"So he's jealous."

"Maybe."

I turned sideways in bed and asked her his name.

"Why you want to know?"

"I just do, OK?"

"I don't like to give you his name, I don't want you upset."

"I already am upset! What do you think when you–when you start talking about some other guy! I mean what was all that in the kitchen? Did you think I was play-acting, messing around? Were *you*?"

I sat upright, pulling my knees up to my chest. I felt her hand on my back, but I needed her to sit up and hold me, promise me it was going to be OK, only she wasn't doing that. I turned my head:

"Sisi, I want you–OK? I've wanted you right from the beginning, the first time you opened your mouth– "

"For blow job?!"

"No, at the dentist, silly!"

And suddenly we were laughing, and I was disarmed again.

I lay back on the crook of my elbow. Those wide, beautiful eyes instilling peace in me.

"Sisi, I love you. But you have to want me, too, it's that simple."

She dropped her eyes to the bed, her fingers, playing with the threads of a hole in the cover.

"Not so simple."

But I couldn't really get from her why it wasn't. Did the ex–or 'kind of ex'–know about the murder? Barely glancing into my eyes, she fudged her answer. OK, so the guy probably did know and was leaning on her somehow. I proposed meeting him and talking things through, man to man. What did he look like? She sighed, deeply vexed, and flopped back onto the pillow.

"Don't ask me so many questions right now–please."

I chewed this over, seriously in the mood to leave. But I let it go and lay back down to gaze up at the ceiling. I suddenly felt ever so tired with all that I'd done and hoped for with Sisi. I felt her hand touch mine and link fingers. A moment later she rolled over me. She wore a half smile that suggested she believed I was too good for her. I didn't want to be too good for her, because too good was the same as not good enough. We kissed. She was hungry for me, one hand already playing with my sex. She smiled impishly as my erection grew and then she kissed me, ever so tenderly all about my face, my neck, my nipples–lingering, as she'd never done before; it was scary, it felt like a goodbye. And yet it was the first time we made love without haste, without any notion of time. Our climaxes rode toward one another without effort, like the ocean's currents.

As Sisi lay in my arms, sleeping, I thought to get up and write Sylvia a text message, but I was through pretending and imagined that prizing myself from my lover would hurt like unpeeling glued skin. As my marital guilt receded quietly, she stirred and turned, curling her hand round mine and bringing it to her breast, pressing her bottom into the cup of my groin, nestling there for protection.

I thought of the murdered man, the so far phantom-like ex she was so reluctant to describe. And I knew I was still a long way from a safe harbour for the both of us.

CHAPTER 16

I woke early to find myself far apart from Sisi in bed. I thought to slip out from under the covers and get quietly into my clothes, but it was already 6.30. I imagined Sylvia waking and thinking, 'He was quiet getting in last night…' I see her lying there, very still, listening out for the muted tinkling of a shower, the clink of a spoon on a cereal bowl, the muted bass muttering of a man's voice in the girls' bedroom. She'd listen… and hear only the echo of her worst fears. Or, rather, what she'd always predicted. Still willing to be proven wrong, she'd look again at the pillow and feel the absence of transferred warmth. And then she'd sit up and look at the empty space beside her and grow aware of its vertiginous force, drawing her down into a well of suppressed emotions. I knew that feeling, the swell of nausea that accompanied the not quite 100 per cent proven realisation your loved one was fucking someone else. I'd never been under Sylvia's spell the way I've been with Sisi, never craved her body, her presence around me. But I'd been sick with jealousy when she'd had a fling in our early days of dating, during the period we ironically termed our 'trial separation' as though we believed we were far too young to be so serious about relationships. After a perfectly timed campaign of patience, understanding and insidious undermining of her new love interest persuaded her to give me a second chance, I vowed never to take her special qualities for granted again. And yet, even before Michaela was born, I'd sometimes felt that the momentous effort I'd devoted to getting her back had permanently depleted my reserves of love for her. She'd tested me so fully that now I had her, I had some warped notion in my head that one day I'd have the right to put her to the test. So now it was 'her turn', at a point when we were already in a terminal phase–would her pain be any less than mine had been?

Supine upon Sisi's bed, listening to the gradual fade-up of traffic sounds, I told myself it made little difference whether I went home now or in two hours'. And if I was going to stay… Yes, I was horny again. How ruthless is the new love–with your cock penetrating the new woman and severing the last remaining ties that hold you to the woman who bore you your precious girls.

I reached to touch Sisi, who was facing me now, her mouth slightly open, a cute little wet spot of saliva on her pillow. I wanted to have my first breakfast with her, even if sex was off. But of course Sylvia wasn't just about to be an ex-girlfriend, she was still legally speaking my wife, she was the mother of our girls and a mature student with a busy weekend agenda. I could picture her now, greeting my return with withering indifference as to my whereabouts the night before. And her point would be this: she'd lost a whole morning waiting for me to come back so she could set off, unaccompanied by whining daughters, to an exhibition somewhere. The frisson of her unswerving pragmatism could almost be arousing.

I pulled myself up, and started putting on my things. By the time I had my shoes on, having sex or breakfast together were no longer on my mind–I simply wanted to see Sisi open her eyes and look me in the face and feel sure that what I'd seen in her eyes the night before hadn't fizzled out overnight. But she was still thick with sleep and I feared rousing the dragon on her shoulder were I to force her awake. So I scribbled a note on a yellow Post-IT and stuck it to the bedside lampshade, signed, 'Love Anthony'. Would she screw it up immediately and toss it in the bin, or touch it lovingly as though it were a petal of love? How mad that I couldn't be sure.

Setting out, I considered my 'story' for Sylvia. The night before, when I'd told Sylvia I was going to a party in the East End, she'd said, "What, in those trousers?" I'd returned to the kitchen in some old Joseph trousers. "These better?" "Yeah, *they're* better." Her smile had conveyed a blend of irony and gentle condescension. (In reality, the irony was all mine: by deliberately dressing in crappy old trousers I'd successfully deflected any suspicion she might otherwise have had that I was hoping to impress a woman at this phantom party.) When I told her it was likely I'd be very late, or that I might even stop over to save on a taxi fare of thirty or forty quid, she didn't even pause in what she was doing. She seemed content to have the whole night before her with no one around–her first chance in days, she'd said, to update the layouts of her portfolio. I'd invented the party just in case things worked out perfectly with Sisi, even though I set out that night bracing myself for an all out row with her–if the row was going to be a bust-up, how wantonly destructive a confession to Sylvia would have been.

Walking down the hill away from the excremental walls and floors of Wembley Central tube station, the urge to come clean became more pressing. Perhaps it was the exercise in the bracing late October air that encouraged me to postpone making a confession and, instead, stick to my lie about crashing on the sofa at the party. In the rare event she actually asked what it was like, I could sketch out a couple of vignettes from an actual party I'd never told Sylvia about, among people Sylvia didn't know and never would. God, I should have been an MP.

The first thing that struck me as I let myself in was the childless silence of the house. I checked my watch–10AM, so they had to be up. The car was in the road. I thought to call out, but decided to do something first in case someone heard me and made an appearance. I heard the hungry chirp of one of the girls' Tamagotchis from somewhere downstairs and thought the kids can't be far away. Silence again. I poured a glass of water and drank in difficult sips. I'd just set the empty glass on the top, when I heard footsteps, the weight of an adult on the stairs. I turned to see Sylvia in her jeans, an old shirt, a rinsed look about her face, a spot on her chin, lips almost pursed, her eyes expectant of an amusing but painful denouement.

"Hello," she said, with a gentle note of query and surprise that instantly took me back in time to when we were still discovering what it was like to live with one another.

I was expecting a question about the apocryphal party, or at least a You OK? but she left the Hello hanging and went straight to the wash basket to begin pulling dirty things from it and was now loading them into the machine. I read her movements for some tell-tale trace of anger, but if she was a little tense that could have simply meant she was tired.

"Well, saved a few quid on a taxi fare, I suppose," I said, as if she'd asked. I refilled my glass, needing something to hide behind.

She shut the machine door, perhaps a tad more sudden than usual.

"Good, was it?" she asked. She'd said the words as if reading her lines and I was immediately uneasy inventing so much as one more word.

"OK… yeah… You get your stuff sorted?" I sipped my water.

She was pouring in the liquid soap. "Sort of."

She shut the soap compartment, twisted the dial, pushed the ON button.

"Where're the kids?"

"My sister's."

Again I was thrown. Her sister lived in Shoreditch. Surely she hadn't driven over there last night.

"When did you do that?"

"Kelly came and picked them up–this morning. They've gone on to the pool."

She was showing me her profile, which not for the first time–the line of her sensible and beautiful nose etched sharper by the melancholy light from the window behind her–hinted at an oncoming and merciless reproach, but I couldn't for the life of me recollect her having mentioned anything about a pool trip I might have been roped into taking charge of.

"They, um, back this afternoon?"

"Why do you need to know?" now rinsing glasses and stacking them.

I moved away–"Just asking. Christ."

"They'll be at Kelly's till Sunday afternoon," she answered with fresh terseness. "I've said you're picking them up. Any problem with that?" drying her hands.

"No."

"Good."

She let out a slight sigh, turned and leant her bum against the kitchen top. She crossed her arms and tucked in her chin. The hint of a sly embittered smile was forming on her lips.

"I thought we should talk."

I felt my throat tighten and reached for the filter jug of water for a swift top-up.

"OK. What about?"

I was aware of a slow tide of blood working up my neck to my cheeks.

"I don't know what you're up to exactly, but…" She was looking at the chairs around the kitchen table, then looked up at the wall and, finally, turned to look at me. And it hurt. She pursed her lips to make a regretful smile, a smile, which as much as it hurt to admit, conveyed more layers of meaning than any smile I'd seen on Sisi's lips to date. "…I think it's time I told you what I'm up to anyway… or have been up to." She paused. The pauses, her style of phrasing had completely fogged my brain. It occurred to me dimly this was possibly her intention. "I'm pretty sure you're seeing someone..." She paused, prematurely, it seemed, but this was very much Sylvia's style, her logic swiftly interrupted by emotion and a fundamental lack of confidence in the effectiveness of words.

Looking into the whites of her large dark eyes, something drained out of me as I noted the absence of their usual warmth–an expression that was chilled not by hate but rather by a purposeful impartiality distilled from weeks and weeks of doubt.

"I don't know if you'd noticed, but I am too." *You might miss that nice turn of phrase, so uniquely English, if you go with Sisi,* I thought to myself. "And I just think it's getting silly–I mean, not talking about it… what we're doing, what we're… *going* to do–y'know?"

Even though my chest was tight and I had no breath to spare for immediate comment, I felt a wave of relief pass through me. I looked away out the window to the overgrown garden–the man who brings flowers, who could never be bothered to grow any of his own for his wife, his family.

"I've tried to tell you," I heard her say, "but… I dunno… you've been so distant, Anthony, I haven't–it's not been–"

"So it's my fault, is it?" Such a ridiculous cheap shot, I knew, even as I was saying it, but I needed to *feel* something, just in case I still cared–I hadn't been prepared for such reasonableness in her, though it made sense upon hearing she was also having an affair.

She gave a little snort of derision that meant this was unworthy of me–she wasn't even going to go there.

"You've said it yourself–there's a gap. There's been a gap for some time. I don't know if it's got something to do with this concussion you had–you tell me there's nothing to worry about, but you won't get it checked–"

"I had it checked and they found nothing–"

"Yes, but you could have had other scans and tests done, couldn't you?" overlapping me. "You still complain of headaches." She paused. "Unless they're more figurative than real." A longer pause. I made no comment. "Maybe you're fine then, but your behaviour since that day at the pool, it's been so… remote." She ended on a note of motherly entreaty, allowing me to make excuses, be forgiven perhaps. When I said nothing, she switched to wry humour: "It's like the bang to your head knocked you into a mid-life crisis overnight."

"Why do you refer back to the accident I had? We haven't had sex for over a year."

"Why do you always have to bring sex into it? Doesn't this…" gesturing the room, the kitchen, the house, the kids, "…mean anything to you?"

"Of course it does," I spat back. "But if we're talking about you and me, the relationship–"

"Why can't you understand it's never been about you and me since Michaela was born."

"Oh, I see, so I'm supposed to abstain from sex until they leave home and then we can have another go. Is that it?"

Sylvia's lips pursed, a mouth much better designed to express moral censure than Sisi's, which with its fullness would always appear to default to variations on the theme of 'an inflamed pride'.

"Anthony, I don't want a fight."

"OK, so–how, when, who… how long?"

She was perfectly still, like a trained spy unfazed by the rat-tat-tat of my question.

"About three months."

"How did it start?"

"I don't think that matters and I don't think I want to go into that right now–"

"I dunno, it might matter," I cut across. "I mean, if it's going to carry on, for one thing, the girls'll be asking me about him, won't they?"

"I don't know if it's going to carry on. I can't tell after three months."

I fell suddenly quiet, like a stone dropping down a bottomless shaft.

Neither of us said anything and, for a moment, I considered walking from the room. But then what? I made a poor attempt at expressing irony with a short laugh but it came out as contemptuous, even self-pitying.

"I dunno–there's me thinking *I* was the one raving it up, staying out late, coming home with a hangover, possibly smelling of some girl's perfume because she rubbed against me on someone's living room floor, but as it turns out–" I paused to express, with an off-hand sort of gesture, the 'reverse is true'–which of course it wasn't.

"Why're you getting like this?" She took the words right out of my mouth. Possibly I was hurting, now face to face with the likelihood that my wife was enjoying a relatively normal, loving relationship, where there were at least a few parameters you could rely on. "Are you saying you're *not* seeing someone?"

I took a medicinal sip of my water, swallowed hard and, as the water went down, my face seemed to clam up. It was if, perversely, just because I'd opened the line of questioning, I didn't have to reveal my hand until she'd given me her story in full.

"Boy at college? Internet? E-bay–?"

"My tutor."

"Your tutor… Right… You mean the guy who–Kings' Cross?"

"Yes."

I nodded thoughtfully. I could see that working: his post traumatic stress disorder and her healing powers through chanting–I dared not even ask if he'd joined her group for fear she thought I was mocking them both. Far from it, I was strangely happy for her–an injured man she could heal steps in for a remote man she couldn't reach.

"Three months? I thought you'd only just started the new term."

"I met him at an end-of-year show in June."

"Oh."

"He's not even my type really," she said, as if a little embarrassed. "He's older than you, he's got a beard and he's even shorter than I am." She gave a little laugh. "But he was around, Anthony–you weren't. I just didn't feel you cared anymore, so… and he was very helpful with my essays and I…it wasn't really a sexual thing, it was more like–I dunno–a companion thing."

But you're fucking him anyway, sucking his balls, his cock, swallowing his cum… I thought to spit out, because I always hated it when women sought to play down the role of sex as though it were purely incidental to, a sort of garnish for, the deeper stuff.

"So it's just my imagination then, is it?" she asked. "You're the–I dunno–the Unambomber."

I couldn't help smiling. She was smiling. And I was suddenly nostalgic for us, remembering that it was this wonderful capacity of hers to look with such a balanced mix of compassion and irony at the things that hurt us that had drawn me back to her after we'd separated years before. It was strangely heartening and yet saddening that we could still share such a poignant connection, such deft irony, even as we hung so precariously from barbed mistrust in this bleak corridor leading to the Exit.

"I–" I sighed, then paused. "Yeah, I have been seeing someone. Like you I–I don't even know if it's viable."

She gave a little shrug as if to say, 'I'm listening'.

I went to the nearest chair and sat down. The way I eased into it reminded me I'd had great sex the night before–my buttocks, my stomach muscles ached from the exercise. Had she been enjoying these aches as well?

Sylvia remained by the washing machine. I asked her if she'd mind turning it off for a minute or two. She pressed the button, without protest.

Silence.

"How long?" she asked.

"About two months," I lied, claiming the moral advantage, knowing it would get worse if or when I revealed her occupation. But she wasn't asking….

She came over and sat down at the table so we were at right angles to one another. She lay her hand on mine. I held hers a moment. Tears welled up into my eyes and I saw there were tears in her eyes–we were both fighting them back, unable to believe that letting them go would wash away our four-way entanglements.

"What do you want to do?" I asked.

"I don't know if I want to DO anything. I just wanted us to be honest with each other."

My thumb rubbing over her silky knuckles.

"Maybe I should move out."

She frowned, like someone who believes you're overreacting to a rash that might soon go away.

"You mean a separation, or a 'trial' separation? I'm afraid I can't really believe in the concept of a 'trial' separation. I don't think you can rebuild a marriage by being absent from it, Anthony. So, for me, it would be–well, the first stage on the way to a divorce. Is that what you want–when neither of us is sure?"

"I dunno," looking at my fingers, now alone on the table. "Perhaps we give it some time then."

She put her tongue in her cheek–I don't think she meant to be ironic but I almost broke into a ridiculous, nervous smile.

"Yeah… we can," she said finally.

I put my hand on hers. She gave me a little smile with one half of her mouth.

"I still love you, Anthony. Always will."

"Hey, me too."

Suddenly her nose was running, the tears dripping onto the table, her chin trembling.

"Hey…" I squeezed her hand. She took it away to wipe away the tears–

"What about the kids?"

"I think we should tell them–without talk of separation or divorce or any of that, just… I dunno, like, you have a new friend, I have a new friend."

"You mean, include these new friends in their lives?"

"No, not yet, just–allude to them."

She exhaled loudly and wiped her eyes.

"OK. We can try."

I got up from the table to tear off a piece of Kitchen Towel. I could have used one for myself, but my tears were in abeyance now that Sylvia's were flowing. The pale brown of her complexion seemed to grow pale and then darker with the tears, as though her various bloods were separating out in this moment of emotional turmoil.

I went to fill up the kettle, asked her if she'd like a coffee. She'd prefer a tea, she said, green tea.

"I'm sorry," she said moments later as the kettle began its ascent to boiling point.

I wasn't sure if she was referring to the tears or her affair, but glancing over my shoulder I said, "Don't be," and pulled off the lid of the container for the green tea. "You deserve to be happy–we both do."

"That's the thing, though, I don't know if I am happy. I just know… I'm less lonely."

"Well, maybe that's a start, hey?"

"And you?"

Now that a relatively grounded person like Sylvia was asking me about where I was with Sisi, I was filled with doubt and said as much. And then hoped so desperately that I was wrong to feel that way.

"Is she someone we know?"

"No."

"A patient?"

"No." Which was a lie, but I knew a Yes would give a totally wrong impression. I was very close to telling her about the day at the pool and what happened after, but delayed answering.

The kettle came to the boil, its hiss and bubble-surge, filling the room. I picked it up before the button popped out, I poured and put the lid on the terracotta teapot. I waited a minute then poured into two small mugs. Sylvia leant against the kitchen table, slightly curving her back, tilting her head, her beautiful shoulder blades showing through a faded Joseph cardigan I'd bought her years ago–like wings, as if she were not so much stretching as straining to fly off.

"Is she young?" she asked, gazing into the steamy green liquid in front of her, moments after I'd joined her at the table. When I didn't answer immediately, she turned to look at me with a child's impassive expression as if she were unconsciously willing herself to reappear before me as ten years younger.

Young… and smooth-skinned and toned and –

For a moment I wanted to vocally dismiss my affair as just one of those sexual things–a forty something cliché–shrug it off as the sexual equivalent of wind that had to be passed out before one could resume the comfortable life. But no, it wasn't. It was something so full and all consuming my mouth felt too small to describe it in words.

"I'll take that as a yes, then."

And she sipped her tea. Then held the mug against her chin, inhaling the vapour…

CHAPTER 17

I wasn't surprised by Sylvia's revelation–the long weekend afternoons out when I hadn't been able to reach her on her mobile, the few nights she'd got in past midnight and arrived home to scoff down a bowl of cereal like a teenager. Her re-emergence from behind a closed door, having been on the phone a long while, and now behaving a little self-consciously about the fact as if she had the uneasy feeling there might still be a residue of chewing gum stuck to her backside. And, of course, the conspicuous absence of any kind of probing recently into my own thinly explained absences. I felt happy for her in a tainted sort of way–somewhat more tainted upon hearing he'd been a heavy cocaine user till he'd given up his job at a big advertising agency and gone into teaching part-time. Not that I could talk–clearly I had my own addictions.

After our drinks that morning, we just got on with things. With the kids out, I felt able to catch up on some reading: a small study that provided 'compelling evidence that Candida albicans converts amalgam mercury into methyl mercury' and other related topics. All things considered, my concentration was surprisingly good. Sylvia had disappeared into the spare room to chant. She'd not so long ago acquired a gohonzon from my sister-in-law, quite a bloody big one, with electric-operated doors, built of rosewood.

She'd set up a little chill-out room in there, with piles of cushions for visitors, neatly arranged on the single bed. The lingering, somewhat choking smell of joss-ticks put me off going in there. *–So if it came to separate beds, maybe I'd feel more at home using the living room sofa...*

It's a funny coincidence how this word 'practice' is so often on our lips, yet meaning such different things. For her it's a verb, for me it's a noun; hers is spiritual, mine is pragmatic. Occasionally–and perhaps that morning was a case in point–I was a tad envious of her sheer willingness to channel her life through this matrix of positive thinking. In the summer months I'd meet up with my brother for a catch-up drink and we'd sit on a ledge overlooking the Thames as the sun dipped to kiss the water as it snaked round to Hammersmith and there'd be a moment just after we'd compared notes about our Buddhist wives when we'd feel ourselves drifting toward death strapped to the wreckage of our own lifelong cynicism, quietly desperate for a means of making more of what they would call our 'potential' for happiness. And we'd smile a smile of acknowledgment, admiring of our wives' energy and optimism even as we felt defeated by their libidinal evasiveness. As I flipped shut a recent copy of Dental News, I wondered what might happen if I now went upstairs to join Sylvia before her gohonzon, if I sat down beside her, hands clasped in prayer and launched my voice into its first atonal round of Nam-Myo-Ho-Renge-Kyo. Would we be rutting like rabbits an hour later, mollified and lubricated by tears of surrender, Animality and Buddhahood united?

Stepping into the garden to stretch my legs, I was reminded of those early, innocent tasks in biology classes when we'd be instructed to check on the progress of seeds in their plots and draw graphs charting their rate of growth. Which would survive and which would shrivel and die?

Standing on the threshold of the door leading back into the living room, I surveyed the ramshackle design of the room and asked myself why I'd never really got into this modern trend of redoing the house you buy. OK, I'd spent thirty grand re-routing the staircase, ripping out the upstairs kitchen and another twenty grand taking out the sweating aluminium windows I'd inherited from the landlord; together, Sylvia and I had refitted the downstairs kitchen in solid wood and German engineering, we'd put down white porcelain flooring that resembled stone slabs, but I'd been lazy with everything else. Over there, for instance: my samurai sword, I'd bought it on a trip to Tokyo–it deserved to be hanging up somewhere. But Sylvia wanted me to erect some shelving on the same wall I'd had in mind for it. We reached an impasse and nothing had been done about either, so now it lay in a corner of the room, behind a cabinet, half forgotten, secondary evidence of a dysfunctional relationship, also a minor safety hazard, although, as I predicted, the girls seldom even noticed it. It's as if having done a couple of major tasks to add value to the house–i.e., windows and kitchen–I was overwhelmed suddenly by the futility of finding happiness through materialist endeavour, as if I could see it all crumbling apart before I'd gotten half way through. Which was odd in a way, because I was almost heroic in my diligence at the practice. I wasn't a slob, and nor was Sylvia, but we both shared an innate mistrust of hubris and, somehow, doing things up seemed to us a sort of hubris, even though we so often returned from a friend's house quietly sighing over the beauty of its newly refurbished interiors. *Maybe it's the tough comprehensive I went to that's to blame–*

mixing with kids who were definitely pre-Thatcherite the way they aped their parents' whingeing about wages and management and class, a national attitude of discontent that brought the economy to a standstill in 79. The truth is, I'd never much liked the house I bought, or the area it was in. We found Wembley's dearth of cafes and bars and shops where you could go and spend idle time in an aspirational environment, an increasingly deadening state of affairs. We should have moved years ago. But by the time I'd had enough money to buy in Acton or Chiswick, say, divorce loomed on the horizon and it seemed so much simpler to walk away from the house we were in than divide a larger, more beautiful one. That sense of possibly being about to move yet making do for now must have passed down to the girls too–evidenced not so much by the fact that they often mistreated the furniture and décor, but rather this sense they gave off of disconnect with their immediate environment. Rather than going out in the street as I had done, they stayed in playing with dolls and soft toys and PlayStation. Had we said they couldn't go out into the street? Or was it just that we hadn't encouraged them to venture out? At the age of eight, Michaela's age, I'd cycled everywhere in a two mile radius–canals, woods, power stations, neighbours' back gardens. Admittedly that was before every parent had had drummed into them that a paedophile was lurking on every street corner. Besides, there were no woods here in Wembley, no places I could see that would have captured my imagination at their age. And the sheer density of foreign tongues and darker skins round here has put them off from exploring on their own, even though they naturally gravitate to making mixed race friendships. We know no one within a ten-mile radius because we've chosen a school in a better area that's a twenty-five minute drive from where we live, populated with kids whose parents work in media and the professions. For a time Sylvia used to talk of moving to the suburbs–more space for your money, better schools, all the familiar pros. But since committing herself to attending part-time art courses and, more recently, to a London university, she's reverted to the song we used to sing when we first met–in praise of the sheer abundance of culture and events in the city. As for me, I liked suburbia no better now than when I'd escaped it at twenty-two, and I didn't think any number of bombs was about to change that feeling.

That same afternoon, as Sylvia went out shopping, assuming it was shopping–yes, it probably was–I went on the internet to look for studio flats in and around W2, just in case the 'waiting period' Sylvia and I had agreed on evaporated overnight due to a sudden and unfortunate misunderstanding that defied a fair hearing. I told myself I was just browsing, getting a feel for what I might have to pay, I wasn't about to buy. But mostly I wasn't searching for myself, I was searching for flats for two. *Hey, kids, I'd like you to meet my Thai prostitute on the run. She's a great cook and very experienced in bed.* I should be grateful the girls weren't yet teenagers.

The rest of the weekend passed without incident. With her own confession out in the open, I'd expected Sylvia to spend some of Sunday with her new bloke, but there was no sign of him, no hint they'd even contacted each other. But that made sense, I told myself: they'd probably agreed to give me a few days' grace before introducing a more open arrangement.

It was a relief to be back at work on Monday. Several batches of inlays had arrived late, so we were busy tracking them down and rearranging appointments, all of which was irritating, but at least my mind was free from reflections of recent developments for hours at a time.

I was just checking some X-Rays, waiting for the last patient of the day to arrive, when I got a call that screamed PRANK!–it was a voice disguised by a clownish distortion effect.

"Hello," the voice began, unctuous to my ears. "You Mr. Anthony."

Already racing through faces and names trying to guess which of my friends might pull such a prank, I was on the verge of letting out a sort of pained guffaw–what stopped me was the fact that I'd already identified an Oriental accent in spite of the distortion.

"How can I help you?" I said, as if prepared to play along for a while.

"You friend wit' Sonia, yeah?"

Alarm bells went off.

"Who is this?"

"She done very bad ting, you know? She making big probrem for us."

The agency. Shit. Heart pounding, my first thought was that it was the velvety-voiced Chinaman in an altered state, but even allowing for the distortion this voice had a youthful edge to it–so could it be someone higher up, like a young enforcer? I caught my reflection in the mirror on the medicine cabinet–and was shocked by how wan I'd turned. The face of a coward? I turned away from it.

"I think you know what we talking about, don't you?"

I cleared my voice. "Who are you?" But I was struggling to express authority with indignation.

"We know what she did and we know you involved."

"Can you please get to the point, I have patients to see."

"If you want girl back, you have to pay."

"Sorry, I don't understand. Pay what, pay whom? What is this?" I sighed as if dealing with the relative of a cranky, hypochondriac patient who had repeatedly ignored sound advice.

"T'irty t'ousand pound."

"Thirty thousand–?! Are you nuts! I don't have that kind of money lying around!"

"We know you can get it."

"I haven't even the slightest idea what this is about!"

Before I could add anything further my ear took a sudden jolt from the man's handset as it was tossed onto a hard surface. There was a muted female cry, then a rattle of the handset, a female cry of pain and Sisi's voice crying my name. My own phone turned to ice in the palm of my hand.

"No one cares about Thai prostitute–but you care, yeah?" The phrasing of the last question seemed like a plain, reasonable question. "You get money, or say goodbye to your stupid whore. You un'stand?"

"No, I don't understand."

The sound of a hand struck across flesh, Sisi's cry, cut off my thoughts. I grit my teeth.

"You un'stand now?"

"OK OK–" I stepped into the toilet and closed the door. Lowering my voice, I said, "Just don't hurt her!" I couldn't believe I was saying these words, like straight out of kidnap movie, but what else was I to say. My arm holding the phone was shaking. Sisi's cries became muted again. "OK, I'll get you the money, but I need time, I can't raise that kind of cash overnight." I licked my lips, my mouth already turned to rubber. "Do *you* understand?" throwing this man's irritating refrain back at him.

"I call you again. You don't call Sonia again, un'stand?"

"Yes."

"We see you near her apar'men', there's trouble, un'stand?"

"Yes."

"She not there anyway. Chinese girl gone too."

"Right."

"Don't worry, she still young and pretty, you soon make money back if you want," the voice went on, now modulating with sleazy consolation. "She work for you, six mont', you get money back. Un'stand?"

How sweet. Fuck. But I said Yes again in the same suggestible state.

"You don't talk to police. It's not good idea, anyway," he added, switching suddenly to an almost convivial tone of voice. "You involved in bad ting. Get you in trouble. Better you pay. You get Sonia back and we go away. End of story."

"What do I call you?"

"No, I call you."

"No, I mean, what's your name, what do I call you?"

"OK, you call me Jack, i's good name. Like Jack Nicholson, yeah?"

Jack. The person I'd been in Earl's Court.

The line went dead before I could comment. I stepped out of the toilet.

"Anthony?"

I span round. It was Andrea, gloved hands in the air.

"Mrs. Verbinski just cancelled. Her car broke down on the way over."

"Right."

"Are you OK?"

"Yeah, um, why don't you head off? I'll finish up."

"You OK?"

My face kind of twitched as a nerve impulse to smile reassuringly collided with planes of worry.

"Yeah, uh…" I remembered having told Andrea about my mum's chronic diarrhoea– "My mum's a lot better, thanks."

"Good."

"Yeah… Anyway, you go. Have a good evening."

She may have smiled sympathetically but I was only aware of the sound of her gloves coming off and her footsteps receding. It occurred to me how lucky I was to have her. Had I expressed gratitude often enough? Possibly not: ever since I'd confided in her as to the sexless state of my marriage, I'd grown a little wary that she might misinterpret gratitude as coming on to her. Shame I won't be able raise her salary this year. I'll probably lose her. Along with 30 grand. My god. The kind of figure I'd estimated I'd need for a new life, not even an extravagant one–a small apartment on my own, as Sylvia continued to explore her new relationship with her former ad exec with an allegedly former coke habit. 30 grand. A payment that would slice off my daughters' university education at the joint. *Sorry girls, you'll have to get a loan, I had to save my whore.* But hey, as the man said, maybe I could redeem the situation by becoming a pimp. Nice.

The blackmailer's call had perforated my already fractured sense of security to its very pulp. I felt suddenly nauseous and dizzy and dove back into the toilet. Retching dry was a pain less painful than the scenarios stampeding through my brain.

"Anthony?" it was Andrea again, just outside the toilet door.

"Yes?!"

"Are you OK?"

"Er, bit of a stomach bug, I think."

"Oh, shit. Can I get you anything?"

"No! You go! Have a good one! I'll be fine!"

I felt so grubby, I could have laughed. I slumped on the floor to one side of the toilet. I could feel Andrea hovering in the corridor a moment.

"Good night then!"

"Good night!"

I heard the door close.

The toilet became a tiny cell, but at least I felt safe in here. My first thought was that I was up against Mafia. Thai? I had no idea. And yet the figure of 30K seemed unusually modest for them. True, they'd know a dentist wasn't loaded, but I'd have expected an organisation to demand a whole lot more than 30 grand for a life. Perhaps they reckoned a customer was unlikely to sell his practice down river for a mere call girl. But if the agency were run by the faceless 'Mafia' and they were behind this call, why not just bring me in, rough me up, have me killed, so that I could never blab about one of their girls' having messed up with a customer? When I'd called the agency last, the booker had seemed totally relaxed when I asked him about Sonia. OK, maybe he'd lied about her having gone off to Australia, maybe he'd been misinformed, either way it didn't seem to fit the prelude to the call I'd just had. No, my gut told me, I'd either been speaking to the guy I'd met at the flat–perhaps Sisi had refused to pay him for disposing the body and now he was seizing an opportunity for swift compensation by an auxiliary root–or I'd been speaking with someone connected to him. Even allowing for the distortion on the caller's voice, the turn of phrase hadn't been consistently Thai or Chinese. 'End of story', for instance, didn't fit with the person I'd met, even if we had exchanged only a few words. So had the guy been working from a script written by someone with better English than he had? In any case, the caller kept saying 'we', didn't he, so I was probably up against a minimum of two…

I got to my feet and stepped out of the toilet. Now I had my ghastly pale reflection to deal with. I thought to run from it as I had a few minutes ago. I thought to penetrate it for a sign of inspiration. All of a sudden my arm came up and I smashed my fist into the mirror – more than once. I gained a moment's gratification on seeing my face splinter into a web of selves before pain took over and I had to stop. My knuckles were bleeding, but I was lucky: there was no evidence of a fracture. *You twat. You need your hand. You need it to keep on making money…* "So you can pay off some lunatic kidnapper–fuck!" I shouted aloud.

Wrapping white bandage round my wrist I thought of boxers and wondered what Neil would have made of my situation. He'd boxed. Maybe he and I could join forces and take on the bad guys… *Yeah, right…*

I swept the blood-flecked pieces of glass into the dustpan and from there onto a topless model from The Sun, left behind by the last patient. I flipped open my phone with my left hand and dialled 999. My thumb hovered over the green phone symbol, then hit the red phone. I closed my phone. I just couldn't get past what Sisi had said about her chances if the Thai police got hold of her for murdering one of their own. I opened my phone again and called my bank.

"No," I said firmly, "I don't want to do this online. I need to see someone as soon as possible, face to face. I can't afford any delays."

"There shouldn't be any delays, really. It's probably quicker online," the woman kindly urged in a broad Brummy accent which of itself seemed to insinuate I must be sadly out of date to think otherwise.

"Look, I've just hurt my right hand, quite badly, I can't even use a mouse, so could you please give me an appointment with one of your loans managers as soon as possible."

After being put on hold twice, I got a date and a time to see someone at my local branch. I'd have to memorise it because I couldn't hold a pen.

"And is there anything else we can help you with today Mr. Price?" the woman asked in her ever so helpful voice upon conclusion of my request.

Yeah, get me a piece, will ya. And some shells.

How soon would that no longer be a joke in my head?

CHAPTER

18

Income tax returns. Digging them out. Bank statements… My brother had just taken out a loan of 20,000 at 5.8% to help him mop up an ulcerous tax bill which had taken a week to come through. I had about 15K in easily accessible savings, so I'd need a top-up of the same. Simple math to save a life. And the weird thing about it? I was better able to deal with this stuff than my own feelings for Sisi; for the first time in my history with her it was clear what I had to do.

"And what would you be needing your loan for, Anthony?" asked my Personal Banker, Jeff, a black athlete (if he'd give up the McDonald's) in a spanking new suit and tie. "Is it OK if I call you Anthony?"

You just did.

"Sure."

I didn't feel he was all that concerned as to what I'd be using the money for but he had to ask in case I said something silly like, 'Semtex'.

"Partly new equipment at the surgery–"

"–and you'll get a lot of that back in tax relief, won't you?"

"Yep…Um… and partly..." I looked away, suddenly tired. We were in an overly air-conditioned glass office, a desk between us, on the first floor overlooking a busy street. It was my lunch hour. I'd nipped out without an umbrella. First mistake. I'd made up quite a list of spurious needs, but now I didn't have the puff to reel them off. Drizzle pissed unevenly upon the double-glazed window behind Jeff. It would soon be Christmas, the end of 2005. What could I wish for in 2006? I was being distant again. Second mistake–

"Well, I'm sure that's fine," Jeff said, cutting across my drifting thoughts, "it's always good to reinvest in a business such as yours. You're clearly doing pretty well," he said, as if to someone just starting out. He took another peek at the recent bank statements and tax returns to remind himself just how well. "And I imagine people are always going to have tooth ache, right?"

Looking at his grinning pretty white gnashers and healthy gums, I wasn't so sure. I smiled obligingly, newly conscious of my racial disadvantage.

Back to it anyway. Jeff now rattling off details from a checklist, which I duly verified and he updated on a computer wherever necessary. The man's flutter of glances from one sheet of figures with my name on to another made me a little nervous... He appeared to have arrived at a little impediment in the proceedings. His crooked finger stirred the air as he put to me, ever so tentatively and with a solicitous frown, "These withdrawals... since July... you've been withdrawing quite large sums–50, 200 at a go–is that something we need to be concerned about?" He raised his eyebrows–unusually fine for a man his size–not wishing to deny me anything, genuinely concerned there might have been something he'd overlooked that he might now be able help me with, another 5 or even 10 grand perhaps.

"Uh, yeah, um, it's just a new arrangement I have with my wife. We're uh–we're going through a separation." I winced as if for the camera and wondered briefly whether there wasn't in fact a hidden camera somewhere in the room.

His face creased with such a brilliant display of instant pity, it struck me like a round of applause. He was really sorry to hear that, he said. Never been there himself, but he was sure it was hard–sucking in his gut as if he'd just missed a savage blow.

"My wife's a mature student," I added, "and she needs extra cash for her studies–travel, that sort of thing."

"Oh, right. Cool. Well, that's good of you, seeing as you're like separated and stuff. Let's hope the courts look on that favourably, yeah?"

I smiled graciously, subtly titling the angle of my face to indicate that we might now get off the subject.

"I was just concerned, um, Anthony, looking at the figures–yeah?–that uh–y'know–the guys upstairs, they'd maybe be lookin' at the tight cash flow you're operating wiv."

"Precisely the reason for my seeking a loan."

He held that thought a moment, then broke into a laudatory laugh, "There you go!" He was blushing, he was young, perhaps new to the loans department. He drew his hand through the air as though drawing a line through the last of any vestigial doubts as to my financial credibility and we finished off with more tapping of keys than clacking of tongues.

I signed and dated the agreements. Jeff shook my hand with assurances that, providing that my credit history checked out, the 15K would be in my bank account within a week.

As I sat in the back of a taxi on the way back to the practice, it occurred to me that only a few days before I'd actually toyed with the idea of investing 5-10K in one of Neil's webcam schemes, assuming, that is, he was able to convince me that he had a proper business scheme and I could reasonably hope for a fair rate of return. It was just as well I hadn't been so easily tempted.

I thought to call the man with the weird voice but remembered he'd blocked his number and had told me to wait for a call. There was nothing to do but carry on as though nothing untoward was going on. As it happened, he called that afternoon. I'd already made some sort of mental adjustment for coping with the spooky, distorted voice and felt no immediate rush of panic and indignation, instead I was aware of savouring an unexpected sense of professional pride in being able to raise the figure he'd demanded in under 7 working days. He hung up on me as I was inquiring after Sisi's well being.

One day merged with the next in a uniform, static silence–and not a word from Jack. I began to wonder if I hadn't dreamed the whole thing. At work I displayed a fairly normal me, if a little rough around the edges, but at home I was wracked with worry. The first couple of nights a bottle of wine was my preferred choice to numb the worry. The second night I told myself this had to stop. I vowed to quit dinking completely and began working out on the patio, skipping for the warm-up then going on to do free weights. After five days of this routine I should have been beaming with re-oxygenated blood cells, but I looked like shit, because I just wasn't sleeping. I'd wake in the morning grappling with this not entirely real villain, like a figure from Sin City, the movie. We'd kill each other a few times over. I'd run off with Sisi, only to run into the Thai police. She'd be anally raped in front of my eyes and dragged from the cell by her hair and have all her teeth kicked out. Neil would come to visit and, dabbing the sweat from his forehead, he'd say, "I tried to tell you mate, they're just trouble."

Sunday afternoon, with the house quiet and time to think, I stumbled on an idea. I clicked on the link I had for Sonia's escort agency and searched the gallery of faces. I saw Li Mei's face. Her agency name was Mercedes. A line of text that said she was away. I scrolled down until I came to Sisi's former flatmate and clicked. I recognised her as much by her fulsome breasts as the fun smile she wore for the camera. She was one of those Thai girls who at a glance could almost pass as Western, or half, in a photo. Sylvia and the girls were out, so I called the number straight away. I got an older Oriental woman this time, who called me 'Dahlin' and asked me if I'd seen 'Angie' before. "She give very good service," she said with lubricious assurance. I suggested a time. Yes, she was free. She would text me the address. Hanging up I could have kicked myself for not having thought of this earlier, but at last I had a time and place for my first possible lead.

I arrived in Paddington around 4PM, as daylight was turning murky and electric lights growing to a bonbon yellow. The streets were half empty and most of the people I passed were tourists, moving much more leisurely than I was. I wouldn't be stopping off at the flower stall this time. In fact my stride was so driven by the need to get on with the job of extracting information from Angie I nearly forgot to withdraw cash from an ATM and had to double back. As I resumed my walk, I grew conscious of the absence of any kind of sexual excitement in my body–I'd always gotten such a rush of adrenalin on the way to Sisi's. It was almost as if my unconscious was preparing me to prostitute myself for the sake of inveigling information from Angie about Sisi.

Angie hadn't moved far–a basement flat in a Georgian Terrace, ten minutes North West by foot from Sisi's old flat. I descended the steps and wrapped on the cracked glass panel of the door. No one came. I peeped through unwashed glass and half open blinds to a living room–sofa, table, empty vase, bowl of fruit. The door opened. A smiling face and long brown hair, honey-coloured skin, big, sensuous eyes all set with a twinkle, full lips, a few cuts of purple chiffon hanging loosely together and, of course, those magnificent, naturally abundant breasts.

"Oh, sorry! You wait long?"

"No no, not long."

I stepped inside. The room's warmth was instant. As it had to be for a girl waiting around in such scanty clothing.

"Cold, isn't it?"

She still hadn't recognised me, so I reminded her and she threw her hands up to her face, laughing, apologising.

"Yeah yeah yeah, you Sonia's friend, yeah?"

"Yeah."

"Oh! Why you not still see her?!"

"Can I take a seat?"

"Sure–sure sure."

She sat beside me on a leather sofa facing the window, a TV, eager for some gossip, it seemed. I undid my coat.

"I have been seeing her, but we–we've lost touch. I don't know where she is. Do you?"

"She same place, no?"

"No, she's not, she moved. She moved in with a girl called Li Mei. Hong Kong Chinese–you know her?"

"Yeah, you mean Mercedes?"

"Yeah."

"Yeah, I know her, she–" Her phone began ringing. "Scuse me. Agency, I think."

She spoke Thai on the phone. It was brief, but when she hung up, she asked if I'd like a drink and disappeared through the open doorway to fix me a glass of water.

"You pay me now?" she asked, returning with a tall glass of water.

"Sure. So you know Li Mei?" Shelling out the 7 twenties and ten I hoped this would cover information too, though I'd brought another fifty just in case.

"Yeah, she on holiday now."

"Yeah, so I was told."

"You come now?" holding out her hand like a nursery school teacher.

She led me down the corridor to her room at the end. The blinds were down, the window was to the left of the bed, otherwise it could have been a duplicate room to Sisi's old room: freshly painted walls, same wood flooring, Ikea style closet and chest of drawers, a couple of framed photos of Angie beaming at camera as she challenged the elasticity of a swimsuit; cheap bedside clock and nappy wipes and, of course, the signature tea-burner candles.

As she lit the candles beside the bed, allowing me a view of her cellulite-free cheeks parted by a black string of nylon, such a strong feeling of déjà vu enveloped me, I fleetingly imagined becoming Angie's regular and forgetting all about Sisi.

As we removed our things, as if for a medical, it was she who returned to the subject of Sonia.

"She doesn't want to see you?"

"I don't know. Actually, I don't think it's that. I think she's got into some kind of trouble."

"Really?"

Hanging up my clothes in her closet, Angie hadn't so much as paused when I said 'trouble'. I handed her my trousers. She took them, holding her hand out waiting for the pants too, no trace of self-consciousness. I slipped them off.

"Yeah. Something's going on with her." I wrapped a white towel around my skinny middle. "She hasn't called. We were friends, y'know?"

"Yeah, she talk about you. She like you a lot, I think."

"Well, she's, like, disappeared."

"I don't think so," she said as if accustomed to indulging the fey imaginations of customers. "Maybe she busy, yeah?"

"No, this is different."

She closed the closet door, smiling as if she were all mine now.

"Angie, can you sit here a minute?"

A spanking white towel in hand–did the agency do her laundry?–she bent so beautifully as she came to sit beside me; she had the lightness of a much younger girl than her Western contemporary. I levelled my eyes on hers to make a reading of her standard 'attentive' expression so I could better read meaning in changes elicited by my questions.

"Have you seen her, recently?"

"Yeah. Um…" She looked at the floor, trying to pinpoint a day. "Maybe five days ago."

"Tuesday?"

"No, I think Monday."

Monday, the day after her 24th birthday. Born on the cusp of Sagittarius and Scorpio. I remembered well her insisting she was a little bit of both; this split between the two Signs was clearly an important part of her self-image. Sisi and Sonia. I'd bought a card– Van Gogh's 'Sunflowers'– and signed it–'with Love'– and put it in its purple envelope. I'd been carrying it around with me in my bag for several days now. It was probably crumpled already.

"She's was OK?" I asked.

"Yeah." She got to her feet suddenly. "Maybe you should call her and speak wit her yourself."

"I can't get through."

"Wait." She crossed the floor to her chest of drawers and her mobile phone. "You want check number?"

She read out the number she had for Sisi. It was the same as the one I had for her. Even so I asked her to call it. She sighed, not happy, but did as I asked. It rang and rang and rang. She took the phone from her ear so I could hear it as if this was proof that Sisi was fine. I pointed out I was getting the same response and never arriving at an answer machine. She hit End and put her phone back on the chest of drawers with a clatter and a little shrug of her shoulders.

"If you want to see her, why don't you book through agency?"

"The agency told me–some guy there told me she'd gone to Australia."

"Australia?!" She screwed up her nose like a little girl catching a whiff of something funny but not threatening. I suspected she practised a kind of denial respecting bad news about other girls. "No no, maybe he think you bothering her, you know?"

"Angie, I'm not bothering her. Her disappearance is bothering *me*."

She put a vaguely proprietary hand on her hip. "I'm sorry, I don't know." A bored look washed over her and there was an awkward pause. "So you want bath now or you want talk more? It's not my business, you know?"

I figured Angie would only dig her heels in harder if I continued my line of questioning; I'd be better served trying again after we'd fucked. So I smiled and shrugged as if it was bound to come out in the wash.

Angie was an even sexier woman than I'd remembered from our brief encounters in her previous flat. Whereas Sisi was bamboo slim and lean, Angie was made of voluptuous curves. I didn't so much want to fuck her as melt into the pores of her smooth, dark, perfumed skin. On the bed she started on me, working to a formula. When I slowed her right down, she adapted to my more leisurely pace as readily as warm liquid running into a deeper mould. Her style was motherly and loving and, as our bodies grew hot, I felt something competitive rise in her and wondered whether she and Sisi hadn't parted on the best of terms.

Closing my eyes I came picturing Sisi in my head. In my last thrusts into Angie's body, I imagined meting out bloody justice to the man who had made Sisi cry on the phone.

"Did you come?" I asked after.

"Yes, small one… but nice."

I smiled, "Do men always ask you this stupid question?"

"That I come?"

"Yeah."

She smiled and ticked my nose with her forefinger. "Some time I can, you know. Depend if I'm tired. Today not so bad. You first customer, so I come, yeah. It's important for you the girl comes?"

"Yeah."

She smiled.

"Can I tell you something?" I said, pressed close to her, raking my fingers through her thick dark hair, as though we'd been lovers for weeks.

"Yes."

"I got a call… from a guy–he might be Oriental, I don't know… he said he would hurt Sonia if I didn't pay him a lot of money."

Her brow furrowed slightly, although I detected no sign of knowledge in her clear brown eyes. I asked her if she understood what I'd said.

"Yes. I don't know. A man said he hurt Sonia? Why?"

I stopped combing her hair. "I'm not sure." I let out a sigh. "The thing is, if you're saying you saw her on Monday… it doesn't make sense: the call I got was before that Monday. Were you alone together with her?"

She shook her head. "She wit' Thai friend–man– and Japanese girl–but she look OK."

"So this guy, did he look like her boyfriend?"

"I don't think she got boyfriend. You have to ask her, not me, uh?" growing agitated.

"I know, I'm sorry to put you in this situation, but I–" I sat up, crossed my legs.

"I don't know about Sonia. Sonia nice girl, but bit strange, you know?"

"Is that why you left her apartment?"

She pulled a face. "She got lots of probrem, you know? I prefer it here. It's good."

I nodded, wishing to impart a sort of respect for her decisions in the hope I might better elicit more information.

"This guy, can you remember his name?"

"I think Arun."

"Arun?"

"Yes."

"Your Thai name, it's Tasanne, right? What's it mean in Thai?"

She smiled. "It mean beautiful view."

I smiled–her parents had got that right and I told her so.

"Tasanee, this guy Arun, did he seem to be… controlling Sonia in any way?"

She shook her head.

I gazed pensively at my bare shins resting against her contrasting smooth dark thighs.

"You in love wit her?"

This girl's voice was so tender and sympathetic it put a lump in my throat. She reached for my arms and drew me to her, a bounty of warmth.

"Don't be sad," she said. "You come see me some time, yeah?"

"Yeah," I said, knowing I never would.

My first tear fell on one of her breasts.

"If you in love wit' her, you need to tell her, 'cause working girl have many men say they love a girl, you know? But it just talk."

"Yeah, I know."

As her arms enveloped me I began to tremble and then I cried. Like a child. Because if what Tasanee was saying was true, it had to mean Sisi had set me up for a 30 grand con.

---

24 hours later I get a call from Jack. Sylvia is home, the kids bursting in and out of the room firing off all sorts of questions about homework and movies. I tell the man to call back in five. He won't.

"Then you'll have to hold while I find a quiet place to take this call."

"I call back, no probrem."

If I lock myself in a room Sylvia will probably assume I'm having a quiet conference call about her affair to a friend–we've had a good day so far and I don't wish to spoil it. So I step outside calling to Sylvia that I'm just nipping down to the post box.

50 yards down the road I take my vibrating phone from my pocket.

"How you doing with money?" Ridiculously it sounds like an offer of a gift.

All I hear is the imprint of my footfall on my breath. I feel like a hero in a Western waiting for the bad guy to draw his gun first. I hear what sounds like the suck on a cigarette… an anxious exhale.

"You got money yet? It's time already."

"Listen pal," I fire back, stopping by the corner of the street, exposing myself to an insidiously damp wind, "you tell Sisira, aka Sonia, if all I mean to her is money, she can fucking *die*, OK? And so can you my friend." I have plenty more to add, but that was on the money so I hang up there and then, totally exhilarated by what I've said and the conviction with which I said it.

I expect to get an immediate call back, so I walk around the block, chin tucked in as I face the sharp wind, hands buried deep in my pockets. I've gone maybe 200 yards, curling round to my own street, when my phone vibrates in my pocket, just the once. It's a video message. I hit play. The screen fills with inky darkness, then grainy low light and dark hair… Sisi's face, bruised, enters frame, her nose bleeding, her shirt torn, one breast exposed. The film looks as fantastical as something out of silent cinema horror. The camera shakes and perches on something. The zoom moves in on her face, the white of terror in her eyes. A figure walks behind her, face off screen, but from the shape, it has to be a man. A rope is casually thrown over her head and pulled tight around her neck by a gloved hand. The rope is pulled tighter and Sisi struggles in vain. I figure she must have her hands tied behind her back because she remains helpless to the torture. I have to watch ten or fifteen seconds of this before the rope goes slack. Sisi coughs and splutters. If she's acting she deserves an Oscar nomination. The clip ends with a zip of white light. My fingers are semi numb from holding the phone, but otherwise I'm in such a state of shock I barely register the cold anymore. I slip the phone back in my pocket and walk back the other way, frantically trying to calculate whether I've blown it and just gotten Sisi killed. But no, think about it. She didn't die in the video, it was a threat, raising the stakes… you've misjudged the situation, you've misjudged them– they're not to be fucked with.

I need time to process this massive about-face before re-entering the house, so I double-back and walk on to the park.

The video and Tasanee's account of having seen Sisi in Arun's company after the first threatening call just don't add up. Kidnappers don't walk around town, stopping to have a café latte in a Starbucks in Bayswater with their product and their product's former flatmate. Unless… Sisi had been in on it and then changed her mind. Or the man who'd called me had radically changed *his* mind. I feel way out of my depth. I so regret not having called the police after the first demand for money. Now that I've called their bluff I've raised the stakes and they'll have fewer qualms about killing Sisi if they so much as smell a cop. And let's not forget the little matter of my having helped her flee a crime scene, otherwise known as aiding and abetting.

As I'm fishing out my front keys by the door, my phone chimes and vibrates again. I flip it open. A text message:

'You got til Wednesday, then say goodbye to Sonia.'

Sonia, I think to myself. I don't know any Sonia. I don't want to buy back a Sonia, I can't even be sure anymore that I want Sisi.

I turn the key and step inside.

The next morning I get a call from my bank to confirm my loan application has been successful and the 15,000 would be in my account within 24 hours. If for any reason it wasn't I should call and ask to speak to Erika. I noted her extension. Was there anything else she could help me with today? How helpful the world appears to be when you feel so helpless to benefit from any help.

CHAPTER 19

The call came in the early hours of the following day, the first school night Sylvia had asked if she might stay out with her new bloke. It rang off before I could get to it. No caller ID. I took the phone back to bed. It buzzed under my pillow a few minutes later.

"Yes?" I'd meant to express ill humour but was surprised to find how light and tolerant my tone was.

"Hello?"

I barely recognised Sisi's voice at first. It sounded deeper, thick with phlegm, older. I reached for the light as though it might help improve my visualisation of Sisi and her words.

"Sisi?"

"Yeah. Sorry I call so late." She was whispering.

There was a rustling then a pause.

"What's going on?"

"Can you come and see me?"

"I dunno. Where are you? What's with this guy, Jack?"

"Jack?"

"Yeah, Jack. Or is it Arun, calling himself Jack. Whichever. Can you do me a favour here and be honest with me for once? What's going on? I mean, tomorrow I'm supposed to pay your *kidnapper* [with sarcasm] 30 grand for your release and here I am in my bed the day before and you're calling me at–"I grabbed my watch–"2.35 AM to say, 'Hello'. What the fuck is going on?"

"I got away."

I had to sit up–

"You got away?"

My chest and head thrummed from this rude awakening.

"My ex-boyfriend made me do this on you."

"You mean, the blackmail?"

"Black–? What s this?"

"The guy asking me for money so he doesn't kill you."

"Yeah. He knows you like me and he need money–"

"Oh, fine, so link up with him and rob me blind, why don'tchya!"

"I know you angry. I'm sorry."

"Sisi I can't get involved in anymore of this–OK?–it's doing my fucking head in. Do you understand?" Christ it was infectious–now I was using the term, bludgeoning her with it.

I thought I heard a muffled sobbing, like she'd taken the receiver away from her mouth and buried it in bedclothes. I resisted the temptation to soften. But what if the guy really had bullied her into it? It would certainly account for the video film I'd been sent. But then how had she gotten away? I'd seen her tied up. What if this was a trap?

"Sisi?" No answer, still the sobbing. I repeated her name more loudly.

"Hello?"

"Sisi, how did you get away?"

"I woke up and he wasn't there. So I just walk out."

"I thought you were tied up."

"No. That's just for the video he sent to your phone. He let me walk around apartment. He thought

I do this thing with him because he promised me some of the money."

Well hey, looks like he was right!

"So where is this guy now?"

"I don't' know. Maybe his house now. I ran away yesterday."

"And where's that, his house?"

"I don't know. North, I think."

I sighed. Terrific on clues here.

"So what about you, where are you now?"

"I got bedsit in Shepherd's Bush. I borrow my friend's phone."

"Which friend is that?"

"My Japanese friend. She got five phones. She very kind…"

Well at least she'd had the sense to move out of her usual two-mile radius.

"I'm sorry, Anthony, I'm very sorry, I–I should have stopped him…"

I cut her off. I couldn't get out of my head movie scenes where the pitiful whore bleats to her nice cop for that one last favour all the while she's setting him up. But then you think of that favourite movie line: 'Everyone deserves a second chance'. I couldn't just abandon her, but nor could I rush off and rescue her from her tears–the kids were on their own, what if they woke to find me gone, it just wasn't on, she'd have to wait. Besides, I needed to see her face in daylight if I was to stand a fair chance of deciphering truth from lies.

"This is what we do," I told her, the tough guy, "you stay where you are and you don't even go out for cigarettes. You don't answer the phone and you don't make any calls. Can you do that for me?"

There was a pause.

"Sisi."

"Yes."

"Can you do that for me?"

"Yes."

"Good, OK. And I'll be round to see you tomorrow afternoon. I will call to warn you that I'm coming. OK?"

"Yes."

"OK. Now let's get some sleep."

Fat chance of that, I thought closing my clamshell.

I was woken at eight, the girls telling me over and over in their sweet voices that we were late, I was late, they'd never get to school on time.

"Come on Dad!"

"Shit."

"Dad said the 's' word," Mia observed gleefully as I sprang out of bed.

Of course I'd barely slept since Sisi's call and then dozed right through the alarm, no Sylvia to rouse me.

"Where's Mum?"

"Uh, didn't she tell you?"

A funny face from Mia as she rotated on the ball of her foot.

"Yeah, she's at her teacher's house," Michaela explained helpfully, apparently not the least bit troubled by this arrangement.

"You haven't done our pack-lunch, Dad!" I was being reminded five minutes later. I seemed to have fallen into the Vauxhall Zafira ad where the kids are behaving like their parents and their parents are behaving like kids.

So I dove into the fridge and rustled up a quick risotto dish with tinned tuna and rice, garlic, soy sauce, fresh basil and Chinese Five Spice, broccoli and carrot and scooped it into their lunchboxes, as Mia accompanied my efforts with a happily sarcastic song gleaned from her mum: "Always tuna and rice, always tuna and rice…" I saw I'd splashed Sylvia's valuable kitchen floor: there was carrot peel on the bin lid and the back of the bin–but what the hell, domestic imperfections hadn't been exactly top of her agenda since she started seeing what's-his-face.

Stomach already tight, I struggled to finish a half bowl of cereal–"Dad, you haven't finished."

I corralled the girls round the basin with electric toothbrushes and floss and hairbrushes and hairbands, then herded them into the car–with my fly undone, Mia pointing this out with great hilarity. Thank god for the girls, I told myself. You'd die of self-absorption if you weren't blessed with their simple, joyous humour.

The working day had promised to be otherwise uneventful, but Georgina P was round, stalking me again. Given the state I was in, I couldn't risk being caught by her–I might explode. So I got Andrea to make up a story to hold her off at the pass in the reception while I slipped out back. We'd been laughing about the situation only a few weeks before, as if it were in the past–now in the light of what was going on with Sisi, I felt seriously disturbed by the woman's delusional state of mind.

I arrived at the address I had for Sisi in Shepherd's Bush at around 4 PM, just as it was turning dark. Her buzzer was on a short row of terraces five minutes south of the Green. For a girl who'd been accustomed to the finer things in life, she had to have made this choice in a moment of desperation. There was litter, lots of it, tossed beside an overflowing wheelie bin. Paintwork was blackened and flaking or, like the purple grey door, awaiting the undertaker. I was greeted by the tell-tale pong of rising damp as I stepped into the narrow hallway where I immediately caught my fleece jacket on the handle of one of the bikes parked against the wall. The stairs were carpeted in dark crimson and were warped to such a degree that going up them actually made you vaguely seasick. A shrivelled rubber plant in a big pot stood gasping its last on a mantelpiece. Mini skirt lengths of peeling wallpaper curled upward as if to entice you with the body rub of a damp, hard surface. Whoever had lain the carpet appeared to have run out half way up the third floor and neglected to return. If her fortunes didn't change soon, she'd be joining the homeless, I thought to myself, pausing to fish out a tissue and blow some of the fetid smells from my nostrils.

Coming to her door, ajar like a trap, I told myself to focus on getting the truth this time, not the honey.

"Sisi?" I called.

There was no answer. I heard the faint tunes of music, most probably from her laptop that she used as a CD player. I pushed the door open and she was there, rushing to let me in, a tissue in one hand.

"You OK?" I asked, stepping straight into the 'studio', (no lobby).

"I got cold," she said, wiping her slightly ruddy nose.

I shut the door.

"You OK?" she asked.

"Yeah, I'm OK." Except I suddenly felt I was missing something–for the first time I hadn't brought flowers.

"Very small," she said, immediately retreating to the bed and holding her hands out to the gas radiator she had there.

The musical melancholy in her voice immediately made me want to take her in my arms, but I planted my butt on the bed, a few feet apart from her. I looked about the room as if searching for one redeeming feature that might help me relax. Hard-wearing squares of grey carpeting covered two-thirds of the floor space–the bedroom end–cheap, B&Q flooring, already splintering, was down at the kitchen end of the room. Stove, kitchen top, kettle, toaster. She hadn't unpacked the vase, it seemed–I assumed because she didn't think the place was worthy of its presence. The small bathroom I caught a glimpse of through a sliding door was tucked around a corner. All I could think was: only the lowest form of customer would pay her a repeat visit here–that's if she was still bent on plying her trade.

I was encouraged by one thing, though: she was fully dressed for once–in a fitting red cardigan and loose scarf, a woollen black mini and black tights. She could almost be the person I'd taken her to be the first time I treated her–namely, a student. Not so good was that her hair was all in knots, she had deep shadows under her eyes and her skin was not in its best condition. It would need one of her best smiles for me to believe she wasn't depressed. –But what was that? As a dentist, I tend to look at a person's mouth before her eyes–and hers didn't look right. I reached forward, hands raised.

"May I?"

I was gentle. She let me lift her lip.

"Shit. What happened?"

"He hit me. With ash tray."

I clenched my back teeth.

"Can you come to the light?"

She let me draw her to the nearest bedside lamp, which I switched on. It was the crown I'd done and it was chipped at a slight angle. She'd lost about 30% of the crown.

"Can I use your bathroom? I need to wash my hands."

A stained basin, stiff taps, a flecked mirror that threw back an uncomplimentary reflection in the wincing yellow light. I returned to her room still drying my hands on the damp towel I'd picked up.

"I need to touch it, OK? ...Did you feel it come loose?"

"Uh-uh."

"I think you might have been lucky; there doesn't seem to be any avulsion–that means, um, loosening of the tooth, yeah?... So–yeah–I think we can wait till tomorrow. But you'll have to come in early, alright? You can't let this go Sisi, or you might lose the tooth. I need to get a proper look at it, under good light, with my extra specs on... We'll have to take an X-Ray as well just in case the root or the peg have fractured."

I paused. The shame in her eyes told me she felt she'd surely forfeited any right to my help by now.

"OK, so... what's been going on?"

She reached for a packet of cigarettes on the bed. I wanted to grab them and fling them across the room–*No more smoke screens!*–but my gut told me she just might flip if I denied her her nicotine crutch after what she'd been through.

"You realise that smoke isn't good for a damaged tooth."

Right on cue, she exhaled from the side of her mouth –and we smiled an improbable smile. I'd nearly forgotten she had an enduring and economical sense of humour.

She said she was sorry for what her ex had done to me–the scam. She'd told him about me, she said, and he'd been jealous. Which was crazy, because she'd never really been his boyfriend, just like friend with sex sometimes, she said, as if she hadn't told me this already more times than I'd cared to hear. But he went crazy, she said. He said he would tell the police about the murder if she didn't carry out the con.

"Sorry, hang on," I cut in, "I'm not getting it. Is this the guy who was there the night you–when you killed that customer, the one who threatened you with a knife?"

"Yes. No, he's his friend. They talk about this together."

"So what's this ex-boyfriend, sex friend, whatever you call him – what's his name?"

"Bobby."

"OK. Bobby. And what's Bobby look like?"

She shrugged. "Like you, so tall," raising her hand, "maybe a bit taller, your age, bigger... blue eyes."

"Blue eyes," I repeated for myself. "Is he Scottish?" wondering about the agency booker who'd lied to me.

"No. I don't think so. More like you."

"London?"

'I think so. But bit different from you."

"What's he do?"

"Businessman."

"OK, so what kind of business?"

"I don't know. Something in Internet, I think."

"That's a lot of people these days. Can you narrow it down a bit?"

She shook her head.

"Agency?"

"No."

"So whose idea was this? It was yours?"

She shook her head. It took her a moment to level her eyes with mine. I read a steady contrition, but a latent defiance too.

"It was his idea. But my fault, cos I tell him about you. You quite rich–"

I interrupted laughing out loud. "Rich, huh?! Sisi, I'm a dentist not a banker. You should talk to my accountant."

"What?"

"Never mind. So this Bobby friend of yours, he came up with this idea–for the kidnap?"

She nodded, eyes on her knees, just the kind of moment when you wish the woman you'd fallen in love with was of your own culture because you'd be in a much better position to read her body language.

"So… how did he find out about the thing at the flat, the murder?"

"My friend call him."

"Arun?"

"Yes. How you know his name?"

"You told me already. Now, why did Arun call Bobby?"

"To get rid of body. He needed help. My friend get stopped by police in his van and he panic."

"He was searched?"

"No. He was lucky, just check his driving licence, but after, he panic and he call Bobby."

"So these guys, they dispose of the body and then they–they look around for some way of getting some money for what they did. Is that it? And they know about my involvement, taking you to the hotel, so they set up this con. Is that it?"

"Yes. I'm sorry."

She stubbed out the cigarette, me taking this in. She stood up and asked me if I wanted a beer.

So she opened two beers and brought them in. We didn't make a toast to anything this time.

"So, tell me… when I didn't pay up, that's when it got nasty?"

"Yeah, Bobby hit me. He think I tell you about him, about his plan. I should have told you, I know, I was really bad person, but I didn't. He was, like, paranoid."

"So that video they sent me, that was for real?"

She lifted her neck and moved forward, pulling down her scarf–faded rope burns.

"Fucking psycho," and I nearly flung my beer at the wall. "Why are you still seeing someone who would do this to you, do this to me?! I helped you, Sisi!"

"Don't shout, please! I know… I know!"

She buried her face in her hands in a display of deepest regret–but I wasn't about to hold her in my arms and say it was all going to be OK.

"How did you get away?"

"I told you he hit me, yeah? I pretend to be KO, you know?" She assumed an unconscious face. "He throw me on the bed and then he left apartment. Maybe for cigarettes, I don't know. I packed one bag and run away."

I noticed then that the chill out music Sisi had put on had come to an end.

"He used to be good guy, but he changed. Maybe drugs change him, I think."

"When you say drugs, do you mean, like, crack?"

She shook her head. "I don't think so, just cocaine…pills. He's got bad memory from too many pills, so he doesn't take so many now."

How reassuring. What were the chances he'd simply forget about me or Sisi?

I sipped my beer. Finding it too sweet and too cold for the weather, the room's damp and the story I was hearing.

"Who knows you're here?"

"You and Kyoko."

"The Japanese girl you visited that first day I came to see you?"

She shook her head. “He doesn't know her. I move soon anyway.”

“What about customers, work? You have to stop.”

“No customers. Not nice place…” gesturing about the room as proof, “dirty, but it’s only thing I could find last night.”

I put the beer on the stained and warped bedside table. I reached out for her beer. She gave it me. I put it beside mine. I sat a bit closer.

“Come here,” I said, and gently took her in my arms. What was I thinking? A dad’s cuddle might make it alright?

Sisi asked, Could I stay the night with her? Sure. She didn’t want sex, though, sorry. That’s OK.

As we got into her bed, I offered to give her a massage. She’d always declined when I’d offered before, probably because she’d been uncomfortable reversing the role of customer and client, but this time, she accepted gladly. I threw her long hair to one side and began on her shoulders and neck, kneading the relatively inelastic skin (as compared to Western skin), slowly working down the beautiful bow of her back to that mysterious darker pigmentation above her bottom.

“How you know this?” she asked.

“My mum was a physiotherapist? So, I learnt something from her–“

“She does massage?”

“Well, she did–but physiotherapy, it’s more than just massage, y’know? It’s a recovery programme for when you get a bad injury.”

“You had injury?”

"Yeah, couple times. Had a bad shoulder once. And that's how you learn the points, y'know?–from feeling other people's hands on your body, trying to ease the pain… That good?"

I asked her if I could remove her panties to do all of her and she said, Yes, I could, in Thai. I drew my thumbs hard across the top of her buttocks, digging my nails in. She said this was the best part–it felt like butterflies were flying out of the base of her spine, she said; she'd never experienced anything like it before. I went to her legs and kneaded her muscular calves, her inner thighs. I gently brushed my fingers against her sex, collecting a little honey dew, which I rubbed back into her skin. I was tempted to do more, slip my pants down and enter her from behind but I didn't want to take her, I wanted only to soothe her. Besides, she was slowly falling asleep.

In the early hours I woke to find Sisi sitting up in bed. Still thick with sleep and charged to fear the worst, my first thought was that she was about to announce that I should leave. But the grey light that was infiltrating the room through ill-fitting, gappy curtains revealed a depleted quality about her posture that suggested she was patiently waiting for me to find her.

"Sweetheart, what's the matter?"

But then she pushed me away as I slipped my arm across her back, just like my own Mia when she most needed to be reassured that her recent temper fit over her drawing, say, didn't mean I loved her any the less.

"What's up?"

She wouldn't lift her face. I reached again but she pushed me away, this time nearly winding me.

"What've I done?"

"You don't understand, it's ME!" She sniffed, thickly.

"OK, what is it I should understand?"

"You can't love me," the 'me' rising in tone as if she'd already put herself in the stocks and was awaiting due punishment.

"Because of this scam, you mean?"

"I betray you. Very bad." Her voice cracked as it uttered the last two words.

I thought a moment.

"We're through that now."

"No! I didn't tell you everything!"

I waited, the cold air wrapping itself around my shoulders like a damp blanket.

"OK. You wanna tell me now?"

"In beginning, when you come to my apartment? That's not dead man. It's just dummy. Not real."

"How do you mean?"

"Dummy! You know, like from shop."

"Not a cop, not a customer?"

She shook her head. "You only see hair, yeah? You see blood, you see knife … sheets with blood on it, so you think someone get killed, but it's just dummy."

"It seemed heavier than a dummy."

"Arun put weights in it," gesturing a man using dumbbells.

"And the blood? It felt like blood…"

"My blood. Period. Sorry."

I was awestruck by her inventiveness.

"I hate my job, yeah?" She sniffed. "You said, maybe you give me money one day, so we can be together, you wanted me to be free so I don't have to work, so… this my plan–yeah?–to get money from you. Now you understand? I'm very bad person."

The hair on my scalp was standing up and I still couldn't quite believe what I was hearing. Perhaps in among that tingling sensation there was the immediate relief that I hadn't in fact been part of a murder because there had been no murder.

"This was your idea?"

"No."

"I thought you just said it was your plan."

She wiped her nose with the back of her hand and finally raised her head. As she looked at me with those large wide eyes, the tears glistening in the moonlight, I still couldn't be sure whether she was sorry for what she was confessing to.

"It was Bobby's idea," she said. "First it was just a joke, you know? But then he want to make plan. I didn't want to, but he said, it's quick way, save me many hundreds of fucks with guys, then I can go home, help my mom and little brother, maybe start business. I said, 'No no, I like Anthony,' but he keep bothering me. Then he says, if I don't do it, he tell agency bad things about me. I said, 'I don't care'. But then I get call from agency and they say customer complaining, they take me off website for one week." She paused to wipe a tear from the corner of her eye with the sheet. "Bobby friendly with Arun and Arun friendly with some guy at agency back in Thailand, so I didn't know what to do." She stopped, mucous was dripping from her nose. I reached for a box of tissues, but there wasn't one. She used the sheet again.

She fell quiet after that. I was still floundering for words.

She stretched out her legs in front of her as though she'd got cramps in her calves. Then crossed them and grabbed her feet in her hands.

"Sisi," I touched her knee, "it doesn't matter now, OK?" though I couldn't possibly know that, I hadn't even processed the truth of what she'd said.

"Yes, it matters, of course it matters! How can you love me now? Always you think of this, always!"

"No no no… no. Look, you were coerced–they–the whole situation, you just got caught up in it. I understand the pressures of this job. I mean–OK, maybe it's fun some of the time, it's definitely good money, but I know how *lonely* you've been, I know how worried you are about your mom, your family." I drew nearer, slipped my arms around her back. "Hey."

"You too kind to me. Break my heart." She began to cry again, in a kind of hiccupping spasm of distress that reminded me of a child's crying.

"Shh," holding her to me, my own beating–yes, breaking–heart.

I got her to lie down with me, in my arms, body trembling uncontrollably, her tears dropping onto my face like some final, painful valediction to the lies that have harmed us.

To the accompaniment of her fading spasms, I reflected on the scene of that night of the 'murder' and couldn't help admiring the brilliant theatre of their con. I'd been so taken in. I felt her head move and sensed she was looking at me now.

"Seems like I was right: you're an actress, a natural." She blinked. I smiled, wanting this observation of mine to be the entire explanation to what had happened, as if she'd used me to prove she had talent. "We have to get you in the movies." I smiled tremulously, tears brimming in my eyes.

In her dense, impassive gaze I read awe, as if she'd discovered new things about me, or about a man, qualities she'd either never known or could barely remember. She reached to touch my face in a way that frightened me because it resembled a farewell gesture–then she laid her hand on mine as if for the first time finding me valuable.

"When I saw you last time, I feel really bad about what we did. I saw you really do care for me. So I tell him, I'm not doing plan anymore… and he got mad, really mad."

"Bobby or the other guy?"

"Always Bobby. Arun quite gentle, but he Bobby's friend, Bobby do him favour like get him drugs and stuff."

Chillingly the video film was only too real now.

"You don't hate me?"

Watching her wipe her runny nose on the sheets I drew some modicum of comfort, because the girl I'd always paid to see had been so meticulously clean, the girl I'd paid to see had deceived me; only by hitting rock bottom could she start over, I told myself.

"I'm just bad for you," she said.

My heart hurt as she said those words, because I knew that on the facts there was a lot of truth to them. I could feel my body tense all over as I clung ferociously to the hope that together we possessed enough integrity, however jaded it might have become, to root out the bad stuff and make a fresh start. I'd reached that point where I was all in, or out.

Our breathing calm and rested now, I asked her if she thought Bobby would come looking for her. She didn't know. I asked her if she knew where he lived. She reminded me she'd told me already, she didn't know; he kept that a secret. But she knew where Arun lived. I asked her to show me. We switched on the light and she got out of bed and hunkered down by her bag, looking for her A-Z. He lived in Harlesden, she said. I asked her to write down the address on a piece of paper and I put the chit of paper in my pocket.

"What are you going to do?"

"I dunno yet, I dunno."

I still had the video on my phone, Sisi's broken tooth was evidence enough of abuse–I made a mental note to take photos as well as X-Rays tomorrow–we'd surely be able to get a restraining order of some kind, deterrent enough for anyone but a psychopath.

Anyone but a psychopath, echoed uneasily in my head.

I switched off the light and Sisi got back into bed with me. We lay facing each other, studying each other's faces.

"I can't be with you Anthony."

I waited a moment. I was afraid she was right. But no matter what the decay, I always try and save the tooth.

I sensed she'd grown cold. I moved a fraction closer until I could feel her fear vibrating against my own skin that she might contaminate me if she let me hold her. With my hand I moved as slowly as an animal handler before an animal he knows well but which has turned a bit crazy overnight, a beast that might bite and kill him if taken too hastily.

"Why you like me?"

I slid my hands up the silky smoothness of her bare thighs to her bare buttocks, and I was surprised to find them cooler than my own hands and was gently gratified I could make them warm. I scooped the other hand under her waist and gently rolled her over on top of me, one hand on each cheek of her bottom.

"You feel that?"

She did.

"Your heart always beat fast for me." She smiled in spite of herself.

I listened to our hearts beating against one another, urgent. When would they beat as one? I wondered. Like in the love songs.

She began to play with me, a wicked glint in her eye like a succubus. She kissed me, warning me to be careful of her broken tooth against my tongue…

I had none of my hang-ups as we made love that night. No longer shackled by time, with no customer about to arrive outside, the blocked chi that so cruelly manifested itself when I'd been with her in Paddington just flowed out of me like a clear mountain stream. I felt I'd come full circle with her: the first time, I'd fucked her with an anger that had scared and thrilled me equally, but that night it was as if this snake-like thing I thought of as an entity writhing beside us as we fucked was now tamed; we'd finally made the transition from the primal to something you might loosely call the spiritual. I'd dreamed of reaching this higher state with her, but I'd always known it would depend on her letting go of the mistrust that came with the territory of prostitution.

"Open your eyes… wider… look at me," I commanded as I read from her sounds that she was nearly there, heading for a big one.

She seemed to struggle to meet my eyes, as though meeting a bright light.

"Look at me," I repeated and I poured my blueness into her aqueous worlds of infinite darkness, until my own vision began to blur... and blur again, as if I were in a car travelling at the speed of sound. With the roof off.

The orgasm was strong, and yet our engorged lips remained hungry for one another, paddling in the swell of post coital waters for many minutes after.

It was the nearest I'd experienced to a sense of 'being reborn'. I could so easily have collided with my anger at the con she'd pulled. I could have frozen with the fear that I was investing in bad stuff. But I chose–

and more significantly, she chose–tenderness, as if it were the only true faith worth holding on to.

CHAPTER

20

Waking that morning I'd roused Sisi as I would have roused my kids for school–with a gentle rub and cajoling sounds. She was so unaccustomed to getting up before noon, I practically had to undress her to get her started. She became a little bad tempered with my encouragements and began insisting that she'd come down to the surgery later in the day.

"No no no," picking her up again from the bed, "I need to look at that tooth this morning. It's possible an infection could set in…"

It's true it probably wouldn't have made much difference had I seen her later that day, but I just didn't trust her to turn up. We'd made up, we'd even made fantastic love, surpassing all my expectations, but there was a contrariness about her that morning that spoke of more than just an unwillingness to cooperate. She'd been so used to a certain style of life, a steady flow of tax-free income, a man in your bed had no right to make demands on her moral fortitude, only the position he'd like to fuck her in. On the evidence, she was probably the type with a tendency to seek out abusive men. Her father had abandoned her and left her to an abusing step-father. This had to mean *she'd* done something wrong, so the prostitution was a natural choice for someone who felt bound to live out her emotion of self-inadequacy. She'd so far preferred to mess around with types like this Bobby character because only with his type was there so little risk of falling in love and then being abandoned as her father had abandoned her. How neat the diagnosis, even smug, but how the fuck did you go about undoing all the damage? My kindness must have been confusing. There was a real possibility she was addicted to empty sex and lies and that regular love and kindness would put her through a kind of cold turkey.

As I watched her finish getting dressed I described what I'd do to fix her tooth, aware that she wasn't listening, but saying the words for my own sake as I knew I'd have a rushed morning ahead of me, fitting her in.

"…and with any luck we should be done in half an hour," I concluded. "Have you anything planned for later?"

"I'm going to the temple." She looked up and smiled diffidently. I couldn't tell whether she was secretly inviting me to join her, or intimating that she wanted to go alone.

"You mean the one in Wimbledon you told me about?"

"Yes." She coughed, clearing her throat.

"Could we go together?"

"But you working."

"Only this morning. I'm free in the afternoon."

She said she had some shopping to do–clothes she needed to buy.

"Fine, I'll meet you after. You can have most of the morning and half the afternoon."

Her non-answer spoke of resistance.

I took her hands and pulled her down onto my lap on the bed. "Hey, I'd like to go with you to this place. You've often mentioned it. Let's go together." I parted her hair back from her averted eyes. "Please."

"OK," she said finally and squeezed my hand and got to her feet, with barely a glance. I tried to shrug the lingering sense that I'd imposed myself on her day.

We left her house, hand in hand, in a pensive mood, beneath a uniformly grey November sky. We sat up top on the bus, seldom speaking. She gazed down upon the streets as though the flow of morning life might take her over a waterfall's edge. I asked her if she was OK and she nodded without looking at me. The only time I saw any change in her preoccupied expression was when she grew aware of a strangely vibrating pattern of early morning rainwater migrating toward her across the window pane to her right. She pointed to it, as if it were alive. No sooner had I identified what was amusing her, than the violent energy in the water began to fill me with foreboding and I was strangely relieved when it dispersed itself.

I called ahead to see how we could fit Sisi in to that morning's schedule. Rebecca was in a distracted mood and I had to hold her hand as we juggled possibilities so that Sisi wouldn't have to wait until midday. While treating my first two patients, I kept popping my head round the corner–I was afraid that Sisi'd lose patience and wander off to do her shopping, but as it turned out my worries proved to be unfounded.

As she sat back in the chair, she seemed just like another patient again. Until I wheeled in close and could smell her perfume, my eyes focusing on those sensuous lips that appeared to have a life of their own. As she opened her mouth, I had to glance at Andrea to block out the picture of me diving my tongue in there.

"OK," I announced, "first, let's get you X-rayed…"

The X-Rays looked fine, no damage to the nerve, so we could numb her up and start drilling off the crown. We took a set of impressions of the core for the lab, Andrea passed the wax and I began building up the stump. I was working efficiently and we were done in thirty minutes. It was even quite a good match. I just had to hope Bobby wasn't about to do anything that would require further reductions and corrections.

After Sisi left, I had to work just as fast to catch up on my morning's list. With the waiting room empty and Andrea getting into her jacket, I reconsidered calling Sylvia–if only to let her know I hadn't been mugged. Was it odd she hadn't called or sent me a text? I knew that if I could, I would want to spend the night again with Sisi because I felt she was particularly vulnerable right now–she'd not only messed up trying to pull a scam on me, she'd antagonised Bobby and possibly this young Thai boy who'd also been in on the scam. She had nothing to do and I worried she'd drink and possibly start calling people I didn't want her speaking to. So I started to write Sylvia a text. But I aborted half way through–it seemed cowardly and unfair. Around lunch I scrolled to her name on my phone. I hardly knew where to begin.

"Sylvia, hi, it's me."

She said nothing.

"Are you there?"

"Yes."

"I'm sorry but I might be out again tonight." No reaction, no blow-up, which would have made it easier for me, now I'd have to plough on, humping my guilt and my doubt on my back. "Um–the girl I'm involved with, she uh… she's trying to get out of an abusive relationship and, right now I'm–I feel I have to help her move house, do all I can to make sure this guy doesn't do anything to hurt her."

Silence.

"Sylvia?"

"I don't know what to say. I mean, if you feel you have to do that…" Her words trailed off into static. "So when will you be home? I mean if we're going to separate, OK, that's on the cards, but I–y'know, we need some kind of plan, I can't–you can't just ring up and tell me you won't be around today because something's 'come up'. I haven't done that to you."

"No, you're right and I wouldn't be saying this if I didn't think it was crucial that I–that I–"

"If it's that bad, why don't you go to the police?"

"I probably will go to the police. But I can't see them doing very much in the short term and, from what I've heard, they don't do much at all until it's too late in these cases."

"Why don't you find out for yourself instead of going on what you've heard?"

"I will, I just told you I will–just not today."

Another pause; inky blackness in my mind.

"So are you saying, we can't expect you home until this stalker has given up? What is it with you and stalkers anyway? You seem to attract them into your life."

"Oh, I see, my karma–"

"Yeah, very much so. Your girlfriends, your patients–" She reined it, but I was already smarting from the eviscerating tone and judgment–it was too horrifying to accept she was right.

"Sylvia–"

But she cut me off, exasperated, her action demanding that she was uninterested in words, I must act if I wanted back into the family.

Presumably her relationship with the other man wasn't going so well. I agonised over calling her back and finally wrote a text saying I'd try and be home later that night. She wrote back: 'I hope your daughters still mean more to you than any new woman'. Knee in the balls, and very effective. And possibly carrying a veiled threat re custody.

I took the District Line to Wimbledon. Coming in to East Putney I got a call from Sisi. She sounded cheerful and I was happy that she'd called to check on my whereabouts. When I arrived ten minutes later, though, Sisi wasn't waiting for me at Wimbledon station and her phone was switched off. When she called me ten minutes later, I nearly vented at her like a worried parent. She'd taken a wander around a shoe shop, hadn't heard my call because of the music–"Sorry!"–and said she'd be with me in ten minutes.

"OK, mai bpen rai," [Doesn't matter] I sang back.

As she came toward me, holding a flimsy pink umbrella, shoulders hunched because of the wet and the cold, I thought how ordinary she was, not in a bad way, actually in a good way, in the sense that I wasn't immediately caught up in her sexual allure; I felt only warmth on seeing her. We kissed and she took my hand and led us off in the direction of the nearest bus stop. She said she'd bought herself a new phone, a RAZR Motorola. She loved its sleek body. She'd put my number in. As if as a joke, I said I hoped she hadn't put Bobby's in. Later I would hate myself for not having asked to see this guy's number, but at the time I was still wary of pushing her away from me by coming across as controlling–after all, I saw myself as a kind of antidote to this type of man.

Ten minutes later we got off the 93 bus on a leafy stretch of road and took a side road to the Buddahpadiba Temple. She took my hand and swung both our arms a couple of times, happy all of a sudden and I felt rather thrown that she'd been able to recapture some of that cheerfulness I had found so endearing when we'd first got to know each other. My skin grew taut with the hope that I could look forward to settling into something like an enduring love with her.

Walking past the properties and their large gardens Sisi said how she loved this area. "Money," I said cynically. She shrugged and smiled as if my remark was irrelevant, as if ownership weren't important to her, just beauty, its capacity to replenish your dreams.

The entranceway was on our right. As we passed through some open gates, along a pathway, a small temple came into view on our left, perched on a sloping incline that overlooked leafy gardens. I felt immediately it was a shame to see it on such a rainy day, I could imagine the gold painting carvings coming alive like flames in the sunshine.

We climbed some marble steps, littered with parked shoes. Sisi asked me to remove my shoes and said I could go inside. I pushed open the heavy glass door and stepped into a room quietly resplendent in various hues of deep red and gold. About 20 feet directly in front of me sat a young monk, in a brown robe, quietly delivering his sermon at the foot of a symmetrical mountain of candles and vases and glass lamps and, of course, Buddhas, which climbed to two prominent and differently smiling Buddhas in the centre. The monk spoke evenly, kindly, as if speaking one-to-one, occasionally pausing to smile, then resuming without gesture or self-important rhetorical flourishes.

Sisi had gotten onto her knees and bowed to the monk and the Buddhas. I sat a few feet wide of her, admiring the beauty of the small interior. The walls were painted mostly in reds, broken up by aquamarine colours and greens–scenes of monks quietly gathered around a wise male, listening to the wisdom he was imparting. The roof, about 40 feet above our heads, was of wood panels painted blood red. Onto the panels had been built various gold-painted frames that might have represented doors to the golden stars they enclosed.

I've never liked churches. Since I was a boy, they'd spooked me with their bareness and images of death and mourning. I could never understand why, with every town we visited on a summer holiday somewhere, my parents had to leave the sunshine to enter the gloom of a church or cathedral. As far as I was concerned they were places that invoked only guilt and morbid emotions, and reminded you of your insignificance in the presence of Christ. By contrast, this room inspired a sense of achievable mental peace with the world. The Buddha figures radiated a benign optimism in such a way as to say it was there for all of us to find if only we stressed a little less about our age and looks. The flowers in the vases at the front were cheerful, various and charming in themselves, not mere symbols of a softer side to rites of supplication. The atmosphere quietly encouraged you to believe in your potential as opposed to dwelling on what you lacked–even if I couldn't help noticing the dozen or so visitors we'd just joined wore decidedly solemn faces.

I shuffled over the red carpet to be beside Sisi. She took out a notebook from her bag and wrote a message for me: 'Tell me when you want to go, we can't talk here.' I nodded, quite content for the time being just absorbing the quietly cheerful beauty of the place.

Stepping outside, Sisi asked if I'd like to see the monks' house, a brown brick building at the foot of the slope on which the temple was built. We entered through a glass door, leaving our shoes outside once again. The very lean monk who greeted us appeared to recognise Sisi. She began talking to him as if about a matter she'd prearranged with him–in fact the case. She asked me to step into a beige-carpeted room with the monk and disappeared. Ahead of me stood a small shrine. The monk sat on the floor with the shrine to his left and his back against the windows. As he was pulling together the collar of his brown robe, I observed in Thai that the weather was cold today. He betrayed momentary surprise as if I'd just flicked an elastic band across the room, then smiled with restored composure, agreeing in Thai. He allowed a pause to elapse before asking me in Thai, if I would please sit. When I sat on the carpet by the wall opposite him he asked me to move closer. He asked me where I was from and was interested to hear I'd never been to Thailand but could speak some of his language. You must go, he said in Thai and then in English. His English was pretty basic and his knowledge of the city remarkably limited given he'd been living in London for two years–but then again, he was a monk.

Sisi reappeared shortly carrying a small hamper in a bronze dish, similar in shape to the iconic Vietnamese hat. She sat beside me and asked me to join her as she passed the offering to the monk. So I put my hand beside hers on the rim of the bowl, while the monk took a rust coloured silk cloth to accept the donation without personally handling it. Sisi explained she was making a donation for someone who'd died. Her father? I didn't ask. Hopefully not her sister, who had been undergoing chemo and radiotherapy a few months ago. The monk instructed her to bring some water. She moved away to pick up two small metal jugs and two goblets. We were to pour water from the little jugs into the goblets as the monk recited some kind of blessing. When that was done, the monk asked me in English to repeat after him, together with Sisi, a kind of litany, which he uttered, eyes closed, hands in prayer, phrase by phrase. I had to concentrate hard to get my tongue round the sounds, occasionally I stumbled, whereupon the monk opened his eyes and repeated the phrase, which I had a second shot at, and so we moved on. He concluded with a kind of tonal amen. There was a pause. The monk picked up a tied bundle of dry grass beside him and dipped it in a bowl and sprayed Sisi and me with blessed water, three times. He smiled, with just the slightest glint of humour, and said we were done. I felt a little bemused Sisi had involved me in this ritual without any warning or discussion, but it also seemed to mark some kind of new acceptance of me.

The monk chatted with Sisi a while, apparently curious as to my relationship with her. I figured he was wise enough to know she'd been a prostitute and wondered what that made me in his eyes. He asked me if I was interested in meditation and gently tried to get me interested in going to beginner classes at the temple. As I waited in a neighbouring anteroom for Sisi to use the toilet, he showed me a rack of books on Buddhism. I began to suspect his interest in me was as much material as spiritual.

The rain had stopped and Sisi suggested a short tour of the grounds, which weren't extensive anyway. We were walking back up the hill toward the Temple, when Sisi paused and glanced back to the monks' house. On the porch there were a couple of women helping themselves to free coffee and tea–and there was a man watching us, hands in the pockets of his baggy outdoor jacket. He had on a red baseball cap. I couldn't be sure, but my gut told me I'd seen him before.

"Is that Arun?" I asked Sisi.

She turned to look.

"Mm… I think–maybe," she said.

"You think he followed you here?"

The man slipped inside as if he'd read my lips from 25 yards.

"I don't think so. Many Thai people come here on Saturday."

"Yeah but–bit of a coincidence, isn't it?"

"You want to go?"

"Do you want me to talk to him?"

"No no," she laughed. "No, please… just trouble with agency."

"But you're not with the agency, anymore, are you?"

"I told you, I take time off. Can we go?" and she threaded her arm through mine.

Reluctantly I let the matter drop and we headed back to the bus stop.

Half an hour later, seated at a table in a spacious bar restaurant adjacent to Wimbledon Station, Sisi was telling me she felt much better for having gone to the temple and made a donation. She said friends often asked her why she didn't go to pub or club to relax, but she preferred to visit temple. It's good to give something, she said. If you never give, you don't have anything in next life, you stay animal. She said her father had gone regularly to the temple, always with some kind of donation. She missed those times, she said. People didn't go to temple so often now in Thailand, she said, because of corruption. Many monks had too much money, rich clothes, expensive cars! Monks weren't supposed to have these things! It was tradition a monk took clothes from a monk who had died, he didn't go to designer shops. And many monks now having sex! she said. Not supposed to have sex. They fight with each other over women. Not supposed to touch women. Everything change. But she still liked to go.

"You must go to my country," she said with the kind of ardour that evoked dialogue from fairy stories where princes found fortune, love and happiness.

"Together," I replied.

And she looked back at me with that waking sort of expression like a child who'd forgotten she wouldn't be alone on a certain occasion. She said she'd like to show me the best places to go–the places that tourists didn't usually see.

"How's your sister, by the way? Her treatment?"

"She better now. Cancer go away for now. I'm very happy." Seeing her smile brightly for the first time that morning, I was suddenly happy too.

"Well that's great, that's really great."

I picked up my glass and proposed a toast to recovery–by which I also meant hers, though she probably wouldn't have realised that.

I asked her what would her family make of me, us.

"They see you want to look after me," she said. But many people would know for sure then that she'd been a prostitute; only prostitutes married with white guys, she said. I asked her if she thought she could stay here with me. She wasn't sure yet. I took her hand in mine, rubbing my thumb gently across her knuckles and thought of Sylvia as Sisi drank from her glass of wine.

We arrived back at her damp studio pretty wet through. For the first time, I ran the bath for us and lit the candles, while Sisi lay on the bed reading making something out of paper. When I asked her what she was doing, she turned her back, shielding her work and told me to listen to music or something.

"The bath's ready."

After a pause, she said, "You go."

"I'm waiting for you."

"So wait then."

I took my Colloquial Thai book, now dog-eared, from my bag, and began reading up on 'torng'–to have to, or must. I read some sentences aloud and she corrected my pronunciation, still busy with her paperwork. Five minutes later she crept up on me with two little paper birds, which she made fly just across my page. I smiled.

"What's this?"

"You know origami?"

"Yeah, sure."

"My Japanese friend teach me. Hai lek kah." [For your children]

I turned to find her smiling sweetly, like a child.

"Thanks."

I took the delicate little paper birds in my hand and lay them carefully on the carpet and reached to take her in my arms. She slipped over my lap, like one identical chair into another. She nestled her face under my chin.

"Y'know, I – " I reached for an envelope in my jacket pocket – "I brought these for you to look at."

I opened the old envelope and took out some photos of Mia and Michaela.

"Oh, so pretty!" she exclaimed and I was touched by the sparkle in her eye as her eyes passed from one photo to the next. "And good pictures. You take?"

"Um, no, Sylvia."

"She very good."

"Yeah… Would you like to meet them some day?"

She kept gazing at the young faces as if she hadn't heard me. Then she raised her head and smiling, exclaimed, "Yes! Tomorrow!"

"Tomorrow?" I laughed.

"Yes, why not?"

I couldn't think why not, I'd have to ask.

"Tomorrow," she kept insisting, as I laughed harder. I had to kiss her to shut her up.

She put the birds in my Thai book and said I should give them to my beautiful children as a present tomorrow.

"Why don't you give them to them?"

"Maybe you can't meet tomorrow," she said, coming slowly down to earth.

I smiled, a little sad to see her lose that glow of spontaneity.

"OK."

"Can I keep them?"

"Sure."

"I make a dragon for when I see them."

And we were cheerful again.

In the bath, I urged her to be careful about giving out her address details to anyone until Arun and Bobby receded from her life. I said now that there had in fact been no murder, she and I should go to the police to report Bobby. She said that was impossible because then she would have to admit to tricking me, trying to get my money. She grew upset, her hand splashing on the soapy water and I had to calm her with a promise we wouldn't do anything for now, only if Bobby came around bothering her.

Our lovemaking that night was much less ardent than the previous night, though she seemed to take a singular pleasure in making the most of my generosity. It was as if she were saying to me, 'Well, if you really do want to devote yourself to me, you must be *my* whore occasionally.' Or perhaps it was her way of leading up to telling me, half an hour later, that she would like to sleep alone tonight. She needed to start getting her life straight, she said, and she couldn't really do that with me around. I said I was fine with that–that's to say, I was, as long as she wasn't seeing customers again.

"No no–you don't want me to–"

"Sisi, you're right, I don't want you to, but it's more important *you* don't want to. I can't stop you doing this, OK? But I want you to know, I'm serious when I say I want to be with you, look after you while you find something better to do."

She answered taking my face in her hands and kissing me on the mouth. It felt inappropriate, a tactic to distract me. She met my eyes with a now almost familiar mixture of fondness and bewilderment – it was as though she read kindness as a sort of sleight of hand.

"It's OK, I have enough money for a while. You don't have to worry."

I wondered where she put it all–in bundles under the bed, in drawers, an overseas account?

Getting into my things, I reminded her I'd booked her an appointment to see Tom, my hygienist, for 5.30 on Monday and she promised she would be there. On balance I felt relieved she'd asked me to go–I'd been aching to get back to see my girls but hadn't wanted to go, abandoning her. It was time too that I put Sylvia in the picture, as best I could–without mention of prostitution, if I could get away with it.

That night was to be the last time we'd make love. I'd later sorely regret not having used a condom, my sperm nesting in a crack where they'd place me in a much stickier situation than I was in already.

CHAPTER 21

I arrived home before 11PM but Sylvia had already gone to bed and didn't stir as I stuck my head round the door. I took spare sheets and blankets from the airing cupboard and curled up on the sofa with the cat.

I woke early, stiff and cold, with Sisi's sore throat. I put some socks on and curled up tighter, but couldn't sleep. I stepped out to buy the Sunday Times at 6.30 and read listlessly until the girls found me around 8.30.

"You're there?" Sylvia said, arriving shortly after, tying the belt of her dressing gown, eyes sleepy, hair tousled.

"Yeah, I didn't want to disturb you."

"Why didn't you use the spare room?"

"Oh, I dunno, seemed easier in here."

"What time did you get in?"

"Late."

"I didn't hear you."

The girls were asking me to pass their cereals, the rice milk, spoons.

Sylvia schlepped about in her moccasins, more heavily than Sisi would. She asked if I'd managed to sort something out, as the girls ran over my reply with their own questions as to where I'd been and why I hadn't slept with mummy. Had I called the police? Sylvia asked.

"Michaela, can you get the milk yourself," she said to our eldest, a little more sharply than was warranted. "You can see we're talking, can't you."

"Oh-kay," replied daughter number one, executing a swift rehearsal for her moodier teens.

"Not yet," I answered belatedly.

"Is this really going to be worth it?" Sylvia asked me, now as composed as if we were discussing a discounted holiday deal.

"Is yours worth it?"

Her face darkened. "Why do you always do that?"

"What?"

"Flip it back to me. Like it's a competition. I'm just trying to–y'know–"

"I didn't mean it that way. I just–I was just trying to establish where we both are."

She sighed as though she would never be done with this apparently obtuse side of my character.

"What are you arguing about?" Michaela asked.

"Daddy's plans–I need to be clear, that's all."

I looked at the girls opposite–from their expressions you'd guess they barely had a clue what was going on, but both of them had asked me questions in private that revealed they knew a lot more than either of us had thought.

"Are you going to be out again tonight?" Sylvia was asking me.

To answer seemed like risking the first foot on a minefield.

"I don't know. But I may be out tomorrow night."

"And you just expect me to fit in with that, I suppose."

I couldn't think how to reply. However I expressed myself, Sylvia would probably take offence and she was not likely to contain herself for the sake of the girls–on the contrary, she tended to act as though she believed that a public flogging of their father served as proof that I was the guilty party.

"I just want to be sure she's safe," I said finally, identifying a growing resentment in me that she might, just for a moment, consider someone other than herself and our kids.

She picked up her tea, looking into it and pursing her lips as if interrupted by the reflux of moral indigestion.

I got to my feet and left the room before she could do anything bitterly ironic with the word 'safe' in its sexual context.

Round lunchtime I called Sisi on her new Virgin phone. She didn't answer. I left a message reminding her of her dental appointment and hoped she was fine. When Sisi failed to show at the practice by six the following day, I called again. And again I got the anonymous voice of her answer machine. Five minutes later, I received a text message from her.

'Sorry need to see you scared please come my place now xx'

My immediate alarm was dampened by suspicion. Because, if she was finally through messing me about, why wasn't she calling me? The only scenario that came to me was of her at her recent, shabby address in the company of her stalking ex or former sex buddy. I pictured a shadowy male figure in the bathroom, as she composed her text, having just enough time to write one line but with no opportunity to speak to me. If he was in fact there, I shouldn't announce my intention to visit her by sending a message, which he might hear arrive and insist on reading–I should just go.

Heading home, I told myself for the hundredth time that I might have to accept that this simply wasn't going to work. But in opposition to this defeatist air, I also saw myself having to confront Bobby or Arun or both–it could get physical. I so wanted to punch this Bobby on the nose, but we weren't in the schoolyard anymore and he'd already proven he had no respect for the law–fists could escalate to knives or even guns.

Normally I'd have made the trip to Sisi's by public transport but that evening I wanted the extra security of a car. If Sisi had fallen ill, or was frightened and needed to move again, I didn't want to schlep from point to point on buses and trains, I needed to show her I could look after her and that meant wheels.

Anticipating resistance from Sylvia, I hit the line with an insistent tone, which I couldn't quite temper to an even one even as she was saying, It was OK, I could have the car. I apologised and now, hearing my pant as I hurried along the street, the pounding of my feet, decided not to ask after the kids in case she threw the question back at me and said, *Yes, how about them?* I said thanks and told her I'd get the car back to her for the morning. The minute I was home, I didn't even enter the house, I just walked into the garage, (which Sylvia had left open), got into the car and drove off.

I must have arrived in Shepherd's Bush around 7.15 PM. I had to park in the road running parallel to Sisi's new house, then walk back. I rang her buzzer but got no answer. I rang her phone again and still no answer. I rang one of the other buzzers and posed as a bloke delivering Pizza to the top floor.

"So ring the bell for top flat," a sulky male voice answered back.

"'er bell don't work, mate, sorry," broadening my London accent.

There was a muttering of curses, then the buzzer was released. I stepped inside. Loud R&B dry-humped the walls in the corridor. I took the stairs with stealthy intent. A round of laughter from two black girls shot through the next door I passed. No sound from the top floor, the stairway getting a fraction steeper and darker as I climbed the last flight of stairs.

I stood before her door and listened. Not a sound from inside. Perhaps she'd given up on me and gone out. The door moved inward a couple inches with the force of my knock. I gave it a push, the hinges squeaking, and stepped inside. I saw the latch was on its clip, so no sign of forced entry. Perhaps she'd gone downstairs to borrow something. But then why turn your light off? The room was in darkness. I fumbled nervously for a switch and stepped into the room. Sisi was there on the bed in her pyjamas and my first reaction was to sigh with relief and shake my head in dismay–a reaction that violently reversed three seconds after it had begun. I couldn't believe what I was looking at. Surely it wasn't her, but rather an uncanny likeness. Taking a step forward I saw that her middle was punctured with multiple stab wounds. Pools of congealed blood, almost black now, had collected around her side like copious amounts of glue that would stick her to the plastic sheeting she had been dumped upon on. Her eyes were slightly open, unseeing, filmy and muted–strangely, this was how my daughters' eyes looked when they were asleep, except no, there was no living moisture about the slither of these eyes exposed to the air. Her mouth had been smashed in with a blunt object; I'm no expert, but it looked like trauma post mortem, or at least while she was already knocked down, possibly unconscious. My brain kept trying to make sense of the visual information but I felt as if I'd become mute to my own stream of consciousness. I stared at her body, the bed, the blood, as though fixing upon an artist's vision of what might have happened to her if her ex had turned crazy. Something in my brain kept telling me the vision would dissolve any moment now and I would 'wake up' and see that she was just taking a nap–I was simply stressed, overworked, hallucinating even. My mouth made gagging movements like a frog unable to croak. I thought of the first 'murder' and clung desperately to the possibility that this was just another prank, I was looking at a dummy of Sisi, it was all just a wind up! Her lips was parted and the jaw tilted slightly–possibly from the force of the final blows–as though she might be trying to whisper the name of her killer now, if I came close enough. With almost no warning my knees turned to gelatine and I had to reach for her chest of drawers to stop myself from falling. A window had been left open and I imagined her killer having magically flown the scene. Now the adrenalin was subsiding I was already shivering from the cold and shock. I thought to cross the indifferent carpeting and close the window, but I found I couldn't move. A logical part of me – floating outside of my body, it seemed – began to worry that I wouldn't be able to react at all until someone found me here, pinned to the side of the chest of drawers, like a man standing on the ledge of a sky scraper peering between his shoes at certain death.

But then my mobile began ringing and out of sheer force of habit my hand moved to my pocket and I was able to escape my paralysis.

Again I thought I was seeing things: the caller ID read: SISI.

To my own buzzing ears I sounded like someone mentally handicapped as I said hello.

"Too bad, huh?" the distorted voice started straight in. Except this time, there was no Oriental accent to the voice. I was thrown yet again. The syntax said second generation Jamaican, London, but the intonation, even allowing for the distortion, was white–so possibly a white boy from down Brixton way, the type whose brittle sense of self comes from Rap, Rasta and fashionable drugs. Not good. "Your fault, man," he carried on. "We offered you a decent looking whore–you coulda made good money from her, man, but you mess up, try and double-cross, think you're clever'n us, yeah?" It wasn't a question it was a rhetorical flourish. "Look out yer window, man," the voice said.

I looked at the window, at first making no sense of the command, then shot over there like a rodent checking its burrow against invading predators. Nothing much to see: a few people passing by; a few parked cars, all empty. A bus at a bus stop… The bus moved away. I saw someone on the other side of the road, or rather a person with an umbrella and noticed it was tilted toward my trajectory blocking off my view of the person's face.

"You seeing me yet?"

I didn't have to ask if he was holding the umbrella. "Yes. Are you Bobby?"

"Never mind who I am–you's in some big trouble man." The figure moved a few steps away from the bus stop. "Let me get to the point Anthony. The price has gone up."

"The price of what? You've just killed the person I was trying to save, you moron."

The man stopped moving.

"Cleaning, asshole."

"What do you mean?"

"Apparently, you and Sonia had unprotected sex last night. Tha's very careless of you, Anthony–how risky with a prostitute!"

My heart began pumping hard and in seconds I was shaking with anger. I only just had the presence of mind to stop myself from making the mistake of sitting on the edge of the bed, spun wide of it and gravitated back to the chest of drawers where I came face to face with the photo of Sisi in her swimsuit, it lay loose on its back, out of its frame, curled at the edges – it briefly wrenched me from the present moment to an illusion I was with her in the past, but –

"My point is…" the voice cut in, "you're in a room with a dead girl and your DNA is inside her body. I'd say that makes you a suspect, wouldn't you? Plus," he raised his voice, like a pontificating radio DJ routinely delighted by his got-it-all-down style of summing up, "the room is covered with your fingerprints… and Sonia's friends know how obsessed you are wiv 'er, always bringing flowers – big Romeo, hey?"

I hurried back to the window. The umbrella man was gone–no, he was there, standing a little way in to a side road.

"…you was scaring 'er, everyone knew, that's why she 'ad to move apartments… but you was always watching 'er… and then, one day, you lost it, 'cause you couldn't 'ave 'er – she belonged to someone else, man…"

It was so surreal listening to this weird voice feed me this abominable lie I could almost have believed it myself the state I was in.

"You're very lucky to have a friend who can help out," the voice concluded unctuously.

I thought to throw my head out of the window and shout to the people in the street, Stop that man! That man with the umbrella, the only man with an umbrella! But my knees simply crumpled, my back slid down against the round knobs of the chest of drawers till my butt hit the floor.

You're fucking insane! I wanted to shout, but I couldn't produce any sound.

"You're a dentist, not a butcher. You need help to get rid of the body… Get up and come to the window, man. Come on." Almost friendly.

I scrambled to my feet and looked out the window. The umbrella figure had disappeared.

"I should keep the window open if I was you, or the neighbours will be round complaining of the smell, know what I mean?"

I glanced at the figure on the bed–a sight my brain still refused to process as real. But I understood this much: I was supposed to pay this thug to cut up my girl and dispose of her so I wouldn't be blamed for her murder. I now also understood *why the plastic sheeting*: it would make his job easier and would minimise the risk of transporting trace evidence; he must have planned to kill her before entering her flat, arriving with tools in a bag, as if she were the frigging failing boiler.

As I turned back to the window, I heard a question but failed to collect the words into a sentence. I asked him to repeat.

"You already have the 30,000, is that right?"

"No. Not yet."

"Better work on that, man, cos the price just went up. We need 20 more for the cleaning job." I merely note the figure, too suggestible to air any protest. "We can only take care of this, to *completion*," he stressed, "upon receipt of our fee. Have you got that,

Anthony?" talking to me as if he were performing a useful, freely-available legal service at a knock-down price.

"20 more–I'll need time to raise it."

"OK, we can do it, like, instalments, OK? 30 in a week's time, 20 two weeks after."

"How do I know you'll–" I stopped, choosing my words carefully, finding it ridiculous I actually felt safer using mafia terminology–"take care of everything?"

"Everything will be cleaned tonight. You pay us the following morning. We will call you. Is that clear?"

"…Yeah."

"Good."

The line went dead. I pulled away from the window and leant against the chest of drawers again. My legs crumpled and I fell on the floor. No, that was in my mind. I simply stood there, too numb to feel anything. Not even tears, just frozen out, as if my mind had short-circuited the moment the phone had gone dead. Slowly I grew aware of the visceral vying with the rational in my senses. I wanted to deal with the visceral alone, but I knew I must somehow encourage the rational, or I was as good as put away for life. Sisi was my first big love in years and now she was my first dead body, my first butchered body. I should go to her, hold her in my arms. I wanted to weep and wail like an Indian Brave – and I might have done, except that in that moment of standing there, now leaning against the wall, I thought of Mia, and then I thought of Michaela, and I knew I had to keep it together for their sakes. I thought to kiss Sisi goodbye, but of course–glancing back at the bed–her killer or killers had denied me that last wish by bashing in her mouth. The tooth I'd recently rebuilt temporarily had been sheered off at the gum. I couldn't help feeling this was a message to me, personally. Strangely I hovered there a moment imagining the work I might have done to repair this latest trauma to her mouth, if only I'd found her alive. I would probably have gone for a titanium post, implanted it into the root, drilled out the fractured tooth from inside the crown, filled the crown with Lutin resin, made a temporary crown, got my guy to make her a new one... But what was I thinking?! The best I could do for her now was to close her lids with thumb and forefinger–even that I did being careful not leave my prints on her make-up. My back straining as I leant over her, I kissed her lids. Clenching my teeth, I withdrew to the bathroom round the corner, hoping that it was far enough away from the bed to allow me one clear thought.

As I leant against the side of the discoloured bathtub, the tide of nausea that had retreated during the call, now returned with a vengeance. I threw my hands at the rim of the toilet seat and opened my mouth. I retched only the once. Nothing came up but glutinous, sour spit. *What a feeble expression of anger and remorse.* I wiped my mouth with some toilet paper and just stopped myself from flushing the toilet–*someone might hear you.* I put the seat down and took the weight off my wobbly legs. A dazed beat later, my cell phone buzzed and chimed once in my pocket. I opened it and read: 'Leave the flat now.'

I shut the phone. He could go fuck himself. I needed time. Time for what, though? Time to study the scene, my rational mind told me. I might notice something that the killer, or killers, had left behind. So I crawled back into the room and propped my back against the chest of drawers, facing away from the window. And I just sat there for a few minutes, passing in and out of the void, until I could start to form coherent thoughts. As so often happens in crisis, my mind cast back to a memory of long ago: me at ten years' old, sitting on a tree stump, holding a fishing rod, waiting for a bite, eyes finely focused on the taut nylon line as it disappeared into the dark waters of the canal… I'd barely noticed till now that Sisi's drawers and things had been overturned. The killer had probably been looking for anything that might tie him to her, such as photos, handwriting... This guy was nothing if not thorough.

I crawled over to a pile of photos that had spilled onto the floor. I turned them over. They were black and white copies I'd given to Sisi–shots of me and her in her Paddington flat, nude together, arms entwined, some a little corny to anyone but us, but most of them were poignantly revealing of how comfortable we'd looked together. This happy me, I now noticed, looked years younger than in any of the recent photos Sylvia had taken of me with the children. In among them, she'd added the photos of my kids that I'd given her in Wimbledon. Sifting through this coloured selection I saw two were missing. It suddenly hit me: I'd given her the last lot of photos in an old manila envelope with my name and address on it–and there it was, torn open, a hole where the name and address had been. *So now he knows where you live.* My family. What the kids look like.

Again, my mind was reeling, but this time I was a scared parent. I got to my feet and scanned the room. No blood spatter was immediately visible. Which suggested she had probably been drugged or knocked out before she–before they– My mind wouldn't go there. In fact my brain was working like a faulty switch: I'd manage one thought, then disappear into blackness. I told myself I must keep moving, physical activity would help clear the effects of shock.

I checked the kitchen area. Knives. None of them bloody. Nothing stashed under the sink. I returned to the bed. No obvious defence wounds, I noted, focusing on just the arms so I didn't have to ingest the rest of the horror–so there'd be faint hope of finding the killer's DNA under her fingernails. *The sheeting,* my mind kept saying. I felt sure there was something about the sheeting that could help me. But what?

My phone rang. SISI. Her name on my phone–a devilish tease that I'd arrived too late to save her.

"We need you to leave now."

"Five minutes."

He hung up.

So he was watching. If the body wasn't disposed of in good time, it would start to smell and then the police would be round and I'd be their number one suspect, just as Bobby said I would be. That's presuming this guy was in fact Bobby. In a disturbing twist of fate I registered a peculiar and distasteful gratitude to the caller for offering to make this body of evidence go away–adding 50,000 to the mortgage was preferable to a stretch of 25 years or more.

I wanted to take something of Sisi's to remember her by, but of course if found in my possession it might have sealed my fate with a jury. But there was one thing I could take. I just needed a pair of scissors and an old carrier bag…

Five minutes later, I switched off the light and left the studio flat as I'd found it.

I stumbled on the stairway and nearly fell. I heard a door open on the second floor, voices, a girl saying her goodbyes to a voice that was all bass and no treble. I waited until the man had reached the bottom of the stairs and shut the door behind him before I continued with my shaky descent.

I glanced about as I stepped into the street. I told myself not to look around, just head straight for the car, following orders–I was being watched.

I fell into my car and closed the door. But for that second call demanding that I leave, I might have started up the engine and driven home. The killer's anxiety to get on with the job had made me think to do some watching of my own.

CHAPTER 22

Once in my driver's seat, I slid back to a state of deep inertia. I felt like someone who wakes in the middle of an operation, can feel the pain of scalpels and fingers cutting and prodding his insides, but is unable to make a sound. Very slowly I grew aware of a faint voice and it was scratching on the inside of my skull–it was telling me I couldn't afford to be in shock, it wasn't over yet, I had to switch to fighting- back mode.

Starting the ignition was like the patient's first step from his hospital bed. I yanked into reverse, carefully put my foot down, mindful of that part of my brain that was telling me to floor the gas and drive into the nearest obstacle. I turned the wheel hard. The exhaust fumes billowed out the rear, clouding my rear view. I ran the vent and wound down the window. A gust of cold, damp air blew away some of the mental fog. I put into first and rolled out of the hole that was my parking spot, nearly as tight as the situation I was in. I drove to the end of the street and turned left. At the end of the next street, looking left, I could see the house Sisi was in. Her room light was still off. I turned right and kept going, checking my rear view mirror every 4 or 5 seconds. I made a full 360° at the next junction and headed back to where I'd come from. No one had made the turn with me.

Within 70-80 yards of Sisi's place, I slipped easily into a parking place and switched off the engine. My first stakeout. I put my mobile to vibrate and zipped up.

An hour goes by.

Then another.

I'm getting cold. Clambering in back it's a relief to find a couple of blankets there and I whisper a few words of thanks to Sylvia, who'd left them there for the kids. I pull the window blinds down so no one can see me huddled up on the back seat unless they peer in from the front.

Around 10 PM, I begin nodding off occasionally. I'm this close already to telling myself I can't hold out any longer unless I have a coffee. But there's no coffee shop nearby. And if I step out of the car, I might miss the killer. Or he might be watching the flat–he'd see me get out of the car, cross the street. So I slap my face to keep myself sharp. It feels crazy, but it works.

One AM. Damn. My eyes are raw. I need to peel these contacts off, they're like fusing to my eyeballs, but I didn't bring my glasses, so they're all I've got.

I peep out between the blinds again. Seconds later, I see a van. It pulls up in front of Sisi's building. As the lights go out, I hear a door open–I can't see the driver, because he's parked street side, back end of the van toward me. The man appears round the back of the van, dressed in black, wearing a ski hat. He has the same stocky muscular movements as the young Thai who got me to help him carry a fake dead body into

Sisi's bathroom. This is not good–I was hoping to find myself up against Bobby by himself. Arun opens the back doors and pulls from the shadowy interior a big suitcase. He stations the case on the sidewalk and takes out a wide plank of wood, about six feet long, and closes the doors. He picks up the plank in one hand and the case in the other and heads over to the front door to Sisi's house. He leans the plank against the doorframe and takes out a key, pushes the door. He glances back down the street as he steps inside, then shuts the door. I climb back into my driver's seat for a better view. A light goes on, top floor, Sisi's bedroom. And only now do I realise I don't want to be seeing this. But I have to.

"OK, license plate," and I dig in my pockets for a pen, scraps of paper. I note it down.

About thirty minutes later the door to the house opens. It looks like my guy. He's carrying the plank he took in with him. He opens the back door of the van and places one end of the plank on the floor of the van and walks swiftly back to the door, left ajar. He disappears briefly and returns pulling the case by its strap. It's heavier. Something in it–Sisi, being wheeled along to the van on casters. He must have used the plank to ease the case down the stairs. And now he's lining up the case with the plank runway. He puts his shoulder into it and gets the case aboard. Slides in the plank after it, closes the doors. He gets in the van and starts it up. I start up mine. He moves and now I move.

First five minutes it's as easy as you see in the movies. But then a taxi pulls out in front of me, I get stuck behind him as he wants to turn right at the next set of lights and the van starts to get away. I put my foot down and make up some ground, but I can't beat the next light and, just as I'm thinking of burning a red, a cop car purrs right up alongside my right. All I can do is sit there and watch the van as it drifts out of sight.

I let the cop car nose ahead of me. He turns off early and I put my foot down, but the van is gone. I keep driving in the vain hope I'll catch up but all I got in front of me is the rest of the night. I pull over and thump the steering wheel. As panic eats up the anger, I hear my dad's consoling voice telling me, "You did your best, son," – and the wish that this could be enough, the way it used to be, just a game of football you lost, nearly makes me weep.

Around 1.50 AM I turn into my road–and brake, suddenly. About a 100 yards ahead of me I have a clear view of the very same van I was tailing. It's got to be a coincidence, I tell myself. Lots of Ford vans around. But I have the licence plate on a chit of paper, in fact I don't even have to dig for it, I remember enough of it already and that's the same van.

He's got his lights off, back end facing me. *What's he doing watching my house?!* I roll my car behind a Smart car and switch off engine and lights. I wait maybe another ten minutes. Then the van door opens, Arun steps onto the sidewalk and goes round to the back doors again. He lets down the plank and rolls the case down it onto the ground. He pushes the plank back inside the van and closes the doors. He drags the case round to the side of the house. OK, so he's leaving it with my rubbish?!

I get out of the car, nudge the door closed. *Don't set the alarm.* I cross to the other side of the street and run behind parked cars till I'm nearly opposite my own drive. Sylvia's closed the garage door. He's not by the bins, he's opened the gate and walked right through to the fucking garden! But my fear and indignation is swiftly is overtaken by that warmer feeling of possessing a home advantage. He must have cased the house a good fifteen minutes before going through. Black windows the whole length of the street, very little through traffic. Sylvia and I have argued about the security issue of that passageway more than a few times over the years. When I'd bought the house, I was single, I'd never worried too much that someone might walk through to the back, because I'd owned only the top flat and had rarely used the garden. Just before Sylvia moved in I had the opportunity to buy the flat below at a favourable price and only then had I looked into building a gate there. But part of the reason I got the property at such a good price was the fact there was this awkward easement running down the side of my and my neighbour's property, allowing them street access through my property. The neighbours made use of the easement maybe twice in one year, usually when workers were on their property and needed some extra throughway to cart materials or debris to a truck at the front, but it was always twice too many for Sylvia. Here's the proof she was right.

Fifteen minutes have gone by and he still hasn't returned. Every minute or so I think I've identified the sound of metal against stone from the end of the back garden. *So he's burying the case, must be.* For once I wish my garden was only half the size. I can't risk following him in there–he might see me. At the end of the garden there are two conical shaped compost bins, just behind the second shed that has Sylvia claimed as her 'temporary' Art Studio. Did Arun cut up Sisi and bag her parts and now he's stuffing them into the bottom of the compost bins? *But he couldn't have cut her up in just 30 minutes, she had to be whole.*

The moment I hear his returning footsteps, I crouch low, slow my breathing. I catch a glimpse of him – no case. I hear the front door of the van slide open, something thrown in, maybe a tool. The ignition fires up and the van drives away. Now it's my turn.

I flash the Maglite around the garden, heading for the larger shed under the pear tree, the uncultivated area to the left of it. The compost barrels look undisturbed, but I have to check them anyway. I brace myself and twist off the lid of the first one. A heady pong of fermented grass and leaves and insect life assaults my nose–but my eyes are spared the sight of body parts. Turning it over, I see nothing has been disturbed. And the second drum is nearly empty. I shine the light along the perimeter, to the far right corner, then all the way back to the left and further on down the easement where it curls round to the neighbour's property. I shine the light on the old work table we have out there, laden with pots and rubbish, a trowel. I laugh at the idea–a *trowel.* But then I see it. My own spade, parked up against the side of the shed. The soil on it is wet, glistening in my beam. If he brought a shovel he must have opted for my spade instead. This time I inch along the floor with the Maglite. The ground here is rough and scattered with leaves and fallen branches. I have to get down on my haunches for a closer look, prodding the earth with my fingers… Is this something? An area of about six feet, all of it softer than the rest. I pick up the spade. I put the Maglite on the table and, using some loose branches as a makeshift tripod, aim it at the patch I'm interested in. Two feet down it occurs to me this guy must have been here in the daytime when Sylvia and the kids were out and at school, because no way would anyone, even a brazen criminal, just walk onto someone's property at two in the morning in the hope of finding a suitable burial place for a dead body...

I start to dig. The scrape of metal cutting through gravely soil is like a dead giveaway and I pause every couple of digs to see if I've startled awake a neighbouring house. But everything stays dark, save for the pool of light I'm working in... I'm just beginning to sweat, my palms starting to blister, when I hit something that feels hopeful. I dig around it, feverishly, having almost forgotten what it is I'm about to unearth. I identify the edge of the case and use the spade as a lever to unearth one corner. I work round to the side till I can get a hold of the handle. I heave upward, every muscle in my back and neck straining to its limit. Thighs quivering. I swear through gritted teeth and somehow that brings it up. I reach for the torch. A purple case. There's no lock on the zipper, it comes open, easy, almost gratifying. Not all the way, though, 'cause she's in there, packed away like a broken doll. My stomach rolls over and I retch, just the once. As the spasm subsides, a voice in my head starts talking to her, as if to comfort a child. Anguish pours in and I zip up the case and the hysteria brewing within. I switch off the Maglite. My mind drifts and my eyes seem to penetrate the black windows into the bedrooms – Sylvia, the kids, sleeping, with no knowledge of this. The disconnect almost makes me laugh out loud. OK. Think. Logical. Back to the exam paper. Twenty years ago. So how could it go? You pay up. They think, *Schmuck*, and demand more, threatening to tell the cops if you don't pay up a second time. Or you don't pay and they make the call within a week. *You'll find a case in the garden at the back under the pear tree…* I can hear that distorted voice laughing at the outcome. But the case won't be here, mate. I just need a new home for the case. That's if I've muscle enough to drag it to the car…

An hour later I step under a hot shower. Muscles stiff from hours of sitting in the cold and frantic digging finally begin to relax. My welted hands are ingrained with soil. It's just as well we use gloves at work, it'll be days before they're properly clean again.

I pop my head round our bedroom door. The bed is empty! Has Sylvia left the kids alone tonight to make some kind of point?! But I find her in Mia's bed, curled up together. Panic turns to warm mushy stuff. I think to pick up some blankets for my kip on the sofa, but, like our cat, who always chooses to sleep nearest an item of his family's clothing left on a chair or sofa, I head for our bed and the familiar smells it holds.

My head hitting the pillow, my only reality is that I've had a tough night waiting in a car, enduring the cold and then digging up a few kilos of sodden earth. I'm in complete denial about what's happened to Sisi. I picture myself like a spy, so busy processing the field he can't afford himself the luxury of pondering the origins of his mission. It isn't until the early hours that the truth properly manifests itself, breaking through layers of dream like a vicious monster rising up from the bed of the ocean. Flashbacks heave up from recent memory like sick and splash onto a screen in my head drenching me in viscous horror and dread. I kick and I jerk and I toss and turn. Even my bones ache with indescribable grief. I have a searing headache. The only release is tears. I bite down on the pillow, fearful of waking my family with my howling. My nails dig like claws into the mattress. When fatigue finally overcomes the tears, I fall into a game world in which I save or just fail to save Sisi–games that my brain is playing in a desperate attempt to wriggle free of the one, true scenario I can do nothing, nothing at all, to reverse.

CHAPTER 23

The girls' arguing tugged and poked me awake around 7.15 AM. It was still dark. Just outside my door in the corridor Michaela was getting exasperated with Mia who was failing to understand Christmas was three weeks, not three days, away and so we wouldn't be going to Grandma and Grandpa's this coming weekend. Mia's voluble heartfelt whine leapt into my chest threatening to trigger some uncontrollable wailing of my own. But then Michaela stomped off and Mia ran back to her room slamming the door behind her and in the vacuum I was able to recollect my thoughts of the night before.

I emerged to find Sylvia and the girls–Mia still sniffing from her tears, but otherwise reconciled–quietly eating breakfast in the half-light. Sylvia's facade suggested she was dourly processing the possible reasons for my late homecoming, but she couldn't hold back a little surprise, a little admiration and even, dare I say it, some female pride in her man, when she saw me appear in my Armani suit.

"So what's this? Don't see you in a suit very often."

"Yeah–conference," aiming for a casual air even though I looked like tooth ache. "I'd almost completely forgotten about it till this morning, but, uh, yeah–"

"Does that mean you're staying somewhere over night?" I don't think she meant to, but in the circumstances it was probably inevitable that a hint of innuendo would creep into her tone of voice.

"Yeah, it does. Birmingham."

"Thanks for the warning."

"It's been a busy week. Like I said, I completely forgot–"

"As you do. As *you* do, that is.'

I was suddenly beset by a fear that if Sylvia continued in this vein of sardonic needling, I might explode with unprecedented violence, smashing plates and god knows what else. So I paused a moment in the hope of slowing my pulse. I reached into the wall cupboard and carefully lifted out my cereal bowl. I collected a spoon and sat down.

"Sorry."

"I need some notice, y'know? I also have a busy week."

I nodded. I thought to say sorry again, but I couldn't get the word past my lips. I didn't know if I could face eating anything.

"I know things have changed between us, but we still have to coordinate with each other."

"Yeah… sure."

I imagined my face smiling to express reassurance, but the skin wouldn't move. It hurt to feel anyone's eyes on me. I was holding the packet of organic brown rice cereal as though I was waiting for someone to talk me through what to put it in and what to add to it. I glanced at the girls opposite and Michaela passed the milk without my having to ask. I imagined saying, Thanks sweetie, but said nothing. I tried to recall whether I'd actually taken anything numbing the night before in order to help me sleep, but reckoned, vaguely, it was just shock still working overtime.

"So what happened last night?" Sylvia asked.

"Yeah, where you been Dad?" Mia asked.

"Why're you sleeping in the guest room?" Michaela asked. "Don't you like sleeping with Mum anymore?" the hint of a smirk that was barely a year short of working it all out.

"I wasn't in the guest room last night. I was in our bed." I glanced at Sylvia, hoping for some sign that she'd help us fudge our way out of this one, at least for now.

"Mum slept with me," Mia chipped in, all smiley face.

"She had a bad dream again," Michaela explained. "She's always getting nightmares. Did you have nightmares, Dad, when you were a child?"

At least we were off the subject of Mum and Dad's sleeping arrangements, but just the very word 'nightmare' had such an unreal ring to it, I turned selectively deaf for a couple of minutes, until Sylvia asked me, "What's the conference about?"

"Um, implants, teeth implants. It's the latest thing," I intoned with muted irony. I poured rice milk over the little mountain of cereal in my bowl. Sylvia took a bite of her toast and got up to pour her coffee. My mind went to the trunk of the car–

"I'm afraid the car broke down last night… on my way back... I had to call the AA…"

Sylvia froze by the kitchen top and shot me a look as if to say, *What the hell next from you?* Looking her in the eye I could see she'd already assumed that because I had no visible facial wounds I hadn't been hurt. Her prime, if not sole, concerns were focused upon the financial damage and the inconvenience to herself. I almost wanted to say to her face that she'd become the kind of person she used to say she despised, but of course neither of us was quite ourselves at the moment.

"I couldn't start it," I resumed filling in the blank of her scolding silence. "And they couldn't either. They had to tow it to a garage."

"You mean it just conked out?"

"Pretty much yeah. Right in the middle of the crossroads. I was lucky no cars went into me. Nasty feeling it's the cam belt."

"I had it serviced only a month ago."

"Well there you go. Maybe that's why you got such a great deal."

"How long are we going be without a car then? I've got stuff to cart around..."

"They reckoned at least a couple of days."

"A couple of days?! No no no– "

"I was planning on going down there on my way back from Birmingham tomorrow night… sort it out– "

Sylvia was talking over me, insisting I should have picked up a courtesy car, she was sure there was a courtesy car on the insurance. Why did I never think of these things? How was she supposed to cope without a car for two days while I was wining and dining in Birmingham?!

"I'm not wining and dining, it's not that kind of conference."

But she'd already got up from the table–"Girls, teeth, please!"–and gone to the living room to look through our CAR files. She was probably right. Now I'd fucked up. She'd find the courtesy car clause and demand I get on the phone to the garage. She had the kids to drop off, pick up, college to go to, shopping to do–she wanted a courtesy car. I didn't have time to get her a courtesy car. She came back with the insurance papers pointing to the courtesy clause.

"OK, I'll call them." *Bitch.*

She reached for the cordless and thrust it at me.

"Can I finish my cereal?"

"No. I need to know now."

"They're probably not open."

"Try!"

I just stopped myself from snatching the phone from her hand. I walked off with it into the living room.

"Why can't you do it here?"

I shut the door behind me, omitting a reply. Should I pretend to be talking to someone who puts me on hold for the rest of the morning, or come clean and tell her I needed the car in order to deal with a blackmailer who'd killed perhaps the love of my life?

The living room door opened. Sylvia stood there with a formidable *Well?* on her face.

"I'm waiting," I explained, with what may have seemed like an uncaring lack of urgency.

I felt a wave of righteousness rise in Sylvia's breast, her eyes nearly screaming at mine for some kind of explanation as to what was going on with me, but her emotions stopped at the brim. She stood there studying my quiet defiance, thinking all manner of things–I had to hope she wasn't going to ask me to put us on speakerphone because I'd actually called my bank's 0845 number and was punching in numbers for options, just so I could look busy–when we were interrupted. Michaela was calling for her. I saw the anger subside in her chest as she listened and called back an answer. Turning to me she said, now in a consolatory tone, that she supposed I could call her on the mobile–she had to go now or she'd never make it to school taking the bus.

"OK."

I began mumbling details of my name and address into the receiver, talking to no one, shaping the fake conversation around the time it would take Sylvia to bring the kids from downstairs to the front door, at which point I would whip up a display of indignation for Sylvia's benefit. I kept it up like this until the girls called "Bye!" and Sylvia stepped into the room waving goodbye and giving me the signal to phone her. She seemed less irate now, adapting admirably to the first obstacle to her day. I nodded, frowning into the phone as I said, "Yes… yes, I realise that, BUT it says here…" The front door slammed, I let go the tension in my shoulders and relaxed my arm.

OK, let's get to work.

First, the practice. Poor Rebecca having to cancel all the appointments. But at least she'd get to go home early.

Next, Yellow Pages, *slap* on the kitchen table, heavy, like a corpse. I looked under Storage and dialled a number. A northern voice asked for my account details. I told him I was new. I needed a small space for a week. Yeah, he can do that. Did I know where they were? I hung up. What was I thinking? I didn't want Storage, I wanted Freezers. And to run a freezer you need electricity; no electricity in storage rooms. So that meant a room. And I'd have to find the room first, because I'd need to give a delivery address for the freezer. Could both tasks be achieved in one day before Bobby made his call? I had to try.

Nice that I had a sharp suit to wear. Everything I would do from now on had to have the edge on who I'd been before. The relatively new black Armani, which I'd worn only once, to a funeral, was just the tonic I needed to sharpen my senses and help me assume the persona of someone self-assured–the person I knew I was anything but. Rings under the eyes, the hint of despair in the uneven symmetry of the sensuous mouth – I needed help. How often have I heard women say they wear perfume not to attract a man, but to feel self-possessed. I sprayed my neck and wrists with a mist of my Paul Smith's eau de cologne and set out to face my next grim task.

Crossing my legs the same way as Petra, the compact and unusually sexy Spanish manager opposite me, I explained that my business plan had been put on hold and I would only be requiring £3,000 today. I smiled cordially and made little of the specious set-back. Petra kindly offered to hold the money in their safe for another week. Muchas gracias. De nada. Her smile told me she could use a little more flirting with well-dressed Englishmen who spoke Spanish. I felt my smile curdle on my face even before I stepped outside into a wet wind. I felt the sweat cooling around my collar. I pressed on.

First, a change of clothes. I couldn't very well be looking at bedsits in my Armani, it'd look odd. The suit would have to come with me, though, just in case Sylvia went looking for something in my closet and found the suit in there when I was supposed to be wearing it to a conference.

Walking up to the car, parked a few streets from our house, I thought–*hearse, a dark navy hearse.* I was to play chauffeur for the day. Drive carefully, sir. Gently over those ramps and potholes... Sylvia had been nagging me to get rid of it–"Why do you always hold on to old stuff, you're so fixed"–and buy something a little more environmentally friendly. Well, today I could be really glad I'd stayed true to the old thing. It wasn't the handsomest model and its interior was now indelibly tarnished with stains thanks to the kids' food and accidents over the years, but at least it had a decent size trunk. I put my tatty old A-Z and list of addresses and times to view bedsits on the passenger seat and composed myself. Considering the cargo I had to transport around with me, aside of the fine film of clammy sweat on my palms, my nerves were pretty steady. I started her up.

Most of us have experienced at least one time in our lives the deprivations of insalubrious accommodation. Twenty years later we forget how bad things can be. We imagine things must have gotten better–surely credit cards have done away with patches of mould and cockroaches, for instance. That phrase *Here's how the other half lives* pops up and slaps you about the cheeks–like, this might be what you have to look forward to if you ever ran into a serious personal injuries claim and you handled badly the impending divorce. I knew of divorced men with good jobs who had ended up in some pretty depressing rat holes. Still, they were all better than a prison cell and I wouldn't truly be moving in, Sisi would. And she wouldn't notice the mould and the cracks in the paint, the mentally challenging wallpaper and the stained mattress. All she needed was the regular hum of the freezer. *Stay cool, baby.* (You know what, as the day moved on, I noticed that I was increasingly resorting to abhorrent, mordant humour to keep myself together. Of course there's a risk with this kind of mental strategy–one day you gotta snap out of it.)

Traffic was congested even outside the Congestion Charge Zone and I was frequently making wrong turns and going half crazy rolling up and down one way systems–with a corpse in the trunk. Mental note: *GPS and automatic, the next time you buy a car.* Around midday, I popped into a chemist for some meds. I spooned down some viscous pink gloop with a vaguely chalky taste–for my nausea–and popped two Ibuprofen for the growing tension headache. I had Valium in the glove compartment and popped one, reasoning that a little mental acuity was a good trade for a more sustainable calm.

London's a big place, so why couldn't I find more bedsits available in one local area? Each stop was 30 or 40 minutes apart. At my first place of call the baggy brown suit and bling refused to give me an answer straight away, even when I showed him cash. He had to see other people, by which I guess he meant he didn't like my face or the colour of my skin. At the second place, the landlord called me on my mobile as I stood outside the mansion block to say he was going to be two hours' late, could I hang on? No, I couldn't. Around three o'clock, as I was viewing a bedsit in Turnpike Lane, Bobby's distorted voice vibrated against my eardrum. I asked the Greek Cypriot showing me the room if he'd mind giving me a minute. He eyed me suspiciously, as if I might be about to pinch the rickety bedside table and flee with it out the rusting French window, then stepped into the corridor. I quietly closed the door. I took out my digital recorder and put my phone on speakerphone. My thumb hit the red Rec button.

"You got the money?"

Straight to the point.

"There's been a delay."

Pause.

"That wasn't what we agreed."

The voice was a little less free with the verbal swagger of before. Serious.

"I didn't agree on a time, *you* gave me a time. I put the first loan on hold last week, because I didn't believe you would hurt Sonia."

"Bad mistake, wasn't it." The glee filtering through the man's distorted voice made the hair on my neck stand up.

"Yes, it was a mistake."

"So when can you get this money to me?"

"Tomorrow. But I need three more days to get this extra money you're asking for."

"50K can't be much for a person like you."

"Oh, believe me it is. I'm not as wealthy as you seem to think I am."

A pause.

"Don't fuck with me, lover boy."

I kept silent.

"You get the money today."

"Three more days. I'm sure you can pay the rent till then. Call me Friday and it's all yours."

I hung up, pressed STOP on my recording device and switched off my phone. I knew he'd be calling me back, but was he really going to call the police falling at the first hurdle? I didn't think so.

I opened the heavy fire-proof bedsit door.

"Can I move in today?" I asked.

The man woke from his melancholy daydream and smiled as if the notes I'd pulled out of my pocket were a sweet little woman.

I took a measurement of the door and the French windows and set off to find a freezer. I went to several stores, but none had freezers with a hook or ring for a padlock. One store assistant was kind enough to do a search on the web for me. We found one. The measurements were good, so I took down the number and placed an order. Again I'd have to take time off work: delivery was between 1 and 6 the next day; I was not going to be too popular with my staff this month. Unless I doubled my budget on their Christmas presents.

Coming up for six and I was done and 24 hours ahead of schedule. I thought to head back home, if only because I didn't know how I'd cope spending a night alone in a bedsit with a corpse. If I left the case in the car, knowing the area, the case and the car might be gone in the morning. If I went home, where the car was relatively safe, I'd have to spin lies about the phantom conference and Sylvia would be on my case again about the car and the state of my health. OK, bedsit it is.

I found a parking space within view of a Turkish café and killed time, reading the newspaper and looking out into the street. After an hour, I moved the car to another spot and did the same. It was like a bedside vigil for my car, my corpse, my dead beauty. Around midnight I parked up outside the bedsit. I watched the street for ten minutes and then popped the trunk. The case I'd wrapped in black bin bags to avoid leaving traces in my car. (I'd even thrown out the rest so no forensic detectives could match the ones I had here with the roll at home. It almost made me smile to think a favourite TV show. CSI, had become more than just entertainment). After hours of sitting in chairs, rounds of bad food and cups of Turkish coffee, my body creaked like old furniture as I lifted the weight. Still, no one was watching, as far as I could see. I shut the trunk and took hold of the strap–and pulled.

Stepping inside the bedsit I shut the door, flipped the latch. I looked at the case, my company for the night, and thought, Home sweet home… (I was still making use of sarcasm to keep my mind alert).

The landlord had left the window open–a fairly futile gesture for clearing the air of some of its carcinogenic spores of mould–and the room was freezing. Which reminded me… I remembered Sisi had hated the London damp and cold as much I had, both of us reedy thin. Now where was I to put her? I moved the case here and I moved it there. Obviously away from the window–which in a room this size narrowed it down somewhat. I didn't want it too near the bed, but I couldn't bear stashing her in a corner, as though she were just trash now. The closet was just big enough, but the base of it was so thin I reckoned the case would fall right through it. OK, we put her middle of the far wall… Damn, no sheets, no blankets. I went back to the car and picked up the two blankets I'd used for the stakeout. Now I knew how a soldier felt the day before battle–all stomach and eyes and ears.

As I sat on the bed, back against a defunct pillow propped against the damp wall, my distracted style of reading the London Metro newspaper took me back to the pool, the first day I ever set eyes on Sisi. How sweet that day seemed now. But seeing her alive in my mind's eye, my mind belly-flopped onto the memory of her lying dead on her bed. My stomach rolled over and I had to bounce off the bed to catch the nausea from balling. I paced up and down the floor for a few minutes, possessed by vengeance, like a live thing kicking inside of me. I admonished myself, slapping my face, punching a fist into my palm… for the first time since Sisi's death tapping hard into my anger, pulling it up and around me like a shield against the demons of despair and self-pity. I dropped to the floor and did push-ups. I put a pillow on the small of my back and I did sit-ups. Sets of threes, rest, then again... Until I felt a twinge in my left shoulder and I had to stop. I flopped on the bed, laughing at the notion I could turn myself into a hard man overnight. At 43. But I knew some yoga, so I eased into that. Twenty minutes later I lay back on the bed, feeling better albeit drained. My throat was sore again. Sisi's bug. All sorts of other bugs growing in her now. I closed my eyes. My ears were singing from the exercise. The stress. My imagination reeled like a drunkard's. I held on. The images slowed down, grew quieter. I found it comforting to wish that I could join Sisi in death. Again I wept with bottomless grief.

CHAPTER 24

I'm lucky: the freezer arrives early the next day. The Italian delivery driver leaves it with me in the hallway, asks me to print my name and sign – I give him my false name – and jumps back into his van. I have to tear off the cardboard it's come in to get this big oblong through my doorway. I park it up against the wall and plug it in. It starts to hum. *We're in business.* I tune into the hum, now gazing at the case. Do I leave the freezer behind when I leave? Do charities sell freezers?

It's home time. Kids in scruffy uniforms eating and drinking fashionable rubbish that keeps me in business pass me by as I sit quietly in my car, scratching the stubble on my face, 50 yards from the semi where Arun lives. I'm parked in a side street in Harlesden. There's barely a tree standing down this road, so I've a clear view of his van's back doors and driver's side. Sisi told me, he worked as a delivery driver. A day off or downtime between the last and next delivery? I don't recall whether Sisi ever said which floor he's on, but it's probably of little relevance to what's going through my mind. The front drive is ankle deep in trash and the weeds have sprung up like happy-slapping gangs. Next door to the house, same premises, there's a very dilapidated brick garage; the tiles on the roof are like loose teeth and the run-in to it has been gated and padlocked. It's that garage I've been thinking about for the past twenty minutes.

It's just turning dark as I see a young, muscular figure leave the house. I note the by now familiar stoop he walks with, his version of the cool outsider, a style that I suspect he nurtures like an imaginary friend. There's something about the way he crawls into the van that makes me think of roaches. How did she ever get involved with this little punk? I wait till his van's plume of exhaust has disappeared and start up my own car. I roll into the parking spot opposite the garage drive and switch off my engine. I think it through. The tools I'll need. If I get my timing right, it could work. I start up the car and roll away into the early evening.

I return to the cell of my operation, the bedsit. The ceiling's taking a beating from a J Lo track I think I recognise. A minute later the sound goes off, a door slams, I hear a key turn in a lock and footsteps descending.

Now I can rest. I lie on the bed and pull the blankets over me. I think. I have to think through every move, just as I used to when I played chess. I haven't played chess in twenty years and I was never too patient. But this is different: the stakes are higher than merely losing a game… My eyes grow heavy. I wake two hours later, surprised I'd finally enjoyed some deep sleep. I take the suit from the closet and start to change. I shave and brush my teeth. Looking in the flecked mirror I see Sisi appear behind me and sling her arms round my neck. She rubs her cheek against mine. She's all in white, with one of the flowers I used to bring her like an arrow through her hair. And then she's gone. My neck stiffens as I remember where she is and how she is. I squeeze a creamy white slug of 'hair play molding paste' onto the tips of two fingers and kick up my slowly thinning, greying hair. This must be the first time in years I've dressed up to look smart for a return to my own house.

I arrived home around 8.30 PM. The lights were on. I let myself in to find the hall littered with sports bags. I heard the girls upstairs. They were romping around with another kid, maybe two. I turned right into the living room where I ran into three large cases, packed. *Is she leaving me already?* Except, I didn't recognise the bags. Footsteps came pounding down the carpeted stairs, and I heard Mia's voice. I saw her nip past the half open door down to the kitchen. I stepped into the hall and followed her. I found her hauling a litre of smoothie juice from the fridge. I startled her and she nearly dropped the carton. She smiled with a flushed face, excited eyes.

"Hi Dad. Bobby and Jasmine are here."

I nearly had a heart attack– 'Bobby?" I blurted.

"Yeah, you know, my cousin."

"OK." *Of course, son of Jasmine, Sylvia's sister.*

"Are they going somewhere?"

"No," Mia answered with implacable clarity. "They're staying here."

"Here?"

"Yeah. Dad, can you pour it?"

I poured the thick fruity gloop into a glass and did one for myself. She gulped hers, I sipped; gulping ended around thirty-one.

"Is Mum upstairs?"

She finished with a great sigh of contentment and nodded, saying a breathy "Yeah." She put the glass on the kitchen top and cast me a concise look of appraisal. "Nice suit, Dad," she said and ran off back to the den of fun.

So let me guess. Jasmine's ex had hit her, thrown her out, wanted her back. So he could hit her again, throw her out, want her back. In the entire time I'd known Sylvia, Jasmine had had only one boyfriend you might not immediately dismiss as a loser. Ever since she decided she had only been exploring lesbianism as a reaction to her father's adulterous behaviour, she's pursued a fatal attraction to guys with addictive personalities and reptilian impulses. Somehow these guys made her feel better about herself, or perhaps less self-hating. She was only four years younger than I was, she was as bright as Sylvia was at school, but her perspective had been so curtailed through years of hanging out with bitter and self-pitying individuals, she still carried this air of a fifteen year old who's dominant sense of self begins with Fuck you. And with that attitude your looks tend to spoil prematurely, even though I still saw the temptation in her. A little heavier in build than Sylvia, she had the same warm eyes, a bigger, fuller mouth, that promised all kinds of sensual pleasures. Her skin was darker, the hair fuller and beautifully spidery, the nose and chin more prominent, her breasts, too, fingers a little less refined than Sylvia's. She wasn't without a sense of humour, but it was cramped by her black and white interpretation of the world as populated by victims and predators. Her eyes were mistrustful of all but her most trusted circle and, even as she smiled, I would feel the air about her contract as if it were charged to accept a distasteful revelation of some kind. She'd been cautious when we were first introduced. I don't even remember shaking her hand. I think she somehow managed to avoid contact by busying herself with her young boy, then an infant, now age ten. She was doting upon her child and upon her recently rehabilitated then fiancé, the father, in a way that seemed to be trying to mimic the cloying security of heroin (as it had been described to me). The father had been similarly wary of me. Later, Sylvia would explain they felt I was judging them. This, mind you, after I'd put on a spread in the garden, given them a couple of bottles of wine to take away with them, toys for their kid. I'd been entirely discreet walking around the subject of heroin and I hadn't at any point given them any grounds I could think of that suggested I was looking down at them. "Well," Sylvia added after I'd pointed this out, "it might just be that they've both had a hard history with men and they don't trust men, so don't take it personally." Sylvia was not unsympathetic to my position. She said her sister had always been difficult, the whole family had had to walk on eggshells around her. So I did my best, offering friendship at arm's length in case I got my hand bitten off for looking as though I wanted to 'twist' something in my favour. Every other gathering, I'd succeed in inveigling a warm smile from Jasmine that told me she wasn't incapable of one day trusting me, but in the past year, as things went to shit again with the third step-dad to come along in four years, she was digging in as–to quote Sylvia–'difficult'. Something dramatic must have happened, though, for Sylvia to have persuaded her to come here with luggage–Jasmine was always broke, but she was proud too and hated accepting help from anyone.

As I drifted back into the hall I heard the women descending the stairs.

"Oh, you're back! Mia said you were–"

"Yeah… Hi Jasmine."

"Hey," she purred coolly. She smiled coyly, swished her hair back. She'd stopped five stairs up, her hand resting on the banister, keeping back as though she might be intruding on my 'emotional space' with Sylvia.

"How's it going… You, um–" I gestured at the bags.

"Oh, yeah, sorry, um–"

"I said she could stay with us for a few days," Sylvia cut across. "It's alright, isn't it?"

Ordinarily I would have said Sure, no problem, but with everything so upside down in our lives I couldn't quite answer straight away.

"Yeah, um…"

Jasmine seemed to rear up before my note of uncertainty as if before a snake in the road and was saying something about having forgotten to show the girls a new PC game she'd brought with her. She'd be back down in a minute. A kiss and Thanks Anthony would have been nice, but she couldn't bring herself to do that.

Sylvia passed me in the hall and headed for the kitchen. I felt obliged to follow.

I stood at the kitchen door.

"Uh… a few days?"

"Yeah. We can manage that, can't we? Or would you prefer to get a babysitter in while I'm down at the hospital waiting for her to come out of a coma?"

"He's hitting her again. And Bobby."

"This guy, Marco?"

"Yeah."

"And what if he comes here?"

"He won't."

"How can you be so sure?"

She sucked the inside of her lower lip as if collecting spit. "Because he's a slime ball, I guess."

I pulled a face, not quite buying the loose logic.

"He's got another girlfriend," she added. "Jasmine was his–y'know–like–his bit of intellectual totty, so I don't think he'll…" She let her words trail off, as if the guy simply didn't warrant any more effort from her lungs.

I watched her fill the kettle–industrious, some vim in her elbows now she'd got a mission on.

"The whole city seems to be full of wife-beating men at the moment," I said in a bid to express solidarity through dismay. "I've just been dealing with a case myself."

Case, I thought. The unintended pun stopped my heart for a moment. I withdraw to a chair. I felt like a man slowly coming to terms with the fact that his house was surrounded by zombies.

"A lot of men have low self-esteem, they can't handle women wanting their own life," Sylvia said, as if she thought I needed this familiar psychobabble. "But they still have the same amount of muscle and aggression, so–" she gestured to mean: 'it's obvious what you get'.

"I'm surprised you got her to come."

"I got her to chant with me."

She popped tea bags into two mugs and started to laugh. "We had to stick her gohonzon back together, though–he'd smashed it up, among other things… But, y'know, we managed. And after that, she said, 'Yeah, OK, I'll come.' I think she's beginning to see it can work for her," she added as though I was part of her group and about to approve of her actions.

It's probably her chanting that's pissed him off, I wanted to say. *If she's completely into that now and not him, being a desperate kinda guy, he'll go for the gohonzon, as if it were a bloke she were screwing.* But that would be about me, me and Sylvia, I don't need that tension right now, so I say nothing. The guy always looked like trouble anyway. A dark skinned, stocky guy, half Scot, half Columbian in his mid thirties, who always made a bee-line for me because I spoke Spanish. Couldn't wait to be asked about the dazzling new Latin act he was managing–turns out, fucking, too–which he claimed Madonna had given her blessing to, because, hey, man, she's Latin, too, you know. (Wow, I never knew that.) Just too many brotherhood handshakes and talk of being part of our family even before I could remember his last name. A tsunami of alcohol breath, dried sweat and sweet eau de cologne at 5 PM, food stuck between his teeth every time you met him, the furtive glances of a man for whom envy was a way of life. I found myself actually trying to like the guy in case he stabbed me in the back thinking I didn't like him.

What was it about these two sisters they both gravitated toward men with victim personalities? Even Sylvia's new guy was an ex cokehead. But how could I forget. Their father. In her late twenties, the twilight of her lesbian phase, Jasmine had undergone repressed therapy with a psychologist. On top of her resentment of her father for his having had an affair for seven years before 'callously' abandoning his wife, her psychologist had got her to explore the possibility – that's to say probability – that she was 'a victim of abuse'. In repressing these troubling memories, she had developed a crippling mistrust of men, sot he theory went. She'd been drawn to women not through a natural sexual attraction to them but rather as a means of 'compensating' for her 'lost memories'. That her father was himself a psychologist and practised hypnotherapy was virtual proof that she'd been manipulated by her father in such a way that she'd 'forgotten' the abuse he'd subjected her to. Neat theory. Pernicious speculation. I'd asked Sylvia if she thought there was any truth in the psychologist's 'findings', and she was quietly dismissive of them. Even Jasmine was later to refute the findings, finally admitting to everyone but her own father that she had probably been used to endorse the psychologist's dubious credentials. As far as I knew, she had never apologised to her father, whose sweet manner and abstracted air was of the kind that rather perfectly fitted the look of a 'dirty old man' man in the eyes of an insecure, invidious child. Though Sylvia was so much more natural and giving with men, having the two women together in the same house felt vaguely conspiratorial at worst and, at best, a no-confidence vote in men.

"So is the car fixed?"

"Yeah, it's fine. There was something wrong with the catalytic converter apparently."

"So what happened with the courtesy car? I thought you said you'd get that sorted."

I dug in my pocket for a little roll of notes I'd put aside for this conversation.

"They apologised." I put three crisp twenties on the kitchen table.

"You got that straight away?" she said incredulously.

"I got them to promise to send a cheque… compensation."

One thing I could be glad of regards Jasmine's visit, at least Sylvia had bigger things to occupy her mind than grilling me on the car.

"Once I started talking solicitors' letters, they became… co-operative."

Sylvia pulled a face, sceptical but impressed. She said she didn't need the money – I could keep it.

"No you keep it… Why don't you…" I stopped just short of suggesting that she spend it on a dinner for two with her new bloke. "…get some… art materials?" She smiled as if that were really sweet of me. As if she'd forgotten I could be tough on her behalf *and* get results when she needed them most.

I went upstairs to take a shower. Under the refuge of the hot spray, time seemed to evaporate and I began to dread stepping out of there, clothes that meant I had to act upon my thoughts. It wasn't until Sylvia knocked on the door calling, "What are you doing in there?" – *hell, she probably thinks I'm masturbating* – that I found the will to get out and dry off.

As I was changing into some rough old clothes, Bobby bounded into the room in baggy pyjamas, all tousled curls and flushed cheeks. He knew me well enough, but he just gawked at me as if he'd stumbled on a big cat sleeping on the bed. His mum hadn't taught him to smile and say Hi. Or close his mouth when he stared at you.

"Hey," I said.

He had a gun in one hand. He raised his arm and fired off an imaginary round, as serious as some low-life thug he'd seen on TV. He expressed mild disdain when I failed to roll over and die and ran off to find more obliging targets to kill.

While the women got the kids into baths and bed, I made myself a chicken stir-fry. My stomach was still tight and bloated with anxiety but I forced most of it down – once the adrenalin eased off I'd be wiped out without a top of good food. Sylvia returned to the kitchen just as I was rinsing my dishes. She told me Jasmine was taking a shower and going to bed early. Asked me if I'd like a tea.

"Sure… thanks."

For nearly two minutes we said nothing, putting things away, walking round each other until I sat down and pretended to scan a newspaper while she stood waiting for the kettle.

"So how was it?" she asked, setting the mugs of jasmine tea on the table. She sat opposite me. She tired but still sporting a lively air from her games with Bobby and the girls.

"How was what?"

"The conference obviously."

"Oh, y'know –"

"No, that's why I'm asking." She seemed about to cast an admonishing smile my way, but then did this thing with her eyelids – batting them, very briefly – as if mentally preparing to deal with any lies I might be about to feed her – or perhaps to warn me off telling any big ones.

"Fine," I replied wearily. When she stared back with slightly widened eyes, I went on to describe the whatever I could remember of the previous conference I'd been to, realising as I did that it had been a long time since she had sat looking at me the last time I told her anything about my work. I dribbled to a pause, afraid she wasn't listening to anything I'd said.

"Anyway, how about you? I hope wasn't too difficult without the car."

"No, it was OK. I took a taxi on the way home. I hope that's OK."

"Sure." Normally I would have asked her – out of habit – if she'd got a receipt, but she always did get them and what did it matter now anyway.

I made a half smile – about nothing in particular, for the years of being together, talking these little problems through. I grew aware of her eyes seeking me out, inviting me to join her in a clearing of some kind. She would have to lead the way, because I was in the dark.

"Is she OK, your friend?"

The mere allusion to Sisi nearly knocked me off my chair. My mind reeled with images of Anthony hurling things at the wall, smashing my head against the German installed teak cupboards… But the moment passed and I just sat there apparently gazing off into space, my fingers tightening around the warm mug.

"I –I only realised tonight, there's like a theme to the women in my life."

I glanced at Sylvia and thought I read a stiffening in her expression as she heard herself being lumped in with 'other women'. "Almost all of them," I continued, undaunted, "have had problems, major problems with their father. He's been missing, or he's been abusive, or he's been adulterous. And for some reason, I gravitate to these kinds of women, or they gravitate to me..." I paused, at a dead end; I didn't know where I was going with this.

"Is she one of those?"

"Yeah."

"Is she still around?"

I looked into her eyes, genuinely stuck for an answer to that. "I can't really talk about her at the moment."

We fell silent.

"*My* thing…" She paused and appeared to study the base of her mug, as though to position it mid-centre on an invisible beer mat. She looked up. "It turns out, he's not strictly a *former* user of cocaine."

Neither of us added anything for a moment.

"How does he afford it on a teacher's salary?" I asked.

"It's getting cheaper all the time. I don't have a problem with the odd weekend, but when it clearly runs a person's life…" She picked up her mug and took a sip. She set the mug down. She gave a little sniff. "Maybe he's not such a hard user, but after today with Jasmine, I just thought… I dunno. It used to be fun, but I have children, it just doesn't sit well, y'know? It's not a moral thing exactly, it's just–it's an aesthetic thing, I suppose." She paused, studying me again. "But on the other hand I like this part of him that refuses to be staid and middle-aged."

"Am I staid?"

She broke into laughter suddenly–"No, you're not!"

I smiled and said, "Just checking."

"No, you're like a child–and that's part of your charm, but at least you don't do coke." She paused, then began to grin foolishly–"Or do you?"

And we laughed together. I was surprised that I could and that it felt good as well as sore.

We chatted for maybe another ten minutes about people we knew, who had changed for the worst, lost their passion, their–oops–sex drive, their sense of humour–and, before today, I would have had a better idea where Sylvia and I fit in among all these people, except now we seemed to have come adrift, with only the kids to anchor us. When I got up, ostensibly to clear the sticky patch near where I'd left my mug, I veered off from the sink and went over to her and gave her a kiss on the mouth – as a token of friendship, really, nothing more – but her lips parted, wanting me, misunderstanding me. *Or did I want her?* I stayed for the duration of the kiss, but then, as I parted, she reached for the back of my head and held me wanting to explore the kiss further. In the first seconds there was a startling newness to our kiss that captivated me. When I tried to withdraw gracefully, she worked her hand into my fly–she'd forgotten none of her old tricks–

"Jasmine could come down… the kids, for a drink or something," I whispered.

She smiled saucily as if that might make it all the more fun.

"Jasmine and Bobby are in the spare room."

"In the single bed?"

"Camp bed for Bobby." As if she'd planned all this over an hour ago.

Before I could say anything further, she got to her feet, her tongue back in my mouth, her exigent hands pushing me in the direction of the living room. She giggled, mouth against mine, as we bumped into things, and it hurt recalling how she used to be when we were lovers. As I swung the door to, she toppled us onto the sofa. She tugged at my belt the second we hit the cushions. I knew what she was trying to do: out-lust the other woman. I thought to tell her she didn't have to do this, that the other woman had gone. And as much as a withered part of me wanted to believe Sylvia's dormant libido had erupted into lasting life, I was experiencing her desire as a kind of rape, because I simply wasn't ready for this, I was grieving!

She peeled off her jeans and panties, surprising me with her bush–I'd gotten so used to Sisi's trimness. She saw me look at her there and brought my hand to feel her open silky wet purse and immediately I wanted to plunge in there–

"Sylvia–"

"Come on–"

"You're fertile, aren't you?"

"You can tell?" she answered, her ironic smile almost lost in her air of reckless abandon.

"I think so–and that would mean, we need a condom, we can't just–"

"So get one, go on. Hopefully they're not passed their Use By date." This humour and the impish light in her eyes, the lascivious moistness about her cheeky smile, was as shocking as a vision of fairies coming to life–where had this girl been for the last twelve months?!

She was waiting and I was hesitating. I glanced at the closed door, hurting inside, as I knew I was about to disappoint her. Soon this fragile but horny moment would expire from lack of heat and momentum and I would have another thing to mourn.

I cast a pained glance at her and sat round on the sofa, elbows on my thighs.

She arrange her hair. I heard her clear her throat. We shrunk back into our skins, even as our blood throbbed in our ears. Now I feared I'd shamed her somehow in front of the other woman, a ghost.

"So, it's not a fling then?"

"It's not that, it's not about someone else. I –"

"You want to be with her. Just say it, it's OK, just tell me instead of all this skulking around – I can't stand it."

"I can't. I can't tell you."

"Why can't you? You're no good to us here, miserable... *pining*."

I did up my belt.

"I still love you Sylvia. I still desire you. But I can't go back to what we had–not just like that anyway."

"Why do we have to go back? I'd like to go forward."

I wondered how much she truly believed that and how much came from slipping into an almost nostalgic view of our relationship as a consequence of her ambiguous interest in her new relationship.

As I sat there on the edge of the cushions, I so wanted to give her hope. I thought to divulge the full of horror of what I was going through now–the case, the body, the blood, the wounds, Sisi's faceless killer–but I feared unravelling in front of her, and so I said nothing. And when I next looked up from the floor, she'd left the room, leaving her wet panties behind as a memento of what might be our very last time.

CHAPTER 25

'My loss permeates everything around the house–it's as though Sisi and I had lived here years together,' I wrote in my diary, early December. 'I see the violence done to her reincarnated in the most innocuous images. A concertinaed sock, for instance. A fallen toy. An overturned bucket in the garden. Even a knife lying on the side of the kitchen top can scare me, as though it knew better than I what I might be about to do with it in some vengeful act of madness. The trauma of Sisi's murder has aged me overnight, turned me into a worrier about the kids' well being. If they're cycling in the road, could they be knocked over? If they're on a school trip, could the bus overturn? I was never like that. I seem to have lost all confidence in my ability to protect the people dear to me. I have to hope this is reversible with time.'

"Look Dad, what's this?"

Mia had found me at my laptop in my study, as I checked my email. A rarefied December sun scaled the rooftops opposite as if to welcome her into the room.

"Dad…" she prompted.

I turned to see she was holding Sisi's two paper birds. She must have found them when I left my

Colloquial Thai book on the shelves in the living room, unable to carry it with me now on my trips around town.

"Did *you* make this?" she asked, clearly doubting I had the skill.

I felt my eyes prick. A hand went to my mouth to stop an involuntary sob. I had this terrible vision suddenly of Sisi in the park with the girls, chasing each other, Sisi swinging Mia round and round…

"No," I said finally. "Do you remember…" I hesitated. Dare I involve her in my grief?

"Remember what, Dad?"

"You remember the photos I showed you, of my friend, the Thai girl?"

"Pretty?"

"Yeah. Sisi. You remember?"

She pulled a face.

"The girl in the pool. She had a broken tooth, you remember?"

"Oh yeah. and you checked it out in that room with the office lamp…" She was smiling as if that day also brought back vivid memories that were worth remembering for a long time to come.

Almost without thinking I turned back to my laptop and looked for the folder I had on Sisi–I wanted her to see Sisi without blood on her face. A row of jpegs. A favourite black and white, seated in a beam of soft light just outside the window of her first apartment. It would hurt to look at it at this moment, but I badly needed Mia to understand something of my loss.

"You remember?"

"Yes."

"She made those birds for you and Michaela."

Mia smiled. "When can we see her?"

Tears were welling in my eyes. I had to break from the desk, the PC and crash on the old sofa we had in there, squeezed into a nook. I reached out my hands for Mia and she came to me.

"I'm afraid, darling, you can't see her… she's dead."

As I hugged my daughter, fighting against a torrent of uncontrollable sobbing, which I was afraid might scare Mia, I remembered so many of those moments I'd clung to Sisi, so desperately wanting her love more than her body.

"Keep them safe," I said, handing the birds back to Mia, even as I knew I would soon find them mangled and forgotten in among toys and coloured pens in a few days' time.

Bobby's' call came the next day, two hours after I'd taken the delivery of the freezer, around 3PM, another still and grey afternoon, early December.

"Three days. Time's up. I hope you have the goods nicely packed and ready to be shipped out."

"What have you done with her?"

"Don't concern yourself with that."

"I want to speak to her."

There was a pause.

"I hope you're not losing your mind, Anthony."

"I love Sisi. What have you done with her?"

"She's nicely tucked away and that's all you need to know."

"I was going to pay you the money, why did you have to hurt her?"

"I'm sorry, but that don't tally with *our* information. You wasn't cooperating. We offered you her as a business package, a whore you could make your money back on, but you didn't take us up on that. She messed us around. I don't want to have to spell this out to you again. Now, 'ave you got the money or not?"

I paused, and then answered: "No" and immediately hung up. I knew that would piss him off. The more I pissed him off, the less careful he'd be as to what he might admit to over the phone.

He rang again about two minutes later.

"This is your last chance, or you're gonna pay another way."

After a calculated pause I said: "Don't you hurt another hair on her head!" and hung up again.

I knew I'd confused him referring to Sisi as though she were alive. And yet, two minutes later, I got a text message that read: 'You have 24 hours and that's all.'

The message was reassuring, if only because it strongly suggested what I was ninety per cent sure of now: that I wasn't dealing with a criminal organisation. The 'we' Bobby kept referring to in all likelihood consisted of him and Arun.

When I got home that evening, without further calls from any distorted voices, I removed the USB clip from my digital recorder and downloaded the digital recordings I'd made of Bobby's recent calls onto my laptop, which I backed up on 2 CDs. I stashed one of the CDs under the floor in the shed, the other in the house with a message to Sylvia to hand over the CD to the police in the event anything suspicious happened to me.

My phone was ringing. Unidentified caller.

"Hello?"

"Anthony, hi, it's Neil, Neil Bantock. Just thought I'd give you a quick call. Sorry I haven't been in touch recently, I've been away on holiday. Just got back–"

"Oh, good… good. Anywhere nice?" having a stab at interested and cheerful mate.

"Brazil. Yeah, nice. Pretty wild again. Some fabulous women. Back at work now," he said, lowering his voice as though phone calls to mates were seriously frowned upon in Immigration. "Just thought I'd see how you are."

"Well, uh–fine, yeah–thanks."

"Any news?"

"News?"

"Yeah, I dunno. That girl, for instance." His optimism cut me to the quick.

"Oh, um, that's finished."

"Really?"

"Yeah," I replied belatedly. "Yeah, it's finished." My throat was closing up on me.

"Just like that?"

"I'd rather not talk about it, Neil, if you don't mind."

"Oh… OK. Any changes, business-wise?"

"No. Everything on hold for a while," I said mechanically. "Bit close to Christmas to be thinking of changes."

"Yeah yeah–too right, too right." A beat. "Well, we should catch up, yeah?–while I've still got this tan."

I said I was very busy at the moment with the various Christmas dos I was going to, which of course I wasn't, but we should certainly try and hook up before too long.

Hanging up, I realised he was the only friend to have called me in the past two weeks. It was as if everyone else knew I was radiating some kind of hurt they'd rather not tune in to.

"Hello Anthony." It was Bobby again, his distorted, vibrating voice sounding ever more like the infuriating buzz of a mosquito as it returns yet again in the night for a little bit more of your blood. I'd just arrived at the practice and the receptionist was remarking that I looked a bit pale before realising I was on the phone. I waved at her, and passed down the corridor heading straight for the back door. I stepped outside in the yard where I took out my recorder and pressed Rec.

"Sorry," I said, "you caught me at work, with a patient."

"I hope you're not thinking of doing anything rash like going to the police, man."

Some of the confidence had gone out of the man's voice and my pause would drain a little more of that juice.

"Why should I believe you?" I resumed, coming at him from a different direction. "You don't bring her to the phone, I don't hear her voice–I think you've killed her. She always said you'd kill her. You just couldn't stand the thought of her turning straight and being with me–that's right, isn't it?"

It was the first time I'd gotten personal and I was hoping it would provoke him.

"She's dead, you fuckin moron, course she's – We're not talking about getting her back here–" But then he cut himself off. Perhaps it had suddenly dawned on him what I was doing, and yet, a moment later, he came back on with renewed confidence:

"You seem to be forgetting something: your DNA is inside her vagina."

"We were in love."

"Bollocks. You were on a trip."

"Which you ended."

"Well, even the rollercoaster has to come to an end, my friend."

"So you've killed her?"

There was a pause.

"You have 24 hours, then I call the cops, and they'll be down on you like flies on shit."

He hung up. Still confident I'd cave in, that I had no strategy of my own.

Predictably I received a text a few minutes later: 'Enjoy the dick in prison'

He's still using Sisi's phone, I noted to myself. A man gets careless when he hangs on too long to sadistic pleasures.

CHAPTER 26

You go over everything in your mind, the true story and the story you've decided to tell. And then you go over it again. It was like taking my Finals again, but with bleaker consequences if I fucked up. I took a mild sedative before I made the call. Just enough so that my voice wouldn't quaver, my hand wouldn't shake, but not so much that I appeared weirdly calm. Only the guilty are calm.

Ten days to Christmas. The kids so looking forward – counting the days, talking about their presents, their wishes and asking me what mine might be.

The afternoon light all but gone, an unmarked car eased into the shiny wet asphalt harbour of the front of the house like a shark. Two silhouettes–one in a jacket, the other in a raincoat–faced the house and approached in unison. The bell chimed with its usual cheerful *ding dong*, as if mocking my dread. Ordinarily the girls would have rushed to the door to welcome the visitors, but I'd already asked Sylvia to take them, Jasmine and her son Bobby to the pictures and then on to a restaurant. I'd spoken to Sylvia the night before to tell her I'd be making the call the next day. The girl I'd been seeing had disappeared. Someone had been stalking her. I feared the worse. I was going to have to contact the police. They'd be coming here.

I sat on the edge of the bed, profile to her, as she sat propped up against two pillows, a book on her lap. The air in the room was so still we could have been miles underground. She asked me again, calmly, how I was involved, what was it I knew? What sort of person was this girl? "For now," I said, "all I can tell you is that I've done nothing to harm her or anyone else." I regretted the terseness in my voice, but it wasn't something I could control. When I finally could bring myself to look at her with more than a fearful glance, I saw all our past reflected in her eyes, everything that was precious and I had put it in jeopardy. But we didn't fight, we didn't cry. I got under the duvet with her and we lay very still as if listening to each other's thoughts.

I felt some mild relief welcoming in men not in uniform – uniforms have always intimidated me, even though I've never had any run-ins with the law – and Detective Sergeants Wallace and Thompson struck me as instantly likeable, rational human beings. *Ordinary men, just doing their job, not here to put me away.* Wallace I put at around fifty-three. He was tall and overweight, with avuncular features, alcoholic and high blood pressure skin that was offset by surprisingly anxious and sensitive blue eyes that lurked behind an unlikely pair of glasses for someone from the murder squad, of the kind you'd more readily associate with an academic. His partner was similarly tall but thin and narrow, economical with his movements, the kind of man whose reticence was in itself a kind of weapon for peeling the chaff off lies.

I invited them into the kitchen and we sat at the table. The minute the cat jumped up onto Thompson's lap, the detective swiftly picked him up and handed him to me as though there was a serious risk of my friendly cat compromising his impartiality. I set Neo down in the corridor and shut the door. I returned to my seat and we began.

I had my laptop open on the table and the downloaded recordings I'd made of my last conversations with Bobby were all set up ready to play. I'd also downloaded the picture messages of Sisi bruised and battered and the more disturbing video clip sent to my mobile phone that showed her being tortured. The detectives huddled around the 15-inch screen as though I were about to show them the replay of a suspect off-side decision that had lost England the match they'd missed earlier in the day. They remained impassive throughout, though – for all they knew I might be making the whole thing up.

Wallace turned to me and asked me why I hadn't gone to the police when the ransom was first demanded.

"Sisi's a prostitute. I panicked."

Wallace stirred on his seat, disappointed, less in me, I felt, than mankind in general. He asked if I'd come down to the station with them. As I demurred, his colleague tapped him on the arm and gave a faintly censorious shake of his head and said it was OK, they had a tape recorder in the car, would I be alright talking to them on that, here in my home?

"Yeah, let's do that," Wallace concurred, stretching in his chair as though were about to settle down to a good movie together.

Before I was allowed to say anything Wallace had us pause to insert a formal caution, which he delivered with a suitably sober but kindly expression as if he were saying grace before we got down to our food.

I started off, dry about the mouth and briefly contemplated excusing myself from the room to take another sedative, but told myself everything would be OK once I got going. It helped to have things I could present – the video, the recordings, copies of my mobile phone bill, the calls to Bobby highlighted in yellow – evidence, I hoped, that I was also a victim. I mentioned that I'd first run into Arun at Sisi's Paddington flat. But I said nothing about the dummy: that side of things would have shown I was capable of breaking the law for Sisi's sake. Bobby and I had never met, I told them. All I could give them was the description Sisi had provided me. I knew of Arun's address because Sisi had given it to me over the phone; she'd wanted me to accompany her on a visit to his place one day. Had I gone to visit Arun?

"No. I thought of going when I got the call that she'd been abducted, but then I thought it was probably a bad idea – if he was the kidnapper, he might hurt her if he saw me anywhere near his place."

"So this Bobby chap, he was one of Sisi's regulars, and somehow he got to know Arun?" Wallace put to me, watching me with clear eyes.

"Yes."

"And you think they kidnapped her, working together?"

"Yes."

"And even though you were just a customer of hers, albeit a regular one, they wanted £30,000 from you – or something would happen to her?"

"Yeah."

"And you didn't want to pay that amount. Understandably."

"Yeah," I said, feeling I had to provide an answer for the tape recorder.

Wallace drew breath. "Thai, is she, this girl?"

"Yeah."

"Got a picture? I mean, apart from that horrible video."

We went to the website.

"Pretty girl," Wallace admitted dryly. "So, your concern is: Sisi, aka Sonia – her escort name – is in imminent danger of her life? From this man, Bobby," pointing to my PC by way of referring to the tapes we'd heard.

"Yes."

The detectives conferred silently with one another–just eyes, a sniff, a scratch of the nose. Like a child at a funeral, my nerves threatened to send me into a fit of grotesque giggling, but the sedatives arrived to gently freeze the impulse and I merely sat there wearing a mask of helpful impassiveness.

The thin one said he had to make a call and got to his feet. Could he use the next room? Sure. He left the room and shut the door. Neither Wallace nor I spoke for a long minute. I figured they weren't telling me what the call was about in order to see if I'd sweat. I refrained from tapping my fingers, any kind of fidgeting. When Wallace finally spoke it was to say something like, "Not the kind of thing you want to be dealing with when you still haven't done your Christmas shopping, is it?" *Bringing us back to the every day, nothing wrong with a little bit of humour in the circumstances, nothing too funny.* I smiled appreciatively.

Scissoring back to the kitchen, Thompson nodded an OK to Wallace and remained on his feet, his backside against the kitchen top.

"Just in case you're wondering," Thompson said, directing his deep-set, pale blue eyes at me, "I was just making sure we can get a warrant to search this guy's premises. We've got a team coming down to rig up your phone in case this Bobby character should give you another call. I'm afraid it might be a long night."

I asked them if they could use a cup of coffee or tea. They glanced at one another and agreed to tea. Milk and sugar for Wallace, milk for Thompson.

Having made their drinks I told them I'd like to call my wife to let her know what was going on.

The kids' voices in the background, Sylvia came on the line sounding quite cheerful. They'd been to the cinema and had just ordered some Chinese food. I told them that the police might be with me for a good few hours yet and asked her if she'd mind driving on to my parents if I could arrange it. But what about school? I don't want them missing school, she said, determined that everything else should go on as normal. I'm sorry. School might have to wait. She sighed as if this were a bigger loss than what was going on with me. Why did the police have to stay so long?

"There's a kidnap situation and they want to tap my phone."

"But why would these kidnappers want a ransom from you?!" she cried.

I think she found the answer for herself in the silence that followed.

"Oh, Anthony," she moaned, just like my mother might have done. "You're incredible." We fell silent. She spoke first, but was interrupted by one of the kids. "I'm talking to Daddy," I heard her say, "wait a minute." I heard Mia's voice and Sylvia's firm "No." A pause. "Let me know as soon as possible, OK?" I said I would, and we hung up.

I called my parents straight after. When Mum picked up I asked her straight away to pass me Dad. Dad wouldn't ask lots of questions, he'd take it that I'd explain later if I felt the need to, so it was enough to tell him the police were questioning me about the disappearance of a patient. And that I'd done nothing to break the law. And with that, though concerned, he was readily assured. He conferred briefly with Mum and came back to say they'd be 'happy' to take the family as long as Sylvia's sister didn't mind sleeping on a mattress on the floor in the living room. I called Sylvia back and said my parents would be expecting her any time before midnight. My doomed love affair was now rippling through my wider family, ever outward.

When we were all seated again, Thompson asked if I'd be alright to continue with the interview. He pressed Rec on his digital recorder.

It wasn't long before the tech support team arrived with two more detectives. They all sounded so chummy with one another, I could have believed they were here to change into their rugby kit. A balding tech guy with protruding teeth happily downloaded whatever useful info he could get off my mobile phone, then rigged it up to a recorder. His colleague, mid forties, stocky, with a light and helpful voice, drew up a seat and asked after my family and whether my wife was sufficiently apprised of what was going on.

Thompson picked up the laptop, reminding me they'd need to keep it a while as it was now evidence.

It's OK, I have a spare one, I nearly blurted out, (the one I was writing all this down on).

"Are we likely to find this fellow at home, d'you think?" Wallace asked, turning in the hallway.

"Sisi said he sometimes works nights."

"Do you know where?"

I shook my head.

"Doesn't matter. If there's no one there, we may have to force an entry." He paused. "OKey-doke, we'll let you know."

I'd grown so accustomed to the dour language and embittered moral rectitude of the detectives of British cop dramas, I was strangely amused and disarmed to the point of a kind of light-headedness by the good humour and reasonableness filling my hallway. I could have believed we'd all be meeting down at the pub later on to compare notes on a safari expedition over a pint. How long, though, would that impression last?

I offered teas and coffees to the replacement team. I brought in newspapers and magazines to supplement their own Sun and Standard and asked if they wouldn't mind my retiring to the living room. They were fine with that. With the door closed, I didn't know what to do with myself. The TV would probably only have irritated me, and might have struck them as far too cool, so I began reading a book. The same page, over and over.

I was very close to nodding off on the sofa when a car's lights swept across the window and I was aware of voices in the drive. It was nearly 3 AM. There was a knock on the door. It was the guy with the funny teeth.

"If you could come and open the door for us, I think we've got some news, sir," he said with the kind of positive pragmatism you'd be wise not to mistake for optimism.

I stepped into the hall to see the stocky tech guy standing by the front door. I went to open it. Thompson and Wallace filled the porch. Their demeanour suggested something indigestible had settled on their stomachs in the interim.

"We've done the search. We've made an arrest," Wallace began, now standing in the hallway. "And I'm afraid–"

"Let's all get inside Frank, can we?" Thompson interrupted him.

"Yeah yeah yeah–let's do that," Wallace said in his whispery, almost caressing, faded Yorkshire voice.

I entered the living room alone. Wallace and Thompson took the stocky chap and his colleague aside and quietly informed them they could pack up. Eyes glanced back at me, no one letting his eyes meet mine. The tech guys collected their gear with practiced efficiency and excused themselves from the room. I heard the door shut, and I was alone again with Thompson and Wallace.

"Alright if we sit down?" Wallace asked.

"Sure."

Both men sat down on the sofa, Wallace with a wheeze.

"There's been a development," Wallace said, removing his specs and setting them on his knee as if they were an encumbrance to human compassion. He paused. His eyes, now naked, looked tired, vulnerable without the heavy frames to protect them. His lips made a slight sucking sound. "I'm afraid, we're pretty sure we've found your friend, and she–"one side of his cheek seemed to wince–"she's dead. Murdered. I'm sorry."

I'd dreaded this moment. I'm no actor, but somehow I had to manufacture surprise, outrage – any one of the emotions I'd already been at the mercy of for days on end. All that was happening for a full ten seconds was that the skin on the back of my neck was rippling up and down. Then my eyes pricked, my throat tightened up as if this really was news.

"You're sure?"

"She had this big tattoo of a dragon on her back, same place on the shoulder, as you described it."

Wallace was adding words to what he'd said– they'd be asking me down to the mortuary to formally identify her in the near future–but I was hearing only half of them. I must have gone into a delayed state of shock. Even as I slowly tuned into their account of how they'd found Sisi's body, I experienced a strange dissociation from the person I'd been in the last five or six days–my mind was playing back key episodes of Anthony Price as someone else, like an alter ego in a dream.

Him – that other, cooler Anthony – with a pair of old bolt cutters a builder friend had left in the smaller shed and long since forgotten. Rusty, but chunky enough for his purposes. Don't show your face in a hardware store buying bolt cutters – camera can see you. It's night, late, cold. Anthony, his gloved hands, cutting the chain – easy enough. But the heavy padlock, fucking cutters keep slipping. A man walking his dog. Anthony slips round the side of the garage and sucks in his chest and turns away from the road and thinks himself into becoming invisible. The dog-walker walks by, no pause in his step. Cutters go back to the thin metal neck of the padlock, crunching down on it. Anthony's arms twist with the cutters and the lock comes away from the rotten wood of the door. An angry splitting sound of wood. It's like the satisfaction of pulling a wisdom tooth. Step inside and pull the door to. Waiting in there, standing by the doors, in case he'd alerted anyone with the noise. All clear and slipping out again to fetch his cargo. Back in the garage removing the bin liners. Stash the case under some cardboard boxes toward the back. He throws the broken padlock into a cardboard box in the corner of the garage. He picks up three broken tiles that must have fallen through the roof onto the dusty floor and, stepping back out, uses them as a means of propping the door back, more or less as it was. He shuts the gate and wraps the chain loosely so that it won't be obvious at a glance that someone has had a go at it. He takes off the bag-like shoe covers, which he pinched from the Small Pool at Acton Swimming Baths, knowing that he would have to be careful about footprints and trace… He draws the car alongside a skip, slips the bolt cutter under a mattress and gets back in his car. Hands stuffing the surgical gloves inside a McDonald's Milk shake in a litter bin. Hands at the basin washing again, as the kids sleep…

"It appears she was murdered some days ago," Wallace was saying. "I can't reveal when exactly, but I'm afraid you'd have been paying up for nothing, so you did well to contact us."

I glanced at the other detective–his silence was oppressive. I knew it was important I let at least some of the emotion show in my reactions, but each time I was terrified of not being able to stop, of turning to jelly-like mush which they could manipulate at will.

They said they wanted to go over again the details of the kidnapping just to be sure they had their dates right, but I could tell they were hoping I might be tired enough to contradict my earlier testimony and give them a point of leverage. I began trembling at one point as emotion overwhelmed me and I had to take a moment to compose myself. The thin man told me to take my time. Wallace reiterated the kind advice. As I waited for my heartbeat to slow down, I feared I might not possess sufficient stamina to retell the story many times over the same way, but like a bolt out of the blue Thompson and Wallace told me they'd let me get some sleep now, it had been a long night, they believed they had enough for now. They said they were hopeful of having a lead within the next 48 hours on finding and possibly arresting 'this Bobby character'. Getting to his feet, Wallace imparted further that, although I wasn't a suspect as such, it would be imprudent of me to leave the country for the time being. I nodded, suggestible to their cautions.

"I'm sorry for your loss," Thompson said with practised sincerity as I saw them out.

I'd heard this phrase so often on CSI, it was surreal to hear it addressed to me, personally. Its neatness–the light word 'loss' attaching to no one, an open concept perhaps, just floating in space–was almost an affront, given the rawness of my emotions, and yet at the same time its very ubiquity seemed to include me in an imaginary community of caring faces. Looking into their professional faces I wondered whether either of them had ever been with a prostitute–they weren't being sympathetic here, they were doing their job.

"Thanks for letting me know. In person."

I held out my hand. Our handshake was purely functional, conferring only a potential for agreement in the future.

Sylvia returned the next day in the car–less the kids and her sister. She'd dropped the others off at a park in Chiswick, so that "we could have the morning alone"–a phrase that might have sounded sexy at any other time. I made us both a Japanese tea and sat down in the lounge. The light was almost dark enough for us to switch on a lamp, but I preferred the shadows. Was I to tell her the true story, or the version I'd given the police, if only to spare her having to lie on my behalf? I told her everything. Everything except that part which concerned the dummy–it seemed irrelevant and would only put me in a dimmer light than I was already. She listened to me fixed with a perpetual frown as though straining to understand an

account in a language she was no longer familiar with. She never once exclaimed or interrupted. We speculated, in fits and starts, over the various possible outcomes, then settled into a desultory analysis of sexual violence in men. Was there more of it these days, or was it just being reported more? Was the wider reporting encouraging the escalating violence? First her sister's bloke, now the man who'd murdered Sisi. How could we protect our girls from similar fates?

The following day, Wallace and Thompson pick me up from the practice at 6 PM. First stop, the mortuary. I pass through rooms threaded with Christmas decorations. How depressing tinsel can be. Deep into the bowels of the place until I arrive at a heavier looking door – which is ajar. *They were expecting me.* Chemicals of death in your nostrils. Grey bag on a gurney, body in a bag. You step forward, as if to look over a precipice. The zip is drawn down. I realise with peculiar violence that this is the last time I'm ever going to see her and suddenly I start to buckle. Even though I can hardly believe it's really her–she looks now like a wax effigy of the corpse I had cared for. They don't ask me anything for a moment, they hover as if waiting for me to collapse. Really they don't need to ask if it's her, they can see for themselves. But procedure has to be adhered to. I ask for five minutes alone in the street before I accompany them to the station. I step outside. It's begun to rain. Quite hard, as if feeling my bitterness. I ask Wallace for a cigarette. It's fifteen years since I smoked one. Wallace's last. It tastes like crap. But just the action of sucking on something, the subtle rush of nicotine, help keep me together.

At the station the detectives tell me again they're sorry they had to put me through that.

"Your first?" Wallace says, peeping over the top of his glasses at me.

I nod. He nods in return. How grim we men are.

They allow a few seconds to elapse before Thompson does the honours with the old tape machine (screwed to the table, which, like the chairs, is screwed to the floor) and opens with a smoothly reeled off caution to which I answer, "Yes, I understand."

"And you're still OK to talk to us without a solicitor present?"

That he's asking this again only five minutes after he asked it, out in the corridor, slightly unnerves me, though I realise it's probably just for the purposes of the recording of the interview.

Leaning back in his back in his chair now, Wallace asks me what was it that drew me to this girl – her looks notwithstanding, of course. *So here's another test. Loosen him up with sympathy or even empathy.*

"I mean, you have money, intelligence, you look pretty fit for your age–plenty better than me–" holding his beer gut as if to bounce a basketball, "you have a beautiful wife… how did you end up here, talking to us – about a murder?"

He allows me thinking time and I take it. I feel so fragmented as to be able to speak only in sawn-off utterances.

"My wife and I, we've been drifting apart for some time." Pause. "I've already told you how I got to know Sisi."

"Yes. She was a patient. Is that altogether ethical?"

"I got to know her outside of the practice. And I didn't know she was an escort til later."

"How much later?"

"She told me after we had sex, the first time."

"So when you saw her subsequently, you saw her as a customer, or as a lover?"

"Both."

They've heard all this, they heard it the first time we met. But this isn't a rehearsal. With repetition new stuff, secrets get dislodged.

"How would you have described the sex you had with Sisi?" Thompson asks. "Normal, kinky, rough…?

"Normal."

So now it's Thompson's turn – and he goes for the more penetrative questions, the ones that make you smart or squirm. When Wallace starts up again, it's to allow, or perhaps encourage, the interview format to disintegrate into chat. Then, just as the chat is on the point of turning into banter, Thompson reins us in with an economically admonitory instruction about 'keeping to the point'. *Wallace the oil, Thompson the screwdriver. Can they get me open all the way up?*

Every few minutes I come close to confiding more than I have so far–the detectives' silences are so beautifully honed to draw truth out of a man, like a pipette working a liquid–but the business with the suitcase has made something of a soldier of me.

The statement I give is finally read back to me, corrected, initialled, (I've never seen the point in initialling, anyone could write AP) and signed.

That same evening Wallace calls me at home to inform me, betraying no excitement, that they've collated enough evidence to make an arrest. They believe they now have the man I know as Bobby.

"What kind of evidence?" I ask. We're in a different room today, different only in size, really, everything else appears to be the same.

"We might get to that later." Thompson is leading off. Wallace looks a bit hungover – following celebrations from last night's arrest? "For now, we'd like you to take a look at a couple of photos."

Thompson draws my surprise from a manila envelope and slides two black and white photos across the table to me, placing them neatly, side by side. Mug shots. After a pause, he asks me, "Do you know this man?"

"I do, yeah. It's Neil Bantock." And all I can think at that moment is they're wanting to go all the way back to the pool incident to run through the whole story again from there.

"Friend? Would you call him a friend?"

"Yeah, uh… a new friend, I suppose. He, um, I met him the same day I met Sisi…" And as I say this, Thompson's tongue flicks out to wet his lips, he tilts his head ever so slightly and I am directed back to the photo, something dead about the eyes and I begin to register a surge of adrenalin rushing through me.

"This man, we believe," Thompson says, tapping the photo, "is Bobby."

"Neil's Bobby?" I begin to laugh, but it's a strange sound – "No no, that doesn't make sense! He's been in Brazil anyway! We were going to meet a few days ago – he said he had a tan!"

"Yes, he has a tan. But he didn't get it from Ipanema Beach, he got that from a sun lounge in West Hampstead. It's our guess he was planning on using his holiday story–and his tan–as evidence that he'd been away, so you'd never suspect him and he could just waltz back into your life, 50 K richer thank you very much and carry on being your 'friend'."

"And with friends like that…" Wallace adds, arms crossed over his big chest.

"Nasty piece of work," Thompson says, as if referring to a malignant tumour lying in a kidney dish. "If in fact we're right, and you're as innocent as you claim to be."

I ignore the last remark and gaze at these messengers with all the incredulity I can muster. But even as I do, fragments of the past come rushing up to me showing me how it could all make sense what they're saying.

"But the tapes, the voice–the accent sounded like South London–"

"Good actor," Thompson interrupts crisply, almost approvingly. "We did a voice analysis and it's the same voice. In fact we even picked up recordings from his flat of him practising his act with you. He does a good slacker's twang."

"Our search of Bantock's flat –" Wallace continues, "we found the device he was using to distort his voice, we also found Sisi's phone–a bit careless–and we can also place him at the crime scene, forensically speaking."

Suffocated by the closeness of the photos staring at me, Wallace and Thompson – Wallace's breath I can smell every time he leans forward – unable to speak, I push the table away, hard, but it won't move of course, it's the same screwed down one as in the other room, and the chair won't move either, so my push propels me upward to my feet – which alarms Thompson, but I move away from him, *I'm not going hit you,* like a crab and shrink against the nearest wall. Pressing my back against it, I slide down it. To the floor, gasping. Now small, I gaze at the opposite wall, waiting for the storm in my head to subside, if it ever will.

Thompson asks me if I'd like a glass of water. He says I've gone very pale, am I alright? He lets me sip from the plastic cup where I've crawled to and observes me from his seat. Wallace cleaning his glasses. I feel lost, utterly confused, as if I've been here for days not minutes. Perhaps I need a solicitor now.

"Apparently, he claims that he was Sisi's girlfriend and you were stalking her… and he was just trying to protect her," Thompson is saying twenty minutes later. I'm back in my chair, on my second cup of water, and I still haven't asked for my solicitor, I've merely asked them to put the photos away.

"That's rubbish. If he really is Bobby, Bobby was a constant menace."

"So how did you get to know him? When did you make his acquaintance? Fill us in–yeah?" Thompson says, twiddling his pen between his fingers.

The questions cast me back in time, like a flat pebble skimming long and far over water until it sinks in the diving end of an indoor swimming pool. I'd never quite made the connection–him and Sisi. I might have done, I tell myself, but for the fact he'd been there with his son. Or if I'd even noticed Neil making contact with Sisi. She hadn't mentioned having recognised him, but then why would she? She'd never even wanted me to visualise him or give me his name. *Never give them your real name.* So maybe she'd only ever known him as Bobby. Had Neil gone to the pool with Sisi and her friend, or had he stalked her, taking his son along to make it look as though, if she saw him, he was there by coincidence? Recalling his outburst by the cubicle it wasn't difficult to believe he could have lost it with Sisi. And yet, hadn't he become my friend?

Days passed and I still couldn't believe that Neil had set out to blackmail me from day one, as the police seemed ready to believe. When I fell for Sisi, he'd latched onto me as a means of feeding his obsession in her, vicariously. I was perhaps also a means of curing him of his obsession: if he could get me clean of Sisi–through seeing other prostitutes, for example–he could cure himself into the bargain. But then he'd seen an opportunity: and chose to make me pay even more for my folly. He knew Sisi wanted out. Anthony Price's naiveté could help them both. His scheme with the dummy would also give him a reason to insinuate himself back into Sisi's life again–he'd have done her a favour ripping me off and sharing the proceeds with her. So he took me out to get me laid, ply me with drugs. (Now I understood why he'd left me with Aisha at Earl's Court: he needed time to stage-light Sisi's apartment, get his props and actors ready.) But of course he couldn't have been there that night, as that would have blown his identity; he needed an accomplice. He'd already got to know Arun through Sisi. Arun's skills as a web designer were of interest to Neil, who had plans for a dot com business. Arun would be cheap because of his Visa restrictions and poor English. The charade had worked a treat. Maybe Neil honestly believed the lesson would do me good. But he clearly hadn't reckoned on Sisi's contrition and then her actually falling for me.

What I found so hard to accept was the measure of premeditation to his murdering Sisi–he'd actually brought along some plastic sheeting to wrap her dead body in. Luckily for me, for justice, he'd handled the sheeting without gloves before transporting it to Sisi's flat. I couldn't have known this, but it had occurred to me that by cutting off a piece of the sheeting and putting it in the case that I might be transferring the killer's prints or DNA or trace evidence from his car or apartment to the body. (I was later to find out that the police had located Neil by way of these fingerprints; they'd come up on computer data, which revealed Neil Bantock had been charged less than a year previously for an assault on his wife, charges later dropped by her.) Neil had involved Arun in the first few calls, probably to make me think I'd fallen foul of the escort agency or even a sex trafficking gang, and then the tidy-up. In return Arun was to receive a cut of the money that I was supposed to cough up. All Arun had to do–and the job was half done for him already thanks to the plastic sheeting–was pack the body in a case, drive a couple of miles down the road, enter a garden and dig a hole. (I remembered having said to Neil I had a big garden but had never done much with it, so he'd possibly gone there himself one day to do a recce for his burial plan.) The question remained, though, had Arun been involved in the murder, or was he just the cleaner?

Like many confessions Neil's came out in bits and pieces, like a rotten tooth. First he'd only hit her, he knew nothing about the stab wounds, they had to have been done by me, or Arun, or 'some other nutter'. He'd hit her and panicked. When the police revealed that they were able to match his prints to two prints on the plastic sheeting, however, he admitted he'd mutilated Sisi's body partly out of anger and partly to terrify me; I was much less likely to try and clean up the crime scene myself, and therefore much more likely to pay up, if the scene was already messy and repelling. The autopsy report corroborated his story inasmuch that it concluded Sisi had died from 'severe head trauma' and that the knife wounds were in fact post mortem. He admitted hitting her with a torch, but had been provoked and hadn't meant to seriously hurt her. The pathologist begged to differ–there was at least one blow to Sisi's face when she was already on the floor, still conscious. The main area of dispute went to intent: had Neil gone to Sisi's flat intending to make up with her, or seriously hurt her? He claimed she'd called him. But his and Sisi's phone records proved the communication must have been telepathic. He changed his story to something along the lines of: "She must have called from a phone box when I was at work." But he ran into the same problem: his phone records at work showed no calls from phone boxes in the Shepherd's Bush area. So maybe she hadn't called, he'd just popped round on the off-chance of finding her in. But then why would he drop by with a heavy torch for a mere social visit? He said he knew she was having problems with her electricity, so he'd brought the torch round in case he had to fix something. How did he know she had problems with her electricity? Arun had told him, Neil claimed. But why would she have kept in touch with Arun, if she'd been running away from Neil, aka Bobby?

To begin with, Arun also denied any knowledge of the crime. But when the police found trace amounts of Sisi's blood on his shoes–he probably hadn't noticed the blood because he'd then gone and got his shoes dirty in my garden–and an escort girl was brought in to say she'd seen him with Sisi on numerous occasions, he started to talk. In the end, it was to be the police's ability to capitalise on the weaknesses in Neil's relationship with Arun that produced two reliable confessions.

Even as the Crown's case grew stronger, instead of relief I was suffering panic attacks, seldom at work, usually when I was relaxing. I would be completely fine one minute and then some smell or visual reference to Sisi, as she was alive or dead, would set me off and I'd be swallowed up into a vortex of high anxiety. On every public bench, every train seat or bus seat, I had imagined conversations with Neil as to what drove him to do it. I also wanted to kill him.

In a bid for some kind of closure and, knowing that Sisi's mother was only modestly well off, I paid for the casket and transportation costs for sending the body home. Sylvia, in a generous gesture, suggested I go too–she knew I'd always wanted to see Thailand, the break might do me good, (somehow she avoided any sarcastic allusion to pretty Thai girls)–but I couldn't, I was afraid of going and not wanting to come home for months on end. I think I was afraid too of being healed. Somehow this broken feeling inside of me was the crutch I needed after my fall. I guess this is grief, isn't it. It wasn't guilt. I knew the difference. I'd done what I could. More than most men would have done. And yet, could I ever escape the notion that it was my love for her that had gotten her killed? So maybe there was guilt from that point of view. There was self-pity too, I admit. But, if there was, it always felt as though I were feeling pity for some other Anthony, not the one I was left with.

I found solace one afternoon in the tranquillity of my parents' beautiful Surrey home, talking to my dad about his dad who had been twice wounded in the First World War. It was Easter Sunday afternoon and all the women had gone out for a walk and we sat together in their beautiful living room listening to a tape my dad's brother had made of my grandfather, by then aged eighty something, talking in an even, almost chirpy voice about the rats and the mud and the stench and the fear of lying in the mud with a hole in your back waiting to be bayoneted by the enemy. And in connecting with my grandfather's strength,

knowing I was of his blood, I found untapped
reserves of my own and a way of moving on.

CHAPTER 27

The press descended on us like vultures, their heads huddled in the collars and hoods of their outdoor jackets–a great source of amusement to the girls in the first few days. Sylvia was determined to ignore them, but was rattled having to brush past them between the street, the car and the front door. Instinctively we knew it wasn't delicate truth they were after. For a time some of the tabloids and local papers had fun punning on words familiar to my profession–'Crown of thorns for dentist trying to save prostitute' was one of the better ones. There was, however, at least one unequivocal and very welcome benefit to be had from their reporting: my own stalker, Georgina P, quit phoning, quit coming to the practice altogether. My staff were of course deeply shocked to hear I was involved in a murder case. They were all perfectly sympathetic to begin with. But then, about a month after the story broke, Tom, my hygienist, handed in his notice, claiming he'd been eyeing a job in the suburbs for some time; he had a kid on the way and wanted better schooling for his toddler and blah blah, so he went. Rebecca, our avid thriller-reading receptionist, developed an unwelcome habit of hovering outside my surgery door in the hope she might gather some clues that had hitherto been missed by both press and police–so I had to be extra careful around her. Andrea, though, was simply rock solid, infinitely patient and kind. Inevitably we received offers of money to tell 'my story', 'the wife's story', 'our joint story' and there were a few persistent individuals who would camp outside the house and even tail us in cars–like stalkers, we said, seizing upon any bit of irony to preserve what was left of our dignity–but I could never bring myself to talk publicly about Sisi. One day I would tell my story, but it had to be in my own time and in my own way. Sylvia might have had something to say about it all, though. Some women in her position might have thought to themselves, *This marriage is over… I could use a bit of cash for my trouble*, but if she ever thought it, she didn't act on it. She could have been hateful and sarcastic. She could have tried to score points in some kind of moral reckoning with me in a pre-emptive strike for who got what in the event we split up. Her quiet and unsentimental display of loyalty would make me feel sometimes that she'd waited all our marriage for this day when she could enter into some huge suffering I might be experiencing in order for us to find a love that she had known was there but which we had not yet had the chance to explore together. She didn't seem to want to know why I'd gone with Sisi, or how it had happened; to have brooded over the past would have undermined her resolve to come through this crisis as a stronger person. I even saw her shed tears for Sisi–very suddenly and unexpectedly, as if she'd just received the news over the phone, one night as we got into bed. I'd just assumed she was shedding tears for the children or the mess I'd got myself into, but they were for Sisi. She was so riven with sorrow that night. The next day, she bounced back with renewed resolve for carrying on as normal–sweeping herself and the girls from point to point, chiding me with a moral terseness which I accepted as my due. I think I'd never seen her looking so beautiful. She wasn't merely being obstinate with whatever forces assailed us, she was being courageous–and when I saw that courage, the radiance in her complexion, I was immensely proud of her and grateful that she was the mother of our kids. Occasionally I would tell her she should get out more, I must be depressing, what had happened to her thing with what's-his-name? I didn't say it too often, though, because I didn't want to push her away and I didn't want her to feel sorry for me, either. Some days she would look hurt that I could even suggest that she go see Steve–if I kept silent about him at least she could keep guessing whether I still wanted us to stay together or not. Toward the end of January, though, she was more likely to smile that slightly cheeky smile of hers when Steve's name came up, as if she'd only ever taken him on so as she could have something to tease me with. It was that smile that always made me think of how she must have been as she was first turning into a woman, her beautiful, big brown eyes twinkling with playful innuendo and insolence as if to say, 'Are you going to make me do something I shouldn't?' And so we'd spend a quiet evening in together, watching TV, and she would ignore her mobile when it rang. Seeing less of Steve was also about the trial, she would say, she didn't want the press finding out and feeding off it at our expense. There was also Steve himself to think about: 'a nice guy', (his coke habit was no longer referred to), who probably wouldn't be able handle a flock of reporters hanging about his home, pecking at his private life for bits of salacious stuff to feed the main bloody story. Intuition and experience told me she was more concerned to preserve her friendship with Steve than their relationship. But, as I say, she liked to keep me guessing.

I remember one afternoon on a rainy weekend at the end of January, coming across her sitting quietly at a table, having a tea and ostensibly reading over some stuff from college. She'd neglected to turn on a lamp as the light faded and her faded image in my eyes warned me I was losing her. As she slowly turned her head, the whites of her eyes shone in the dying light, and she watched me quietly like an owl. I sat at the table and said something like, "The girls are very quiet this afternoon." She didn't seem to hear me. Her eyes gazed upon me, quietly beseeching that I make the bad stuff go away. I pictured myself reaching out to touch her, but we'd already discovered that watching each other was more comforting. I wanted to cry out to her, *I'm here for you*, but I simply didn't know where I was. Everything was so still and yet shifting under our feet, a sort of insidious earthquake that could open up at any moment and swallow us in minutes… or not.

During February, we dared to look forward to spring–and yet how strange it was to hope for more light and sunshine at a time the dark story of Sisi's murder would unfold in the law courts. I would have to relive the story all over again, but not as I'd really known it, as it had to be retold to a jury–in question and answer form, with quantifiable assumptions and brutal conclusions. I would be a significant witness for the Crown. I would have to perjure myself in order not to undo the confessions the police had elicited from Neil and Arun.

Then came that night, February twenty something, when one of the uncertainties running through our lives came to an abrupt end. As I was flicking listlessly through channels on the TV, I saw lights and I heard Sylvia's car arrive in the drive. Something was wrong with this. We'd argued that morning and, for the first time in several weeks, she let me know that she would be stopping over at Steve's that night–"So I don't want the kids up all night, get them to bed before nine… and none of those stupid PlayStation games you let them have!" I switched off the TV, expecting her to come in any second. When, after ten minutes, she still hadn't appeared, I went to the window to look outside. It was definitely her car; (I'd bought her a secondhand Nissan, partly in order to make it easier for us both to elude the press). The door opened and Sylvia got out and came inside. I moved through to the kitchen to find her, still in her coat, pouring a glass of water. She'd been crying and could barely make herself face me.

"Hey, are you OK?"

She didn't answer. Just grabbed the Kitchen Roll and sat down at the table, sniffing.

I sat down, one chair away, and waited patiently.

"Did you fight?" I asked when she failed to say anything.

"Can you turn that main light off, it's too harsh on my eyes."

I turned on the table lamp that gave its 60W bulb an orange glow and switched off one of the spotlights. Then sat down again

She let out a tired, tremulous sigh. "We didn't fight," she said. "Steve died."

I wondered if I'd heard her right. I waited a moment and simply queried, "He died?"

She nodded–"Yeah"–and wiped her nose. She sighed again, her mouth slack and moist. "I didn't even know until this evening, but he died three days ago, while he was on holiday. I'd got an email from him asking me round for dinner at his place–he must have written it from an Internet café. But there was no one there when I went round tonight. I called him–I don't know why I didn't call earlier… no, maybe I did, but anyway I didn't speak to him obviously–and I got a friend of his on the phone–and he told me." She drew breath to continue. "We were breaking up really, but–" She broke off.

"I thought you were stopping over."

She gave me a look as if to say 'dumb male never quite understands woman'. Once she felt that had sunk in – she'd gone to break up with him – she continued:

"He wanted us to go on a holiday, together… and I said I just didn't think it was the right time… and I wasn't even sure I wanted that. He wanted to go skiing–he even bought tickets for us both. But I said, 'No… No, *you* go. It'll do you good.' He said, 'I'm not going without you.' But I insisted he go–without me. So in the end he went. He went with a few students from our college, so I felt at least he wouldn't be on his own, y'know? But then he had an asthma attack. His inhaler, it didn't work. The people with him, they thought it was maybe too cold–like, my camera, for instance, it won't work when it gets below a certain temperature, so maybe it was that: the cold. He had another inhaler but it was back at the chalet and they were just too far. They managed to get him back, someone rushed to get the inhaler, but he died before they could get it to him."

"Christ, that's terrible. I'm so sorry."

"I told him to go! *I* told him, Anthony! After all this, after trying to put things right somehow. I could have just gone, been his friend–you said I was free to do that–but I said no, because I didn't want him to think –" she sucked in her breath – "…that we had a future, y'know? Now *he* doesn't have a future."

I saw her eyes prick with tears. I felt woefully unqualified to say anything of any use. I thought to get out of my chair and give her a hug, but she was still talking, gesturing, angry with herself, with recent horrific turns of events, so I let her carry on, all the while conscious that there would come a point when she would register my inaction as a lack of caring. My cue came when she got to her feet. I went to her and gently wrapped my arms around her. She sobbed a moment and broke away, talking the language of inconsolable disbelief.

I ran a bath for her. I picked up her clothes which she tossed just anywhere as she undressed. She thanked me and crept round-shouldered into the bathroom and locked the door.

She was a long time. I was just beginning to worry about her when I heard the bolt drawn across.

I was under the covers in the spare room by then. I heard a creak of hinges and turned in bed.

"You OK?"

She didn't answer, except by way of entering the room and slipping under the covers with me, the way the girls used to after a bad dream, her face averted, wanting nothing except human warmth.

In the morning I noticed she must have cried again on waking, probably as I was rousing the girls, but a steadfast look in her eye seemed to beseech me not to ask her if she was alright.

A few days later she revealed that it was hurtful words Steve had said about me and Sisi that had caused the last of their relationship to bleed out, ironically, just as she'd begun thinking it might have more to offer than she'd thought. She didn't wish to repeat what he'd said, but she said she'd found his attitude profoundly mean and crass and, from then on, hadn't been able to see him without finding something small about him. "That and his penis," she added with a guilty smile, which immediately prompted her to exclaim, "Oh, God, poor man, I can't believe I told him to go!"

In March Sylvia and I returned to a routine of sleeping together. For maybe a month the most contact we ever had in bed was holding hands. It was a moment like no other in the day; a symbol of fortitude. A pleasure, too, to rediscover the character and architecture of her fine, elegant fingers, the unexpected strength in a woman's consoling grip. She would hold my hand tightly as if guiding me across a treacherous path on the way to unconsciousness and I'd usually have fallen asleep before she let go. Some nights, as we faced each other in the dark, moved by her sadness and her patience with me, I'd feel a fragile urge to touch her in a sexual way. But even before I could move my arm, memories of Sisi came up thick and fast, bringing waves of nausea in their wake and the impulse died. I think anyway we were more fascinated reading each other's faces, trying to see how – or whether – hope was separating itself from the turmoil and damage. Occasionally I would turn my head in bed and find her looking at me with innocent eyes as if she might be wondering how or when she might possibly let me take her virginity. She'd make a little smile, as if unaware she'd done it, her gaze opening a fraction as she waited for some sign that she could bring her body closer to mine. I was always tempted, if only because I wanted to quench some of that longing in her eyes, but I couldn't bear the thought of being inside her and dreaming of Sisi. I was still so spent emotionally I wasn't even confident I could maintain an erection long enough for us to enjoy it. One bad go and we would have to face what we suspected was true: that it was all over. For the time being doubt was the cotton wool we needed to cover our wounds.

During the trial, which I find too sickening to relate in these pages, we ceased looking into each other's eyes with sexual curiosity; we were like two people besieged again. To my disgust, Neil Bantock, whom I could barely bring myself to look at in the court room–he never once looked at me when I was looking at him–was sentenced to a mere 14 years for manslaughter and kidnapping and other lesser criminal charges. He would be out in roughly 10. Arun was sentenced to 3 years for perverting the course of justice.

The trial took a lot out of me – even though I wasn't there much, just knowing it was going on was a sickening reminder of what had happened.

"Are you and mum going to split up?" Michaela asked one morning when we were alone.

She was the first to have used the words 'split up' and they rather shocked me.

"I hope not," she said when I gave my hesitant answer.

During the next couple of weeks Sylvia began to show impatience with what she called my 'lost look'– the trial was over and it was time to move on. Only at night would I read undimmed fascination in her eyes as she looked into mine trying to grasp what it was about this other woman that had had such a hold on me. Her own affair had been so lightweight by comparison. She said the experience had made her question whether she was even capable anymore of falling passionately in love. She wasn't sure she even wanted to.

In the first few months after Sisi's death I now think Sylvia believed it was just a question of time for us–if we could just get past the trial without some huge, impulsive bust-up, time would heal our wounds and I would come to her because our love for one another, however undernourished in recent years, remained true, and true love lasts. Part of me wanted the same as she did, but by the time I could imagine having sex with Sylvia without immediately being overwhelmed with grief for Sisi, I came up against another barrier: the tartar of old resentments. I'd been suffocating a long time before I'd met Sisi and I wasn't prepared to slip back into our old routine. Even if my experience with Sisi hadn't profoundly altered something inside of me, I couldn't face going back to the cycle of war and peace that had been our sex life. I also knew I was bored and that she was probably bored too, if she could only admit it.

When I first raised the question of separation, as in separate flats this time, I winced as I saw I'd caught her completely by surprise. She'd thought things were mending, she said. She laughed and couldn't help scoffing at the possibility I was actually dating another Thai prostitute. I let that pass. She asked me if I'd come to this decision because of her thing with her tutor? I said, No, not really. Didn't I love her anymore? No, I did love her, of course I did, I always would. So what then?! It would have been demeaning to try and explain, so all I could say was that I felt I had to be on my own for a while. She said I didn't mean 'a while', I meant forever. What about the children?! What about them?! Why's it always about you! And then she became irrational and I grew frightened that I was making the wrong decision. But somehow my decision stuck to me, like barnacles.

I moved out the following weekend–of all places, to the flat above my practice. It had become vacant round the time the trial had started and I'd put down a deposit the day it ended. I didn't plan to stay there for long, but for the time being at least it was a place that was close by and already familiar to them.

Shortly after Christmas, I'd called my mum to ask her if she could remember what had happened to the girl my brother and I had hurt with our aerosol games. Knowing much of what I'd gone through, she gave me a straight answer without asking me why I wanted to know. She said a close friend of hers had bumped into the mother at a local hospital only six months ago and had been told that the daughter was living in Brighton now, married to a doctor. "Of course we haven't really said more than a few words to the mum after that accident," she said. "But she's still living in the same house. Do you remember it?"

I got in the car after work and headed out to Chertsey, a town not far from where I'd spent my adolescence. I arrived at my destination as it was getting dark. A quiet suburban street of mostly detached houses built after the Second World War – houses which had struck me as very lacklustre back then, but which carried a certain nostalgic appeal now that I owned a house of my own. There were lights on in number 29. I turned off the ignition and sat there for a while, still not entirely sure what to do. I opened my bag and took out the package I'd taped up and labelled. I'd written a letter – several actually, and deleted them all. In the end I settled on this: 'For Chrissie Walters. I wish this could have come sooner. Anthony Price'. Would she remember my name? Five grand. I had to put my name or the mother might worry that she was expected to do something illegal for the money. I didn't know what the daughter could do with it. Certainly couldn't buy herself a new eye, but at least it might help her start the New Year with a smile on her face.

As I approached the glass door, I was in two minds whether to drop the package through the letterbox or ring the bell. But was there really anything to say? The package landed with a soft flop on the carpet floor. If someone heard it, no one came. I returned to my car without haste and started the engine straight away. At the road's exit I turned right and right again… and when I realised I didn't know where I was, I reversed in a tranquil side street and stopped. I switched off the engine, and I began to cry. Like a man who'd arrived at the end of his journey only to realise it wasn't yet the end. And there never would be an end. What was I even doing here! What was I hoping to achieve with this belated gesture of apology! The gift might only agitate the woman and her family, bringing unhappiness. I thought to knock on the door and invent a lie for retrieving the package. Would the mother recognise me? Would she still be mad at me? How naïve to think the gesture would have a healing effect…

A month or so after moving out I ran into Li Mei, the Chinese girl who'd shared with Sisi. I'd just been to see a movie on my own at Whiteley's in Bayswater and was feeling peckish. It must have been around four in the afternoon (on my day off). I'd just entered a café in Queensway when I spotted her at the end of the queue. I tapped her on the shoulder and said hello. It took her a moment to recognise me. We took a seat at the back of the café and, of course, started in comparing notes about Sisi. She'd read nothing in the papers about the case, only knew what she knew through friends and gossip. Not that there was much gossip – "Bad for business," she said gravely. It was the first time since Sisi's death that I'd spoken to anyone who knew her. I was again taken by Li Mei's smouldering sensuous beauty and deep voice.

"I miss Sisi too. Mm," she said thoughtfully, a couple of times, her melancholy eyes inclined over the table.

The two of them had discussed setting up a bar together in Bangkok, she reminded me. "Mm," she said again, with her signature languor as she pondered the dour prospect of having to find a new partner.

As we were preparing to part ways, I thought to ask her out, but I let go the impulse pass and waved goodbye. Not long after our chance meeting, I went to see Wong Kar Wai's sumptuous *2046* and was struck by the physical likeness of Li Mei to Zang Ziyi, the sometimes call girl in the story. I returned home to find her face on the agency's gallery. Mercedes. Did they get to choose their names or were they given them?

My intuition had been right: we had chemistry. Or perhaps I had simply learnt the art of being with a

prostitute through being with Sisi, a way of peeling off the layers of self-consciousness in a short space of time and focusing intently on the art of sharing sexual pleasure as if it were the last thing on earth I might enjoy. There was nothing playful about Li Mei, nothing light. She spoke little and her proud mouth would seldom know when to break into a smile, which was a shame, as her smile truly lit up her otherwise rather opaque expression and melancholy almond eyes. Her style in the bedroom and bathroom might have been described as 'sensuous, with particular attention to detail'. In fact I'd never been with a woman who knew so precisely how to arouse a man around his balls and his perineum–with her massaging fingers, her tongue and mouth. Her skills in controlling the ebb and flow to my groin, the soles of my feet, the base of my spine could have persuaded me I'd gone to see her for some kind of holistic treatment, not sex alone. I did my best to reciprocate and, when she fell chronically ill with a cold, I brought her food and vitamins and flowers and found it was a way of reconnecting with the best memories I had of being with Sisi. As early as the second visit I'd begun to feel something for Li Mei–our sex was deeply soothing–but I was relieved that my emotions were modest compared to anything I'd felt with Sisi. I had no cravings to see Li Mei outside our hour together, no illusions about a relationship other than the one we had in her room.

I began seeing other South East Asian and black girls too. Almost all of them had tragic stories to relate. Many had left children behind. I was moved by the numbers carrying physical scars, too–operations, beatings from ex-boyfriends, accidents. I came across a few who were chronically unwell and/or depressed. Then one day, after a few weeks' absence, I returned to see Li Mei, who'd agreed to a booking in spite of being in quite some pain with a migraine. She was always having headaches and I was beginning to suspect they couldn't all be blamed on her chocolate addiction or MSG. I insisted she let me take a look in her mouth. She laughed and said I must be deaf–it was her head! She had no idea it was in fact two impacted wisdom teeth that had been giving her the headaches. She had become so house-bound in her mentality, sleeping almost all day, seldom eating, waking to provide sexual services, then retiring to bed until her phone woke her again, that I nearly had to drag her out of her apartment and into a taxi. She was afraid that 'agency security' would see me taking her off somewhere, she was afraid of not being available to the agency 24/7. And she hated me telling her what to do, even though I was trying to help her. So I called her agency and explained what was going on. I whipped out her wisdom teeth that week, treating her for free, though I was half in mind to bill her agency. After Li Mei, there were others. I treated them all without a fee. Of course they could all have afforded to pay me, but I didn't want them to; I wanted to show them, or remind them, that their days didn't all have to be about money and sexual services. You might think I did this out of guilt, or out of an ulterior motive for further sexual favours, but no. In terms of my own gain, I did what I could for them because I needed to. I'd got to the age of forty something able to live reasonably comfortably, I'd had my family, I'd made money and I had some standing in my local community–before the press kicked me in the teeth, anyway–but I'd somehow forgotten what it felt like to help people without thinking of my fee. My brother joked that I thought of these girls as my harem. I laughed, and yet, in a funny sort of way maybe he was right, although in no way did I see myself as 'owning' the girls I helped. Perhaps I was motivated in part by personal vanity, but I had to start somewhere building a new me. I couldn't have gone back to being the person I was after witnessing what had happened to Sisi. I couldn't accept that Sisi was the end of the story, either; she/us had to be the beginning of something–and, however odd it may have seemed to most people, fixing call girls' teeth was my small contribution to making sure Sisi hadn't died in vain.

I supposed I would try dating again some day, but whenever I thought of following up invitations or emails from strangers on websites, a wave of indifference would wash over me and I'd know I still lacked the patience to try and be attractive to a woman, never mind manage a relationship. For a while it was enough to be in love with my two girls– they needed me now, more than ever. And Sylvia and I were learning to be best of friends.

July 2006, a year after I first set eyes on Sisi, I begin at last to consider making a trip to Thailand. I've continued teaching myself Thai in my spare time, with a textbook and CD. A few months ago I met and got to know a Thai girl studying for an MA at London University. She is perhaps just pretty enough to be an escort girl, but she isn't one. By an odd coincidence, she's studying tourism, the subject Sisi dropped out of at university. She'd phoned me in answer to a posting I'd put on a language school noticeboard offering English tuition in exchange for the same in Thai. We now meet on average once every two or three weeks. I've reached a level in my speaking ability which would have given me greater insight into Sisi if she were alive now. Though she possesses none of Sisi's sexual beauty, Sumarlee has a charming spontaneity about her, she's sensitive and she's a good listener. Above all, I feel soothed by her company. I have grown to see these lessons as the equivalent of sessions with a shrink. Instead of confessing and weeping and venting before a professional, I must force my mouth to make very different tonal sounds from any I've learnt before and by having something to do that connects me to Sisi I am better able to disentangle the good from the bad memories and put them in boxes, creating order where so much chaos has reigned. I have told Sumarlee almost all I have to say about Sisi and me, and having seen her enthralled has helped me come to terms with what happened, though I will never forgive Neil for what he did to her. I could imagine falling in love with this girl, but I suspect my professed ardent love for Sisi has made that impossible from her point of view. Which is fine, I'm in no rush to test my heart again. For weeks she has encouraged me to go to Thailand and seek out Sisi's family again (we were in touch for the sending home of her body for burial)–she's sure they would welcome me. And so that's what I've been organising. Early September, I fly out to Bangkok to be met by Sisi's older sister at the airport. I'm to be their guest for as long as I want in their suburban town just north of the city. Back at the new flat I look at Sisi's empty vase on the table. Finally, I feel something inside of me opening up, the courage perhaps to go down to the flower seller and buy myself some flowers, a big bunch of sunflowers, like the bouquets I used to buy for Sisi.

Printed in the United Kingdom
by Lightning Source UK Ltd.
135281UK00001B/390/P

9 781849 230780